The Secret Letter

BOOKS BY DEBBIE RIX

The
Secret Letter

Debbie Rix

bookouture

Published by Bookouture in 2019

An imprint of StoryFire Ltd.

Carmelite House
50 Victoria Embankment
London EC4Y 0DZ

www.bookouture.com

ISBN: 978-1-78681-701-3
eBook ISBN: 978-1-78681-700-6

For my mother and father –
whose experiences, diaries and letters
inspired the characters of Imogen and Freddie

In War: Resolution. In Defeat: Defiance.
In Victory: Magnanimity. In Peace: Good Will.

Winston Churchill

PROLOGUE

The letter landed on the mat, just as Imogen walked into the narrow hall from the kitchen. She usually ignored the uninteresting brown envelopes that slipped through the letter box. They lay undisturbed for days in an untidy pile until she was forced to gather them up simply to open the door. But even at a distance this handwritten envelope was intriguing. In spite of her arthritis, she bent down slowly and retrieved it, along with the pile of bills, and carried them through to the conservatory at the back of the house. Winter sun streamed in as she sat down in her favourite wicker armchair. She laid the unwanted mail on the kelim-covered footstool in front of her and examined the handwritten envelope, noting the German postmark and slid her long elegant finger under the flap.

Dear Imogen,

I hope you will forgive this intrusion, for we have never met, but please let me introduce myself. I knew your husband when I was a young woman living in a small village in Germany. We lost touch after the war, but it was with great sadness that I heard of his death, only recently, from a mutual friend. I understand he died nearly two years ago and had I known, I would have made the journey to England to meet you then and offer my condolences in person.

You will be wondering how we met – he and I. Let me explain. He lived with me and my family for a few brief, but significant, days in the last months of the war in 1945. He was one of the bravest men I have ever met and certainly the most noble. Your husband showed great courage and performed an act of huge kindness in our village and I have long wondered how to thank him for it.

I have decided to arrange a ceremony of thanksgiving and reconciliation next Spring – to commemorate what happened. As your husband cannot be there, will you come to Germany, in his place? This was a dark time in our history and I will explain more in due course. You would be welcome to stay with me. I live on a farm outside the village and we would be delighted to welcome you.

I look forward to hearing from you.

Yours

Magda

Imogen removed her reading glasses and gazed out at the wintry garden. Frost still covered the lawn and a robin perched on the edge of her bird feeder, clinging to the wire structure with its tiny claws. She stood up and walked over to the French windows to get a better look, but the robin, ever alert, flew away.

'Magda,' she muttered under her breath. She caught a glimpse of herself in the glass – still tall and erect in spite of her arthritis, her hair unnaturally dark for a woman of her age, streaked with broad swathes of silver. Magda... the name seemed familiar and yet had been lost to her, somehow, over the years. She lifted the lid of the pine chest that stood near the French windows. Brought from her father's house after he died more than thirty years ago, it had lain relatively undisturbed since that time. She had been preoccupied then, in her early sixties, still working full-time as an architect, helping her young adult children, and had neither the time nor interest to investigate its contents. She knew it contained mementoes of her family's past, photograph albums and so on, but now she wondered if it might also contain some clue as to the identity of Magda.

She opened a small, dark red leather box and found her father's medals from the first war; in a small cardboard box was the King George medal her grandmother had been sent, with a letter informing her that her other son, Bertie – her father's brother – had been killed. A sepia photograph had been tucked between the folds of the letter. It showed a young man in uniform, with a high forehead and bright pale eyes staring into the camera. 'What a waste,' Imogen muttered. She sat down heavily on the kelim stool and picked up her father's old pipe. She held it to her nose, inhaling the familiar scent that had somehow clung to it for nearly thirty years.

She rummaged deep in the box, finding photograph albums filled with small black and white photographs of long-lost family members. Among them, she found a picture of seven little girls wearing white pinafores over their dark dresses, standing in a row on a line of wooden palings on a stony beach. Written beneath the picture, in her mother's neat handwriting, were the girls' names: *Mimi, Bella, Amelia, Rose and friends. August 1902.* There were pictures of her mother as a young woman – so pretty and vivacious, tiny in her corset, her hair piled on top of her head. Her parents' wedding photograph... her mother in a nineteen-twenties wedding gown, her father so tall and upright in his top hat. Her own wedding photograph: Imogen wearing a long cream satin dress, and a veil that pooled on the ground. At the bottom of the chest was an old shoe box from a store in Newcastle called Bainbridge & Co. On the lid was a picture of a woman wearing a flowing full-skirted dress next to the words 'fine feminine footwear'. Imogen smiled. Her mother had always loved pretty shoes. Imogen opened the box and found that it was full of letters. As she inspected the dates and postmarks on the collection of pale blue, cream and green envelopes, she recognised her own girlish hand and realised they were letters she had sent home to her mother when she was a girl. It was touching that her mother had kept them – neatly curated in date order, and curious they had lain undisturbed all this time.

She removed one letter from its cream envelope. It was dated 6th October 1939 – the start of the war. She had been fifteen, and recently evacuated with her school from her home in Newcastle to the safety of the Lake District.

> '*I wish you were here,*' she had written to her mother, '*to help me solve all my difficulties – Miss Linfield is so beastly and Helen is not nearly so nice as she looked at first, and I had a pain today again and my maths won't come out and Helen is just going to see her Mother and Daddy for a whole week next week…*'

To her surprise, tears came into Imogen's pale green eyes, as she reflected on that young girl, alone and hundreds of miles from home. The letter seemed filled with self-pity – not a characteristic she was aware she had ever possessed. As she rifled through the faded envelopes, she tried to remember what it had been like in those first few weeks of the war, when everything had seemed so simple and straightforward…

Part One

The Phoney War

1939–1940

As a National Socialist and as German soldier I enter upon this struggle with a stout heart. My whole life has been nothing but one long struggle for my people, for its restoration, and for Germany. There was only one watchword for that struggle: faith in this people. One word I have never learned: that is, surrender... If our will is so strong that no hardship and suffering can subdue it, then our will and our German might shall prevail.

Adolf Hitler, speaking to the Reichstag, 1st September 1939

I am speaking to you from the cabinet room at 10 Downing St. This morning the British ambassador in Berlin handed the German government a final note stating that, unless we heard from them by 11 o'clock that they were prepared at once to withdraw their troops from Poland, a state of war would exist between us. I have to tell you now that no such undertaking has been received, and that consequently this country is at war with Germany.

Neville Chamberlain, Prime Minister, 3rd September 1939

Chapter One

Newcastle, England
The last days of August 1939

Imogen Mitchell ambled along the cul-de-sac, dragging a long stick that bumped against the railings with a satisfying thud.

'Bumpety, bumpety, bumpety…' she murmured in time with the rhythmic clattering.

'Imogen Mitchell! Stop that!'

It was Mrs McMasters, who lived across the street from Imogen's imposing Victorian red brick house. Mrs McMasters was in her front garden pruning the fading florets of the hydrangea bushes. She wore a knee-length skirt and a pretty grey blouse that looked as if it was made of silk, Imogen thought. Mrs McMasters' hands were protected by immaculate leather gardening gloves and as she dropped the florets into a basket Imogen noticed her neatly shod feet encased in pale cream leather brogues.

'Sorry, Mrs McMasters,' Imogen called out in a sing-song voice. Imogen hated Mrs McMasters. No, that wasn't quite correct. She didn't hate her because, as Mummy always said, you shouldn't 'hate' anyone, really. But she found her irritating. Mrs McMasters was always complaining about something, and really, if you thought about it, she had nothing to complain about. She lived in a lovely house, had a nice enough husband, expensive shoes and three handsome sons. She also had a maid as well as a cook, and a gardener who came twice a week to mow the lawn and 'do the heavy work'. Imogen wasn't sure what 'the heavy work' meant, but it was obviously useful.

Imogen hoiked her stick into her hand, and began to plant it firmly in front of her, just as her father did with his walking stick, or his umbrella. In fact any stick-like object that her father held in his hand was used in this fashion – as if he was marching in time to a military band.

Imogen muttered the marching rhyme her father had taught her as a tiny child, adjusting her stride so that her feet hit the ground on the words 'left' and 'right'.

'I had a good job and I left,
Serves you jolly well right.
Now you've got it now you keep it,
Left, right, left, right.
I had a good job and I left…'

Her steps were now magically in synchrony with the rhyme, the stick hitting the ground with military precision.

She opened the garden gate to her own house and walked up the drive past the neat borders of annuals and the well-trimmed lawn. Standing her stick in the corner of the tiled porch, she removed her front door key from the pocket of her bottle-green school tunic. As she opened the door to the dark hall she inhaled the comfortingly familiar scent of floor polish and beeswax, overlaid with the sour smell of overcooking vegetables and just a hint of dog.

Honey, her cairn terrier, bounded up to her.

'Hello girl,' said Imogen, scratching the little dog's blonde ears.

The cairn bounced around at her feet, delighted that Imogen was home and available to play.

'Not now, Honey,' said Imogen. 'I'm starving.'

She meandered into the morning room that led into the kitchen. She could hear the sound of the maid, Hetty, singing tunelessly in the scullery. Imogen opened the biscuit barrel that her mother kept on the dresser and took a piece of homemade shortbread, before retreating into the hall.

'Is that you Miss Imogen?' Hetty called out in her broad Geordie accent.

'Yes… it's me,' replied Imogen, already half way up the stairs.

'Do you want some tea?'

'No… no thank you,' Imogen said, skipping up the last few stairs and into her room, closing the door with a satisfying click. The dog scratched at the door, whining piteously to be let in. Imogen, holding the biscuit between her teeth, ushered the little dog into her room, snapping the door shut the moment Honey jumped on the bed, her black claws catching on the silky paisley eiderdown.

'Oh Honey…' said Imogen, lying down next to her dog. She broke off a little piece of biscuit and fed it to the dog, which licked her fingers, hoping to extract every last crumb, each last sweet taste.

'Lie down, there's a good girl,' said Imogen as she lay crunching her own share of the buttery shortbread, gazing out of the bedroom window at the large copper beech that dominated the back garden.

The sound of the front door slamming shut interrupted her daydreaming.

'Ginny?' She heard her mother calling her name from the hall. Imogen went out onto the landing.

'Yes Mummy… I'm here.'

'Oh good – well come down darling, there's something I want to discuss with you.'

Imogen found her mother, Rose, in the drawing room at the back of the large double-fronted house. The room always struck her as particularly feminine and was very much her mother's domain. It was here that Rose played bridge twice a week, serving tiny sandwiches and slices of homemade fruit cake. Her mother made a new cake for each of these occasions – not trusting Hetty with such a task.

'That girl hasn't the least notion of how to bake,' her mother often said, despairingly. 'I've tried to show her, but she really is as dim as a TocH lamp… It's as if she can't retain the simplest piece of information. How I do wish Edith would come back.'

Edith was the Mitchell's regular maid. She had been with the family for nearly twenty years, but had recently returned home to care for her own dying mother and Hetty had replaced her. Imogen wished that Edith's mother would either hurry up and die, or get better, so that Edith could come back to them. Then her own mother would be happier and life would return to normal. Imogen knew it was wrong to wish someone dead, but as her mother always said, 'we all have to die sometime.'

Rose stood by the fireplace. Although a tiny woman, she had the ability to command a room. She had been a teacher before she married, and emanated a quiet sort of strength. It was not difficult, Imogen thought, to imagine her holding forth in front of a class of children.

'Come here darling,' Rose said. Imogen's feet sank into the silky pile of the pale cream Chinese rug as she walked towards her mother. Kissing her lightly on the cheek, Imogen inhaled the scent of lily of the valley.

'Did Hetty give you some tea? I left a cake cooling on the rack before I went out and asked her to ice it for me and make sure you had a slice. I know you're always starving when you get home.'

'No…' said Ginny. 'I just had some of your delicious shortbread.'

'I see,' said Rose, 'well sit down Ginny; there's something I need to discuss with you.'

Imogen sat down on the sofa. It was covered in lilac-coloured linen decorated with large white wisteria flowers and contrived to be both feminine and charming.

Imogen had a bad feeling about this 'chat'. She had played a bit of a prank at school that morning – pretending to faint in assembly. Two teachers had rushed to Ginny's aid and carried her to the sick room. The last sight she had of her two best friends – Joy and Norah – was of them rocking with suppressed laughter as she was carried bodily out of the assembly hall. Had the headmistress realised she had been pretending? And if so, had she since been in touch with her mother? A sense of dread spread up through Imogen's body, working its way up her legs, until it reached her stomach, where it sat like an undigested meal, heavy and uncomfortable.

'No need to look so worried, darling,' her mother said, sitting down beside her on the sofa and taking Imogen's hands in hers.

'You're shaking, Ginny! What on earth is the matter?'

Imogen blushed. 'Nothing,' she mumbled.

'I suspect you've been up to mischief, haven't you?' her mother said with mock seriousness. 'Well don't worry – you're not in any trouble. Now... I'm sure that you must be aware that things are not going well with Mr Hitler.'

Imogen sat up, and looked intently into her mother's amber-coloured eyes.

'Yes Mummy. Our form teacher was telling us about it this week.'

'Yes, well…. The thing is – it looks like war is on the cards.'

Imogen's eyes immediately filled with tears.

'Is Daddy going to have to join the army again?'

'No, Imogen; not at all – he's far too old. He did his bit last time. No, it's not that. But if things proceed as we all fear they might, the school has been told that Newcastle is likely to be a target – what with the docks and shipbuilding and so on.'

Imogen looked blankly at her mother.

'Target?'

'Yes darling… for bombs.'

Imogen reached over and gripped her mother's cool hand.

'Now, Imogen, I realise it sounds scary, but really it's not. We might never be bombed; nevertheless, there's been a decision taken that children like you, who live in big cities, should be evacuated.'

Imogen stared, uncomprehendingly, at her mother.

'Do you understand?'

Ginny shook her head.

'Your school will be moved – to somewhere in the countryside, where you'll be safe. The headmistress was informed this morning and is making the arrangements now. It looks as though you might be off to the Lake District. Just imagine Ginny, all those lovely lakes, and mountains and fresh air. It will be marvellous.'

'And leave you and Daddy, and my friends?'

'Not your friends – they'll be going too. It will be a real adventure.'

'But for how long?'

'Oh… just until things settle down. It might only be a few months.'

'But I don't want to leave you and Daddy,' cried Imogen.

'I know darling. And we don't want you to go, but it's sensible to keep you all safe.'

'But who will keep you safe?' Imogen asked, logically.

'Oh we'll be all right. We've already been through one war and it's not so bad. But if the school was hit by a bomb, your education would be interrupted, and then you couldn't do your exams and… well… it would be a disruption.'

Ginny sensed the faltering in her mother's voice, the tears hovering in her eyes.

'But how will I bear it,' she asked her mother, gripping her hand, 'being so far away from you and Daddy?'

'Well, you already go away in the summer on your own to visit Granny in Aberdeen, don't you?' her mother said briskly, recovering her composure slightly. 'But instead of staying with her, you'll be with all your chums. It will be fun, Imogen, you'll see. And Daddy and I will visit you. We can drive across the Pennines from time to time and I'll bring you a cake or two.'

Honey crept into the drawing room and snuggled around Imogen's feet.

'And what about Honey?' said Imogen, scratching her beloved dog's ears. 'I'll never see her.'

'We'll bring her to see you.'

The tears that had been hovering in her mother's golden eyes now spilled over, trickling down her powdered cheek. Realising that she should be brave for her mother's sake, Imogen pulled the dog up onto her lap, and said simply:

'Yes, of course you will. And, as you say, it might be a lot of fun.'

She leaned over and kissed her mother's soft cheek, tasting Rose's salty tears on her lips.

Chapter Two

Färsehof Farm
On the outskirts of a small village
a few miles from Augsburg, Germany
September 1939

Magda Maier, her school rucksack digging into her shoulders, hurried up the lane to the farm where she lived. Surrounded by fields as far as the eye could see, the farmyard was enclosed on three sides by buildings – the ancient farmhouse itself, half timbered, its walls painted yellow ochre, was flanked by a pair of wooden barns, pine-clad with tiled roofs. One was filled with farm machinery, supplies of feed and bales of hay, and the other housed the milking parlour and dairy. That afternoon, as Magda ran towards the house, the yard was filled with cows on their way to milking, their hooves clattering on the cobbles, their udders full, their soft noses nuzzling one another.

'Oh good,' Magda's father, Pieter, called out across the noise of the herd, 'you're home. Come and help with the milking.'

'I can't, Papa…' she called back, over her shoulder, 'I've got a school project to finish.'

'Do it later,' he said firmly. 'The cows need milking now. Take off your coat, and put on your old boots.'

That evening, with the milking done and the herd back in the fields, Magda warmed her stockinged feet on the old range, her school project laid out but not yet begun, on the pine table. Looking across at her mother, Käthe, she noticed an envelope standing up on the dresser, addressed to her in familiar careful handwriting.

'It's a letter from Karl!' she exclaimed excitedly to her mother, who was skinning a rabbit by the sink. 'Why didn't you tell me?'

'You had homework to do,' said her mother calmly as she severed the rabbit's head with a strong downward stroke of her meat cleaver. Magda shivered. Her mother's hands were covered in bits of fur and blood, as she peeled the rabbit's skin off the smooth pink flesh. Its head lay abandoned on the kitchen worktop, its pale grey eyes staring vacantly at Magda.

'I can't concentrate on a letter with that thing looking at me,' Magda said, snatching up the envelope and grasping it to her chest.

'You won't be so squeamish when I serve this rabbit up in a nice tasty stew later,' her mother said, laughing.

As Magda ran up the creaking stairs to her bedroom, she passed her brother's room. Nine years his junior, she had always admired her older brother – revered him almost. She stopped, as she always did, and gazed around the orderly space. The bed – not slept in for two years – was still covered by the knitted quilt their mother had made for him as a child; the academic diplomas and certificates, framed by her mother, still hanging in pride of place over his desk. Their father had hoped to hand the farm on to his only son, but Karl had no interest in farming, preferring to hide away in his room with his books. Pieter had initially been disappointed, but when Karl's teachers had explained to his parents how very intelligent their son was, his despair had given way to pride. Magda could still recall the celebratory dinner the family had held when Karl had gained a place at Heidelberg University back in 1934.

'My boy, a university graduate,' Pieter had said, raising a glass of schnapps to his son. 'No one in our family has ever been to university.'

'Well now one of us will,' said Karl gently. 'I just hope you'll forgive me for not taking on the farm?' His voice had faltered slightly. He was anxious, Magda realised, not to upset their father.

'Well I've known for a while now that farming wasn't your passion, my boy,' Pieter had said, philosophically. 'To be honest, I'll be relieved that you're away studying.'

'Why?' asked Karl.

'It will get you away from those bully boys in the village – the Hitler Youth.' He spat the last words out.

'Oh Pieter,' said Käthe, impatiently. 'The boys in the village are all right.'

'No Käthe, they are not,' said Pieter. 'We used to have boy scouts, but they got kicked out and replaced with the Youth. At first I hoped it would be all right – they still went camping and hiking and Karl seemed to enjoy it.' Pieter looked across at his son, who nodded. 'But things changed…'

'Not in front of Magda,' Käthe whispered, nodding towards her daughter who stared intently at her food, hoping no one would notice that she was listening eagerly to the conversation.

'She's only little,' Pieter said, impatiently, 'she's not interested in our conversation. Now,' he went on, warming to his theme, 'the Youth has become a training ground for the military. Karl has told me about how they force them to adhere to the cause. It's not right.'

'He's right, Mutti,' Karl had said. 'The National Socialists are determined to create a generation of young people indoctrinated with their ideology. They fill their young minds with propaganda about racial purity, of the automatic superiority of our race and the inferiority of every other – especially the Jews.'

'They spend their time marching through the local villages,' interjected Pieter, 'declaring Herr Hitler has the answer to Germany's problems. And mark my words – no country's problems, economic or otherwise, can be solved by young men marching around the streets, bullying people.'

Karl had smiled.

'You are very wise, Papa, very wise indeed.'

Three years later, in 1937, when Karl had finished his first degree, he was offered a place to study at Oxford University in England.

'Please don't go,' Magda had begged, when he told the family his news. 'Why not finish your studies in Munich… or stay in Heidelberg,' she suggested brightly, 'then you could still come home at the weekends?'

'Because I cannot remain in Germany,' Karl said.

His parents looked at him, perplexed.

'The universities here…' Karl went on, 'have no academic freedom any more. Every teacher, every lecturer must follow the party line – you must see that?'

His parents looked bemused.

'But a British university will be different, I think. I've won a scholarship and it's a great honour, don't you understand? I have been working towards this since I was a teenager. Soon I'll be among "that sweet city with her dreaming spires".'

He had looked around hopefully at his little family, as they sat in front of the fire in the kitchen, willing them to understand, his face alive with excitement.

'But I'll miss you,' Magda had bleated.

'I know little monkey,' he'd said softly, holding out his arms to her. 'But we can write to each other.'

Mollified slightly, she ran towards him and he hugged her, twirling his fingers around her blonde plaits.

'Ouch!' she had complained, pulling away, 'you're hurting.'

*

Now, aged thirteen, Magda walked on, down the corridor, past his room to her own small bedroom. She threw herself on her bed and eagerly tore open the letter. It had been months since Karl had written to her and she was anxious to hear his news. Perhaps, she hoped, he would be coming home to visit.

My darling Magda,

How are you, little monkey? I hope you are working hard at school. I miss you all, but am enjoying my time here in England. I have joined the choir at my college, and have been told I am a good tenor – can you believe that?

Magda could believe it. Her brother had always had a beautiful singing voice. As a boy he had been a soloist in their local Lutheran church. She read on.

Now, there is something I need to explain. It is hard because I know that you will not have been told the truth but it is vital that you understand something. For many years you have been taught falsehoods. I was lucky – I left school just as these lies were becoming widespread. You have been taught in school that 'our' people – the Aryan race – are superior to all others. You have been taught that the Jewish people are our enemy, and that anyone who disagrees with the National Socialist principles is dangerous, and unpatriotic. Some German people are unhappy with Hitler and his party, but they are fearful of speaking out. You mentioned in your last letter that you have to go to school wearing your German Girls' League uniform; that you must stand and salute the Führer every morning, and sing nationalistic songs – something you say you hate. You are right to feel this way. This fanatical devotion to Hitler is wrong; the indoctrination of young people is a disgrace. Now that I am in England I have been able to see more clearly, to reflect on what is happening in our country. Herr Hitler is a warmonger; his occupation of the Rhineland is just the beginning. He wants total European domination. There will be a war, Magda, which Hitler will blame France and England for starting. Do not believe this. Hitler and his government of National Socialism are evil. You know what they have done to our Jewish friends, don't you? Did you know what happened in November last year on Kristallnacht? They encouraged people to smash up all the Jewish shops, and burn their synagogues. Jewish people were murdered that night in cold blood and many thousands more were sent to concentration camps. Since that time innocent Jewish people have been rounded up and sent away from the villages and towns they know and love. They will be forced to move to the cities, or worse – imprisoned. In Munich they have to live in a 'Jew Camp'. Can you believe it? Some have managed to pay huge fines and have been allowed to leave the country travelling to America and Britain. But many more are trapped in Germany – unable to pay fines, unable to escape. They have been disenfranchised, Magda… their livelihoods taken away, their lives destroyed. We have their blood on our hands. It is wickedness Magda, and must be stopped. Hitler is determined to take over the neighbouring countries to the East. He tells you all that these people want to be part of Germany and maybe some people do, but you cannot just invade another country and take it for yourself. I suspect you know nothing of this, safely tucked away in our village, but it is happening Magda, believe me.

I have made a decision – to stay on here in Oxford and do what I can to help the resistance in Germany. If I were to come back, I would be called up for military service, and I cannot fight a war I disagree with.

I will write to our parents later and explain everything to them, but I wanted you to hear this from me. Say nothing to anyone about my reasons. I don't want you to be drawn into this, or blamed in any way. People will say terrible things about me – let them. Ignore them. Denounce me if you have to. As a girl, you will not be forced to fight and Papa is too old, thank God. I pray that you will be left in peace. If I can find a way to get you out of Germany, believe me, I will.

Look after Mutti and Papa. I love you, little sister and we shall see one another again soon – once this madness is over.

Your loving brother
Karl

PS destroy this letter – please. If it was found, it could be used in evidence against you or the family.

Magda lay on her bed, perplexed and upset by her brother's letter. She adored Karl, idolised him, and yet surely, what he was saying just couldn't be true. She recalled the conversations Karl had with their father before he left – about the way young people were being indoctrinated, and she understood that. But to suggest that these views were actually leading to cruelty, to the banishment of people in their village, seemed unimaginable. She folded the letter and placed it back in the envelope. 'Destroy it', Karl had written. Why should he ask that of her? She re-read the last line. 'It could be used in evidence.' What did that mean? Who exactly would use it? How would anyone even know she had the letter? It made no sense. Besides, if she were to destroy it, how would she go about it? She could burn it in the range in the kitchen when Mutti wasn't looking. But Mutti had eyes everywhere. Or she could tear it into tiny pieces. She held the paper in her hands, steeling herself to begin. But the thought of destroying her beloved brother's letter seemed unbearable – she hadn't seen him for two years and had kept all his letters carefully stowed away in her chest of drawers, tied together with a ribbon. Could she not merely slip this amongst them? She looked again at his instructions. If she was not prepared to destroy it, then she must hide it. She peered under the bed, but Mutti would find it when she changed the linen. Her wardrobe was quickly ruled out as her mother was always tidying and sorting out her clothes. Desperately casting around for anywhere secure, her eye fell on the wooden bookcase and the bible she had been given for her confirmation. Picking it up, she ran her fingers over the smooth leather cover and gilt edging. As she opened it, she noticed a little paper pocket on the inside back cover, where she was supposed to keep copies of her favourite prayers. It was empty, and she slipped the letter into the pocket and smoothed it flat, until just a faint outline of the paper was visible. She returned the bible to the bottom shelf next to her fairy stories. It would be hidden, but in plain sight. Isn't that what people said?

This task completed, she felt the need to get out of the house, to walk and think – to make sense of what her brother had written. She felt so conflicted and confused. As she passed Karl's room, she looked again at the brightly coloured bedspread, the diplomas on the walls, the photographs showing him proudly holding his first degree, his dark eyes so full of hope, before closing the door. The boy who had lived in that room was not the young man who had written that letter, so full of incomprehensible lies. Surely, she reasoned, as she walked down the creaking pine stairs, they must be lies. In the kitchen her mother was frying the rabbit pieces, filling the kitchen with the comforting scent of supper. Magda's school project on 'the importance of purity' lay untouched on the kitchen table. As she stepped outside into the yard, she heard her mother call her name.

'Magda? Where are you going?'

Her father was washing down the dairy after the evening milking. She rushed past him and down the lane towards the road that led to the village. A horse and cart plodded slowly towards her driven by a man and a young girl. As they drew closer she recognised Erika and her father, Gerhard, from the neighbouring farm. Magda and Erika were in the 'Young Maidens' together – part of the German Girls' League. The female equivalent of the Hitler Youth, the Young Maidens were taught the importance of becoming good mothers and housewives. This was bad enough, as far as Magda was concerned, but worse still were the lessons on the sliding scale of 'racial purity' the National Socialists thought so important. They were taught that the Nordic peoples, with their taller than average builds, narrow, straight noses and 'dolichocephalic' skulls were at the top of the racial 'league'. Erika, who had recently become a team leader, had been delighted to be singled out at their last meeting to have her head size measured and be declared a 'class one Aryan'. Everyone in the group, apart from Magda, had cheered wildly. Since then Erika had become increasingly overbearing and bossy.

Now from her seat on the cart, she waved enthusiastically at Magda, who reluctantly waved back. She did not like Erika, but it would not be sensible to make an enemy of her. Relieved that they did not stop to talk, but instead continued on up the lane, Magda crossed the road swiftly and ran into the woods on the other side. The autumnal sun filtering through the tall pine trees cast long shadows as she ran downhill, heading for the stream at the bottom of the valley. Slithering down the slope, she inhaled the sharp tang of the pine forest, her mind clouded by her brother's words – 'Hitler is evil'. Evil… what did he mean? How could the leader of their country be an evil man? Her teacher at school had taught them that Hitler was inspirational; that he had saved their country, and given everyone back their jobs and their pride. As for invading neighbouring countries – surely he was only taking back what was rightfully theirs?

At the bottom of the hill, as the ground levelled out, was a copse of deciduous trees – oak and ash – already turning golden with autumn colour, their fallen leaves forming drifts underfoot that crunched as she walked. In the centre of the copse was a small clearing where she and Karl had often set up a camp when they were young. Karl had always been the leader – enthusiastically erecting the tent, and building a little fire on which they could cook their supper. As she helped him stir a pot of stew, or bake potatoes in the embers, he would guide and protect her. After supper they would lie under the stars and Karl would tell her stories. Later, when it was time to sleep, he would tuck her up in their little tent and they would lie next to one another, listening to the rustle of woodland animals outside. With him beside her, she felt no harm could ever befall her.

Sometimes, he would suggest she brought a friend, and the person she most often invited was Lotte Kalman, the doctor's daughter. Lotte had long brown hair and bright blue eyes, the colour of forget-me-nots. The two girls shared a birthday, and had much in common – most especially their love of camping. Magda thought about their last camping trip, when she and Lotte had been around nine years old. It was just before Karl left for university in Heidelberg. He brought his guitar down from the house, and once they had cooked their supper, they had sat under the stars singing folk songs – not the nationalistic songs that were encouraged by the Hitler Youth, but Russian and Norwegian folk songs. The girls had loved that weekend. A few months later, on their tenth birthday, Magda was informed she was now old enough to join the Young Maidens. Excited at the prospect of further camping trips in the woods she had rushed to find Lotte, but found her crying in the corner of the playground.

'What's the matter Lotte?' she had asked her friend, putting her arm around her.

'I can't join,' whimpered Lotte.

'What do you mean – join what?'

'The Young Maidens…'

'Why not?' asked Magda, innocently.

'Because I am… I am Jewish.'

On her first evening with the group Magda asked the youth leader, Fräulein Muller, why her friend Lotte – who had eyes as blue as Hitler's – was not allowed to join the others. Magda remembered the expression on the Fräulein's face to this day; it was a look of shock – revulsion even.

'Because Jews are at the bottom of the racial scale of non-Aryans,' Fräulein Muller replied, furiously. She spoke to Käthe about it that evening when she came to collect Magda. Waiting to go home, Magda had watched, guiltily, as her mother was harangued by the youth leader, her face contorted with rage. Her mother, by contrast, had looked upset, even a little frightened. After that Käthe no longer suggested she brought Lotte home to play, and often made excuses when Magda was invited to visit Lotte's house. Then one day, the Kalmans simply disappeared. It was rumoured they had moved to Munich, and Magda imagined they must have chosen to go – perhaps they had family there, she told herself. But she remembered women muttering together in the village shop about how you couldn't have a Jewish doctor.

'It's a disgrace,' one woman had said. Magda thought this was odd, as Dr Kalman had always shown her great kindness, on one occasion sitting by her bed all night when had the measles.

'They have been rounded up,' Karl had said in his letter. What did that mean? Had Lotte and Dr Kalman been rounded up? She thought of her father herding cattle. Is that what had happened? She didn't like to think of the Kalmans suffering in any way. Perhaps Lotte and her family had gone abroad? She hoped so – poor Lotte…

It had rained heavily the night before and the stream was full to bursting, bubbling over the stony bed, each rock crested with foam. Magda sat on the river bank, thinking of all the times she and Karl had come down together to throw stones into the stream, watching the ripples spread out across the water. They had fished here too, taking river trout back to Mutti to cook in lots of butter for their supper. Although much older than her, Karl was her best friend – the one person, apart from her father and mother, she admired and trusted completely. But now it seemed something had happened to him since he had moved to England. Perhaps they had imprisoned him and forced him to write these terrible things to her. Might that be the reason he had told such lies? Her teacher at school had explained how, under Herr Hitler, Germany was becoming the most successful economy in Europe. Other countries, he had told them, envied that success. Had the English been so envious that they had imprisoned her brother and forced him to write these lies against his will? The thought of her beloved brother locked in a dark, dank prison cell brought tears to her eyes and she ran hurriedly back up the hill, through the pine forest, back to the farm.

In the kitchen, Käthe was serving supper.

'Ah Magda… good, you're here. Where did you go in such a hurry?'

'Just for a walk,' Magda said, washing her hands at the kitchen sink.

Her text book, notebook and pens had been tidied away by her mother and lay on the dresser.

'You've not started your project yet,' Käthe said, ladling rabbit stew and potato dumplings onto Magda's plate.

'I'll do it later,' said Magda.

'How is Karl? Can I read his letter?'

'No!' Magda said, abruptly, remembering Karl's instructions that she should 'Say nothing to anyone.'

'Oh, why not?' her mother asked.

'He said he would write to you; this letter was just for me.'

'I see,' said Käthe, her eyes betraying the hurt she felt. 'Well at least you can tell us his news,' she said, hopefully.

Magda stabbed a piece of rabbit with her fork but felt unable to eat. The memory of the rabbit's head oozing blood on the draining board made her gag. '*We have their blood on our hands…*'

She stood abruptly, knocking her chair to the ground, and ran from the table and outside to the yard, where she vomited violently.

Later, resting in bed, feeling her mother's cool hands stroking her forehead, she brooded over Karl's letter.

'Mutti,' she said, 'why did Lotte and Doctor Kalman leave the village?'

'What an odd question,' her mother said. 'What makes you ask that now?'

'I just wondered. They left so suddenly. I liked Lotte.'

'Yes… well… they went to be with their own people. It was better that way.'

'So they are with their friends and family?' asked Magda, hopefully.

'Yes… now stop worrying about silly things and tell me – was there something in Karl's letter that has upset you?'

Magda's eyes filled with tears, but she blinked them away and turned over in bed to face the wall.

Her mother stroked her hair.

'Well, maybe you'll tell me tomorrow. Try to sleep now.'

Käthe blew out the oil lamp and closed the pine door with a click.

Chapter Three

Keswick, The Lake District
September 1939

The train journey from Newcastle to the small Lakeland town of Keswick would take most of the day. Imogen stood beneath the vaulted ceiling of Newcastle station saying her farewells to her parents, alongside her best friend Joy Carr. The two girls had met, aged eleven, on their first day at Newcastle Girls' High School. Joy's first words to Imogen had sealed their relationship forever.

'Are you naughty?'

'Yes,' said Imogen, uncertainly. 'At least I think so.'

'Excellent,' Joy had said, disarmingly. 'You and I are going to be the best of friends.'

Now, standing on the windswept station platform, Joy jiggled with excitement as she said a cheery goodbye to her parents. Imogen by contrast was overcome with nerves, her stomach jittering with butterflies.

'You will remember to write, won't you?' Imogen's mother insisted, holding onto her stylish rust-coloured felt hat, as a gust of wind blew through the station.

'Of course, Mummy.'

Imogen could tell that her mother was doing her best to be brave and she was determined to reciprocate. But she could feel her eyes smarting with tears, her throat aching as she swallowed back the sadness.

'And don't get into too much mischief,' her father added.

'No Daddy…'

'Not much chance of that,' her mother said, smiling, tears brimming in her eyes. 'Come here darling.'

She held Imogen to her so tightly that she could scarcely breathe.

'I love you,' Imogen whispered into her mother's neck.

'I love you too,' Rose replied.

All around them children were wishing their families goodbye. Amidst the tears and last-minute instructions, the guard blew his whistle. The train expelled a great draught of steam from its funnel.

'Quick,' Rose said. 'Get on… you don't want to miss it.'

Imogen's father efficiently stowed their luggage in the overhead rack.

'Don't speak to strangers,' he instructed as he kissed them both goodbye on the tops of their heads.

Then he was gone, the door slamming behind him. On the platform Rose was flapping her hands, trying to say something, but Imogen couldn't hear her. She finally dropped the window down just in time to hear her mother shouting, 'open the window'. The girls waved bravely at their parents, as the train drew out of the bustling, dark station and into the sunlight as it crossed the glistening Tyne.

The train had been specially commissioned, and was filled with children from a variety of schools – some as young as four or five years old. Imogen and Joy shared their carriage with three very young children who, judging by their uncanny likeness to one another, were all from the same family. The little trio consisted of two boys who wore matching caps and long socks that sagged around their ankles and a little girl with blonde curls peeking out beneath her blue beret. They sat snuggled up against one another, with labels pinned to their woollen coats, their belongings wrapped in cream cotton bags, looking utterly forlorn and lost, their faces smeared with tears, their noses running.

Imogen removed a handkerchief from her pocket and offered it to the eldest boy, who stared at it blankly. So she took the handkerchief and one by one wiped their faces.

'It's all right,' she said, smiling encouragingly. 'Joy and I will look after you… won't we?' She nudged her friend who had already opened the small picnic hamper her mother had given her and was inspecting its contents.

'Sure,' Joy said cheerfully, while secretly wishing her friend had not volunteered their services. This was an adventure and she was determined to enjoy it, not to play nursemaid to a posse of small children.

Once they were out in the countryside, the train chugging contentedly along, the little children drifted off to sleep. Imogen and Joy, relieved – at least temporarily – of babysitting duties, began to enjoy themselves. They shared their packed lunches and planned the fun they would have away from home.

'It's going to be terrific,' Joy said, cramming a potted meat sandwich into her mouth. 'I'll be away from my mother and her strict bedtimes. School will be chaotic – probably with no homework either. It will be like being on holiday. Oooh you lucky thing, you've got cake!'

Imogen broke her piece of cake in two and handed one half to Joy.

'Thanks,' Joy said, stuffing it into her mouth. 'Your mother's cakes are always the best.'

The youngest child – a boy with liquid dark brown eyes – woke up and gazed longingly at Imogen's piece of cake. She halved it once again and handed it to him.

'Have you got any lunch?' she asked him.

He shook his head mournfully. Imogen nudged Joy.

'Give them one of your sandwiches,' she said.

'Must I?' asked Joy.

'Don't be so mean,' said Imogen as she laid out a white napkin supplied by her mother with a selection of sandwiches and a small piece of cake for each of the children.

As the little ones ate, the train rattled across the bleak brown landscape of the Pennines, stopping at Carlisle station, where they were all herded onto a branch line train called 'The Merry Carlisle'. Now heading south, the train climbed over moorland, before clattering downhill through the little station of Troutbeck, and on past the granite quarries, gorging smoke up into the atmosphere. As the hills of the Lake District rose up on either side of the line, the train criss-crossed gurgling rivers before arriving finally at Keswick station late in the afternoon.

Climbing out of the train, Imogen admired the pretty Victorian station buildings and the distant grey mountains – their summits already covered with a sprinkling of snow. She and Joy helped the little children out of the carriage and along with hundreds of others, they were ushered into the ticket office, where a tall woman wearing a dark blue suit and grey trilby hat stood behind a table.

'Evacuees – queue here please.'

The little boy with liquid brown eyes looked up, bewildered, at Imogen.

'That's you,' she said, gently. 'Queue up here, and give your name when they ask you.'

Once they had all been ticked off someone's list, they were herded onto buses and driven into town. As a rain-sodden mist descended, the younger children, exhausted from the journey and frightened at the unfamiliarity of it all, began to cry. As Imogen gazed out of the rain-spattered bus at the dark stone buildings of Keswick, she clutched at Joy's hand, still sticky from cake. 'We will be all right, won't we?' she whispered.

Arriving at a church hall, they were allocated, in alphabetical order, to local families. To their horror, Joy Carr and Imogen Mitchell were to be sent to opposite ends of the town.

'I can't believe it,' said Joy, indignantly. 'We're not going to be together.'

'I know,' said Imogen, tears welling up. 'I thought at least we'd be in the same house and could help one other. I'm going to be with Helen!'

'Poor you!' said Joy. 'She's an awful wet… and such a goody-two-shoes.'

'I know!' said Imogen. 'But what about you – where are you going to live?'

'I'm with some family called the Metcalfe's,' said Joy, gloomily. 'Mrs Metcalfe is over there, crying. I hope that's not my fault! I'm not that bad am I?'

'No, of course not,' said Imogen, encouragingly.

'And not only that,' Joy continued. 'I'm sharing with that poisonous creep Millicent Clark. I hate her!'

'Oh Joy!' said Imogen. She looked around the hall searching for the little children they'd shared the journey with. A kindly looking woman with red hair was kneeling down, talking to the eldest boy, whilst holding the hand of the little blonde girl, who sucked her thumb, sleepily, and leant gratefully against the woman's shoulder. At least they'll be all right, Imogen thought. 'Well, maybe it won't be so bad,' she said encouragingly to Joy. 'I'm sure Millicent must have a good side, and although Helen is a bit wet, she's not an altogether bad person.'

Imogen and her housemate Helen were introduced to their new landlady, Mrs Latimer. She was grey-haired, with soft peachy skin, beautifully manicured hands and kind grey eyes. She smiled sweetly at her two charges.

'Well girls,' she said, 'I'm sure we'll all get along famously. Do you want to come with me?'

Imogen waved a forlorn goodbye to Joy who was standing sullenly next to Millicent and the weeping Mrs Metcalfe, and climbed into Mrs Latimer's battered Austin Seven.

The Latimers' house stood in a commanding position overlooking the town. Built at the turn of the century it was a detached pebble-dashed house, painted off-white, the window frames and front door picked out in dove grey, topped by a dark slate grey roof. There was a tidy front garden with well-clipped shrubs and hedges. It reminded Imogen of her grandmother's house in Aberdeenshire.

The room she was to share with Helen was at the back of the house. Single beds stood on either side of the window, beneath which was a small writing table and chair.

'This was my boys' room,' Mrs Latimer said, as she showed the girls around. 'They're both away now. They've already joined up, so the room was sitting empty, and I thought it would be nice to have some company.'

This explained the 'masculine' decoration, Imogen thought, as she noted the dark blue curtains and matching bedcovers.

'Come down, as soon as you're settled,' Mrs Latimer said. 'And I'll show you the view.'

The girls spent the next half hour unpacking their things and arranging the room to their satisfaction. The Latimers had thoughtfully provided a mahogany dressing table mirror, which they had placed on the table. But after Mrs Latimer had left them alone to unpack, Imogen and Helen, preferring to keep the table for homework and letter-writing, moved it onto the tallboy next to the door. It now stood next to a silver-framed photograph of the Latimer's two sons: tall fair-haired boys, wearing hiking boots and corduroy knickerbockers, standing at the summit of one of the local landmarks, smiling in the sunshine.

Imogen thought them rather handsome, and was disappointed to learn they no longer lived at home. The tallboy had been cleared of its contents – spare linen and so on – in readiness for the arrival of the two girls, and they filled it with their school dresses, night-clothes, underwear and 'home' clothes. They had arrived with just one suitcase each, so the tallboy was far from full. Nevertheless, Mrs Latimer had also cleared a space in the small hanging cupboard in one corner of the bedroom. Pushing Mr Latimer's best Sunday coat and Mrs Latimer's ancient fur to one side, the girls squeezed in their school coats, hats and walking boots. They hung their satchels over their bedposts, and, satisfied that the room was ready, came downstairs to find Mrs Latimer.

Standing in the back garden of the house in the fading evening light, Mrs Latimer led Imogen and Helen down a crazy paving path that ran alongside the flower beds on either side of the garden.

'We'll pick a few apples later,' Mrs Latimer said, indicating an orchard at the bottom of the garden that led onto an area of common land. 'There's a good crop this year.'

Beyond the orchard and the common land stood the hills and mountains that formed the startling backdrop to the market town. They rose up majestically – green at the foot, blending through to purple and grey near the summit.

'There's Skiddaw, just to the left,' Mrs Latimer explained, naming the various hills. 'And Blencathra straight ahead.'

Imogen had spent many summers with her grandmother in the north of Scotland and was used to mountains and lochs, but the hills behind the Latimers' home were truly remarkable.

'Soon they'll be covered with snow,' said Mrs Latimer dreamily. 'It's a beautiful sight. We're so lucky to live here.'

She looked down at Imogen and Helen, and smiled.

'Come on girls, let's go and have some tea.'

Delighted at the thought of food, Imogen and Helen scampered back up the path and into the house. At the back door, as Mrs Latimer headed for the kitchen, Imogen caught Helen's arm.

'She's nice, isn't she?'

'She is,' agreed Helen.

'I think,' said Imogen, 'compared to poor Joy, we've rather landed on our feet here…'

'Yes,' said Helen, agreeably, 'I think you might be right.'

A couple of days later, after attending church, and eating a delicious Sunday lunch, Imogen wrote her first proper letter home.

3rd September 1939
Keswick,
The Lake District

My dear Mummy and Daddy,

I think that I am really settled down now at the Latimers. As I told you, I am sharing with Helen, who is really quite nice – but poor Joy is very unhappy I think.

She is with Mrs Metcalfe whose four sons have just gone to war. All she does all day is weep. *Well! I call that a very cheerful sort of hole! And she's sharing with a horrid girl – called Millicent. I feel so sorry for her, poor kid.*

Mr and Mrs Latimer are so sweet (Mrs L is writing to you).

They are a retired school master and school mistress. The house is white, has a dining room, sitting room and kitchen with a lovely garden front and back. Upstairs are bathroom, WC and three bedrooms – spare, ours and Mr and Mrs L's.

The predominant colour in the house is Presbyterian blue, although the Lats are C of E and I went with Joy to St John's this morning with a school party.

Has the car been requisitioned yet? Do come to see me if poss.

Well, tons of love and take care of yourselves,
Imogen

PS Have just heard War declared. Mr and Mrs L invited
Helen and myself into the drawing room to listen to
the radio and we heard Mr Chamberlain. I thought he
sounded rather upset. It all seems an impossibility when
you stand on the shores of Lake Derwentwater and look
at the wonderful scenes.
PPS please send brogues and other brown shoes and
Macintosh (either one) and if poss my yellow coat and
brown hat – not Breton (don't bother with hat if you
cannot manage).
Love once more, Imogen

The following morning, just as Imogen was leaving the house, adjusting her school hat in the hall mirror, a letter floated down onto the Latimer's door mat addressed to her in her mother's meticulous hand. Imogen snatched it up eagerly, determined to read it as she walked to school.

3rd September 1939
Gosforth,
Newcastle-upon-Tyne

My darling Imogen,
I received a postcard yesterday giving me your new address.
It's good to know that you have arrived safely and have a roof
over your head. I look forward to hearing your news and
hope the family you've been assigned to are good and kind.
We are all well here. We heard Mr Chamberlain speaking
on the radio – did you? I thought he sounded very gloomy
indeed and it's hard to keep one's spirits up.

Imogen, absorbed in her letter, crossed the road without looking either left or right. She was startled by the ringing of a bicycle bell, and the sound of screeching brakes. She looked around to find an elderly man lying in the road next to his bike, extremely red in the face.

'Sorry,' she said, helping him up. 'I'm so sorry.' He pushed her aside irritably, and brushed himself down, muttering, 'stupid girl!'

'Well – if you're quite all right?' she asked anxiously, before running the rest of the way across the road and watching him weave his way, uncertainly, down the road. Heading towards the town, she found a bench and sat down to finish the letter in peace. She skimmed over her mother's description of a bridge game she had played the previous day with their neighbours. Mrs McMasters, it seemed, had been complaining about the unfairness of her two adored eldest sons, Jonnie and Philip, having to join up. But Imogen's eye was drawn to her mother's mention of Freddie, the McMasters' youngest son.

> *...Only Freddie is still at home. He's studying architecture at King's College, Newcastle, and as it's considered a reserved occupation, he's been allowed to complete his first two years. But he's joined the RAF squadron at the University.*

Imogen leaned back and looked up into the clear blue sky, and thought about Freddie. At nineteen, he was four years older than Imogen, but in spite of the age difference they had become close over the last couple of years. After Freddie's older brothers left home for work and university, he had found himself slightly at a loose end, and had occasionally invited Imogen to play tennis with him at the local club. Slightly to his chagrin, he discovered she could beat him hands down, through sheer guile and determination – at least that's how he later explained the score line.

'Well done!' he'd said to her in the tennis club bar, where he bought her lemonade. 'I'm impressed.' He sipped his pint. 'But don't you dare tell my brothers you can beat me!'

'Maybe I will, maybe I won't,' Imogen had replied teasingly.

Imogen began to walk towards her school, daydreaming about Freddie. How like her mother to mention him – it was as if she had an ability to see right into Imogen's mind, and understood the appeal of the older boy for her daughter. After all, Imogen thought, how could she not be a little bit in love with Freddie – with his wavy dark hair flopping over his pale grey eyes, his adorable laugh and sweet nature? To a fifteen-year-old girl he seemed impossibly glamorous and grown up. But reading about his exciting life at university in her mother's letter, Imogen realised, gloomily, that he was bound to be snapped up by an older girl, maybe even married, while she was stuck in the Lake District.

As she approached the school gates, reading the final paragraphs of her mother's letter, Joy called out to her.

'Hey there stranger. I've been waiting for you.'

'Oh hello,' said Imogen. Joy was carrying her lacrosse stick. Her brown hair was, as usual, tied up in pigtails that stuck out at a jaunty angle beneath her school hat. She peered over Imogen's shoulder at her letter, her brown button eyes shining with curiosity.

'What've you got there?'

'Just a letter from home,' Imogen said, folding the letter up and putting it in her blazer pocket.

'Anything interesting?' Joy asked as they walked through the playground towards the main door.

'Not really. Just a bit of news about Freddie McMasters.'

'Do I know Freddie?' asked Joy, opening the door.

'No, I don't think so. He's a neighbour. I don't think you've met him.'

'Well, by the look on your face,' said Joy, 'I think it's time you told me all about him.'

Chapter Four

Färsehof Farm
October 1939

Karl's letter, secreted in Magda's bible, became a source of constant anxiety. Every morning when she woke, Magda wondered whether today would be the day she should show it to her mother. As she washed her face and hands in the china bowl in her room, as she brushed her hair, twisting it into the long blonde plaits that hung on either side of her oval face, as she dressed in warm stockings with the navy skirt and white shirt of the Young Maidens, she tussled with her brother's instructions that the letter should be kept a secret and destroyed. By preserving it, she had already broken his trust. To show the letter to her parents would be a double betrayal.

Magda knew her mother was desperate to know what was in the letter. Every morning at breakfast, her mother would lean forward expectantly, her mouth half open to ask a question but finally saying nothing. Magda understood, and felt guilty for upsetting her. If she was honest, she wanted her mother to read the letter – to explain what Karl had meant. Why did they have the blood of the Kalman family on their hands? Surely they were not dead… they had simply moved? But then she remembered her brother's instructions to 'say nothing' and once again resolved to keep the letter hidden.

An added complication was that Magda knew her mother would be unable to resist looking for the letter. This complicated game of 'hide and seek' was familiar: for whenever Magda tried to keep anything private her mother would search for it. Magda had learned to leave little tell-tales around her room – a piece of thread on her bedside table or in her desk drawer. If, when she came home from school, the thread had been moved, she knew her secret had been discovered. There was a boy at school named Otto. A year or so older than Magda, he had developed a crush on her, writing her love letters which he left in her desk at school – letters which she brought home and read in secret, before stashing them away in the bottom drawer of her clothes chest. They both horrified and delighted her. She was thrilled that anyone should love her, but hated the way he expressed it. He wrote of wanting to put his hands on her body, to 'touch her in secret places' – an idea which filled her with fear and revulsion. It would have been logical to destroy his letters, but she felt compelled to keep them – as part of her relished the feeling of power she had over him. So she wrapped them in newspaper, with one corner of the paper turned down, and buried them in her bottom drawer beneath a layer of nightdresses. One afternoon, she had come home from school to find the clothes had been slightly rearranged and the neatly turned corner on the newspaper parcel had been flattened out. The thought of her mother reading these obscene missives was appalling and shameful. But rather than confront her mother, Magda resolved instead to find a better hiding place, moving them to the bottom of her wardrobe beneath a broken floorboard.

One dark evening at the end of October, Magda sat at the kitchen table after school, swinging her legs rhythmically against the chair, watching as her mother prepared a large vat of damson jam on the range.

'Lotte loved that jam,' Magda said.

Her mother, hot from the steam, pushed her fair hair, irritably, away from her face.

'It's damson jam, isn't it?' Magda asked.

'What?' her mother said, crossly.

'The jam… it's damson isn't it?"

'Yes Magda. I have a large crop this year, so I'm making jam.'

'Mutti…'

'Yes Magda…'

'Mutti… please tell me why Lotte and Dr Kalman left the village.'

'Oh for heaven's sake!' Her mother sounded exasperated. 'Why do you need to know?'

'Because she is my friend,' Magda said simply.

'*Was* your friend, you mean.' Her mother was picking stones out of the jam with a spoon, and laying them on a large plate.

'What do you mean?' asked Magda.

'You cannot have a… Jewish friend,' her mother said impatiently. 'I'm sorry but that's the way things are now.'

'Why?' Magda asked. 'That's unfair. Tell me… do you know what happened to them?'

'You really want to know?' Her mother swung round furiously, and sat down heavily, opposite her daughter, her arms folded in front of her.

'Yes,' said Magda, nervous suddenly of the truth.

'I was in the haberdasher's shop in the village,' her mother began. 'I was buying fabric for a new dress for you. I was holding a piece of pale pink cotton up to the light… you know how dark it is in there, and I wanted to check the colour… that it would suit you.'

Magda nodded.

'I saw Dr Kalman coming into the square with Ester his wife, and the children – Lotte and her little brother Ezra. They were carrying their suitcases. I had seen Ester a few days before. She had been very quiet, I remember… upset. I tried to get her to talk, but she wouldn't. I was going to go out into the square, and ask them where they were going. But Mr Wolfahrt, the haberdasher, held my arm. "Don't," he said to me.'

'Why were they leaving?' Magda asked. Käthe's grey-blue eyes filled with tears.

'Some of the villagers spat on them; young men from the Hitler Youth – that boy you know, Otto – he was one of them.'

Magda blushed, remembering the letters.

'They pushed and shoved them,' Käthe went on. 'I remember thinking, why are those boys not in school? The truth is, they run wild. They have become informers, you know… on villagers who they think are not patriotic enough.'

Magda's eyes widened. 'Really?'

'Oh yes,' said her mother. 'We have spies in our midst, Magda, and they are children. They even reported one of your teachers. They said he did not show enough respect for the Führer – can you imagine? When I was a child we were expected to show respect for our teachers. Now these boys are in charge.'

Tears ran down Käthe's face and she fidgeted nervously with the edge of her apron.

'But what of Dr Kalman?' Magda asked softly.

'I saw people I knew – people we sit next to in church – bullying them, pushing them. They shouted "You're not welcome here… get out – back to your own people." I was shocked. I thought these women were my friends, but the way they treated the Kalmans – their own doctor, who was a good man, and his wife and family – it was disgraceful. Then the boys started up again – shouting and spitting. I said to Mr Wolfahrt, "Those boys should show more respect. Dr Kalman is a professional man, for heaven's sake." My hand was on the shop's door handle and I was about to go out into the square and argue with the young men, reason with the others, when Mr Wolfahrt leaned over and locked the door. "Leave them, Madam Maier," he whispered. "I'm afraid you can do nothing for them now. Let them leave the village… hopefully they will find peace somewhere else.'"

Tears poured down Käthe's flushed cheeks, and she wiped them away roughly with the edge of her apron.

'I let them down,' she said. 'Maybe I could have stopped it, but I was afraid.'

She stood up again, and turned back to stirring her jam. 'I thank God that your brother Karl is in England,' she said. 'Do you remember a very devout Catholic boy called Klaus who lived in the next village? He tried to stand up to the Hitler Youth. He accused them of being un-Christian, and begged them to atone for their sins. They took him away. No one has seen him since – not his parents, nor his brother…'

She turned around and leant against the range, looking at her daughter with tears in her eyes.

'So Magda, my darling, however sorry I feel for the Kalmans, I love you and Karl more, and I would do anything to protect you. I can't help Ester and Dr Kalman and I can't stop the hatred in our village. But I can watch over you and I can pray that Karl is safe. I just wish I knew how he was.'

Magda went over and wrapped her arms around her mother's waist, burying her face in her mother's breast. Käthe leant over and kissed the top of her head and Magda suddenly released her and ran upstairs, returning with the letter.

'Mutti… I'm sorry,' she said, holding it out to her mother. 'Here is Karl's letter.'

Her mother broke into a broad smile. She hurriedly wiped her flushed face and sticky hands on the edge of her apron and took the letter from Magda, kissing the envelope. She sat down in the big pine chair at the head of the table and read. When she had finished, she folded it back into the envelope.

'Come,' she said, holding her arms out to her daughter, 'let me hold you.'

Magda sat on her mother's lap, resting her head on her shoulder, her arms wrapped around her neck.

'I understand why you felt you could not show it to me,' Käthe said softly. 'You didn't want to betray his trust.'

Magda nodded. She felt as if a huge responsibility had been lifted from her shoulders.

'It is shocking what he says about this country,' her mother went on, 'but I'm not surprised. Karl has often spoken of his fear about the way everything is going. Before he left for England, he and your father would sit up long into the night, discussing it. I sometimes wondered if it was just talk – men do like to talk, Magda. Often they'd rather talk than act. But Karl is doing something now he believes in, and I must respect that. He's such a clever boy, I know he wouldn't say these things lightly.'

'Should we show it to Papa?' Magda asked.

'No,' Käthe said. 'I don't think so. He would insist on us destroying it.'

'So you don't think we should get rid of it?'

'Of course we should,' Käthe said, fingering the letter. 'But we won't, will we? Neither of us could bear to do that – it might be the last letter we ever receive from him.'

'Oh Mutti, don't say that, please.' She nuzzled into her mother's neck. 'I'm frightened, Mutti.'

'I know, *Liebling*,' her mother said, stroking her hair. 'So am I.'

Chapter Five

Imogen woke just after dawn. Silently she crept out of bed and padded down the chilly lino-covered corridor to the lavatory. Embarrassed at the noise made by the vast overhead cistern as she pulled the chain, she scurried back to the room she shared with Helen. Her room-mate sighed and rolled over in bed, pulling the paisley eiderdown up over her ears.

The room was cold. The bedroom window between their two beds was milky with condensation. Imogen resisted the urge to get back into bed and bury herself in her own eiderdown. Instead she wiped the window with the back of her hand, creating a small porthole through which she could watch the sun coming up over the hills that rose up behind the house. It must have snowed sometime in the night because the summits of the craggy hills were no longer the iron grey of the previous evening, but were sprinkled with the first light snowfall of the year. They sparkled in the autumn sun, pale pink and enticing, like something out of a fairy tale.

Later that morning as Imogen and Helen helped to lay the table for breakfast in the dining room, Mrs Latimer called instructions through the hatch from the kitchen.

'Use the second best cloth girls – the pale blue one. It's in the middle drawer of the dresser. And you'll find plates and so on in the cupboard there... on the right. Use the ones with the little apples and pears. Napkins as usual in the drawer.'

Once they were all seated, boiled eggs arranged on china plates, toast resting in the celadon honeycomb china toast rack, Imogen asked Mrs Latimer if they might go for a walk in the hills later that morning.

'We thought we'd go up Skiddaw,' suggested Imogen, 'the sun on the snow at the top is so lovely.'

'Skiddà, you mean,' murmured Mr Latimer from behind his copy of the *Penrith Observer*.

'I beg your pardon, Mr Latimer?' enquired Imogen politely, cracking open the top of her boiled egg.

'It's pronounced Skiddà... with the stress on the last "a". If you go around saying SkiddORE...' he emphasised the last three letters with a 'received pronunciation' accent, 'the local children will never let you forget it.' He peered across the top of his paper and winked at Imogen, before disappearing once again behind the broadsheet.

'Well thank you very much indeed, I'm sure,' said Imogen, winking herself at Helen, across the table. 'We'll be sure to say it right.'

After breakfast, Imogen and Helen cleared the table and washed up, while Mrs Latimer made them a packed lunch. Back in the hall, as the girls put on their school coats, berets and scarves, Mrs Latimer laid an Ordnance Survey map out on the hall table.

'I think Skiddaw is a bit ambitious for your first walk, girls,' she told them. 'I'd suggest the little hill of Latrigg to start off. Follow Spooney Green Lane here...' Her manicured finger ran along the dotted line of the footpath. 'It will take you up through the forest to the top of the hill. From the summit, you'll have a lovely view of the town and right across Derwentwater and the hills all around.'

Folding the map carefully, she handed it to Imogen. 'And you'd better put on your walking boots,' she said, glancing down at the girls' shoes. 'Those will be no good at all.'

When she went through to the kitchen they slipped out of the door and down the back of the garden, without changing their shoes.

'We won't need boots!' Imogen declared boldly, as they ran towards the back gate. 'Really, what a fuss – it's just a little walk.'

Helen, who was not quite so confident of the wisdom of wearing her day shoes, had already begun to regret not taking their landlady's advice, but decided against complaining. Imogen could be rather intolerant of people who were 'weak and weedy'. But after half an hour, even Imogen was regretting her hasty decision – as water seeped through a small hole in the sole of her new brown brogues, saturating her sock. Ever the optimist, she tried her best to ignore it as they trudged along the footpath, past green fields, and instead gazed up at the snow-sprinkled summit.

'Mrs L said it was about three and a half miles if we just go as far as Latrigg,' said Imogen brightly. 'We should be able to do that easily… don't you think?'

'Yes, I suppose,' said Helen doubtfully, gazing up at the crest of the hill looming over the pine forests on the lower slopes. 'Can you really read that map, Ginny?'

'Of course,' said Imogen proudly. In truth, she was not quite sure she really understood the map, with its complex pattern of footpaths intersecting the circular brown lines that indicated the gradients of the hills over which they were walking.

But keen to show leadership, after they left the relatively easy incline of the lane, she steered them onto a path that traversed the side of a hill. A pine forest rose up imperiously on the right, sunlight filtering through its dark canopy in vertical shafts. Deciduous oaks – their leaves a blaze of autumn colour – dropped away to the left.

As they emerged from the woods onto the open hillside once again, they were presented with a stunning vista of snow-covered hills. Gradually the path began to zig-zag towards the summit. Although still well below the snow line, the path was icy and slippery and the girls – in their unsuitable shoes – began to slip and slide. Imogen fell more than once, tearing her woollen stockings.

'Damn,' she said, 'they're my best pair… I'll have to mend them now.'

'Oh, Ginny,' said Helen, 'perhaps we ought to go down.'

'Down!' exclaimed Imogen. 'Don't be daft… we're nearly there.'

They scrambled to the top and as they triumphantly reached the summit, stood together, looking down over the little town of Keswick and beyond to Derwentwater and the fells on the other side.

'Oh!' said Helen. 'It's so beautiful…'

'Yes it is, isn't it?' said Imogen. 'I knew it would be worth it. Let's sit down for a while and have our picnic.'

In spite of the overnight sprinkling of snow, the sun was now high in the sky and the snow had all but melted. The girls removed their coats and laid them down on the damp ground, lining side up.

'It's so hot we could sunbathe,' said Imogen, sitting down on her coat. She unwrapped their sandwiches and cake and laid the food out between them.

'What… take off our clothes?' asked Helen, horrified.

'No, silly… not completely. But we could take off our jerseys and undo our blouses. I was reading an article in a copy of *Screen Play* magazine the other day. There was an article about Greta Garbo sunbathing. She was in the South of France, and was wearing such wonderful little shorts and a sort of top that stopped under here.' Imogen indicated an area just beneath her bust line.

'What – so you could see her stomach?' asked Helen, breathlessly.

'Yes…' said Imogen, dreamily. 'I asked Mummy if she could make me something similar.'

'What did she say?'

'She would think about it!'

Imogen undid the buttons on her blouse and pulled it up, revealing her stomach.

'Ginny!' said Helen. 'What if someone saw us?'

'What! Up here? Don't be stupid.'

Imogen lay down, her white stomach bared to the weak autumnal sun. Helen gingerly undid her own shirt, but modestly tied the two shirt-tails together.

'Up here,' Helen said, sitting with her hands wrapped around her knees, 'where it's so quiet and peaceful, it seems unimaginable that there's a war somewhere.'

'I know,' said Imogen. 'I said the same to Mother in a letter the other day.'

'Perhaps it will be over soon,' Helen said, shivering slightly as she ate her slice of cake. 'I mean, surely the grown-ups will be able to sort it out?'

'Mmmm,' said Imogen. 'I'm not sure. Grown-ups don't always have all the answers, do they?'

'Well I hope they do,' said Helen. 'My big brother's away fighting and I do worry about him.'

'I'm so sorry,' said Imogen, sitting up and putting her arm around Helen's shoulders. 'I had no idea. My cousins are fighting and I worry about them too, but it's not the same as a brother. I'm sure he'll be all right, Helen. Come on – lie down – let's enjoy the sun while we can.'

After half an hour, as the sun crested and began to slip over the side of the hill, the air began to turn chilly.

'Come on, Ginny,' Helen begged, buttoning her blouse and hauling on her coat. 'I'm cold… we ought to get back.'

'Oh, all right,' said Imogen, reluctantly, tucking her blouse back into her tweed skirt, and pulling her jersey on over her head.

Standing up, she shook the damp grass off her coat, and after putting it back on, they began their descent.

Slipping and sliding their way back down the zig-zag path, they became disoriented. The sun was dropping fast behind the hills, which had taken on a dark purplish hue, and light levels were getting low.

'Oh Ginny,' bleated Helen, 'we're lost.'

Imogen, who was just as nervous as her friend, nevertheless ploughed on, struggling in the half-light with the map.

'No, no… we're fine. I'm sure we passed that tree on the way up,' she said, waving airily at a massive oak, its branches overhanging the path.

'Did we?' asked Helen anxiously, 'I don't remember.'

Truthfully, Imogen was not sure she remembered either, but she marched boldly on, nevertheless.

'If we keep going downhill,' she declared confidently, 'we'll get back to town eventually – it makes sense.'

The path took an upward turn.

'Ginny,' said Helen, catching her arm, 'we're going up again… Ginny!'

Imogen turned irritably towards her friend.

'You're lost!' Helen blurted out, her eyes filling with tears. 'Admit it!'

'Well,' Imogen said, swallowing hard in an attempt to control her own rising sense of panic, 'you're lost too! *You* read the map if you're so clever.'

She threw the now ragged map onto the stony path and slumped down on the grass verge, removing her brown shoe and examining the sole which had developed a hole the size of a guinea coin. Her stocking was soaking wet and had rucked up under her heel causing a huge blister.

She wanted to cry, but was determined to put on a brave face in front of her friend.

There was a rustling sound in the undergrowth nearby.

'What was that?' whispered Helen.

'I don't know,' said Imogen. 'A rabbit?'

'It was too loud for a rabbit.'

'A deer then… there are deer up here on the hills.'

A stifled laugh emanated from a nearby bush and two boys, aged around fifteen, exploded from the woodland, guffawing and clutching their sides.

'Oh!' said Imogen, sharply. 'It's just two silly boys. Come on Helen… we're off.'

She shoved her shoe back on, stood up and taking her friend firmly by the arm, marched off up the path.

The boys stood together and laughed openly.

'You'll not do any good going that way,' they called out, 'unless you want to spend the night on Skiddà.'

The boys turned and ran in the opposite direction, laughing and whooping.

Imogen waited until they were out of sight, before grabbing Helen's arm once again and chasing after them.

As the sun sank in the west, and the moon rose over Skiddaw, the girls found themselves back on the path that led through the pine forest. In fading light, they ran until they reached the welcome familiarity of Spooney Green Lane. As they arrived, out of breath and panting, on the outskirts of the town, the two boys were waiting for them, leaning on a post and rail fence.

'You made it then,' the tall one said, smirking.

'Yes, thank you,' said Imogen with as much dignity as she could muster.

She was aware that her stockings were torn and the sole of her damaged shoe was flapping wildly as she walked.

'Not too chilly up there… for sunbathing?' The boys guffawed.

Helen blushed the colour of beetroot and grabbed her friend's arm, whispering. 'They saw us! Oh Ginny, how could you? They saw…'

'Well, I don't care,' retorted Imogen sharply. 'It was very nice, actually,' she said to the taller of the two boys. He had bright blue eyes and floppy blond hair. 'You should try it sometime. It might make you look a bit less pasty-faced…'

She turned on her now rather squashy heel and marched off towards Manor Park, followed closely by Helen. When she got to the corner of the road, she turned round and noticed the tall boy watching her, a smile playing on his lips. She could have sworn that he winked at her.

Chapter Six

Färsehof Farm
December 1939

Every year, on the first Saturday in December, Käthe prepared the Advent wreath. Piles of greenery lay on the kitchen table, filling the room with their scent. She had gathered branches of pine, bouquets of mistletoe, and late berries from the hedgerows to weave around a circular base made of straw. Velvet and gingham ribbons, meticulously folded and reused each year, were spilling out of a small circular box. Four new red candles stood waiting to be inserted into the wreath. One candle would then be lit the following day – the first Sunday in December – the second one week later and so on, until Christmas Eve.

Magda, wearing her Young Maidens' uniform, came into the kitchen from the yard. She had been to a special meeting of the Hitler Youth to discuss a mid-winter festival their leader wanted to hold in the village.

'Oh I'm glad you're back,' said Käthe, weaving mistletoe between the prickly pine leaves, 'do you want to help me with the wreath?'

Magda had always loved the preparations for Christmas and the making of this wreath was something mother and daughter had done together since Magda was old enough to bend the springy green plants into shape.

'No,' said Magda, heading towards the stairs.

'Magda?' her mother called after her. 'Is something the matter?'

'I'm just tired.'

Magda ran upstairs to her bedroom and slumped down on her bed. Käthe followed her and stood anxiously in the doorway.

'Magda?' *Liebling…* tell me, what is the matter?'

'I hate it!' said Magda. 'I hate the Young Maidens and all those girls. I hate Fräulein Muller. I hate it all, and I don't want to go any more. Please say I can stay at home, Mutti.'

Käthe came into the room and sat down beside her daughter. She put her arm around her.

'Oh little one – are they being mean to you?'

'No, it's not that,' Magda said, impatiently. 'They don't like me particularly. But I don't care about that – I don't like them either. I just don't want to go any more. They are changing everything – even Christmas.'

'What do you mean?' asked Käthe.

'We can't even call it Christmas, any more. It's "Julfest" now. Fräulein Muller says that for hundreds of years before Christmas existed we had a mid-winter festival and that's what we have to celebrate – the Aryan family, gathered round the fire, telling stories of bravery.'

'Would that be so bad?' asked Käthe.

'And we aren't allowed to mention Jesus Christ the Saviour. Now, the only saviour is the Führer – can you believe that?'

Käthe shook her head sadly.

'And there is no Father Christmas – our presents will be delivered by Odin now, a horrible old man in a white robe.'

'Well…' said Käthe, 'does that really matter?'

'Yes, it does matter! Don't you see? Everything's been changed. We can't even put stars on our tree because they are a symbol of communism – or worse, the Star of David. We had to make swastikas and paint them with gold paint.'

'That sounds nice,' Käthe suggested. 'Where's yours?'

'I threw it in the hedge on the way home.'

'Oh Magda…'

'And they won't even let us sing carols. They've changed all the words... turned them into ... what is that word? Propaganda... that's right – propaganda for the party.'

'I'm sure that can't be true...'

'Fräulein Muller says we must have a fire in the village and we all have to go and sing songs.'

'But that might be nice?' suggested Käthe, gently. 'Singing – whether it's carols or not – might be fun?'

'No Mutti! I had to practice them today; they're awful.' Magda began to weep. Her mother hugged her tightly.

'Magda,' she said calmly. 'I'm sorry you don't like it, but you must go. It won't look good if you don't.' Käthe had heard stories about a family who had discouraged their child from attending Hitler Youth meetings. The father had recently been put in a work camp.

Magda looked at her mother. 'I thought you'd understand...'

'I do,' Käthe said. 'But we will get in trouble if you don't go. Remember – you can sing the songs and wave the flags, but you don't have to...' she hunted for the right word, 'you don't have to believe it...'

Magda looked into her mother's blue eyes. 'So I have to pretend. I have to lie?'

'If you like,' said Käthe. 'I know it's hard, Magda. But we are living in dangerous times. Come downstairs. Help me finish the wreath. That's still the same... it's not changed, has it? They can't take that away from us. Then maybe we can cook together – make some cinnamon biscuits; you'd like that?'

'No, Mutti,' said Magda. 'I don't feel like it – I'm sorry.'

The 'fire' celebration took place the following Saturday. It had snowed hard the previous night, and the whole village was swathed in a blanket of white snow.

The wintry weather had forced a relaxation of the uniform rules and the young people had been allowed to wear their own winter coats, boots and hats. The girls looked pretty with their ears and hands muffled in fur, wearing fur-lined embroidered boots and coats. Even the boys looked less militaristic, wearing rabbit-lined hunting hats and brightly coloured scarves. As Magda looked around at her contemporaries, it struck her that even Otto – wearing a red woollen scarf knitted by his mother – looked more like a normal boy, and less like the threatening bully her mother had described haranguing Dr Kalman and his family. That this boy could behave so cruelly seemed at odds with the image he presented of a rosy-cheeked young man in a woollen scarf and fur hat.

The boys of the Hitler Youth had spent the afternoon gathering firewood from the woods around the village. They piled it up in the centre of the square, while the Young Maidens set up tables covered with black and red table cloths decorated with swastikas. As they laid out their homemade cakes and biscuits, it struck Magda that it looked more like a National Socialist rally than a celebration of Christmas. The only traditional 'Christmas' decoration was a large fir tree that had been chopped down a few days earlier in the forest, and put up at one end of the square. In spite of the sparkling swastikas hanging from snowy branches, Magda had to admit that it looked beautiful. As dusk fell, the villagers gathered together and members of the Hitler Youth passed around collecting tins in aid of the 'Winter Relief' fund – a National Socialist initiative designed to raise money for the deserving Aryan poor.

Before the boys and girls were due to sing their Nationalistic songs, Erika and Otto, as team leaders, were handed tapers and invited to light the candles on the Christmas tree.

'Here you are,' said Erika to Magda, handing her one of the tapers. 'Light the candles with me.'

It was an act of friendship, Magda realised, and while she hated everything about the evening, she couldn't suppress a little sense of delight at having been chosen for this duty. There was something eternally joyous about the sight of a candle flickering in the darkness, she felt. Magda and Erika worked their way around the base of the tree, while Otto stood on a ladder and lit the candles at the top. As he climbed back down, he bumped into Magda.

'I'm sorry,' he said, blushing. 'I didn't see you there.' His politeness unsettled her. He was such a contradiction. She found it hard to reconcile his apparent gentleness with the unpleasantness he had shown her friend Lotte.

After the celebrations, the girls cleared the tables and the boys smothered the embers of the fire.

'May I see you home?' Otto asked Magda when everything was tidied away.

'You don't have to,' she said. He would only try to kiss her, and that was something she dreaded.

'I'd like to take you…' he persisted.

'I'll come too,' said Erika, enthusiastically. 'I live next door.'

For once Magda found herself relieved at Erika's intervention. Otto, clearly irritated, reluctantly agreed, and the three young people set off through the forest on the edge of the village. The tall fir trees cast eerie shadows in the moonlight, and Magda was relieved when they emerged into the open fields that led to the farm.

As always, when in the company of other members of the youth movement, Magda felt tongue-tied. As Erika prattled on about how beautiful the ceremony had been, how proud she was of the Führer, of the Young Maidens, of the cakes they had made, Magda simply smiled and said nothing.

'It was so wonderful when the villagers joined in with the singing – don't you think so Magda?' said Erika.

'Yes,' said Magda, without enthusiasm.

'I don't think Magda enjoys these evenings very much,' said Otto perceptively.

'I did enjoy it,' Magda protested, trying to sound enthusiastic. 'I love Christmas… I mean Julfest, and I thought the tree looked very beautiful.'

'And what of the songs?' asked Otto. 'You didn't sing very loudly. Anyone would think you disapproved.'

'What a ridiculous thing to say,' she said, glaring at him before striding ahead of the others, making deep ruts in the snow with her boots.

'My house is just over there,' she called back to Otto and Erika. 'I can go on by myself. Why don't you take Erika home, Otto?'

'Don't I get a hot drink,' he asked, clearly disappointed, 'before I set off for home?'

'I'll give you one,' said Erika, excitedly.

Magda quickened her pace. Arriving at the farm gate, she turned to wave at them both.

'See you soon,' she called out, running up the farm track and hiding behind the dairy, from where she had a good view of the road. Erika, she noticed, had taken Otto's arm and was gazing up at him, as if in rapture.

'Poor Erika,' muttered Magda, before running to the farmhouse and into the sanctuary of home.

Chapter Seven

The girls from Imogen's school shared a building with the local co-educational Keswick Grammar school. It was an unsatisfactory arrangement, and required intricate planning and timetabling on the part of the staff. The girls and boys were segregated in their classes, but as the bell sounded to mark the end of each forty-minute session, the corridors were filled with boys and girls marching past one another in single file to their next lesson, and no amount of sharp-eyed teachers could prevent them fraternising. Notes were passed surreptitiously between the sexes at these 'crossings'; dates were made and relationships inevitably formed. As a pretty, vivacious girl, Imogen had her fair share of male attention, and was frequently passed little notes by admiring boys, their hands slipping into hers as they passed in the corridors. Occasionally she would follow up on these invitations and agree to meet a boy in a café in town. She might even allow one of them to accompany her to the weekly Saturday morning film showings at the Alhambra cinema, although she resisted their invitations to sit in the back row and 'neck'.

Rather to her disappointment, the tall fair-haired boy who had followed her and Helen up Latrigg had not, as yet, featured among her clutch of admirers. She observed him, from time to time, around the school. Sometimes their eyes met and he would smile at her, but she felt it was a cynical smile, as if he was laughing at her. Consequently, she took to walking in the opposite direction if she saw him coming towards her.

As the end of term drew near Imogen and Joy were excited at the prospect of going home for Christmas.

'Let's meet in town after school,' Imogen suggested, 'I want to get a little present for the Latimers.'

'Well I'm not buying anything for my horrid landlady,' said Joy bitterly. 'She does nothing but complain and I'm sure she's only doing it for the government money. She hardly spends anything on food – I'm permanently starving.'

'Oh poor Joy,' said Imogen. 'I do wish you were with me at the Latimers' instead of Helen. She's nice enough, but she's never going to be a really good friend.'

'Perhaps she'd swap?' suggested Joy, optimistically.

'I hardly think so,' said Imogen. 'Everyone knows how awful your landlady is.'

'Well it's just not fair,' complained Joy. 'You're *my* best friend, not hers.'

'I know,' said Imogen, sympathetically. 'Maybe we can change things around next year.'

'Oh I do hope so,' said Joy, earnestly.

'Now, I must find something pretty for Mrs L. She's a bit sad because she's not sure her boys can get home this Christmas.'

'What are you going to buy her?'

'I don't know yet,' said Imogen. They stopped outside a little gift shop that sold mementos of the Lakes. 'What about in here?' suggested Joy.

As the girls wandered around the small gift shop, Imogen became aware of someone watching her. As she turned to look, she noticed the tall, fair-haired boy smiling at her through the shop's Georgian windows. Blushing, she turned away, grabbing Joy's arm.

'He's outside,' she whispered.

'Who is?' Joy whispered back.

'That tall fair boy I told you about. The one who followed me and Helen up the mountain – the boy who's always laughing at me – you must remember.'

'Oh him! The one you don't like, you mean,' said Joy.

'Exactly. I think he's rather supercilious,' Imogen said grandly, before taking Joy's arm and marching to the opposite side of the shop where she picked up a snow globe and shook it, so the white specks fell onto the little Lakeland village below.

Suddenly, the boy materialised next to them.

'Hello again,' he said, a smile playing mischievously on his lips.

'Oh hello,' she said dismissively.

'You been sunbathing recently?'

'What on earth is he talking about?' asked Joy, staring at her friend.

'Oh it's nothing important,' said Imogen, blushing. 'He's just being silly. Come on Joy… let's go.'

Imogen walked determinedly out of the shop, pulling her friend behind her. As they turned towards Main Street she noticed the boy was keeping pace, a few steps behind them.

'Will you stop following us? If you don't, I'll tell someone.'

The boy smiled. 'Just walking through town – same as you. It's a free country.'

'Well, do you have to do it so… close?'

The boy hung back and let a little distance develop between them, but with his long stride, he soon caught them up. Once they'd arrived on Main Street, bustling with shoppers, the impressive clock tower of the town hall ahead of them, the hills rising up in the distance, the boy patted Imogen's shoulder.

'Fancy a milkshake? There's a milk bar round the corner – opened a couple of years back.'

Imogen knew she should say no. It would serve him right if she marched off in the opposite direction with Joy, but she had never had a milkshake before – milk bars having not yet travelled as far as Newcastle.

'All right,' she said, 'as long as you're buying?'

'I am, but I'm not paying for your friend,' he said, pointing at Joy.

'Charming,' said Joy. 'Well I ought to go anyway – I've got maths homework to do. Yuck! See you tomorrow Ginny…'

The milk bar on the high street was filled with girls and boys from the surrounding schools. The tall fair-haired boy found a space for them by the window.

'What can I get you?' asked the waitress, licking her pencil.

Imogen studied the menu, uncertain what to order.

'Chocolate milkshake, please,' said the boy, leaping to her rescue.

'Same,' said Imogen. 'So… what do they call you?'

'Me? Dougie. Douglas really.'

'Are you Scottish? I am… well my parents are anyway.'

'Yes, I suppose I am. My father was born in Edinburgh. He's a teacher.'

'Oh – at our school?'

He nodded.

'What's his name?'

'Henderson,' said Dougie.

The milkshakes arrived and Imogen sucked on her straw, savouring the velvety sweetness.

'Mmmmm,' she murmured. 'Lovely. Oh yes, Mr Henderson, of course. He doesn't teach me, but he always seems nice in the corridor. My grandmother was a Henderson before she married Grandpa. Maybe we're related?' She smiled, relaxing a little at this superficial connection between them.

'Maybe. Quite a popular name in Scotland, though isn't it?'

The pair sat in awkward silence, trying hard not to slurp their milkshakes.

'How old are you?' asked Dougie, finally.

'Fifteen… nearly sixteen. I'm moving to the sixth form next autumn. You?'

'Seventeen. I'm a year ahead of you; when I leave I'll have to join up, I suppose.'

'Poor you,' said Imogen. 'All the young men I know have been called up. It's awfully worrying. I suppose I'll have to do something too when I leave school; although maybe it'll all be over by then… do you think?'

'I doubt it…' said Dougie, pushing his blond hair away from his face. His skin was smooth and clear, Imogen noticed, and his eyes were bright blue – the colour of forget-me-knots.

'What would you do?' he went on, 'join the army?'

'No, nothing like that. I don't think so, anyway. I've not really thought about it. The Wrens maybe? I rather like the uniform.' Imogen was aware, suddenly, of how superficial she sounded.

'You'd look nice,' he said, blushing.

Outside, as the pair left the milk bar, rain was beginning to fall.

'I ought to be getting back,' Imogen said, pulling up the collar of her school coat. 'My landlady doesn't like us to be late.'

'I'll walk you.'

'You don't have to.'

'I'll walk you… you might get lost.'

'You're very cheeky,' she said, laughing. She tucked her dark hair behind her ears, self-consciously. 'I assure you, I'm perfectly capable of finding my own way.'

At the garden gate, she found herself wishing he could stay.

'You could come in if you like.'

'No,' said Dougie, looking up at the house. Mrs Latimer was staring down at them from one of the upstairs windows. 'I don't think she'd like that,' he said, nodding discreetly towards the window above. 'But thank you.'

'Thank *you*… for the milkshake.'

'Can I see you again?' he asked, as she opened the gate.

'Why not?' she said, turning to look at him, trying to imagine what it would be like to kiss him. They stood looking at one another, both aware of Mrs Latimer watching from the bedroom above.

'Well… goodbye then,' she said.

When she got to the front door she turned to wave, but found he'd already gone; much to her surprise she realised she was disappointed.

As Christmas loomed, school days were filled with preparations for end of term plays, carol services and school parties. Imogen and Dougie occasionally found time to snatch a cup of tea together after school, or a stolen moment in the corridor. On the last day of term, as Imogen was coming out school with Joy, she found Dougie waiting outside the school gates.

'I'll be off,' said Joy, discreetly. 'I'll see you tomorrow. What time is your father coming to collect us?'

'Around one o'clock. We'll pick you up…'

As Joy struggled off carrying her school and kit bags, her lacrosse stick slung over her shoulder, Dougie offered to carry Imogen's school bag.

'Thank you,' she said, taking his free arm.

'So… you're off tomorrow then?'

'Yes. My father is collecting us both.'

'Seems odd – you going back to Newcastle. Odd that they think it's safe…'

'Yes I know. But I think the idea was for our schooling not to be disturbed. If we die in the holidays that's not so important.' She giggled, making light of it.

'Don't say that,' he said, grabbing her by the arms. 'Don't ever say that.'

'I'm only joking,' she said, tenderly. 'I'm sure nothing will happen. My parents have been in Newcastle all this time and have been perfectly safe. It's rather ridiculous us all being here.'

They carried on in silence.

'Do you want a cup of tea?' he asked suddenly as they passed a little tea shop in the centre of town.

'I'd better not,' she said. 'I've got to pack this evening and wrap a present or two.'

They walked on in companionable silence until they arrived at the Latimers' house. He put down her bag, and fished around in his school coat pocket. 'I got you something.'

'Oh! That's so sweet.' She blushed. 'I didn't get anything for you – I'm sorry.'

'No matter… open it, then.'

The parcel had been inexpertly wrapped in gaudy red and green paper. Inside was the snow globe she had seen in the gift shop the day he'd taken her to the milk bar.

'Oh Dougie – it's lovely, thank you.'

'I remembered you shaking it. I thought you'd like it.'

'I do.' She reached up and kissed him lightly on the cheek. 'You're very sweet. I hope you have a nice Christmas.'

'And you,' he said.

'Well then…'

'Aye… you'd better go in.'

'Yes,' she said, glancing up at the house. Mr Latimer was watching them from the sitting room window.

'Who was that?' asked Mr Latimer when she met him in the hall.

'Just a boy I know,' she replied.

'Looks keen,' he said, smiling.

'Does he? He's very sweet. He's a lovely boy, but… well, he's just a friend.'

'If you say so,' Mr Latimer said.

*

The following day, Imogen had just finished packing when she heard her father's Wolseley draw up outside the Latimers' house. She raced down the stairs to meet him.

'Oh Daddy,' she said, flinging her arms around his neck as soon as he climbed out of the car. 'It's lovely to see you. I'm so glad you managed to get enough petrol.'

'Yes. It was a bit of a struggle, but we got there in the end. Now I don't want to be too long – we must get home before dark, and it's a long drive back across the Pennines.'

'Yes Daddy. You do worry so.' She took his arm as they walked towards the house. 'I promised Joy we'd give her a lift – I hope that's all right?'

'Yes, of course,' he said. 'And what about Helen?'

'No. Her mother came for her yesterday.'

While her father stowed Imogen's belongings in the boot of the car, she said her farewell to Mr and Mrs Latimer.

'I do so hope you have a good Christmas,' she said, removing a small neat parcel from her coat pocket, and handing it to Mrs Latimer. 'I bought you a little something.'

'Oh… you didn't have to do that. I'll save it for Christmas Day, shall I?' But noticing the slight disappointment on Imogen's face, Mr Latimer nudged his wife.

'Oh open it now, lass.'

Inside the pale pink wrapping paper nestled a small blue bottle with a crystal stopper.

'I hope you like it,' said Imogen. 'It's called "Soir de Paris".'

Mrs Latimer removed the stopper and dabbed a little of the perfume on her wrists. 'Lovely,' she murmured as she brought her wrist to her nose. '"Soir de Paris" – how romantic it sounds.' Her eyes welled up with tears.

'I'm sorry,' muttered Imogen, 'I didn't mean…'

'Well,' said her father, interrupting, 'we ought to be getting off. Thank you so much both of you for looking after Imogen.'

'Oh,' said Mr Latimer, 'she's no trouble.'

Joy was in high spirits as she climbed into the car.

'I am so relieved to be getting away from that terrible woman,' she said, sinking into the leather seats.

'Poor Joy,' Imogen explained to her father, 'is with the most awful family. The mother does nothing but weep over her four older boys who are all fighting in the war and ignores her four younger children; and there's never enough to eat – is there Joy?'

Joy nodded her head, mournfully.

'I do wish we could help her move somewhere else,' Imogen pleaded.

'Well there's nothing we can do about it now,' said her father from the front seat. 'Settle back girls and enjoy the drive.'

Back in Newcastle, the household was busy with Christmas preparations. The scent of cinnamon and nutmeg wafted out of the kitchen, as Imogen's father, Joe, put her bags down in the hall. Her mother emerged wearing an apron, her hands covered with flour.

'Darling girl,' she said, hugging Imogen to her. 'I have missed you so.'

'And I've missed you too,' said Imogen, weeping slightly with relief at finally being home. 'Something smells lovely,' she said, wiping her eyes with the back of her hand.

'I'm just making a batch of mince pies – in case people drop by unexpectedly. They're threatening us with food rationing in the New Year, so I thought we'd make the best of it while we still can.'

'Have you done the tree yet?' asked Imogen, peering around the hall.

'No,' her mother said firmly. 'I told Daddy we must wait for you to come home, as I know how much you love decorating it. It's outside in a pot in the back garden.'

In the days leading up to Christmas, Imogen relaxed and spent much of her time helping her mother in the kitchen. Rose taught her to make pastry and they assembled a game pie together. Wrapped in greaseproof paper, it was stored on a marble slab in the larder, next to the large goose Rose had bought for Christmas Day. In spite of the war, most people were determined to enjoy the holiday, and Rose and Joe had invited family to share the celebrations with them. Two of Rose's brothers were due to arrive on Christmas Eve, bringing their combined brood of half a dozen children. Imogen, as an only child, adored her cousins and found herself counting the days until the celebrations could begin.

'We shall go shopping,' Rose said to Imogen one morning over breakfast. 'You've grown such a lot and nothing seems to fit you any more. Fenwicks, I think.'

'Really Mummy – are you sure? That would be lovely.'

They chose a new skirt, two new shirts, some underwear, and a dark green woollen dress. It was quite unlike anything Imogen had ever owned before – figure-hugging and grown up, at least to Imogen's eyes.

'You can wear that at the McMasters' do,' said Rose, as the shop assistant wrapped the dress.

'Are they having a do?' asked Imogen.

'Yes – the day before Christmas Eve. I expect all the boys will be there.'

Rose turned to look up at her daughter as a faint blush spread across Imogen's pale face.

Imogen hadn't thought much about Freddie since being sent to Keswick. Convinced he would find her childish in comparison to the girls at university, she had dismissed him from her mind and had instead occupied herself working hard at her lessons – and, of course, going out for the occasional date with Dougie. But standing next to her mother in Fenwick's, Imogen realised the lure of handsome, debonair Freddie was as strong as ever.

On the evening of the party, snow was forecast and Imogen's bedroom – in spite of the fire her father had lit in her room – was chilly. Imogen stood back to admire herself in the dark oak cheval mirror. The new green dress was perfect, she decided, but her shoulder-length hair hung childishly on either side of her heart-shaped face. Recalling a photograph of Rita Hayworth she had seen in a movie magazine with her hair piled fetchingly on top of her head, Imogen sat at her dressing table and pinned up her own hair. Finally applying a slick of red lipstick, she tried to imagine what Freddie would think when he saw her. Would he be entranced by her? Perhaps they would spend the evening talking together, reminiscing about their tennis days – and the following day he might even invite her to go for a romantic Christmas Eve walk…

'Imogen,' her mother called up the stairs, interrupting her romantic fantasies. 'It's time to go.'

'Coming,' she shouted. With one last look in the mirror, she swept down the stairs, her green eyes sparkling, her neat figure shown off to perfection in the new emerald-green dress.

The party was in full swing when the Mitchells arrived. Leaving their coats on a long upright sofa in the hall, they found the drawing-room filled with local people drinking sherry, the air thick with smoke from the men's cigarettes and cigars. While her parents were being greeted by their friends, Imogen looked around hopefully for Freddie. Nursing a small glass of Dubonnet and soda – the only drink her father allowed – she was delighted when Philip McMasters, Freddie's elder brother, tapped her on the shoulder.

'Hello little one,' he said. Imogen was not sure she liked this term of affection. She realised he meant well, but it made her feel like a child and she had tried so hard that evening, with her new figure-hugging dress, to look as mature and elegant as possible.

'Hello Philip. How are you? You look marvellous in your uniform.'

'Thank you,' he said smugly. 'You look rather good yourself… have you grown?'

Imogen blushed – flattered and irritated in equal measure.

'Are you home on leave?' she asked, trying desperately to make adult conversation.

'Yes – just for a couple of days… got a new posting in the New Year.'

'Anywhere interesting?'

'Not allowed to say.'

Imogen fingered her glass, wondering what to say next.

'Is Freddie here?'

'No,' he said. 'He's gone to some university squadron do tonight.'

Noting the disappointment on Imogen's face, he added: 'Were you hoping to see him…?'

'Oh… you know,' she said as casually as possible. 'We've just not seen one another for a while. I was hoping he might give me a game of tennis.' In light of the fact that snow was forecast, this last remark was clearly absurd.

'Ah yes – your tennis.' Philip smiled indulgently. 'Quite legendary, I gather. He admitted he'd been absolutely trounced by you.'

'Really? Did he? I wouldn't say that, but I was a little better than him, it's true.'

'Well good for you,' said Philip, laughing. 'I'll tell him you missed him, shall I?'

'Oh, it doesn't matter,' Imogen said, as casually as she could. 'I'll see him next time, I expect.'

That night, as she lay in bed dressed in her girlish pyjamas, she thought longingly of Freddie McMasters and of his floppy dark hair and clear grey eyes.

Back at school after the holidays, she told Joy about her unrequited love.

'Oh Joy... it's just so unfair. He's quite the most handsome man I've ever known. But I never see him. I hate this war.'

'Oh Ginny, you poor thing. He does sound dreamy. But he's quite a lot older than you, isn't he? Don't you think, that... perhaps, he might already have a girlfriend more his own age?'

'Oh don't say that!' Imogen snapped. 'He can't have anyone else. I thought he really liked me – but perhaps I've just been fooling myself all this time.'

Imogen was not somebody to wallow in despair. Her nagging anxiety that Freddie might already have a more suitable girlfriend forced her to abandon any hopes she might have once had for their future relationship. Over the next few months, as the days grew longer and the cold days of winter turned to spring, she began to see more of Dougie. They walked in the hills together after school, lying on the grass amongst the bracken.

'It's so peaceful up here... It's like we're the only boy and girl left on earth – like Adam and Eve,' Imogen suggested, innocently, one afternoon.

Dougie, his shirt sleeves rolled up, revealing strong forearms, rolled over to face her.

'Adam and Eve, eh? So are you going to tempt me then?'

Imogen sat up abruptly, crimson with embarrassment. 'I didn't mean that. Oh... you know what I meant. It's just so tranquil and quiet – one can't imagine all those boys, like you, doing battle with Hitler and his horrible, horrible army over in France.'

Tears came into her eyes.

'Hey,' he said, gently, reaching up and rubbing her back. 'Don't think about it, lass. I don't. There's nothing we can do anyway. Lie down.'

She lay, feeling the sun warming her body… Dougie leant over and kissed her tenderly on the mouth. It was the first time she had ever been kissed, and she was amazed at the softness of his lips.

'That was lovely,' she said, stroking his cheek.

'I'll do it again then, shall I?'

As he kissed her she forgot about Freddie, about missing home, about the war itself. She was just a girl lying in the arms of a boy in the spring sunshine.

Chapter Eight

Pieter came in from the yard, leaving his muddy boots outside on the step.

'Käthe,' he called out. 'Is breakfast ready?'

'Yes,' she shouted down from their bedroom, 'I'm just coming.'

As he waited for his wife, he sat at the table, twiddling the dials of the Volksemfänger radio that sat on the kitchen dresser. In order to encourage ordinary Germans to listen to National Socialist propaganda put out by Goebbels from Berlin, millions of these inexpensive radios had been produced by the State. Listening to foreign news stations was illegal, punishable with a year or more in a concentration camp. In an attempt to prevent foreign news infiltrating the airwaves, the authorities had destroyed radio transmitters across Europe. But the BBC had a German language service which could be heard all over Europe.

As Magda came down the stairs for breakfast, she heard the disparate staccato snippets of radio programmes as her father turned the dial – classical music, a woman's voice reciting poetry, curious whistling sounds, all edged falteringly into the room, until they heard an English voice saying in German:

> *In London this morning, it was announced that the Prime Minister, Neville Chamberlain has stepped aside in favour of the First Lord of the Admiralty – Sir Winston Churchill…*

The signal dipped. Standing in the doorway, Magda watched as her father turned up the volume.

First news of the German invasion into the Low Countries reached London at dawn…

'Papa… what are you listening to?'

Pieter held his fingers to his lips. 'Ssshh… come here… the signal's so bad, I can hardly hear it.'

Magda listened intently.

In a proclamation issued to the German armies in the West, Hitler said: 'The hour has come for the decisive battle for the future of the German nation'. Reports from Holland said German troops crossed the border during the night. The Dutch destroyed bridges over the rivers Maas and IJssel to prevent the German advance.

Pieter looked at his daughter, his eyes wide. 'Well? What did they say?'

'It's something about our troops being in Holland… The Dutch have blown up the bridges to try to stop them.'

Pieter turned the dial to a German station. The familiar hectoring voice of the Führer rang out: *The battle beginning today will decide the fate of the German nation for the next thousand years.*

'What's going on?' asked Käthe, coming downstairs.

'We're trying to listen to the news,' said Magda.

'Why? What's happened?' Käthe eyes were fearful.

'Our troops have moved into Holland,' said Magda.

Käthe walked across to the stove and riddled the fire. She threw on the last of the coal from the bucket, and filled the kettle from the rattling tap.

'Well, there's nothing we can do about it,' she said, putting the kettle on the stove and taking a basket of eggs from the windowsill. 'How do you want your eggs?'

There was a knock at the door and Pieter swiftly turned off the radio.

'Open it,' he whispered to Magda.

Standing outside in his Hitler Youth uniform, was Otto.

'Hello,' Magda said, as casually as she could, wondering how long he'd been standing there.

'May I come in?'

'I suppose so,' said Magda, stepping aside.

He filled the kitchen with his presence. In his khaki-coloured shirt, always immaculately ironed, and dark tie, his blond hair swept away from his high tanned forehead, he looked like a poster boy for the Youth.

'I thought I heard the Führer's voice,' he said, peering around the room.

Magda blushed. 'Oh yes. We were just listening to him on the radio.'

Otto looked from Magda to her father. 'What was he saying?'

Magda, anxious to prevent Pieter revealing something that could only have come from a foreign news organisation, quickly interjected.

'Just that the battle has started. The Führer said it would decide our fate for the next thousand years… It was very stirring, wasn't it Papa?'

'Well…' said Pieter, standing up. 'If you'll all excuse me, I have work to do.'

As he got to the door, he turned and looked pointedly at the young man. 'Heil Hitler,' he said, raising his arm in the familiar salute.

'Heil Hitler,' said Otto, crisply, snapping his heels together, before pulling out a chair and sitting down at the table.

Käthe, standing behind the young man, looked across at Magda and raised her eyebrows. 'Why is he here?' she mouthed silently.

Magda shook her head discreetly.

'Would you like breakfast, Otto?' Käthe asked, politely.

'Thank you – yes,' he said. Magda's heart sank, but she got up and laid the table for three.

'Are you on your way to school?' she asked him, as she set out a plate and cup for him. 'You're a bit out of the way here, aren't you?'

'I was coming this way – I just thought I'd drop in.' He smiled at her, but his eyes were cold. 'I thought we could go to school together.'

Their breakfast finished, Magda went upstairs to her room and brushed her hair. Her father was out in the yard, pushing the cows into the milking parlour. He looked agitated, Magda thought. He hadn't even had breakfast. When she came back down into the kitchen, Otto stood ready to escort her. As they walked down the farm track towards the road, Magda turned to wave and noticed her parents talking intensely to one another.

'Why did you really come here today?' she asked Otto.

'That's an odd question,' he replied. 'I thought you liked me… I thought we were friends.'

'Of course I like you,' Magda said hurriedly, anxious not to upset him. 'Although I think Erika likes you more.' She attempted a laugh, trying to diffuse the air of tension between them.

'Huh,' he said dismissively, 'Erika is an idiot…'

'She's team leader,' said Magda defensively.

'Only because she sucks up to Fräulein Muller. You should be leader, really.' He glanced shyly down at her, admiring her gold hair, her clear skin. He was sincere, she realised.

'Oh no!' Magda replied, modestly. 'I'm really not…' She cast around for a suitable phrase. 'Not the right sort of person.'

'Why not?' Otto asked. 'You're intelligent, blonde, Aryan… you're perfect.'

Magda's route to school took her along the main road, before she cut across fields and through the wood, which lay on the edge of the village.

When Magda was alone, she would often run the last part of the journey, nervous of hidden demons and strange sounds that lurked between the tall fir trees. Now as they entered the dark wood she felt more afraid of what Otto might do while they were in such a secluded place.

'Come on,' she said, walking briskly ahead. 'We don't want to be late.'

He grabbed her by the arm and pulled her towards him, kissing her fiercely on the mouth. She turned her face away, wriggling free of him.

'What are you doing?' she asked, backing away from him.

'Kissing you, of course. What's wrong with that?'

'Because I'm not your girlfriend.'

'But I want you to be.' He glared at her.

'Well…' she began, casting around for anything she could say to dissuade him, without offending him. 'I'm too young,' she said at last.

'You're only a year younger than me.'

'I've known you all my life…'

'What has that to do with it?'

Unable to come up with any suitable argument she finally turned on her heel and marched off, shouting behind her, 'Oh Otto…do let's go on. We don't want to be late.'

Reluctantly he followed her, walking sulkily behind her. Magda was relieved when an elderly woman came towards them carrying a foraging basket. Magda began to run, only pausing briefly when she reached the edge of the wood, where the sun broke through the darkness of the trees. She hurried on, arriving at the outskirts of the village, walking past the Kalman's old house and into the village square, which was bustling with shoppers. Only then did she stop and wait for Otto. They walked in silence through the square, and down the lane that led to the school.

As she was about to walk through the school gates, he caught her arm once again.

'No Otto – not here.'

'I heard,' he said. He was smiling, but his blue eyes were icily cold. 'I heard you listening to the foreign station.'

'It was a mistake,' Magda said, hurriedly, her heart racing. 'Papa was looking for the German station.'

'I could report you to the authorities,' he said. 'You know what happens if you listen to foreign news broadcasts.'

'Otto… please don't do that. It was not deliberate.'

'Well, we'll see, won't we? I wouldn't want my girlfriend to get into trouble.' He snaked his arm around her waist and pulled her towards him. She smelt his breath, felt it hot on her cheek. Then he released her suddenly and walked away – leaving her panting slightly, sweat breaking out on her forehead.

Chapter Nine

Keswick
May 1940

One afternoon Imogen, Helen and the Latimers gathered around the large Bakelite radio in the sitting room of the house in Manor Park listening to the early evening news:

> *In Parliament today, Winston Churchill made his first address to the House of Commons as Prime Minister. He spoke of the importance of creating a government of national unity, and reminded the House that the country faces an ordeal of a most grievous kind, with many long months of struggle and suffering ahead. He had nothing to offer, he said, 'but blood, toil, tears and sweat…'*

The Latimers sat together on the sofa, and, unusually, Imogen noticed, were holding hands. She wondered, as she observed the concern etched on their faces, whether her own mother and father were also sitting side by side listening to this momentous broadcast.

Mrs Latimer suddenly stood up, clutching a handkerchief to her mouth and ran from the room. Imogen and Helen exchanged glances. Mr Latimer followed his wife to the kitchen.

'She's worried about her sons,' said Helen, knowingly. 'I heard her on the phone last night, talking to a friend. The boys are both in the army – being pushed back by the Germans.'

'Oh that's awful,' muttered Imogen. 'Poor thing.'

*

In the week that followed, Mrs Latimer retreated to her room. She would appear briefly in the morning in her woollen dressing gown, collect a cup of tea from the kitchen before returning to her bedroom, where she would stay for the rest of the day. Imogen and Helen did their best to help Mr Latimer prepare breakfast and tea when they came home from school, but the strain was felt throughout the house. Although she was not a mother, Imogen could well imagine the torment of not knowing what was happening to one's beloved children, facing peril and danger on a daily basis. She often studied the photograph of the Latimers' two boys – James and Arthur – wearing corduroys, hiking books and Fair Isle sweaters, standing in the sunshine at the top of Skiddaw. In another time, Imogen often thought, she might have fallen in love with one of them. Now, it occurred to her, she might not even get a chance to meet them – they might be killed in this terrible war, and Mrs Latimer would never leave her bedroom again.

A few days later, when Imogen came home from school, she found Mr Latimer listening, once again, to the radio in the sitting room.

'Listen,' he said, holding his finger to his lips. 'It's the PM…'

> … *A tremendous battle is raging in France and Flanders. The Germans, by a remarkable combination of air bombing and heavily armoured tanks, have broken through the French defences…*

'Oh dear,' said Imogen, with tears in her eyes, 'your lovely boys…'

'I know lass… listen to Churchill.'

… side by side, the British and French peoples have advanced to rescue not only Europe but mankind from the foulest and most soul-destroying tyranny which has ever darkened and stained the pages of history. Behind them – behind us – behind the armies and fleets of Britain and France – gather a group of shattered states and bludgeoned races: the Czechs, the Poles, the Norwegians, the Danes, the Dutch, the Belgians – upon all of whom the long night of barbarism will descend, unbroken even by a star of hope, unless we conquer, as conquer we must; as conquer we shall.

Centuries ago words were written to be a call and a spur to the faithful servants of Truth and Justice. 'Arm yourselves, and be ye men of valour and be in readiness for the conflict; for it is better for us to perish in battle than to look upon the outrage of our nation and our altar. As the will of God is in Heaven even so let it be.

'Amen,' said Mr Latimer as tears poured down his cheeks.

The following week Imogen received a parcel from her mother. It was delivered to the house just as she was preparing to leave for school. She ran upstairs immediately to open it and, along with a letter from her mother, found a new summer dress in pale green Liberty print cotton, and a cream silk blouse. Helen, who had been brushing her teeth in the bathroom, came into the bedroom just as Imogen hung up her new clothes up on the door of the wardrobe.

'Oh… something new to wear – lucky you,' she said, sulkily.

'I know,' said Imogen. 'I am lucky. But I've grown such a lot and everything I have is too short. Mind you, this dress looks a bit long. Still, I can take it up, can't I?'

Helen shrugged and pulled on her school skirt and shirt. Clearly, she would not give Imogen the satisfaction of admiring her new clothes and Imogen could hardly blame her. To get pleasure from something as trivial as a new outfit, when a few hundred miles away young men were dying, seemed quite wrong. And yet, she had to admit that she did feel pleasure.

Walking into town after school with Joy, Imogen mentioned her new clothes.

'It's such a lovely frock – although when I'll wear it, I don't know. What I really needed was new shoes… I did ask for some money so I could buy a pair, but she doesn't seem to have taken the hint.'

'Oh Ginny,' said Joy suddenly, 'do stop talking about clothes. I've been trying to tell you something for ages.'

Imogen looked at her friend, and was surprised to see tears in her eyes.

'Oh Joy… what's the matter?'

'I simply can't bear that house I'm in any longer, Ginny. We have to do something about it. Couldn't we live together?'

'You know I'd love to. But I'm stuck for the moment with Helen and poor Mrs Latimer – who's jolly nice, obviously, but the poor thing is so worried about her sons – I don't want to cause her any bother.'

'I understand,' said Joy, blowing her nose. 'Poor Mrs Latimer. I shouldn't be so selfish.'

'You're not being selfish, but I'm just a bit torn at the moment; I'm sure you understand.'

'Yes, of course I do. I just thought, if we spoke to our parents about it, maybe they could find us somewhere else, together?'

'I tell you what… if Mrs Latimer's boys are all right, I promise I'll have a word with Mummy.'

Back at Manor Park, Imogen let herself into the hall. She could hear someone moving around in the kitchen and Mr Latimer called out.

'Imogen, is that you?'

'Yes, Mr Latimer…'

'Could you come in here please?'

Imogen hung her school coat and satchel over the banisters, and went into the kitchen at the back of the house.

'Could you give me a bit of help? I really don't know what to do – I've never cooked spam before, but there doesn't seem to be much else.' He opened the kitchen cupboard, revealing bare shelves. Imogen looked a little dubiously at the small oblong tin sitting on the Formica worktop.

'Well, quite honestly,' she said, 'neither have I, but I'm sure it can't be that hard – can it? We could fry it perhaps… in slices? And do some potatoes. How about that?'

Together they cooked tea and afterwards went into the sitting room to listen to the news. Mrs Latimer remained in her bedroom, unable to bear any reminder of what was happening in Northern France.

When the broadcast was finished, Imogen offered to take Mrs Latimer a cup of tea. 'She's had nothing to eat this evening,' she told Mr Latimer, 'and I ought to go upstairs and reply to my mother's letter and thank her for the lovely clothes she sent me.'

Sitting at the table in her room overlooking the hills behind the town, she sat staring at a blank piece of writing paper, her pen in her hand, wondering what to write. She would thank her mother for the clothes, obviously, but somehow there was so much to say.

Should she mention Joy's predicament? In all honesty, what could her mother do about it, back in Newcastle? She thought about mentioning her new friend, Dougie. But it seemed inappropriate somehow when the war was getting so much worse. Besides, her mother might not approve of her getting to know a local boy – she could be funny like that. 'I'm not prejudiced,' Rose was fond of saying, 'but I do discriminate.' Her mother's letter had mentioned painting the kitchen, but it seemed such an odd thing to do when your house might be blown up at any time. Suddenly she was overcome with homesickness. She thought of her mother choosing paint colours – of how she would have asked Imogen's advice had she been at home. 'You have a good eye,' she often said to Imogen, 'what colour do you think it should be?' Imogen's eyes filled with tears, her throat constricting as it always did when she was about to cry. She swallowed hard and thought about the Latimer boys – and all the others in trouble across the Channel – and began to write.

22nd May 1940

Dear Mum and Dad,

Isn't the news awful? What is wrong with the British and French armies – why can't they stop this awful advance?

Today they say the Boche is fourteen miles from the Channel. Does it mean that the Allies are waiting for them with a trap, or that we are being hopelessly beaten? Couldn't the Fleet, if the Germans take the channel ports and the French citizens have been evacuated, bombard them?

You'd think God would defend the right – but will He? Has He?

I don't feel exactly optimistic today.

Yes, Mummy the frock and blouse fitted – thank you very much, but I will have to turn up the hem of the frock.

What colour is the kitchen? Not the same? What's the good of painting it when Hitler is about to walk in on us?

Today is not so warm as the days previous, but even so – it's fine.

Well, I must finish my homework now, so I'll say cheerio.
Tons of love,
From Imogen

PS – Mrs L is very worried about her two sons, who are in Northern France. She's not managing to do much shopping

and I'm starving! Please could you send a little extra money
so I can buy food?!
PPS if they invade Britain <u>I'm coming home</u>!

In spite of the terrible news from France, Imogen managed to maintain a cheerful exterior. And her meetings with Dougie, which took place almost every day, cheered her more than anything. They went to the cinema, and visited the tea shops. They walked in the hills and around the edge of the lake where they held hands and kissed. At night she thought about him – the softness of his skin against hers, the way his fair hair tickled her forehead when he kissed her. Sometimes, when she unpacked her satchel at the end of the day, she would find little notes from him – notes he must have placed there when they were together.

One afternoon, at the end of May, Dougie walked her home and they stood a few doors down from her house kissing, hoping they couldn't be seen.

'Dougie… I must go in. Mr Latimer needs help.'

'Stay a bit longer,' he begged, stroking her neck.

'No!' she said firmly. 'I'll see you tomorrow. Good night.'

As she walked through to the kitchen, she found Mr Latimer sitting at the small kitchen table, listening once again to the news. He held his hand up as she walked in.

'Listen…' was all he said. Helen came downstairs and as she opened her mouth to say something, Imogen put her finger to her lips and pointed to the radio.

'A number of appeals for recruits have been issued today.
The Admiralty want men experienced in marine internal
combustion engines, or service as enginemen in yachts or
motor boats. Others who have had charge of motor boats
and have good knowledge of coastal navigation are needed as

uncertified second hands. Applications should be made to the nearest registrar, Royal Naval reserve, or to the fishery officer.'

Mr Latimer sat staring into space when the broadcast had finished. Imogen switched on the light and peered into the cupboard for something to eat.

'What do they mean?' she asked. 'Why do they need recruits?'

'To bring the boys out,' said Mr Latimer. 'They're trapped on the beaches at Dunkirk. Thousands of them, being strafed by the Luftwaffe. Sitting ducks. Hundreds… dying. The navy can't rescue them all – so they've asked for little boats. God, I'd go if I could.' He put his head in his hands.

'Oh,' said Imogen, looking anxiously at Helen. 'Does Mrs Latimer know?'

'No… thank God. She won't listen to the radio. It's better that way.'

'What can we do?' asked Helen, kindly.

'Nothing, girls… you're all right.'

'Well, we can make supper,' said Imogen brightly. 'We've got to eat.'

'I'm sorry – I've done no shopping, I've been that worried.'

'I'm sure there's something we can use,' said Imogen, optimistically.

The girls peered into the deep recesses of the Latimers' larder.

'Right,' said Ginny. 'There's jam and flour, and a small piece of cheddar, and the end of a loaf. I'm sure we can make something out of that.'

'I've no eggs; we've had our ration for the week.'

'Cheese on toast then?' said Imogen, 'and a spoonful of jam for pudding…'

*

Later that night, as the girls lay in bed, their stomachs rumbling, they listened to Mrs Latimer sobbing – an almost childlike crying, interjected only by the soft, gentle voice of her husband trying to console her.

'Poor Mrs L,' said Helen. 'Do you think the boys will be all right?'

'I hope so,' said Imogen. 'I really do hope so. The thought of anything happening to them is just too awful to contemplate. I just don't think she'd survive.'

Chapter Ten

Färsehof Farm
June 1940

Magda stood in the bathroom of the farmhouse, a pair of scissors in her hand. The following day would be her fourteenth birthday – the age at which she had to join the young adult section of the League of German Girls. It was a momentous day for other reasons too. The 22nd June was the day the Führer was going to sign an armistice with the French, giving Germany control over Northern and Western France. German troops had already arrived in Paris and German tanks were rolling unopposed down the Champs-Élysées towards the Place de la Concorde.

Magda's local Hitler Youth group were planning a weekend of activities to celebrate the defeat of the British on the beaches at Dunkirk, the capitulation of France and the signing of the armistice. Thousands of Allied soldiers had been killed on the beaches of Northern France, although thousands more had been spirited away on a fleet of little boats and troop ships back to England. In the higher echelons of the German armed forces, the fact that so many troops had escaped was considered a critical mistake, but in the towns and villages all over Germany the propaganda machine was insisting that it was a great victory, and the beginning of the end. As the League of Girls had gathered the previous week to discuss arrangements for a street party to celebrate the victory, they had been greeted by their leader Fräulein Müller – in an ecstatic mood – quoting one of the Führer's speeches delivered after the battle.

'"Soldiers of the West Front!"' Fräulein Müller said, her face shining with pride. '"Dunkirk has fallen… with it has ended the greatest battle in world history. Soldiers! My confidence in you knows no bounds. You have not disappointed me."'

Magda's fellow league members cheered. Some even had tears in their eyes. Magda was bewildered by their euphoric response.

'We will have the most wonderful party, and I want everyone to bake a cake to demonstrate your culinary skills,' Fräulein Muller went on, inspecting the line of girls. She stopped in front of Magda.

'I'm talking particularly to you, Magda Maier. You will be fourteen next week on the day our Führer is signing the treaty. It's an auspicious day, and I expect great things from you. Don't disappoint me.'

That evening, Magda had asked her mother if she could spare her this torture.

'Please Mutti – could you make the cake for me? You know what a terrible cook I am…'

Now, as she stared in the mirror, and considered her long plaits – the hairstyle of choice for all League maidens – Magda took the bathroom scissors and snipped through the two long ropes of blonde hair, just below her chin. The sense of rebellion and liberation this act produced in her was remarkable. She shook her head and ruffled her hair, then picked up the two plaits and took them into her bedroom, stuffing them into the bottom drawer of her chest of drawers.

Downstairs in the kitchen, Mutti was taking an apple cake out of the stove, when Magda came in. As she turned around, holding the cake in her hands, Käthe gasped.

'My God, Magda! What have you done?'

'Cut my hair,' said Magda, sitting down at the table. 'Is it a problem?'

'But *Liebling*, girls don't have… you looked so nice with…'
Käthe fell silent.

'Girls don't have short hair?' said Magda, defiantly. 'Well, I do. I like it. Can you neaten it up for me?'

Her mother put the cake onto a rack, and took the scissors from her daughter.

'Very well. Let's at least make it look tidy.'

As the smell of apple cake drifted across the kitchen, Käthe snipped nervously at her daughter's hair.

'I made your cake for you,' Käthe said.

'Thank you Mutti… it smells lovely.'

'Well I hope they all enjoy it.'

'I hope it chokes them,' Magda said gloomily. 'I can't see what there is to celebrate.'

'I just worry,' Käthe said, as she clipped away at her daughter's hair, 'that you are so out of step with everyone. All around us, people are celebrating our victory over the British at Dunkirk and the fall of France. If you don't seem happy about it people will notice.'

'How can I celebrate the death of so many soldiers dying on the beaches? Fräulein Muller told us all about it, and she was so delighted – it sickened me.'

'I blame your brother,' Käthe said, wiping the snipped ends of her daughter's hair away from her white neck. 'If he hadn't written that letter you would be happy along with the others. He included you in something that was not your business. He's an adult, and he can make these decisions, but you're just a child.'

'I'm not a child,' Magda said, defiantly, running her fingers through her newly-shortened hair. 'I'm a young woman and I have eyes and ears and can see what is true and what is not.'

'Well,' said Käthe, sweeping up the clippings from the floor, 'I just hope your short hair doesn't upset too many people.'

*

At school that morning, her new hairstyle, predictably, caused a stir.

'Magda Maier! I hardly recognised you,' Herr Schmidt, her teacher, scolded. 'Do you have some sort of infestation that necessitated you to do this?'

'No!' Magda said indignantly. 'I just didn't want plaits any more.'

'I see,' he said sternly. 'Well sit down. I suppose it will grow.'

But that morning, in the break between lessons, several girls came up to her and admired her short hair.

'I'd love a hairstyle like that,' Erika said. 'But my mother won't let me. She says that long hair is the mark of a true maiden.'

'Well I don't want to be a true maiden,' Magda said briskly. 'I just want to be me.'

Returning to school after lunch, Otto bounded up behind her.

'Magda,' he called out, 'I've been looking for you everywhere.'

'Well you found me,' she said.

'Why did you cut off your beautiful hair?' He touched her short golden bob. 'I liked it the way it was.'

'Well, I didn't,' she said, moving her head away from his hand. 'It annoyed me. Everyone looking the same – it's odd. I'm not like everyone else. I'm an individual.'

She knew this was a provocative thing to say. Individuality was not encouraged. But she felt unable to quash her sense of defiance. She knew she had affronted her teachers and peers, and it delighted her. It was an outward symbol of rebellion that she could impose on the people around her who, increasingly, she despised.

Otto flushed. With what she couldn't be sure... anger, perhaps. Certainly anger was an emotion he expressed only too frequently. He had stood up in class the previous day, and criticised the teacher for not saluting the Führer at the start of afternoon school. The other children had sniggered in admiration, but the teacher, Magda thought, had looked genuinely scared, as if this young boy had the power to destroy him.

As junior leader of the Hitler Youth, Otto had become increasingly overbearing. He had recently joined an elite group within the Hitler Youth called HJ-Streifendienst, which would give him automatic entry to SS officer training when he was old enough.

'Well I hope it grows soon,' Otto said, 'you looked prettier with long hair.'

When school finished, the children assembled in the village square to arrange the tables for the feast they had been instructed to bring the following day.

'All the girls will bring cakes and biscuits,' Fräulein Muller said. 'Erika will make a list of what you all intend to bring. The boys, led by Otto, will perform a demonstration of their rifle skills. Otto – you may set up a rifle range in the centre of the square.'

'Magda,' said Erika. 'What cake will you bring?'

'An apple cake,' said Magda, remembering the cake her mother had made that morning.

'That's very good,' said Erika, with surprise. 'I thought you hated cooking.'

'I do,' said Magda, defiantly. 'My mother made it.'

Erika regarded her with disdain. 'You should learn,' she said. 'It's your duty… as a German woman.'

Magda wanted to scream at her: 'my duty is to fight people like you.' But she remained uncharacteristically silent.

Before the meeting broke up, Otto took it upon himself to speak to the group.

'Tomorrow,' he began, 'we will spend the day celebrating the signing of the greatest treaty in our history – the capitulation of the French!'

The young people cheered, stamping their feet. Otto held up his hand. 'We will now pray,' he said.

'Führer, my Führer, given me by God.
Protect and preserve my life for long.
You saved Germany in its time of need.
I thank you for my daily bread.
Be with me for a long time,
Do not leave me, Führer, my Führer,
My faith, my light. Hail to my Führer!'

The other children repeated the last phrase 'Hail to my Führer', but Magda, appalled at the deification of Adolf Hitler, remained sullenly silent.

When she got home she threw her school bag angrily into the corner of the kitchen.

'Magda,' said her mother, 'what on earth's the matter?'

'They are saying prayers for him now… as if he is God himself!'

'Who? Who is God?'

'Hitler of course. Otto and his little friends – they pray to him. It's terrible.'

Magda stomped upstairs and Käthe heard her bedroom door slamming shut. Following her, she knocked quietly on her door.

'Magda… *mein schatz.*'

'Leave me alone,' Magda said, her voice thick with tears.

'I have something important to tell you.'

There was silence.

'Magda, I had a letter from Karl today.'

Magda threw open her door.

'Why didn't you say?'

'You didn't me a chance.'

'He says he cannot come back,' said Magda, skimming the letter. 'He says he's been interned!'

'I know!' Her mother dabbed at her eyes with the edge of her apron. 'Is that the same as prison?'

'I don't know,' said Magda. 'I suppose so. He says his professor at the university has been kind… that he spoke up for him with the authorities.' She looked up, hopefully, at her mother. 'He says that this man is trying to help him – that he might be able to work on his farm.'

'It's almost funny,' said Käthe, 'all these years he's hated farming – and now he'll be forced to do it.'

'It's better than fighting,' said Magda, handing her mother the letter.

'I suppose so,' her mother said, sniffing.

'And now you can tell everyone that he is "doing his bit",' said Magda. 'He's in jail, after all.'

Käthe began to cry. 'Yes. Yes that's right… Of course. And the best thing of all – is that we will know that he's safe.'

When Pieter came in from milking the herd that evening, he read his son's letter with tears in his eyes.

'Thank God he's not here,' he said, laying the letter aside.

'Perhaps now,' said Käthe, 'the war will be over quite soon – the French have surrendered already, haven't they?'

'Hmmm,' said Pieter. 'They have. But the British are another matter. I can't see them giving up that easily.'

'But if we have already taken Paris?' Käthe began.

'I don't know. They say it's a matter of months, but I don't believe it.'

That night, lying in bed, as Magda grimly anticipated the 'celebrations' planned for the weekend, she re-read Karl's first letter. That slim, flimsy sheet of paper was, in some ways, the only truthful thing in her world – a world that was dominated by lies and deceit and cruelty. Her life on the farm was protected from much of this, of course. The family's life together in the countryside seemed a haven of sanctuary compared with the horrors of war. The daily rituals of farm life gave an outward semblance of calm and security – the cows gathering twice daily to be milked, clattering contentedly across the yard, the sight of her father leading the horses out to the fields to plough, or sow, or harvest. Her mother in the kitchen, churning butter and making cheese to sell at the market; the rows of bottled fruit and salted vegetables lining the larder, the rabbit stews and freshly roasted chicken her mother produced for supper. Magda slept in a clean bed, she drank warm milk and had enough to eat. But, at night, as she read Karl's letter over and over again, she saw that this cosy country life was an illusion. Behind this veil of security, a whole generation had been taught that Adolf Hitler was a god – that his every proclamation was an inalienable fact, whereas the truth was that thousands of men were dying fighting a war. German citizens were being denied their liberty and their lives because they were Jewish, or because their Catholic faith set them at odds with what the Nazis wanted everyone to believe. Karl, through his letter, had shown her the truth. And now it was time for her, Magda Maier, to make a stand. That was what Karl was doing, after all…

Chapter Eleven

Keswick
June 1940

Dear Mum and Dad,

I heard from one of the teachers, Mrs Burnett, who's just come back from Newcastle, that German planes had been flying over the city at night, but did no damage. She'd looked out of the window and saw them caught in the search lights! Mrs Burnett said that on the third alarm she tried to get her husband Roger up and out of bed – to go to the shelter – and all the response she could get was 'Let 'em come! I'm going to stay here and be bombed!' Wasn't that funny? But I do wonder why they didn't manage to bring a few down? It doesn't say much for our anti-aircraft batteries. Still the wet weather has set in – it's been pouring all day. I think it's just as well, as rain may hinder the Nazis.

I think signing the 'peace' in the same place as in 1918 is beastly – the poor French people. What on earth will happen? Do write and say what you think as children's opinions of the situation are probably incorrect.

I have been thinking you won't be getting much sleep these nights – I hope Daddy's indigestion doesn't get worse.

Tons of love,
Ginny

Imogen was just addressing the envelope when she heard the doorbell's insistent ringing in the hall. Moments later she heard a wail – an animal-like sound that reminded her of a fox caught in a poacher's trap.

Abandoning her letter she raced downstairs and found Mrs Latimer crouched down on the hall floor, a telegram lying on the floor beside her, the telegraph boy standing helplessly on the doorstep.

'I'm sorry,' he said in a small voice, 'I'm so, so sorry...'

'It's not your fault – thank you,' said Imogen nodding goodbye and closing the door.

Mr Latimer, who had been down in the garden, heard the commotion, and came rushing up the path and into the hall. He knelt at his wife's side.

'Moira, Moira... what is it?'

Imogen handed him the telegram.

'Bastards,' he said, reading the telegram. 'Bloody, buggering bastards.'

Imogen stood rigid, pinned to the spot. She had never heard anyone swear in such a way. And it seemed quite out of character for mild-mannered, dear Mr Latimer.

'It's our Arthur,' he said, looking up at her, his face wet with tears. 'They got him at Dunkirk... like rats in a trap, they were.'

He stood up, putting the telegram on the hall table, helped his wife up to her feet and through to the sitting room.

'I'm so, so sorry Mr Latimer,' said Imogen.

At school the following day, she and Helen were invited into the headmistress's study.

'Ah girls – good. Sit down. Now, as I'm sure you're aware, the Latimers have had a terrible piece of news.'

Imogen and Helen both looked down at their shoes, tears springing to their eyes.

'Poor Mrs Latimer,' Imogen blurted out, 'she started crying the moment she heard the news and she's not stopped since.'

'Well it seems that not only is their eldest boy... I can't remember his name...' The headmistress shifted sheets of paper around on her desk, searching for the information.

'Arthur' said Imogen.

'Yes, Arthur... not only has he tragically lost his life, but their youngest son, James, has been injured. It's not too serious, but he's coming home to recuperate when he leaves hospital, and understandably they need the room for him.'

'Oh, of course,' said Imogen, looking at Helen.

'So we'll have to find you a new billet. He won't be back for a couple of weeks, so I've asked if you can stay for the time being, but with term ending soon, I wanted you to know that you'll be in new digs when you come back in September. If we need to move you before then, I'll find something temporary. Very well – you can go.'

The girls crossed the head's study and were opening the heavy oak door to leave when she called them back.

'Oh... and girls... I imagine I don't really need to say this, but do all you can to help the Latimers at this time – cooking and tidying and so on.'

Ten days later Imogen's parents arrived to collect her. In spite of the recent spate of bombing in Newcastle, the school was closing for the summer holidays and as many children as possible were being sent back home. Imogen's mother took charge of clearing and tidying the room she had shared with Helen, anxious not to add to Mrs Latimer's burdens.

'I don't want her to have to do anything after you've gone. Imogen – bring me a broom from the scullery, and a cloth and some polish. And strip that bed and put all the linen in the pillow case – there's a good girl.'

The bed stripped, Imogen was standing on the landing, the bag of linen in her hands, when she spotted an ambulance driving down the road. It stopped outside the house and a couple of orderlies opened the back doors and manoeuvred a young man out of the ambulance. Her father pushed past her, carrying her suitcases.

'Jump to it Ginny, open the front door for me.'

'All right, Daddy. I think the Latimers' son has just come home.'

As her father walked down the garden path to his car, Imogen watched the young man being lifted carefully into a wheelchair. He was no more than nineteen – sandy-haired, with pale blue eyes and a full sweet mouth.

'Hello,' he called out to Imogen in his soft, gentle Lakeland accent; he reminded her of Dougie.

'Hello,' she replied, walking towards him. 'You must be Jimmy – sorry, it's James isn't it?'

'Jimmy's fine,' he smiled. 'Yeah that's me; and you're…?'

'Imogen. I've been billeted here with another girl from school since last September. It's been very nice; your parents have been very kind. We're leaving today, though. I was so sorry to hear about…'

'Arthur. I know. I can't believe it. Both getting clobbered on the same bloody beach, who'd have thought…'

'Excuse me, lad,' said the orderly, 'but we need to get you inside.'

At that moment, Mr Latimer came to the door of the house. He walked steadily down the garden path and stood opposite his son, gazing down at him – as if he could hardly believe he was there. Then he knelt down and embraced him, sobbing into his son's shoulder.

Imogen, uncertain what to say or do, retreated back up the garden path.

'I ought to say goodbye to Mrs Latimer,' she muttered nervously. She found her mother with Mrs Latimer in the sitting room. They were standing at the window, watching as Mr Latimer wheeled their son up the path.

'Well, we'll let you get on,' Rose was saying. 'I'm so glad your boy is home. Thank you for all you've done for Imogen – we are so grateful. God bless you.'

Imogen, standing in the doorway, was uncertain what else she could say; her mother, as always, had said all that was necessary.

The sound of the wheelchair clattering into the hall made any words superfluous, as Mrs Latimer rushed past Rose and Imogen, and threw herself at her son.

Rose put her arm around Imogen's shoulder.

'Come on poppet… let's leave them to their reunion.'

As the car drove away from Manor Park, Imogen spotted Dougie standing at the corner of the road. He was looking anxiously around.

'Daddy, please stop the car,' implored Imogen. 'There's someone I need to say goodbye to.'

As the Wolseley pulled up at the kerbside, Imogen leapt out.

'Dougie… there you are.'

'Oh Ginny – thank God. I thought I'd missed you.'

'I know… I'm sorry I've not seen you. It's been so difficult these last few days – the Latimers' eldest son, Arthur, was killed at Dunkirk and Helen and I have been doing our best to look after Mr Latimer. I'm leaving today, for the summer.'

Dougie's eyes filled with tears and he took her hands in his. Imogen was aware of her parents craning their necks to study the young stranger. The car door opened and her father got out.

'Imogen… who's this young fellow? Aren't you going to introduce us?'

'Yes, of course. Daddy, this is Douglas Henderson – he's at the school next to ours.'

'How do you do, Douglas,' said her father, holding out his hand.

'How do,' said Dougie, blushing.

'Well, Ginny dear…' said her father, 'we must get going – it's a long drive and we need to be back before dark.' He climbed back into the car.

'Yes Daddy, of course. I'll write, Dougie,' she said, turning to him, 'I promise. And we'll be back in September.'

'I won't be here,' he said.

'Why?' she asked, alarmed.

'I've joined up.'

'But you don't need to yet; you had another year at school.'

'You've heard the news. We're needed. Fighting men.'

'But you're not a man. You're a boy.'

'I'm seventeen, nearly eighteen. I'll be off in a week – army.'

'Ginny,' her father called from the car.

'Yes, coming…' She turned back to Dougie; tears were coursing down his cheeks.

'I'm so sorry,' she said, wiping his tears away with her fingers.

'I'll think of you,' he said, leaning over and kissing her fleetingly on the mouth.

'And I'll think of you, too,' she whispered.

As the car drove away she turned to look at Dougie through the rear window. He seemed so young suddenly, standing watching the car, his hands thrust into his trouser pockets. He was just a child, she realised, not even shaving yet, on the verge of entering a man's world. She pushed aside the thought that she might never see him again. It was too upsetting to contemplate.

Part Two

Plotting

1942–1943

This is not the end. It is not even the beginning of the end. But it is, perhaps, the end of the beginning.

Winston Churchill

Chapter Twelve

Gosforth
April 1942

Imogen ran down the stairs of her parents' house. She was relieved to be home for the Easter holidays. On the cusp of her eighteenth birthday, she was due to leave school in a few months, and was looking forward to the next phase in her life – going to university to study architecture.

That evening her mother was having a small party for friends and neighbours including, much to Ginny's delight, Philip and Freddie McMasters. Imogen had not seen Freddie for over two years and she was intrigued at the thought of meeting him again.

'Edith,' she called out, as she walked through to the kitchen. The Mitchells' maid Edith had been back with the household since the death of her own mother a year or so earlier. Hetty had last been heard of working in a munitions factory on the other side of the Tyne. 'Is my mother at home?'

'No, Miss. She's gone to Bainbridge's… to buy some trimming for her hat.'

Imogen looked blank.

'For Easter Sunday, Miss – she wants to smarten up her hat.'

'Oh I see. I just wondered what time the guests were coming?'

'Seven-thirty, she said.'

'Is everything ready? Anything I can do?'

'No Miss – you know your mother… it's all organised. The bits of food are all ready, the sitting room's laid out. She asked me to remind you to change your frock.'

'Of course I'll change my frock. Mummy remade that old green summer dress of mine. She's so clever – it was too short so she added an edging round the bottom, in plain green fabric and made a matching belt – it looks really rather stylish!'

At the party that evening, as Imogen assisted Edith handing round plates of food to guests, she listened to snippets of conversation.

'So tell me, Philip,' said her father to Mrs McMasters' son as he poured whisky into his glass, 'how's life in the navy?'

'Oh interesting… demanding. I'm part of the Home Fleet. I'm moving to a new ship in the Atlantic when I leave here. We're hoping that now the Americans are in the war, things might get easier.'

'And what of your brothers?'

'Well Fred's in the RAF; he's just about to start proper training in Canada – lucky bugger, and Jonno is stationed in North Africa. Not heard from him for a while, but I think he's OK.'

'Well that's good to hear,' said Joe. 'And what of your university chums? Are they all doing all right?'

'Yes – as far as I know; scattered, like the four winds. Most are in the army, one or two, like me, joined the navy. Interestingly, there were a couple of Germans in my year at Oxford – a Rhodes scholar among them.'

'Germans?' Joe asked. 'Didn't they go back when the whole thing kicked off?'

'One did… yes, but another chap – Karl was his name… was rather on our side. He was studying economics like me, but was a bit older – a brilliant scholar. He had an interesting perspective on things. I think he's been interned now. Bit of a shame, really. He seemed keen to help.'

'What? To work against the Fatherland?'

'I know – odd. But he'd long felt the Nazis didn't have the right idea. Anyway, he's locked up for the duration.'

'Good,' said Joe. 'Best place for him, I imagine. Well, I must move on. The natives will get restless.'

Imogen spotted Freddie standing in the bay window of the drawing room, nursing an empty glass. Wearing his RAF uniform, which matched his grey-blue eyes, he was sandwiched between his own mother and Imogen's mother Rose. The two women were discussing plans for an imminent church social due to take place on Easter Sunday and although he was doing his best to appear interested, it was clear he was bored. Imogen, keen to both rescue him and get him to herself, was just about to interject, when her father appeared at her elbow.

'Another drink, Freddie?' Joe asked proffering the whisky bottle.

'Yes, sir – thanks.' Freddie held out his glass.

'Tell you what,' Joe said, winking. 'Perhaps you could do me a favour, and help yourself. The drinks are just over there.' He gestured towards a table laid out with spirits on the far side of the drawing room. 'Imogen will show you, won't you darling?' He smiled at his daughter, who blushed faintly.

'Of course,' said Freddie. 'I'd be delighted.' He and Imogen pushed through the throng of guests towards the drinks table. 'Jolly decent of your father to rescue me,' Freddie said quietly, pouring himself a large whisky. 'Can I top you up?'

'No… I'm all right thanks,' she said, indicating her full glass of Dubonnet and soda. 'I'm not sure church socials are the most interesting topic of conversation, are they? Would you like something to eat?'

Imogen retrieved a plate of anchovy toast from the bottom shelf of the drinks table and Freddie took a small morsel of food and crunched down on it.

'Mmm delicious – your mother's work, I presume?'

'Oh absolutely… definitely not mine. I'm the most terrible cook. Growing up with Mummy and Edith – I've just never had to learn. It's awful isn't it?'

'How's school?' he asked, taking another piece of toast from the plate.

'Oh… so boring. I'll be leaving this summer and can hardly wait. It's not much fun living away; we're billeted in a sort of boarding house now, which is easier than living with a family, to be honest. But it's not the same as being at home.'

'Ah, boarding school! I remember it well,' said Freddie, sipping his drink.

'Where were you?' she asked, 'somewhere down south?'

'Yes. I was in the West Country. Made me the man I am today,' he said, laughing.

'Well you certainly look very dashing in your uniform,' Imogen said. 'When did you join the RAF?'

'I joined the college squadron when I started university, but I'm off to Canada in a few days. I'll be there some time for a period of intensive training. I'm rather looking forward to it.'

'Oh,' she said, disappointment etched into her voice. 'I was hoping we might see something of one another while I'm home.'

'Me too. But I'm not off till after Easter Monday – so I've got another couple of days. Maybe we can go into town?'

'I'd love that,' she said, thrilled to be finally asked out. 'I really would.'

'Imogen,' her mother called out across the room. 'Are you going to pass those toasts around?'

'Yes Mummy… coming.' She smiled at Freddie. 'Duty calls!'

'I'll give you a ring,' he said. 'Tomorrow.'

They met at seven o'clock in the bar of the Station Hotel. Freddie was waiting for Imogen in a small booth off to one side.

'Oh there you are,' she said, cheerfully. 'I couldn't see you… thought you might have stood me up.'

Freddie leapt to his feet. 'I'd never do that! I just thought it would be nice to have somewhere peaceful to chat. What would you like to drink?'

'Gin and it,' she said, confidently.

'Really?' Are you sure?'

'Yes,' she said. 'Why?'

'No reason... it's just a bit strong. But if you're sure – "gin and it" coming up.'

Truthfully, Ginny had never even tasted a 'gin and it'. A mixture of gin and vermouth, she had only seen sophisticated women ordering it in films and, desperate to impress Freddie, thought it would make her seem more grown up.

As she took her first sip, she struggled to conceal her disgust.

'All right?' he asked gently.

'Yes, absolutely. Delicious,' she said. 'So, this is nice. I haven't been here before. I've been stuck in the Lakes for so long and they don't have many nice hotel bars over there. Besides, we'd never be allowed in. We'd be spotted as soon as we walked through the door.'

'Why?' asked Freddie.

'We have to wear some bit of uniform at all times, even on Sundays – a school coat, or beret or something – so if we break a school rule, we can be identified! Makes sneaking into pubs and hotel bars nigh on impossible.'

'How frustrating,' said Freddie, sipping his pint.

'It's more than frustrating – it's inhuman!' She laughed and took another sip of the drink, her taste buds gradually adjusting to the sour flavours. She began to relax, feeling the alcohol spreading through her body.

'And have you?' he asked.

'What?'

'Broken some rules?' He smiled encouragingly.

'A few,' she said teasingly.

'Tell me more...'

'No,' she said, sipping her drink. She was keen for him to see her as something other than a schoolgirl. 'You tell me instead about Canada. That sounds far more interesting than a few schoolgirl pranks.'

'Nothing much to tell, if I'm honest. I've never been there. But I gather it's a big place – lots of wide open spaces where we can crash the planes.' He laughed.

'Oh please don't do that,' she said, grabbing his hand. 'I simply couldn't bear it.'

'I won't,' he said gently, squeezing her hand. 'At least, I'll try not to.'

As the evening wore on, they chatted easily about Freddie's ambitions after the war.

'I'm looking forward to learning to fly, obviously, but really I just want to get back to university.'

'You're training to be an architect, aren't you?'

'I am,' he said.

'I know you probably think it sounds silly… but I'm hoping to be an architect too. I've always been rather good at drawing and my maths is not bad. I've applied to the School of Architecture in Newcastle – like you.

'That's wonderful,' he said. 'Your mother mentioned you wanted to study engineering, like your father.'

'Yes – that was my first idea. But it turns out the university won't let me.'

'Really? Why?'

'Because I'm a woman I suppose. They said it had never been done before… ridiculous isn't it?' She shrugged her shoulders.

'Well, architecture's great. You'll love it. Much more interesting than engineering anyway, and they're going to need us when this is all over.'

'Really?'

'Yes! Think of all those houses that will need rebuilding. Oh Lord…' he said, glancing at his watch. 'I had no idea it was so late; we really ought to get going.'

'Oh we don't have to go yet, do we?' Imogen had a profound sense that this might be her last chance to tell Freddie how she felt about him. He'd be going away to Canada soon and she would be back at school. It might be years before they had a chance to meet again. 'You're so easy to talk to and I've had such a lovely time,' she said, blushing slightly. 'I don't really want it to end.'

He reached over and squeezed her hand. 'Neither do I if I'm honest. You're a very special girl – do you know that?'

'Only when I'm with you… everything makes sense when I'm with you.'

He looked at her, his grey eyes widening. 'You're very sweet,' he said. 'But I really think we should get back,' he said at last. 'I told your father I'd have you home by nine.'

Outside the hotel he held the door to his little Morris car open for her. As she slid past him, their faces just inches away from each other, she looked up into his eyes, willing him to kiss her. He leant down and brushed her lips with his own. She felt her head spinning, her legs giving way slightly.

'Hey,' he said, catching her in his arms. 'Are you all right?' He helped her into the car.

'I'm fine,' she said, smiling up at him. But as they drove north through Jesmond Dene on their way to Gosforth, she began to feel a little queasy, the sour taste of the 'gin and it' repeating on her, her mouth filling with saliva. She was about to ask him if they could stop, when they heard the mournful wailing of the air-raid sirens.

'Damn!' said Freddie. 'Come on, we'd better pull over. They'll probably be heading east towards the docks. We should be safe enough here.'

As he pulled over at the side of the road, Imogen began to struggle with the door handle.

'I've got to get out,' she said, clutching at her mouth.

'Don't do that, sit tight – we'll be all right.'

'I think I'm going to be sick.'

'What now?' he asked calmly. 'Well, we'd better get you out of the car, hadn't we?' He opened the passenger door and guided her to the side of the pavement.

As a row of searchlights picked out the line of German Heinkel bombers flying low over the city, Imogen vomited against the garden wall of a large red brick house while Freddie held her dark hair away from her face.

Soon the sound of her retching was drowned out by the sound of bombs falling.

'That was a bit too close for comfort,' said Freddie. 'Come on Ginny – back in the car. I think we're sitting ducks here.'

'I can't,' muttered Imogen, retching one more time.

'You must! Throw up in the car for all I care. We're getting out of here – now!'

As he drove the car down the road, his lights dimmed to avoid detection, there was an earth-shattering sound a few hundred yards behind them. Pieces of masonry spattered noisily against the car, and Freddie jammed his foot down on the accelerator pedal. Parking a few hundred yards further on, he looked back through the car's rear window, and watched as the bombers flew down along the Tyne towards South Shields, their route lit up on that moonless night by successive explosions.

'That was a close shave,' said Freddie. 'I'd better go back and see if there's anything I can do to help.'

As he walked away from the car, he heard Imogen racing after him. 'I'm coming too.'

'No… go back. Wait for me in the car.'

'No! I've done first aid at school. I might be able to help.'

As they ran down the road in the darkness, it seemed there had been very little damage.

'Everything seems fine,' said Imogen. 'Perhaps we were wrong – and the bomb fell further away from here.'

'No, it was definitely right behind us. It must be a bit further on,' said Freddie.

On the other side of the crossroads, Ginny looked around. There was a break in the clouds above and a glimmer of moonlight illuminated the road and surrounding houses.

'Where's that house... the large one, where I was sick?' she asked.

'It was here,' said Freddie, gesturing towards a gaping hole in the ground. Just one wall remained vertical, its violet-coloured wallpaper flapping incongruously in the breeze. The rafters of what remained of the roof hung precariously from the wall. The rest of the house and its contents had been completely destroyed. Even the garden wall, where moments before Imogen had been so sick, was gone.

'The people... where are they?' begged Imogen.

'I don't know,' said Freddie. 'I can't hear anything. Perhaps they were away. God I hope so.'

It was unexpectedly still and silent, the peace only disturbed by the occasional sound of a piece of falling masonry crashing into the void. People in the neighbouring houses gradually emerged and stood next to the young couple, gazing in consternation at the space where a family had once lived.

'We can't see anyone moving around,' said Imogen to a tall well-built man standing next to her. 'We thought maybe they were away?'

'No, they were in. We had supper with them just an hour ago. I'm going to look,' he said, striding over the rubble.

'Shouldn't you wait?' asked Freddie, 'for the wardens, or the fire brigade? You might get hurt – falling masonry and all that.'

'Maybe,' said the man, 'but I'm going in anyway.'

*

When Freddie rang on the doorbell of Imogen's house an hour later, her father opened the door within seconds.

'Thank God,' he said, ushering them into the hall. 'We heard the bombs. They sounded close. We've been so worried.'

'Oh Daddy,' said Imogen taking off her coat, 'it was awful.'

'Were you hit?' her father asked, brushing dust and rubble off her coat.

'No… but we'd stopped moments before at the very place it happened. Fortunately, we'd just got back in the car and as the bomb fell Freddie put his foot down. He saved my life…' She looked over at Freddie, his uniform covered in dust, his face and hair blackened from digging in the rubble looking for survivors. 'He was so brave,' Imogen went on.

'Thank you Freddie,' said Joe, wrapping his daughter in his arms.

'You're welcome,' said Freddie quietly. 'I'm just so sorry…'

'We went back to help, Daddy,' continued Imogen. 'This house – a house just like ours, had completely disappeared into a huge hole in the ground. We tried to help – moving bits of wood and bricks and things, looking for people.'

Imogen began to cry.

'Was that wise?' Joe asked Freddie.

'What else could we do?' Imogen said, pulling away from her father. 'Just abandon them? We had to see if anyone was still alive.'

'And were they?'

'No, I don't think so. The fire brigade arrived and took over, but I think all of them – the whole family – are dead.'

Rose came into the hall from the drawing room, and pulled her daughter towards her. Although nearly a foot taller than her mother, Imogen nevertheless crumpled into her arms.

'Thank you for bringing her back, Freddie. Can I get you a drink?' Rose asked.

'Thank you, but I'd better be getting off. I think Ginny needs her bed. It's been quite an evening.'

Imogen turned to look at him, her hair and face still plastered in dust.

'Will I see you again?' she asked.

'I'm not sure. I'll try,' he said, opening the door.

'I'll write,' she called out as he walked down the path towards his car.

'Thank you,' he said, raising his hand and waving goodbye. 'I'd like that.'

Chapter Thirteen

Färsehof Farm
June 1942

Magda woke to the familiar sound of cattle clattering on the cobbles in the yard beneath her bedroom window, bellowing insistently – as they always did when their udders were full. She peered at the little clock on her bedside table. It was a quarter to seven. Normally her father woke her at half past six to help with the milking – banging on her bedroom door as he went downstairs. But the evening before, he had promised she could have a lie-in, as a treat for her birthday.

She lay back and pulled the feather-filled quilt over her head, trying to slip back into sleep but her mind was already alert – racing ahead to the coming day at school. She eventually gave up, rolled out of bed, poured water from the jug into the bowl on her wash table and splashed her face. She brushed her short blonde hair, clipping it back on one side, then put on her League of Girls uniform of dark blue full skirt, short-sleeved white shirt and tie, and went down to the kitchen.

Cooling on a rack was the cake her mother had promised to make for her birthday. She leant down and inhaled the scent of cooked cherries, her mouth salivating, and tasted a few of the crumbs that had fallen onto the dresser. It was delicious. As she listened to the comforting sounds of her parents ushering the cows into the milking parlour, she laid the table for breakfast. She was just loading wood onto the stove, when she heard a knock on the door. Opening it she found the young post boy, Andreas, holding a sheaf of envelopes.

'You have a lot of letters today,' he said, almost accusingly. Andreas was in the same class as Magda at school and was one of Otto's little gang of followers; they were constantly whispering conspiratorially in corners. He had a reputation for being a sneak and a busybody and for that reason alone Magda had little time for him. She had also begun to suspect him of being one of the child 'informers' – reporting evidence of unpatriotic behaviour. Magda hated the fact that he delivered their post, as he seemed far too interested in the contents of the family's mail.

'It's my birthday,' Magda replied unapologetically, and closed the door.

She watched from the kitchen window as he crossed the farmyard, surrounded by cows ambling shambolically out of the milking parlour heading for their field. A large heifer butted against him with her flank and he stumbled, stepping in a huge cow pat. Magda laughed out loud as he leant down to untie his boot and hopped awkwardly, cursing the cow, towards the grass verge on the edge of the track to wipe his soiled boot.

Satisfied that he had finally left the farm, Magda flicked through the envelopes. There was a card from her mother's sister in Leipzig, another from a godmother in the village. But one envelope stood out. She knew immediately from the neat, orderly handwriting who had sent it.

'Mutti, Mutti,' she called out to her mother who, having finished the milking, was heading towards the kitchen garden with a bowl of scraps for the chickens.

'Come quick! There's a letter from Karl.'

Her mother threw the bowl of scraps onto the ground and ran into the house.

The envelope lay in glorious isolation on the kitchen table.

'Open it,' her mother said, anxiously. 'Quick.'

Inside the envelope was a postcard. The picture was of a charming collection of red brick Georgian townhouses, their small gardens filled with a riot of spring colour – tulips, daffodils and apple blossom. Printed on the back were the words: 'Hampstead in the Spring' and a simple handwritten message: Happy Birthday little monkey.

Magda turned the card over. She peered inside the envelope.

'Is that it? Is that all he can say after this time – "happy birthday"?' She threw the card, disconsolately, down on the kitchen table.

Her father came into the kitchen and stood with his back to his wife and daughter, washing his hands at the sink.

'Good morning Magda – happy birthday,' he said, cheerfully. 'I hope you enjoyed your lie-in?'

As he turned around, drying his hands, he looked from his wife to his daughter.

'Magda… Käthe – what's the matter? What's happened?'

Magda handed him the card.

He read it, turning it over more than once, studying the words, and examining the photograph.

'Is that it?'

'Exactly.'

'Karl never does anything without a reason,' Käthe said. 'He's trying to tell us something. What's the picture of again?'

Pieter read out the caption. 'Hampstead in the Spring.'

'Well, it's not a prison is it?' said Käthe. 'It looks beautiful.'

'So maybe he's not in jail after all?' Magda suggested, hopefully.

'And maybe he's living here… in this place?' Her mother peered intently at the picture.

'Maybe he can't say any more,' said Magda. 'He's trying to protect us.'

'The postmark is not from Britain,' said Pieter, examining the envelope. 'It's a German stamp, posted in Berlin. How did he manage that?'

Her father began to sift through the other letters on the table. There was a second thick brown envelope, also postmarked Berlin, addressed simply to 'The Maiers'.

'This envelope is also addressed in Karl's handwriting,' Pieter said. He took a knife from the table and sliced through the thick paper, sealed with layers of tape.

Inside was a plain paper package, also taped. As he carefully slit open the package, a clipping from a newspaper fell onto the table.

'It's a British newspaper,' said Pieter. '*The Daily Telegraph*. I presume he wrapped it in paper to prevent anyone being able to read it through the envelope.' He handed it to Magda. 'Can you read this?'

Magda, who had become relatively proficient at English at school, began to translate:

Germans murder 700,000 Jews in Poland... Travelling gas chambers...

She looked up at her father, bewildered.

'What does it mean? I don't understand... what are travelling gas chambers?'

'No! I don't believe it,' said her mother. 'That cannot be right. It must be British propaganda – surely, Pieter?'

'I don't know,' said Pieter dispassionately. 'It could be true. Quite honestly, anything could be true these days.'

Pinned to the newspaper front page was a second, smaller clipping, which Magda began to translate.

'"*Enemy Aliens enlist*"... I don't understand exactly what that means, but I think it says that some Germans in Britain – "enemy aliens" – people like Karl, I suppose, have joined the British forces.'

'Karl is fighting with the British against the Germans?' asked Käthe, aghast.

Her husband shrugged his shoulders.

'Is that all you can do?' she asked, angrily. 'Shrug?'

'What else can I do?' said Pieter. 'He's made a choice. Maybe he's right. I hate this government. I hate everything they stand for. I admire him – standing up for his principles. But he took a huge risk sending these clippings to us. The envelope doesn't appear to have been tampered with, but if someone had opened it, they would know what he was up to. While he was in jail in England, he was safe, and us too; but if anyone found these, he'd be a marked man, and us with him. Burn them – the articles and the card. Put them on the fire.'

'But, Papa,' pleaded Magda, 'the card is from Karl! Don't make us do that.'

'Look – if we've worked out he's working for the British, living in… where was it… Hampstead? Then others will do the same. Do as I say. And burn the envelopes too. Everything must go.'

'We'd better do as he says,' said Käthe reluctantly, after Pieter had gone back out to the yard. She ran her finger over her son's handwriting on the card, as if by doing so, she could imbibe some part of him. The thought of burning this last missive from her beloved child seemed like a violation. She opened the range door, and the flames from the fire flared momentarily as she threw on the newspaper cuttings, followed by the card. Shutting the range door, Käthe and Magda looked at one another, both wondering if they should also burn the secret letter, hidden away upstairs. But some unspoken understanding kept them from doing so.

The following day Magda was due to visit Munich with fellow members of the Hitler Youth. They were to attend a rally on the Königsplatz with other groups from Bavaria. Magda did not relish these 'outings', but Fräulein Muller would frown on her if she refused to attend. Besides, she had never visited Munich before, and had begun to imagine a life for herself, once she left school, following in Karl's footsteps and attending university. Munich had a fine university and she was intrigued to see it.

Otto insisted on sitting next to her on the train as they travelled from Augsburg to Munich.

'Did you have a nice birthday?' he asked, settling himself next to her.

'Yes. How did you know it was my birthday?'

'Andreas told me, of course. He said you had all sorts of mail yesterday – including a couple of letters from Berlin. Who do you know in Berlin?'

Magda blushed involuntarily.

'I have an aunt there,' she said, as casually as she could. 'Although I don't know what it has to do with you?'

'Really?' said Otto. 'And one aunt sent two letters? Or maybe it was a card and a package?'

Magda's heart began to race.

'It was a present. She sent me a book and she forgot to put the card in with it.' Magda breathed rapidly, trying to calm herself.

'An expensive mistake,' Otto said, sarcastically. 'Having to send two envelopes. It's funny – I've never heard you mention that you have relatives in Berlin. I thought your aunt lived in Leipzig?'

'That's my mother's sister,' Magda said indignantly. 'My father has a sister too. Anyway – I really don't think it's any of your business, do you?' She regretted this last comment. It would only annoy him.

'It's my business,' he replied arrogantly, 'because I am your boyfriend. We should have no secrets from each other.' Since the morning he had overheard Pieter listening to the BBC, Otto never missed an opportunity to remind Magda that she was in his debt. Now she played along with his insistence that he was her boyfriend – it was the only way she could pacify him.

She feigned a smile, and bit her lip.

'I got you something,' he said, reaching into his jacket pocket, 'for your birthday. That's what boyfriends do, isn't it?'

He handed her a small brown paper parcel.

'Thank you,' she said feebly, and began to unwrap it, watched intently by Erika sitting on the other side of the carriage.

Inside the wrapping was a dark red leather jeweller's box. Opening it, Magda found a silver brooch and matching earrings, set with blue aquamarines surrounded by crystals. They were pretty, Magda thought, but more suited to an older woman, and far too expensive for a boy like Otto to be able to afford.

'To match your beautiful blue eyes,' Otto said. 'Here, I'll pin the brooch your shirt.'

As he fumbled with the clasp, his fingers touched her breasts. She inwardly recoiled, her heart racing.

'Don't I deserve a kiss?' he whispered in her ear.

Blushing, more with fury than desire, she pecked him briefly on the cheek.

'You can do better than that,' he said, breathing heavily into her neck.

'Not here,' she whispered, embarrassed. Looking around the carriage she realised everyone was looking at them, including Erika, who had tears in her eyes.

'I shouldn't wear it now, anyway,' she said briskly, unpinning the brooch and putting it back into the box. 'It's against regulations, besides, I might lose it.'

'All right,' he said. 'But wear it later…'

Magda slipped the leather box into her pocket and inched over towards the window in order to put some physical space between herself and Otto. She was relieved when he began to joke noisily with the other boys and she was left alone to stare gloomily out at the passing countryside.

At Munich station, they walked in a crocodile up the platform, through the station, and outside where they gathered excitedly, waiting for their team leaders. As they were being assembled, a group of fifty of so people – men, women and children – shuffled onto the concourse. Each one carried a suitcase, as if departing on a long holiday. But they showed no sense of expectation or delight – rather, they looked pale and frightened, and in spite of the warm summer weather wore overcoats and hats. As soldiers surrounded them, barking orders and prodding them with their rifle butts the women began to scream, and the children to cry.

The Hitler Youth, led by Otto, began to shout.

'Jews, Jews,' they chanted, hissing and shaking their fists. Magda, appalled and ashamed, kept her eyes trained firmly on the concourse's cobbled surface.

'Where are they taking them?' she whispered to Erika.

'I don't know,' Erika replied, crisply. 'And I don't care. Away from here… I hope. We don't want them any more.'

As the travellers were pushed and shoved, cowering, towards the station, Magda noticed a young girl at the back of the group. She wore a shabby grey coat, and as she turned to stare at the Hitler Youth, Magda recognised her pale pinched face.

'Lotte!' she shouted, pushing Erika and the others aside as she ran towards her friend. Otto tried to restrain her, grabbing hold of her arm, but she broke free of him and sprinted across the concourse.

The two girls fell into each other's arms, but a soldier brandishing a gun pulled Magda roughly away and planted himself between them.

'What are you doing?' Magda demanded, angrily. 'Where are you taking them?' The soldier ignored her and stared implacably ahead.

'Oh Magda,' cried Lotte, her hand reaching out to grasp at her friend. 'We had to leave our flat, and all our things. Magda, I'm scared!'

'Where are your parents?' asked Magda, desperately.

Dr Kalman pushed his way through the group to stand at his daughter's side, but the soldier hit him sharply in the stomach with the butt of his gun.

'Get back to your place,' he shouted.

'Leave Dr Kalman alone,' Magda shouted defiantly. 'He deserves your respect!'

'Go back to your unit – now!' said the soldier to Magda. 'This is nothing to do with you.'

'But there's been a terrible mistake! This man is a doctor. You must let him and his family go – they've done nothing wrong.'

Dr Kalman reached over and grasped Magda's hand.

'Thank you Magda… for your friendship, but you must go now – for your own sake.'

Fräulein Muller bustled across the concourse and pulled Magda forcibly away, muttering to the soldier: 'I'll speak to her, don't worry.'

'Get them out of here,' said the soldier wearily, gesturing to Magda's companions, who stood gawping at the scene.

Magda was dragged bodily across the concourse, calling her friend's name:

'Lotte, Lotte…'

'Why did you do that?' asked Otto furiously, as they marched away from the station towards the centre of the city. Magda wept openly, looking over her shoulder in case she could still see Lotte, but the Kalmans had already disappeared, swallowed up into the station building.

'She's my best friend,' Magda sobbed. 'They were driven away from our village. My mother told me you were there – spitting in their faces. How could you do that? She was at our school…' She sank to her knees, weeping, in the street. Otto hauled her up.

'Don't stop… keep moving.'

'Where are they taking them?' she said, stumbling, trying to force her feet to fall back into the rhythm of the group as they marched up Luisenstrasse.

'A work camp, probably,' Otto said dismissively.

'A work camp? What sort of work?' She thought about the newspaper article her brother had sent. Before she could stop herself, she asked Otto: 'Are they going to be killed?'

Otto came to a sudden halt. 'Why do you say that?' he said, staring at her. 'Why do you care? They are nothing to you – scum.'

'They are not nothing!' she shouted, her misery turning to rage. 'Dr Kalman is a doctor – a good man.'

'Jews are not allowed to be doctors.'

'But he *is* a doctor!' protested Magda. 'What are you talking about?'

'It's against the law,' said Otto calmly.

'Well the law is stupid and cruel and wrong,' said Magda, glaring at him.

'Don't say that! Never say that!' Otto's blue eyes flashed icily. 'Now – march.'

'Are you ordering me?' asked Magda.

'What's going on here?' asked Fräulein Muller, pushing through the rest of the group. 'Magda Maier – start marching, now!'

The rally took place on the Königsplatz. This vast square was surrounded on three sides by neo-classical buildings, modelled on the Acropolis in Athens. It provided a magnificent backdrop for National Socialist rallies and was filled that day with thousands of young men and women from the Hitler Youth, standing in regimented rows, cheering as various announcements and speeches were made from the platform. A phalanx of senior SS officers was assembled in front of the monumental Propyläen – the central building complete with pediment atop a set of Doric columns. On either side of the stage were flaming torches shimmering in the heat.

The grandeur of the square and the sheer energy emanating from the thousands of Hitler Youth was overwhelming. All around, Magda's fellow league members cheered and saluted. Their eyes were filled with passion, as if they had lost their hearts and minds to the cause and to the men who stood on the stage.

One by one, young men who had showed 'leadership', or 'devotion to the cause' were called up to the front and presented to the officers. Otto was amongst them, walking proudly up the steps and across the stage where the officers shook his hand and slapped him on the back. He bowed and raised his arm in the Hitler salute. The crowd roared in delight. Once all the chosen boys had been presented, they were lined up on the stage and a senior officer spoke to the crowd.

'These young men have served their country well. They will be given the honour of becoming part of a new elite military group – the W-E Lagers. They will be sent to special training camps in preparation for their eventual call-up to the military.'

The crowd was ecstatic – screaming and cheering. The officer held up his hand and they fell instantly silent.

'This programme begins in November; support them, nurture them. These young men are our heroes. They are our future.'

The crowd cheered again and the boys walked off the stage, buoyed by the mass hysteria. Just one boy, at the end of the line, looked anxiously around, as if confused by this announcement. He looked frightened, Magda thought.

As Otto squeezed back to his place at the front of his troop, he looked back at Magda, hoping, she assumed, for some sort of acknowledgement – a smile or a wave. His handsome face was shiny with sweat, his blond hair pushed away from his forehead, his blue eyes filled with zealous pride. She took no pleasure in his elevation. His cruel comments about Lotte and her father had been so repugnant, and his lack of remorse for the way he had treated them so appalled Magda that she couldn't bear to look at him, and turned her face away. The hard leather jewellery box in her skirt pocket pressed, uncomfortably, against her leg. Something about that brooch had seemed familiar, she thought – as if she had seen it somewhere before.

One girl from each troop had also been selected for special recognition. Erika, with her long blonde plaits and eager personality, had been chosen to represent their village. Now she joined a group of other girls and walked to the front of the crowd. Thirty or so young women, aged no more than fifteen or sixteen, were lined up facing the stage. Dressed in their uniforms of dark skirts and white shirts, their blonde hair plaited and tied neatly across their heads, their faces free of any trace of make-up, they were the perfect vision of German womanhood – ripe and ready for childbirth. The officers walked down the steps and along the line, inspecting the girls. They chatted to some, admiring their pretty faces, their firm bosoms. The officer who had previously spoken to the crowd stopped opposite Erika. He patted her arm and leant towards her, whispering in her ear. She blushed and giggled, and when she returned to the group taking her place next to Magda, she had a look of sly contentment, like a cat. One or two of the other girls whispered to her – presumably asking what the officer had said to her, but she tossed her head coquettishly and said loudly enough for everyone to hear, 'It was a private conversation; I'm not allowed to say.'

Magda observed all this with cool detachment. She was grateful she had not been selected for this particular inspection. She hated the way the officers admired the young women; it reminded her of her father inspecting heifers at the market. This attitude – that girls were there for the pleasure of men – permeated the whole Hitler Youth. She had heard the boys talking amongst themselves when they went on camping trips. They would sit around the fire laughing and sniggering, talking about girls who had agreed to have sex with them 'for the Führer'. They called them the 'mattresses'.

Two girls in Magda's own troop had left the village suddenly after one such trip the previous summer, and rumour had it that they left because they were pregnant. The other girls seemed full of admiration – as if it was some significant rite of passage. Magda, by contrast, had been horrified. The pregnant girls deluded themselves that the boys cared for them, whereas it was obvious to anyone that they were just using them, laughing at the girls behind their backs.

Magda clung faithfully to the idea that to have a child was a responsibility to be shared between a man and a woman, and their local pastor still preached that to have a child out of wedlock was a sin. But Fräulein Muller told the girls that motherhood should be the pinnacle of every young woman's aspirations. 'To have an Aryan child is the ultimate gift a girl can give the Fatherland,' she was fond of saying. And in the last few months, she had even gone so far as to advocate children out of wedlock. 'It doesn't matter if a girl is married any more,' Fräulein Muller had said. 'The union of two perfect Aryan young people is a beautiful thing.'

It was hardly surprising, Magda thought, that the boys tried to take advantage of the girls in the League; they knew no one would reprimand them.

Now, having seen the way the officer spoke to Erika, and overheard her comment about their 'private conversation', Magda wondered if the girls were being selected to have children with SS officers. She did not like Erika, but she would not wish such a fate on anyone. The officer who spoke to her was old enough to be her father.

When the rally was finally over, Fräulein Muller assembled her group together. 'We will go back to the station now by a different route – down Brienner Street – and pay our respects to the Honour Temples. I expect you all to behave properly.'

The Honour Temples contained the sarcophagi of sixteen members of the National Socialist party who had been killed in the abortive 'Beer hall putsch' on 10th November 1923. During this failed coup attempt, Hitler and his supporters were confronted by armed police outside the Feldherrnhalle – a monument built in 1844 to honour Bavarian soldiers. In the riot that followed, four policemen and sixteen National Socialist members were shot, and Hitler himself was arrested and imprisoned. In 1933 Hitler turned the Feldherrnhalle into a memorial to the failed coup, guarded at all times by the SS. In 1935, he erected two temples next to his own headquarters on Brienner Street to house the graves of these 'martyrs', and they had since taken on an almost mythical significance.

Magda and the rest of the troop set off for the temples, marching in tight formation. Otto, revelling in his new status as part of an elite fighting group, predictably strode out in front, followed closely by Erika. As they passed the temples, they saluted smartly, before carrying on down the road, past the Karolinenplatz obelisk, and turning right towards the station. Magda, unnoticed, gradually slipped to the back of the column, and as the rest of the troop turned right, she hung back and ducked into the doorway of a small café, watching as her troop marched away. When she was sure they had gone, she slipped inside and hid behind the door.

'Can I help you?' asked a waitress.

'Oh, no thank you,' said Magda, shifting nervously from one foot to the other.

'Would you like a table?' the waitress asked, clearly confused by the young girl's strange behaviour.

Magda sat down at a dark corner table, peering anxiously out of the window, in case anyone had returned to look for her, and ordered a glass of water.

When the waitress set the glass down, Magda asked her where she would find the university.

'Oh, you mean Ludwig Maximilian. It's not far. It's just north of here. You can walk up Ludwigstrasse, or you could go through the Hofgarten and then on through the Englischer Garden – that's very pretty at this time of year.'

The park was filled with families enjoying the summer sunshine. Couples sat together in cafés enjoying a beer or a coffee. Children ran laughing to their mothers. Faced with a scene of such tranquillity Magda wanted to scream at everyone: 'Do you know that a few miles away from here, families – just like yours – are being herded onto trains, taken to work camps, or worse. Don't you know what's happening in your name?' As she skirted the large pond, the sun filtering through the trees, she remembered what Otto had said on the station concourse: that Lotte and her family were 'nothing'. How could that be true? They had as much right to a good life as these families here in the park.

As Magda approached the main university building, its white stone walls gleamed impressively against the bright blue sky. A tall bronze fountain, green with age, spilled water into a wide stone pool. Groups of students, chatting and laughing, perched on the stone edge, dragging their hands in the cooling water, their bulging bags and bicycles abandoned on the green lawn. Compared to the ritualised behaviour of the Hitler Youth rally she had just left, these young men and women laughing together and discussing ideas seemed so relaxed and happy. Magda had been indoctrinated with the idea that women should be discouraged from further education, and yet, here they were, studying on an equal basis to men. She sat down nervously on the grass, hoping – in spite of her uniform – to blend into the background, while eavesdropping on snatches of conversation.

'He's such a letch,' said a girl with short brown hair. She wore slacks and man's shirt tied in a knot around her waist and was lying languorously on the green lawn, her head resting on her rucksack. 'He told me yesterday that I would get an A* if I let him kiss me.'

'No! Really?' said another.

Magda, fascinated, leaned towards the group, surreptitiously trying to hear what the others were saying. The girl with short brown hair looked over at her and smiled.

'Hello,' she said, rolling over onto her side and propping herself up on her elbow. 'You look a bit lost. Can we help you?'

'Oh… no, thank you,' said Magda, blushing. 'I'm just visiting.'

The girl shrugged, rolled back over and resumed her conversation with her friends.

Magda stood up, intending to leave. But as she brushed the grass from her skirt, the girl with short hair smiled at her again and Magda felt emboldened to speak to her.

'I'm sorry to bother you,' she began. The girl jumped up and came and stood next to Magda.

'It's no bother,' she said.

'It's just that I'm sixteen, and people keep telling me that girls don't need to go to university. But I'd like to come here one day.'

'I understand. I was discouraged from coming too. I had to do war work for a year before I came here. I worked on a farm – it was terrible.'

'I live on a farm,' said Magda, smiling. 'It's not so bad when you're used to it. But my brother always hated it. He went to university and I want to go too.'

'Where did he go – your brother?'

'Heidelberg and then to Oxford… in England.'

The girl looked surprised.

'Really. When was that?'

'Before the war. He left in '37.'

'And now?' she asked.

'He stayed there and was put in jail – at least I think that's what happened.'

The girl smiled. 'So he didn't come back to fight.'

Magda shook her head.

'He sounds interesting, your brother.'

'He is,' said Magda, uncertain how much she should reveal. 'I miss him.'

'And you're in the League,' the girl said, gesturing to Magda's uniform.

'Yes. I had to go to a rally in the Königsplatz today. I hate it.'

It was a risky thing to say. You never knew, these days, who you were speaking to, but something in the girl's demeanour made Magda feel she could be trusted with such unpatriotic thoughts.

'What – the rally or the uniform?'

'Both,' said Magda.

'I understand. I hated it too,' the girl whispered. 'We're all going to a café soon – for a meeting. Come with us.'

'No,' said Magda, 'not dressed like this. Besides, I ought to get back to Augsburg; they'll be angry that I missed the train.'

'Then take this with you,' said the girl, reaching into her pocket and pulling out a leaflet. 'A group of us are spreading the word. I have a feeling you might be interested.'

She pressed the leaflet into Magda's hand.

'Only read it when you're alone. I hope you get to study here one day.'

On the train home, sitting alone by the window, Magda pulled the leaflet out of her pocket and read it with growing amazement.

Since the conquest of Poland, 300,000 Jews have been murdered in a bestial manner. Here we see the most terrible crime committed against the dignity of man, a crime that has no counterpart in human history. Is this a sign that the German people have become brutalised in their basic human feelings? That they have sunk into a terminal sleep from which there is no awakening, ever, ever again?

It seems that way… if the German does not arouse himself from this lethargy, if he does not protest whenever he can against this gang of criminals, if he doesn't feel compassion for the hundreds of thousands of victims – not only compassion, no, much more: guilt. Everyone shrugs off

this guilt, falling asleep again with his conscience at peace.
But he can't shrug it off; everyone is guilty, guilty, guilty!
We will not be silent. We will be your bad conscience.
the White Rose will not leave you in peace!

Magda folded the leaflet and put it back in her pocket. Staring out of the train window as it rumbled through the outskirts of Munich, she shaded her eyes against the sun, hanging like a vast red orb over the dark buildings. Magda, exhausted and confused, closed her eyes. So much had happened that day: the appalling treatment of her friend Lotte; the rally with all its pomp and ceremony and nationalistic pride; her surprise meeting with the brown-haired girl at the university. But as she fingered the leaflet in her pocket, she felt something she had not felt for years – hope. For the first time since she had read Karl's letter, she realised she was not alone in her feelings of revulsion and anger. There were people like her, young people who cared passionately, just as her brother did, who wanted to make a difference. Who wanted to stop the madness and the cruelty. And she was determined to be part of it.

Chapter Fourteen

As Imogen and Joy approached their final few weeks of school, the weather grew hot and balmy. During the previous year their school had moved into a large mansion outside Keswick on the shores of the lake. Rather than being billeted with families, most of the pupils now shared dormitories in a couple of boarding houses on the edge of town, which created a sense of shared camaraderie; it also meant Imogen and Joy could finally be together. One morning, as they prepared for school, Imogen received a letter from Freddie.

'Joy,' she said, grabbing hold of her friend. 'You go on ahead of me to school. I just must read Freddie's letter. I've not heard from him since that night we went out at Easter.'

'All right…' said Joy. 'I'll get the bus. Don't be late though, will you? You're taking the register for the Lower Fourths, remember?'

'Don't worry – I'll be there…'

Freddie's letter was full of news: he had been selected to fly bombers, training initially on Oxfords and Ansons. It was all very intense, he told her. There was theory to study, in addition to one hundred hours a week of flying experience. He loved it and felt, at last, he was doing something important.

Included with the letter was a photograph: it showed him leaning casually against his plane on a brilliantly sunny day, wearing his RAF uniform and a pair of aviator sunglasses, looking sophisticated and handsome. Lying on her bed in the dormitory, Imogen propped the photograph against the alarm clock on her bedside table and gazed at it. Disappointingly, he had made no mention of their last meeting in the letter; nor was there was any reference to the brief kiss they had shared. She had spent the previous few weeks day-dreaming about him, and secretly she had hoped for some sort of declaration in this letter – even a 'PS I love you...' would have been enough. She turned the letter over and her heart leapt when she saw that he had written an extra note on the back.

> *Dear Ginny, meant to post this earlier, but got dragged out to a dance in the town. The locals here are so friendly and the girls are really pretty – so natural. We had a wild time.*
> *With love,*
> *Freddie*

She lay back on her bed, her eyes filling with tears. It was as if he had completely forgotten their evening together. He made no mention of the kiss, and certainly no mention of loving her. She felt a fool for having nurtured such romantic fantasies; they were nothing but girlish dreams, she realised. While he was living a glamorous life in Canada, she'd be taking her final exams. Their lives were poles apart. Of course he didn't love her. He'd simply indulged her that evening. Tearfully, she put his letter, along with the photograph, into the bottom of her suitcase beneath her bed.

Having missed the school bus, Imogen set off for school on her bike. Half way round the lake, she stopped to watch a flotilla of little dinghies scudding across the sparkling water. Dougie had taken her sailing one afternoon, she remembered. They'd had a lovely time, tacking back and forth across the lake. Now, as she sat miserably on the wooden bench in the sunshine, she realised she had not thought about Dougie for months. She had written to him once or twice soon after he'd left for the army, but had never heard back. At the time she'd been relieved that he seemed to have forgotten her. She'd always suspected their relationship wouldn't last. Now she wondered if she would ever be able to feel such indifference for Freddie. Somehow she doubted it.

Glancing down at her wristwatch, she realised, to her horror, that she was due at school in five minutes to take the register for the Lower Fourth. Pedalling fast, she careered into the school grounds from the main road, her bike juddering over the cattle grid. As she raced down the gravel drive towards the main door she braked sharply and the bike skidded on the gravel, throwing her off. Her school hat flew up into the air and landed ten feet away on the lawn. Momentarily stunned, she lay quite still, watching the wheels of her bike spinning hypnotically in the sunshine. Closing her eyes, she became aware of a throbbing pain in her lower leg.

'*Cosa è successo?* Are you all right?'

Opening her eyes with a start, she was surprised to find a handsome dark-haired young man leaning over her. Imogen didn't recognise either him or his accent, but it sounded a little like French. She smiled bravely and tried to stand up, but the pain was too severe and she collapsed back down on the gravel drive.

'Let me help you,' he said, effortlessly picking her up, and carrying her into the school hall where he lay her gently down on a battered old sofa.

'I will get your things,' he said, returning a few minutes later with her hat and school bag before walking off down the corridor, revealing a red circle on the back of his jacket.

'Where are you going?' she called out.

'To find someone.'

The school secretary came bustling out into the hall.

'Oh dear, Imogen. What's happened to you?'

'I fell off my bike, Miss Fuller. This kind man picked me up.'

Miss Fuller looked askance at the young man. 'Oh Sergio – yes. He's helping in the gardens. He's Italian,' she said to Imogen, as if his nationality was all the explanation that was required. 'You can go now, Sergio,' she said to him, flapping her hands as if shooing away a flock of birds.

He removed his cap and bowed low to Miss Fuller, and then again to Imogen.

'At your service,' he said, in his deep, dark voice.

Imogen's grazed leg was bathed in iodine and bandaged up in the school sanatorium. As the day wore on, it stiffened and she was let off games and most of her prefect duties. At four o'clock, when she came out of school, she found her bicycle leaning against the front wall of the building, next to the front door. Sergio, she presumed, had left it there. It struck her that he had the same dark good looks as Tyrone Power in *The Mark of Zorro* – a film she had recently seen with Joy. Tyrone Power was a 'dreamboat' according to Joy, and Imogen had to agree. She slung her bag into the basket on the front of her bike and climbed onto the seat. But as she began to turn the pedals, the pain in her knee and shin was so severe she had to climb off and limp slowly towards the school gates, wheeling her bike.

Sergio appeared from the direction of the vegetable garden.

'Hello again,' he called out. 'How is your leg? Does it still hurt?'

'Yes – rather a lot, as it happens.'

'Let me help you,' he said, taking the bike from her.

'Miss Fuller said you're Italian.'

'*Sì* – yes.'

'And how did you end up here – in the Lake District, of all places?' she asked.

'I was shot down in an aeroplane.'

Imogen looked momentarily confused.

'I was in the air force,' he explained.

'Oh,' Imogen said, brightly, 'what a coincidence, I have a friend in the air force.' She blushed. 'How silly of me – he's in the *Royal Air Force*, of course.'

The Italian smiled.

'But you're not a prisoner, are you? I mean, you work in the garden – that's hardly a prison, is it?'

'Well at first I was in a camp, but they need help on farms and in the quarries. I like gardening and farm work; my father was a farmer and I'd rather be working.'

'Your English is very good,' she said, wondering if all Italian farmers had such impressive language abilities.

'I am a teacher,' he said, as if reading her mind. 'In Torino. I teach English to school students.'

At the junction to the main road, he held the bike steady for her to climb onto.

'Where do you live?' he asked.

'Keswick – it's about two miles.'

'You cannot go so far. Wait here. I will find help.'

'You're very kind,' she called after him, as he ran down the drive. A few moments later he reappeared in a truck being driven by Jimmy, the head gardener.

'Hello there, Miss,' said Jimmy, jumping to the ground. 'You been in the wars?'

'Yes, I have rather. But this nice man has been a huge help.'

'Well climb in. Sergio will put your bike in the back. I'll give you a lift back to town.'

Installed in the cab of the truck, Imogen waved at Sergio as they headed towards Keswick.

'That man… he's a prisoner, isn't he?' asked Imogen.

'Yes. We've been assigned a couple of them. Well, there's no young men left here to do the hard work. Sergio works on a local farm most of the time, but we're allowed to have him a few hours a week. It's a big help. I can't keep up otherwise. He does the vegetable garden for me.'

'And is he nice? He seems nice.'

'Oh Sergio's OK. Not a big fan of Mussolini, I gather, or Hitler for that matter. He's a teacher, really. Bit wasted doing the garden. But he's a good bloke.'

A few days after she had fallen off her bike, Imogen, out of the blue, received a letter from Dougie.

> *Dear Imogen,*
>
> *Thanks for your letters. I'm sorry I've not replied sooner – your letters take an age to arrive, and it's hard to find the time to write back – it's been that busy here… more like hell to tell the truth. I'm not allowed to say where we are, but it's hot, I'll tell you that. Hot and dirty and frightening.*
>
> *It's odd to think of you back in the Lakes, with all that rain and water and clean grass. I miss it. I miss you. I thought, joining up, I'd be a man, but truth to tell, I feel like a frightened boy most of the time. I think of you often, and miss you – the softness of your skin, the silky feel of your hair, your laugh. I won't ask you to wait for me, that wouldn't be fair. But I hope I get to see you again sometime soon.*
>
> *All my love,*
> *Dougie*
> *Xxxx*

The letter disconcerted Imogen. It was clear that Dougie was still fond of her and although he had said, sensibly, that she shouldn't wait for him, she now felt responsible, in some way, for his happiness. She fretted about whether she should reply. He had said he missed her, but she could not honestly reciprocate. She would not lie and pretend to love him. If she loved anyone – however hopelessly – it was Freddie, who was thousands of miles away training to be a pilot in Canada.

The irony of her situation was not lost on her. There were two men in her life: one, a brave soldier boy whose love she could not return, and the other, a handsome airman who she adored, but who was immune, it seemed, to her charms.

During that final school term, she resolved to put love behind her, and concentrate instead on revising for her exams. To her delight, she was accepted by the School of Architecture in Newcastle, and she began to look forward to a different sort of future – as an adult woman with a career of her own. Her friend Joy had decided to learn shorthand and typing when she left school, and on the afternoon of their final exam, they wandered down to the shores of the lake, and lay down beneath a weeping willow tree. They listened to the water lapping rhythmically nearby, as bees buzzed lazily around them.

'Oh Ginny,' said Joy, 'isn't it marvellous? No more school. No more uniform. We're adults at last.'

'I suppose we are,' said Imogen, 'although I don't feel "adult" quite yet. I'm excited, obviously, about university. But there's still a war on, remember. Out here in the countryside, you'd hardly know it was happening. But Mummy told me in her last letter that Newcastle has been taking quite a battering recently. And remember – I was nearly blown to smithereens when I went home at Easter. If it hadn't been for Freddie I don't know what would have happened.'

'You're still pining for him, aren't you?' said Joy, sympathetically. 'I noticed you'd put his photograph away.'

'Yes,' Imogen said sadly. 'It's utterly hopeless. He's thousands of miles away having a wonderful time, and I don't really think he even knows I exist.'

'But he wrote you a letter,' Joy insisted.

'Yes. A letter in which he told me he was a having a marvellous time with other girls. He was obviously trying to tell me, basically, to forget him.'

'Oh Imogen. Don't say that. No man writes to a girl unless he likes her; besides, you've still got Dougie. He adores you.'

Imogen sat up suddenly. 'Please don't say that. I feel bad enough about Dougie as it is.'

'What do you mean?'

'I know Dougie cares for me. And he's sweet – he really is. But, oh, Joy…'

She flopped back down and lay on her side, facing her friend, tears in her eyes. 'I don't love him. I don't think I ever did – he was just a crush. It's Freddie I love, but he doesn't love me.'

'Oh Ginny,' Joy leaned over and stroked her friend's cheek. 'What a mess.'

'No,' said Imogen, wiping her eyes. 'Don't say that. It's not a mess. It's just the way things are. I've been thinking about this for a while – and I've made a decision. There will be no more men for me, at least not for a while. I'm going to get on with my life, start university, enjoy being at home, and not look back.'

Joy, lying on the damp grass, listening to the sound of the lake water lapping against the stony shore and the distant bleating of sheep on the hillside, smiled at her friend.

'That's what I love about you, Ginny. You're the most optimistic person I've ever met – apart from me that is.' And they laughed.

On the final Saturday before the end of term, Imogen and Joy met up with Helen in the tea shop in town. It was bustling with housewives taking a break from shopping, and the odd holiday-maker dressed in hiking gear.

The girls had decided to have one final hill walk before they left the Lakes for good. After two years they were experienced hikers, and were properly dressed for the occasion in corduroy slacks and boots.

'Oh Ginny, do you remember that first walk we did?' said Helen, pouring tea into their cups. 'Honestly Joy, you should have seen us – we went off in our school shoes! Do you remember, Ginny? We ended up slipping and sliding. We were lucky we didn't break a leg.'

'Oh Helen,' said Imogen irritably. 'You do exaggerate. But I agree – trousers and boots are best for walking. I've got maps and a packed lunch, too. And I bought some biscuits yesterday, although I found some of the fourth form trying to steal them.'

'Mrs Latimer would be proud of us,' said Helen. 'Properly prepared at last!'

'She would,' said Imogen, taking a bite of her toasted teacake. 'I often think we were so lucky with the Latimers. They were such a sweet pair.'

'How's their son – James, is it?' Joy asked.

'I don't know,' said Imogen. 'Last I heard, his leg was healed up and he'd been sent abroad – North Africa I think. God, I hope he makes it. Poor Mrs Latimer, she couldn't cope with losing him too. She never really got over losing Arthur. I saw her at church last week, weeping over his grave. It was so sad.'

'Have you heard from Dougie?' asked Helen, pointedly. She had always been rather jealous that Douglas had preferred Imogen to her.

'Not for a while,' said Imogen, wishing Helen wasn't always so interested in her personal life.

'I'm surprised,' said Helen, 'I thought he was sweet on you.'

'He was, for a bit. I was on him I suppose, but… the war has changed everything, hasn't it?'

'Right then,' said Joy, anxious to steer the conversation away from Dougie. 'It's time we were off. Skiddaw here we come.'

*

The three girls left the tea shop and set off for the hills in high spirits. The sky was azure blue and the sun shone as they walked past a small hill farm on the lower slopes. They waved cheerfully at the farmer before crossing a beck, which was full to bursting after heavy rain. They jumped nimbly from stone to stone, landing safely on the other side. The track was a gentle incline at first, winding through green fields of grass and bracken. Gradually the hills and fells came into view.

'I'm going to miss all this,' said Imogen. 'These hills are so beautiful.'

'Maybe we'll come back one day,' said Joy, hopefully. 'After the war, I mean.'

As they climbed higher, they crossed streams that bounced and coursed down the shale-covered valleys. They passed a sheepfold that had been set up on the hills, and watched as a shepherd in the far distance drove his flock towards them.

Gradually, as they climbed higher and higher, mist began to roll across the landscape.

'Oh, I hope it won't rain,' declared Helen.

'Well, what if it does?' said Imogen. 'We have to get to the top. I'm determined to do this before we leave.'

They walked along the Cumbria Way with Great Calva to their right, covered in heather, just a few weeks away from flowering. In September the hillside would be swathed in purple. They passed an old stone building called Skiddaw House and headed on across moorland, reaching Skiddaw Ridge just as the sun broke momentarily through the clouds.

'Can we stop now?' asked Helen. 'We must be nearly at the top, surely?'

'No!' insisted Imogen. 'It's not far… that's where we're heading.'

The three looked up towards the looming grey summit, as the sun retreated behind dark, threatening clouds.

'Oh, Imogen – I really think we should go down,' begged Helen. 'I thought you had a bad leg, anyway?'

'It's much better, thank you,' said Imogen, walking on determinedly. 'Now, do stop moaning.'

The path became stonier as the group trudged towards the stone column that marked the summit. When they finally arrived at the top, they stood panting, catching their breath.

'We made it!' said Imogen. 'Just look at that view.' Beneath them lay a patchwork of green fields, and nestling on the water's edge, the little town of Keswick.

'You can just see the school down there,' said Joy.

'And the church in the distance,' said Imogen. 'Shall we sit down and really enjoy it?'

'This might be the last time we ever see this,' said Joy dreamily, wrapping her arms around her knees. 'Next week we'll be back in Newcastle. You'll soon be off to university, and I'll start secretarial college. What about you Helen?'

'I'm going to be a teacher,' Helen replied.

'Really?' said Joy. 'I can't imagine anything worse than working in a school. I can't wait to get away.'

'I like it,' said Helen. 'You know where you stand in a school… rules and so on.'

'Well good for you,' said Imogen. 'You'll be a good teacher, I'm sure.'

'Thank you,' said Helen.

'I know we've not always… got on,' said Imogen. 'But I am fond of you – you do know that?'

'Yes, I know.'

'Well,' said Imogen, jumping to her feet, 'I think we should all be very pleased with ourselves.

'*To the future!*' she shouted, the words ricocheting around the ring of grey-green hills surrounding Derwentwater. '*To love, happiness and excitement!*

'I thought you were giving love up?' said Joy, peering up at her friend.

'Well I am,' said Imogen, smiling, 'but not forever!'

'Well that's all very well,' said Helen, standing up. 'But at the moment, all I can see are dark clouds. I'm sure it's about to rain. Please can we go down now?'

As the girls began to trudge downhill, the shale paths soon turned to stone, and the steep heather uplands merged into grass as the landscape became gentler. Once again the path took them through sloping green fields and they could hear the distant bleating of sheep. But as the sky darkened dramatically, rain began to lash the hills. Imogen, in the lead, approached a winding stream and as she made her way gingerly across, slipped on a stepping-stone, badly twisting her ankle.

'Ow!' she cried out, collapsing onto the opposite bank and unlacing her boot. 'Look – it's already swelling up. I don't think I can walk.'

'You have to,' said Helen. 'We can't stay here.' She looked around her at the rain-sodden hills. 'There's nowhere to shelter. Get up Ginny, please.'

'I can't. You'll have to go for help,' whimpered Imogen. 'I'm sorry but I really can't walk.'

'I'll go,' said Joy cheerfully. 'You stay here with her,' she instructed Helen. 'And do try not to moan.' She set off at a run down the hill.

'Let's try and make a shelter,' Imogen said brightly.

'What with?' asked Helen gloomily.

'The hillsides are covered with bracken. I used to make camps with it in the Highlands when I was little. See if you can pick an armful and bring it back and we can make a sort of roof with it.'

Helen wandered off, reluctantly, returning a few minutes later with armfuls of greenery. Imogen in the meantime had hobbled over to a little stone gulley and together they erected a roof of wide bracken leaves, which kept the worst of the rain off.

'Oh heavens, where is she?' asked Helen frantically, as the minutes ticked by.

'She'll have gone back to the farm,' said Imogen. 'It'll take a while. Just keep calm.'

Helen glared at her. 'This is all your fault... You keep calm.'

After half an hour, the girls were cold and wet. In spite of the bracken 'roof', rain lashed in at right angles, stinging their faces and drenching their clothing. Even Imogen was beginning to worry, when she heard a dog barking in the distance, followed by the sound of a man's voice and that of a girl.

'It's somewhere over here,' the girl said, 'I'm sure that's where I left them.'

'Joy,' Imogen shouted, struggling to her feet, 'we're over here.'

In the gathering gloom, a man ran towards them.

'Sergio!' said Imogen. 'How wonderful! What are you doing up here?'

'I've come to rescue you.'

'He works on the farm down in the valley,' Joy explained. 'He was herding those sheep we saw earlier – putting them in that pen half-way down. Weren't we lucky?'

'Here,' Sergio said, 'put your arm around my shoulder.'

Once again, he swept her up in his arms and carried her back down the hill.

The farmer's wife, Dorothy, ushered the girls into the farmhouse kitchen.

'You'd better come in here, she said, clearing space around the kitchen table. 'You're wet through, all of you – give me your coats, I'll put them on the range to dry and then I'll put the kettle on. Sergio, go and get George for me, would you?'

He nodded and went outside.

'George's my husband,' she explained. 'You girls are from the big school, are you?'

'Yes we are,' said Imogen, removing her boot and rubbing her swollen ankle. 'I'm so sorry to cause you all this trouble.'

'You're lucky Sergio was up with the sheep. You could have had a cold wet night up there. Now have a mug of tea and piece of my cake.'

Once they had warmed up and their clothes had dried a little, they thanked the farmer's wife and Imogen limped outside, where Sergio lifted her into the front seat of George's old Landrover.

'Thank you so much Sergio,' Imogen said. 'That's twice you've rescued me. I'm in your debt.'

'You're welcome,' he said politely.

'Right,' said George. 'You go back to your billet, Sergio, and I'll take the young ladies home.'

As they set off bumping down the stony drive away from the farmhouse, Imogen looked back and watched as the handsome Italian raised his hand and waved.

'He's utterly dreamy,' cooed Joy. 'You are lucky, Ginny. I can't imagine anything lovelier than being carried down a mountain by a man like that.'

'He's the enemy!' Helen declared. 'How can you possibly say anything so traitorous?'

'He's not the enemy,' Imogen said calmly. 'He's just a nice man, caught up in a war he doesn't believe in.'

Lying in her bed that night, Imogen thought back over her two years in the Lakes. Of the Latimers and their poor dead son. Of

Sergio and his kindness and of Dougie, a young man who was
fighting a war that hadn't turned out the way he had expected.
In a few days' time they'd leaving school forever. She would go to
university and a new phase in her life would begin. She leant down
and pulled her suitcase out from beneath her bed. She flipped it
open and removed the photograph of Freddie. Perhaps she had
misjudged him. Perhaps he did care for her. Perhaps, one day, she
would see him again.

Chapter Fifteen

In the weeks following the Hitler Youth rally, Magda often thought about the intriguing brown-haired girl she had met at the university. Re-reading the leaflet she had been given, she began to envisage a role for herself supporting the group with their campaigning. The only flaw in this plan was that she lived deep in the Bavarian countryside, and so rarely got the chance to visit the local city of Augsburg, let alone travel to Munich. Her problem, she realised, was a lack of transport and she began to plan how she might acquire a bicycle, or even a motorbike, to liberate her from the seclusion of the farm.

'Papa – I was wondering if I could ask you something,' she began, one evening after she had helped him bring in the herd.

'You can ask…' he replied, settling down to milk the first cow.

'Could I have a bicycle perhaps, or maybe even a motorbike?'

'No! Definitely not a motorbike,' replied her father, 'it's too dangerous. Maybe a bicycle, but you'll have to contribute in some way – I'm not just going to buy one for you.'

'I know Papa. I'll do extra work I promise. All the morning milking, maybe? Then you won't have to get up at all.'

'Well, maybe not all, but if you do half the week for me, that would be helpful.'

A couple of weeks later she was standing in the kitchen looking out of the window, when she saw her father unloading something from his cart.

'What have you got there?' she asked, coming into the yard.

'A surprise,' he said, whipping off a piece of old canvas to reveal a tatty bicycle, its front wheel slightly bent, but a bicycle nevertheless.

Magda threw herself at her father and hugged him. 'Oh Papa, thank you so much! I'm so grateful.'

'I bought it from a farm sale – they've gone out of business, poor things. I know it's a bit shabby, but with two new tyres and a bit of paint and oil, it will be as good as new.'

The bike was repaired and repainted a smart navy blue. Käthe bought a basket to put on the front, and as Magda buckled it onto the handlebars, her mother hovered in the yard next to her, fretting about where she was intending to go for her first cycle ride.

'Maybe it's best just to go to the village for your first outing,' she suggested.

'I could do that,' said Magda, 'but I'd like to go a bit further.'

'Where?' her mother asked, alarmed.

'Augsburg maybe,' Magda ventured. She was lying of course. Her real destination would be Munich, but she realised her mother would worry if she went so far.

'Augsburg? Why do you want to go there?'

'It will be fun to cycle round the city and see how the bike handles the roads.'

'What if you fall off?' Käthe asked anxiously, 'or something happens to you?'

'Why will anything happen to me?' Magda replied. 'I'll be fine… stop worrying.'

Cycling down the farm track later that morning, and onto the main road heading for Augsburg, Magda felt a huge sense of liberation. At the railway station, the guard of the train helped her load the bike into his van. 'Come and collect it get it when you get to

Munich,' he told her. From Munich station, she cycled straight to the university, determined to find the girl who had given her the White Rose leaflet. Wandering around the university grounds, wheeling her bicycle, she saw the girl leaning casually against a wall, smoking a cigarette. She wore trousers and a loose man's shirt, and to Magda's eyes, seemed impossibly glamorous.

'Hello,' Magda said, shyly, to the girl.

'Hello,' the girl replied, inhaling deeply on her cigarette. 'Have we met?'

'Yes, a few weeks ago. I was in my Girls' League uniform. You gave me a leaflet.'

A look of recognition passed over the girl's face as she exhaled cigarette smoke. 'Oh yes, of course. The little League girl with the interesting brother.'

Magda smiled. 'That's right.'

'You look different.'

'I'm in my own clothes,' said Magda, blushing.

'Well it's a definite improvement,' said the girl. 'I'm Saskia by the way.'

'And I'm Magda.'

'And what are you doing here, little Magda?'

'I want to help.'

'Do you?' the girl said, dropping her cigarette butt beneath her shoe. 'Mmmm,' she said, observing Magda. 'Maybe you can. Do you want a coffee? I'm just off to meet some people. Come with me.'

'Thank you,' said Magda, delightedly. 'I'd like that.'

The coffee house was in a dark basement on a small side street close to the university. Saskia darted down the metal exterior staircase, followed closely by Magda. It took a few moments for Magda's eyes to adjust to the low light levels.

'What is this place?' she asked Saskia.

'Just a private room in a bar. But they're... sympathetic.'

'To what?' asked Magda, innocently.

'To the movement,' the girl whispered in Magda's ear. 'I thought you said you read the leaflet?'

'Yes… yes I did.'

'So you know what we're about.'

'I suppose so,' said Magda, uncertainly.

'Do you really want to be part of it?' the girl asked. 'Because once you're in… you can't get out.'

'I understand.' Magda said, her heart beating loudly in her chest.

'Come on then. I'll introduce you to the others.'

A small group of young men and women sat in a dark corner, huddled around a table covered with spent coffee cups and saucers overflowing with cigarette butts.

'Hi there,' said Saskia. 'This is Magda – she's keen to help.'

A thin young man with dark hair and even darker eyes inhaled deeply on his cigarette and looked suspiciously at Magda. He stood up and, yanking Saskia's arm, dragged her across the bar to the other side of the room. He looked angry, Magda thought. Saskia waved her arms around and Magda heard her say,

'Yes, she's young. But she's sincere.'

A few minutes later, the pair returned.

'You need to understand something,' the young man said. 'This is not a game. It's dangerous. We all know the risks. We're prepared to die for what we believe in – do you understand?'

Magda had a momentary frisson of fear. She thought longingly of the farmhouse kitchen; of Mutti baking apple cake, of the cows in the yard. She could leave now and forget all this. But something made her push those thoughts away.

'I understand,' she said. 'I cannot stand back any more and do nothing. I can't live a lie.'

The young man smiled and touched her shoulder. 'You're very young,' he said, gently. 'How old are you?'

'Sixteen, nearly seventeen,' Magda said. It was a lie, for she wouldn't be seventeen for another nine months, but she felt the need to impress him.

'We are all older than you – Saskia's twenty-two, I'm twenty-four. I worry you don't really understand what you're getting into.'

'My brother is in England,' Magda said, firmly. 'He's fighting on the side of the British. I love him and if he cannot support this government then neither can I. And yes I'm young, but I can't watch the people I love – like my friend Lotte who is Jewish – being hurt any longer.'

The group welcomed her; she became their little mascot. They shared their plans, their dreams, their hopes of a better future. Max, the young man with dark eyes, was one of the ringleaders. He was filled with zeal and passion, Magda thought. She admired him, perhaps even fell a little in love with him. But most importantly, she felt she was doing something at last; something that might help Lotte and millions of others like her. Over that summer and into the autumn of 1942 four leaflets were produced under the heading: 'Leaflets of the White Rose'. Six of the group were responsible for writing, the others concentrated on distribution. The leaflets were not left arbitrarily in the streets, but instead posted to academics and intellectuals they hoped would be sympathetic to their ideas.

Over the following months Käthe learned to trust that Magda would return safely from her cycling expeditions. Emboldened, Magda finally admitted that she sometimes went as far afield as Munich, although she kept the real purpose of her visits a secret.

'I don't know why you need to go to Munich so often,' Käthe complained one Saturday morning as Magda prepared for another outing. 'What do you do all day?'

'I wander around,' Magda said, evasively. 'I want to go to university there... after the war. I need to get to know the city. Besides, I like it. It feels free somehow.'

'But I worry about you,' said Käthe. 'You're still very young.'

'I'm sixteen, Mutti. In a year or so I will be doing war work.'

'Oh let the girl alone,' said Pieter. 'She's got a sensible head on her shoulders. She helps on the farm, she does her schoolwork. Let her have some freedom.'

One Saturday evening at the end of October, when the air was caught between the warmth of summer and the chill of autumn, members of the White Rose group filed up the metal staircase from the basement of the bar into the moonlit evening. Magda climbed onto her bike, preparing to cycle back to the station.

'I need to get back,' she said to Saskia. 'It's late; my parents will be worried. I left without saying goodbye this morning.'

'It's nearly nine o'clock,' said Saskia. 'Why don't you stay with me?'

Magda was tempted.

'I'd better not,' she said.

'Your parents know you're sensible,' said Saskia. 'Better to spend the night in a warm flat than risk cycling back in the dark.'

Magda felt a glow of excitement. To spend the night with a friend in the city seemed a dream. She worried that her mother would be sitting at home fretting about her, but her father would reassure her. 'She's a sensible girl,' he'd say, 'she'll be fine.'

'All right,' she said. 'I'll get the first train home in the morning and be back in time for breakfast.'

She walked contentedly with Saskia through the streets of Munich, wheeling her bicycle. They stopped outside a five-storey corner building with tall, graceful windows. The middle three floors were decorated with ornate metal balconies overlooking the street.

'Is this your house?' asked Magda, gazing up at the elegant building.

'Yes… not all of it,' Saskia said, laughing. 'My apartment is at the top. It's not as glamorous as it looks from the outside!' She led the way up a set of stone steps and unlocked the main door. 'Leave your bike here,' she said, indicating an area of the hall littered with a tangle of bicycles. 'It'll be all right.'

The concierge, an elderly lady who sat in her little kitchen off the hall with the door left ajar so she could observe the tenants' comings and goings, grunted as Saskia and Magda walked past.

'Come up,' Saskia said to Magda, 'it's only five flights.'

The apartment consisted of one large room. There was a little makeshift kitchen in one corner, with a tiny gas ring and a sink, a big tin bath in the opposite corner, a small double bed against one wall, and under the window a shabby armchair and a desk littered with papers.

'The lavatory's on the landing out there,' said Saskia, filling a kettle. 'Do you want tea?'

'Yes please,' said Magda. She felt shy, and curious; Saskia had mentioned 'we' quite often.

'Do you live here on your own?'

'No,' said Saskia, lighting a cigarette, 'I thought you realised. I live with Max… from the group.'

'Oh,' said Magda – surprised and a little disappointed. She blushed at the romantic thoughts she had harboured for the older man.

'But don't worry,' said Saskia, 'he's not coming home tonight. He and Willi are spending the night at Willi's place – they've got some more leaflets to write. He won't be home till the morning. You can share the bed with me.'

She toasted a piece of bread on the gas flame, and spread it with damson jam.

'My mother makes this jam for me,' she said, handing the toast to Magda. 'It's good.' Magda had never thought of Saskia as having anything as prosaic as a mother.

'What's she like?'

'My mother? She's a doctor. She lives outside the city – a long way away. I don't see her very much.'

'Does she know about you and the movement?' asked Magda.

'Yes, she knows. My father too; they both support us. My father's already in jail for his views.'

'I'm so sorry,' Magda said. 'That must be terrible.'

'It's hard. We all have to be careful. My whole family is being watched. Me too, I suspect. But we take care to keep things small, you know?'

'Why did you let me join? Surely, that was a risk?'

Saskia lay on the bed, sipping tea and inhaling her cigarette. 'Max was against it – he thought I was mad letting you in. But there's something about you. I just know we can trust you.'

A siren – piercing and insistent – disturbed the peace of the attic room.

'Oh no,' said Saskia, swinging her legs off the bed, her cigarette hanging from her lips.

'What is it?' asked Magda.

'It's a siren, silly,' said the older girl. 'Surely you've heard one before?'

'No,' said Magda, innocently.

'Oh, of course; you live in the country. It means bombs are coming. We had the same thing a month or so ago. Come on – we'll have to go down to the basement.'

Magda and Saskia ran down the five flights of stairs, joining a throng of people from the other flats dressed in every variety of clothing – evening dresses, pyjamas, even a young man in an SS uniform. Magda had a frisson of fear when she saw him. But Saskia slapped him on the back.

'Hi Klaus – you well?'

'Sure,' he replied, running ahead of them down the stairs.

Magda marvelled at Saskia's cool exterior. To be able to be so calm and casual in the presence of a uniformed soldier – the enemy – seemed extraordinary to her. Down in the cellars, the tenants gathered. There was a gaggle of sleepy children clutching teddy bears, being comforted by their mothers, some of whom wore dressing gowns, their hair in curlers. The concierge had a list of everyone who lived in the building and was laboriously ticking off each name as they entered.

'The Beckers from apartment three are missing,' she said, looking around the room, accusingly.

'Perhaps someone should go back up and knock on their door,' suggested Klaus.

'No,' said a woman in curlers. 'It's not safe. The bombers must be close now.'

The building shook; there was a sound of crashing, and then a sort of roaring sound, louder than anything Magda had ever heard before. The inhabitants of the cellar gasped, the mothers gathering up their children, the men wrapping their arms protectively around their families.

'Perhaps we'd better stay down here,' said Klaus pragmatically. 'If the Beckers are up there, it's either too late, or they'll be down here soon enough.'

'They've gone away,' said another man impatiently. He was wearing a silk dressing gown. 'I saw them leave earlier from my window.'

'Why didn't you say?' said the concierge irritably, from her hiding place beneath a small table.

'It doesn't really matter now, does it?' said the woman in curlers, clutching her two children to her breast.

The building shook again. There was another violent explosion, closer this time. The group, most of whom were sitting on the floor, their backs to the wall, their arms wrapped defensively around their knees, instinctively hid their faces. The children began to weep, their mothers comforting them as best they could.

'That was close,' said the man in the dressing gown. 'Too bloody close.'

There was another explosion, followed by another…

When the All Clear siren finally sounded, the group staggered upstairs. Their building had miraculously survived, but the sky outside was red with flame and vast aching gaps had appeared where apartment buildings had once stood. From the hallway, they stared uncomprehendingly through the shattered glass front door at the sea of broken bricks, glass and furniture strewn across the road. Somewhere beneath the piles of rubble, people moaned and screamed. A child ran, bleeding, down the road, crying for his mother.

Saskia put her arm around Magda's shoulders as they surveyed the carnage. 'There's nothing we can do,' she said.

'But we should help,' said Magda, her eyes filled with terror.

'Others will do that. Come on little one, let's get you upstairs to bed.'

Saskia guided her up the five flights of stairs and gently removed her jacket, encouraging her to sit down on the bed.

'You're shaking,' she said. 'Here… take off your skirt.'

Magda sat on the edge of the bed and pulled off her jumper. Saskia knelt in front of her, and removed her boots and stockings.

'It's all right,' she murmured, 'the bombers have gone now. They won't come back again tonight.'

She swung Magda's legs into the bed and covered her with the quilt. As Magda lay down, still shaking, Saskia sat on the edge of the bed, stroking Magda's forehead.

'Rest little one, rest now,' she said and slowly Magda's eyes closed, her eyelashes fluttering as she fell into a deep but troubled sleep.

Chapter Sixteen

As Imogen walked through the impressive red-brick façade of the student union building, rain poured out of the sky in waves – dense droplets that hammered against the leaded windows, and bounced off the grey paving, splattering her stockings with dirty water and soaking through the thin leather of her dark brown court shoes. She ran the last few yards into the School of Architecture, holding her leather briefcase over her head. An impressive mock gothic building with stone-mullioned double-height windows, its red brickwork covered in ivy, it still gave Imogen a thrill every time she walked through the large wooden doors. As one of just two women out of a year group of sixty, she was proud to be a part of it, and felt, perhaps for the first time in her life, that she had truly found a real purpose.

Upstairs, in the drawing studio, with its vast windows overlooking the quad, she removed her wet coat, shaking off the raindrops, before hanging it on the pegs by the door, aware of the other students' eyes on her neat figure. With her dark hair and green eyes, Imogen found herself the subject of constant attention from men trying to persuade her to go on a date – a situation that both pleased and irritated her.

'Morning Ginny,' Giles, a fellow student, called out. 'How's my best girl? Changed your mind about marrying me?'

'I'm fine, Giles, thank you,' she said, walking across the studio to her drawing board. 'And no… I'm still not available.'

Already at work was Marion, the other female in the group. Taller than Imogen by several inches, the 'boys', as she and Marion called them, felt slightly intimidated by her. She had a wicked sense of humour, which Imogen loved, smoked incessantly, and had a habit of wearing corduroy trousers.

'Giles is being his usual patronising self, I see,' said Marion, winking at Imogen. 'Still, you can't blame him for trying.'

Imogen smiled and took the cover off her drawing board, studying her work from the previous day. She was flattered, of course, by the boys' attention, but was determined not to be side-tracked. She had worked hard to get to university and although she would only have the chance to complete the first year of her degree course before she was required to join up, she wasn't going to waste her time going on pointless dates with men in whom she had no interest. Her lectures covered subjects as varied as the history of architecture, which she loved… to engineering which she found interesting, if challenging… to complex mathematics which she struggled with. But determined to succeed, she worked hard, taking her maths homework back to her father in the evenings for extra tuition. Beyond the academic work, she was also required to study life-drawing and painting, which she shone at, developing a real eye for the human form.

Imogen and Marion worked hard all morning and at lunchtime Marion suggested they go to the canteen.

'The boys are off to the Shit and Twigs,' Marion said. 'We might get a chance to have a peaceful lunch for once.'

The Crow's Nest pub at the end of the road, affectionately known as the Shit and Twigs, was the students' regular haunt and the two girls often joined the boys there in the evenings. But at lunchtime they both preferred to remain sober, so they could work hard in the afternoon.

The rain had let up by the time they pushed out of the big double doors into the quad, and the sun was making an appearance, pushing through the granite grey clouds overhead.

The canteen was busy and they queued in a long line, inspecting the various options, finally choosing cock-a-leekie soup and bread. They found a table in the corner of the canteen.

'What are your plans?' Imogen asked Marion as they spooned soup into their mouths.

'What do you mean?'

'Next year – when we're nineteen... when we have to join up.'

'Oh that. Apart from the unlikely prospect of Hitler suing for peace, you mean?' Marion laughed, put her spoon down, and lit a cigarette. 'I really don't know,' she said. 'The Land Army, maybe? I rather fancy those corduroy breeches they wear.'

'Working the land?' Imogen was horrified. 'That would be awful.'

'Not really,' said Marion. 'My father's a farmer. Well, a landowner really, but I'm familiar with tractors and engines and all that. Or the ATS – drive a big truck around the place. What about you?'

'The Wrens, I think,' said Imogen. 'The hats are nice.' She giggled. 'Seriously – I'd quite like to push those little ships around. I've a cousin in the Wrens who's a plotter, and she was telling me all about it. Or a radio operator – that might be fun. I can't bear to think about it really. I'm loving it here so much, the thought of having to give it up for a while is rather painful.'

'Now stop this,' said Giles, interrupting, and putting his lunch tray noisily down on the table. 'Budge up Marion, there's a good girl.' He sat down on the bench next to Marion, smelling strongly of beer, belching loudly and began to shovel shepherd's pie into his mouth. They were soon joined by a gaggle of young men, anxious to chat and show off.

Back in the drawing studio, the afternoon sun poured through the double-height windows, filling the space with light. Imogen had begun work on a preliminary design for a public building inspired by classic 1930s architecture. It was a project that she would have to complete over the next few months, involving detailed working drawings, culminating in a hand-painted finished image of the final scheme. Concentrating hard, she looked up, briefly, across the sea of student heads and saw a flash of dark grey uniform. Ex-students often called into the studio so this was not unusual, but the owner of this uniform was Freddie McMasters. She hadn't seen him since the night of the bombing in Jesmond – before he went to Canada. Over the past year she'd done her best to forget him, but now, seeing him again, she felt her heart beginning to race.

He was standing on the other side of the room, laughing with their tutor. Frustratingly, Imogen was unable to make out what they were saying. Desperate for Freddie to notice her, and too shy to simply walk across the crowded studio and speak to him, she stood up suddenly, knocking her pot of pencils off her desk with a loud clatter.

Everyone, including Freddie, looked around, startled by the noise. She blushed as she bent down to pick up the pens, and then, deeply embarrassed at her own clumsiness, waved at him. He said something to the tutor, who patted him on the back.

'See you later,' Freddie called back to his tutor, as he walked towards her, across the studio.

'Hello there,' he said, kissing Imogen fleetingly on the check. 'I had no idea you'd already started here. Somehow in my mind, you're still at school.'

'Oh no, I left last year. This is my second term here.'

'I remember now,' he said, 'you wanted to do engineering, didn't you?'

'Yes, but it turned out universities don't accept ladies who want to study engineering. You were the one who suggested I did architecture instead, don't you remember? Anyway – here I am.'

He walked around her drawing board to study her work.

'Not bad,' he said, his chin resting in his hand.

She blushed again. 'I've only just started it… it'll get better.' She felt tongue-tied, uncertain what to say. 'Well…' she began.

'Yes…'

'So you're home? Are you coming back to university?'

'No, no… sadly that will have to wait till Mr Hitler has given up. No. I'm just back for a couple of days. I've finished my training – I got back from Canada yesterday actually. Just wanted to see my folks, and thought while I was in Newcastle I'd pop in – see my old tutor; make sure he doesn't forget about me.' Freddie nodded towards their drawing teacher standing on the other side of the room. 'I'm off to join my new squadron in the morning.'

'Oh,' was all she could say. 'That's good.'

'Well,' he said, biting his lip, 'maybe see you later – in the pub?'

'Yes,' she said, too quickly. 'I'll be there.'

He smiled briefly, a distant smile, she thought, and walked back across the studio. He said something else to their tutor, accompanied by an easy laugh, a manly slap on the back, and was gone, the doors of the studio swinging into the room, the sound of his footsteps echoing as he strode off down the corridor.

'Who was that?' whispered Marion conspiratorially, as Imogen attempted to busy herself, putting her pens neatly back in the pot.

'Just an old friend,' she said.

'Pretty dishy,' said Marion. 'Always did rather fancy a flyer…'

Imogen glared at her.

'Ooh… sorry,' said Marion. 'Is he yours?'

'No, not really. I thought he might have been once. But somehow we just never… never seem to connect at the right time.'

The Crow's Nest was busy with locals and students all fighting to get to the bar. Imogen and Marion squeezed in through the doors and Imogen could see Freddie in the centre of a group of young men, hanging on his every word. All first year students, many of whom would be joining up themselves soon, they were eager to talk to an older student, already a glamorous flyer in the RAF. He was a hero to them and the pub was filled with the sound of laughter as they listened to his tales. It felt exclusive somehow – these men sharing stories together. She wanted desperately to be part of it, wanted him to notice her… to call her over and say to everyone, 'Here's Imogen – I must get her a drink.' And they'd all stand back and watch as he put his arm around her, and made her feel special. Truthfully, she wanted everyone else to leave, to just be alone with him, to be able to tell him what she had felt all these years.

Marion fought her way through to the bar.

'Two gin and tonics please,' she shouted to the barmaid, who ignored her, choosing instead to serve a handsome young man standing next to her.

Giles came to the girls' rescue. 'Two g & t's for the lovely ladies when you've got a moment, Barbara,' he shouted to the barmaid, who nodded in acknowledgement.

'It's so annoying,' said Marion. 'Why won't she just accept my order? It's humiliating having to depend on you, of all people, Giles.'

'Thanks a lot,' said Giles. 'Next time, I'll leave you to die of thirst.'

Clutching their drinks, Marion suggested they find a table, but Imogen was desperate to speak to Freddie.

'You go and sit down with Giles; I'll be over in a moment,' she whispered to her friend.

She fought her way through the throng, ducking under the arm of a tall student who was standing between her and the object of her desire. She materialised in the centre of the group, as if by magic.

'Hello again,' said Freddie, cheerfully.

'Hello,' she said. 'I hope you don't mind… I just thought we ought to have a chat.'

The young men looked at one another and gradually slipped away, forming other rings of laughter and banter, leaving Freddie and Imogen alone.

'Oh, I'm sorry,' said Imogen. 'I didn't mean to break things up.' She felt embarrassed, rather than guilty.

'It's OK,' he said, kindly. 'Let's go and sit over there. I haven't got that long.'

He found a small table in the corner, near the door.

'So,' he began, 'how have you been keeping?'

It was the sort of question people ask a distant cousin, or a maiden aunt, and Imogen's heart sank.

'Fine…'

'Your parents… are they well?'

'Yes… yours?'

'Oh yes.'

'And… Philip and Jonno?'

'Yes, both OK – thanks. Phil's ship took a bit of a battering but he got out before it sank.'

'How awful. I hadn't heard. Is he really all right?'

'Yes. You know Phil – nothing gets him down. And what about you? You know, I'd forgotten you were going to study here. I was rather surprised to see you earlier in the drawing studio.'

'Were you?' she asked. 'We'd talked about it that night when you took me out – last Easter. The night the bomb fell.'

'Oh yes,' he said, 'that awful night; that poor family. How could I forget? What must you think of me?'

'Well it was a long time ago; and such a lot has happened, particularly to you. How was Canada?' She had been dreading asking him, fearful he might reveal a secret marriage to one of the girls he'd met. Was that why he was being so distant with her?

'Oh great fun. I had a wonderful time. It's a marvellous country and fantastic to be able to learn to fly out there – there's so much room.'

'You sent me a letter,' she began.

'You didn't reply,' he said.

'I… I thought you sounded as if you didn't need me to write back,' she stumbled.

'What made you think that?' he asked, studying her face. 'I wouldn't have written if I hadn't wanted you to write back. I thought you weren't interested.'

'You said you'd met some wonderful girls. "*The girls are really pretty,*" you wrote, "*so natural. We had a wild time.*" I think you'd been to a dance with them.'

'You remember what I wrote?' He seemed surprised. 'I can't remember what I did yesterday, let alone what someone put in a letter a year or so back.'

'I do remember – every word, as it happens.' She blushed. 'How pathetic is that?'

'Ginny.' He covered her hand with his. It was cool and firm.

'Yes?' She looked, hopefully, into his grey eyes, willing him to kiss her.

'Look, come outside, we can't talk in here.'

'I thought you wanted to see your friends.'

'I do… I will. But I need to say something to you first.'

He guided her out of the pub. It had begun to rain again, and they stood in the doorway of the gentlemen's outfitters shop next door, listening to the patter of raindrops.

'Look Ginny… I know we said a few things to each other back then. Before Canada.'

'Yes,' she said, gazing up into his eyes. She could smell the rain on his hair, the slightly musty scent of his uniform.

'I like you Ginny, I really do,' he said.

'But,' she said, her hopes sinking, 'there's someone else isn't there?'

'No!' he said, placing his hands squarely on her shoulders. 'No, that's not it at all. The thing is – I'm off to… well I can't say where. I'm part of a special squadron. But it's dangerous stuff, Ginny. And I've had to come to terms with something since I began my training. I might not make it. What we do is dangerous. Flying at night, flying low over enemy territory, taking flak… I've already lost mates. And once I really get started, I'll lose a lot more. I might die myself.'

She shivered. 'Please don't say that.'

'I've come to terms with it – it's the best way to think. I say to myself: "The worst that can happen is that you'll die, so just get on with your job, do your best, be brave, don't hold back." He spoke as if giving instructions to himself.

'That's awful,' she said, with tears in her eyes.

'Not really, it's just sensible. And I've made a decision. I won't break someone else's heart. I've seen too many blokes with girls back here – girlfriends and wives – and how will they feel if their man is blown to smithereens? I won't do that to someone. So I've decided not to get involved with anyone till after the war – if there is an after.'

'I don't understand,' she said, 'do you mean you would get involved with me… if you could?' She was clinging to some longed-for future where she and Freddie could be together.

'Don't read too much into it, Ginny – please. I'm not saying that. I'm just saying, don't depend on me. I might not come back. Get on with your own life. Study hard, be a wonderful architect. But don't wait for me.'

He kissed her briefly on the cheek and was gone, pushing through the swing doors of the pub, the noise and laughter from inside seeping out into the rain-sodden darkness, leaving her alone and crying in the doorway.

Chapter Seventeen

Färsehof Farm
February 1943

Magda came downstairs early one morning to find her father once again listening to the radio. Unusually, it was a German voice she heard, and not the foreign tones of a BBC announcer.

We are interrupting your programme for a special bulletin, the announcer said solemnly. A slow drum roll was followed by the second slow movement of Beethoven's Fifth Symphony. Finally the announcer spoke again:

> *The battle for Stalingrad is over. True, with their last breath, to their oath to the flag, the Sixth Army, under the inspirational leadership of General Field Marshal von Paulus, has been defeated.... They died so that Germany may live.*

'So,' Pieter said, turning off the radio. 'It looks like it's the beginning of the end.'

'Really?' said Magda. 'How do you know?'

'It's the only thing that makes any sense. We've lost on the Eastern front, and the Allies are getting stronger by the day. We've not been so affected here – in the middle of the countryside – but the cities in the north are being bombed mercilessly. I don't think people can take much more.'

He stood up and riddled the fire, removing the box filled with embers and taking them outside to throw on the rose bush near the vegetable garden.

'Maybe Karl can come home now,' Magda said, when her father came back inside, stamping the snow off his boots before leaving them by the door.

'Well, these things take time,' he said, slotting the box back into the range. 'It won't be over tomorrow, there's still a long way to go. But there's a sense that things are changing. I remember the First War and how that ended. So many men on both sides dead, our best soldiers killed, pointlessly. By the end our army was exhausted. We were just a group of boys and old men. We'd lost heart and we knew the Americans had joined the war, and were arriving in their thousands in France by the end. We could never beat them. I have the same feeling now. All those men lost in Russia. How much longer can they carry on pretending this is a war we can win?'

After breakfast Magda sat by the range pulling on her snow boots. Outside, large flakes of snow floated dreamily out of the sky before settling on the hardstanding outside the farmhouse.

'Can you deliver some cheese for me to the shop in the village?' Käthe asked as Magda pulled on her coat, adjusting her fur hat.

Käthe wrapped the large rounds in muslin. 'Put them in the basket of your bike. And try not to get them wet, or dirty will you?'

'Yes Mutti,' Magda said, taking the cheese from her mother. 'I'll be careful.'

'And make sure you deliver them before you go to school – Herr Fischer is waiting for them. He'll give you the money; look after it for me.'

'Yes Mutti, I won't lose it.'

As the shopkeeper weighed each cheese carefully, counting out the notes pedantically for Magda to take home to her mother, she overheard several women muttering about that morning's radio announcement.

'I have a cousin in Munich,' said one woman, quietly, to another. 'The city is filled with refugees from cities in the north – they've had so much bombing up there. There's nowhere for anyone to live any more, it's a disgrace.'

'I know,' said another, conspiratorially. 'My friend in Heidelberg said the same thing. There are people arriving at the railway station every day. Where they are supposed to put them, I don't know?'

The mood in the village was one of quiet fury, and as she cycled away from the shop, Magda decided to go to Munich as soon as possible. She was desperate to speak to Saskia; to find out how the bad news from the Eastern front might impact the work of the White Rose. Might they be able to stop their work now, or would they instead become emboldened, she wondered? As she cycled towards the school gates, her heart sank. Otto was waiting for her.

'There you are,' he said. 'You're late.'

'I know,' said Magda irritably, wheeling her bicycle into the school yard, and placing it in the rack. 'I had to deliver some cheese for my mother.'

She picked up her bag of school books and began to walk into the building, but Otto held her by the arm, pulling her towards him.

'Stop it,' she said, 'what are you doing?'

'I follow you sometimes,' he said.

'What are you talking about?'

'Where do you go each week?'

'We're late, Otto. I've got to get to class.'

'You cycle to Augsburg – every Saturday. What do you do there?'

'How do you know I go to Augsburg?'

'I see you cycling in that direction; where else would you be going?'

'Magda, Otto,' said Herr Schmidt walking towards them. 'Get to your classes.'

Magda avoided Otto for the rest of the day. After school she ran out of the building and cycled home, peering over her shoulder from time to time, checking to see if Otto was following her. She woke the following morning with a sinking feeling in the pit of her stomach. It was Friday, and that evening she would be forced to spend time with him as the Hitler Youth and the League of Girls met in the village hall.

Käthe was chopping turnips for soup, her fair wavy hair falling over her eyes. She pushed it away with the back of her hand.

'Mutti,' said Magda, sitting at the table, and buttering a piece of bread. 'I don't feel well. I don't think I can go to school, or to the meeting tonight.'

'Oh dear,' said Käthe, putting down her knife. She walked over to Magda, standing behind her, her large hand resting on her daughter's forehead. 'You have no temperature.'

'Don't I? I still don't feel well.'

Käthe sat down with her daughter at the table. 'You shouldn't miss school… unless you're really ill.'

'I am – honestly.'

'Magda,' her mother said, gently. 'Is there something worrying you… or someone you don't want to see?'

She gazed at her daughter with her clear blue-eyed stare. Tears came into Magda's eyes.

'No, it's not that – I promise.'

'Well,' said Käthe, 'unless you have an illness, I think you must go to school, and to your meeting tonight.'

Tears fell down Magda's cheeks, and Käthe wiped them away with her thumbs.

'Dearest Magda – you must try not stand out from everyone else. I worry for you otherwise. About what people will say. Just go to school, please. And get it over with.'

Reluctantly, Magda did as she was told. At school, she hid in the cloakroom between lessons, desperate to avoid Otto. But that afternoon, at the village hall, Otto was waiting for her.

'I didn't see you at school,' he said, accusingly. 'Where were you?'

'I was there, but I wasn't feeling very well.'

'We never finished our conversation the other day,' he continued, ignoring her explanation.

'What about?' she asked impatiently.

'Augsburg.'

'What about it?' she said irritably. 'I go there, sometimes... yes – to the cathedral.' She was surprised at her own lie.

'I didn't know you were interested in such things.'

'It's not the religion particularly, but I like to listen to the organist.'

She smiled defiantly, pleased with herself.

'Why?' he asked. 'You don't even play.'

'I may not play myself, but that doesn't stop me appreciating an artist. He's very good. He plays... stirring German music.'

Delighted at her fiction, she ran across to join the girls in her group. They stood in a noisy gaggle, gossiping and giggling.

'Where's Erika?' Magda asked.

'Haven't you heard?' Bette, a tall blonde girl whispered conspiratorially.

'Heard what?' asked Magda.

'She's gone to a special camp... to have a baby with an officer!'

'No!' said Magda, genuinely shocked.

'That SS officer – in Munich,' the girl went on. 'He organised it.' She sniggered.

'That's disgusting,' said Magda. 'She's younger than me.'

'Yes, but she was desperate,' said Bette. 'It's not her first time you know. She's done it with several of them.' Bette nodded towards the boys standing on the other side of the hall. 'Otto and Erika – they were at it for weeks. I wouldn't be surprised if she was already pregnant, and the camp is just a convenient way to cover it up, to make her look patriotic.'

Magda looked across at Otto. He smiled at her – with his tight, mean-lipped smile.

'I didn't know,' she said to Bette. 'Poor Erika.'

Later that evening, as they left the hall, pulling on their warm coats and fur hats, Otto caught up with her.

'I've got to go,' she said, irritation in her voice. 'Mutti is expecting me.'

'Oh stay a little,' he said, slipping his arm beneath her coat where it snaked around her waist.

'No Otto… I can't.'

'I think you can,' he said, pulling her around the side of the building. He pushed her against the wooden panels of the hall. She could feel it cold against her back; her feet were chilly in the snowy ground.

'All that stuff about Augsburg and the organist… it's a lie, isn't it?' He held her face in his hands. She could feel his fingers, icily cold, against her cheek. 'Kiss me,' he said, his icy breath spilling out into the dark night air.

She could hear Bette and the others saying their goodbyes, the cheerful sound of bicycles being wheeled down the road. She heard the youth leader muttering under her breath as she locked the door. Listened as she too, climbed aboard her bike and wobbled heavily down the road towards the village. She and Otto were quite alone in the darkness with just the distant sound of an owl hooting in the woods nearby.

Otto pressed his mouth against hers. She tried to resist, but he was stronger than her and held her head firmly in his hands while he kissed her, forcing his tongue deep inside her mouth.

'There,' he said when he'd finished. 'That wasn't so bad, was it?' His hands slid down her waist. She felt them as they clutched at her backside, pulling her towards him. She felt him hard against her stomach – an unfamiliar sensation that appalled her. She felt sick, but attempted to smile – desperate to placate him and to wipe away the feeling of his wet tongue inside her mouth and on her lips.

'I'm old-fashioned,' she said, moving his hands away from her body and trying to pull her coat protectively around her. 'I ought to go.' She slithered away from his grasp busying herself with putting on her gloves, adjusting her hat, discreetly wiping her mouth with the back of her hand.

'Erika didn't feel that way…' His face, lit only by the moonlight, was flushed with anger.

'No,' she said, moving away from him, 'and look what happened to her.'

She regretted the words as soon as she had uttered them. He looked over at her, his eyes narrowing.

'What do you mean?'

'She's gone to a special camp, I hear… to have a baby.'

His face relaxed, and he smiled. 'Oh that. Well she's just a little tramp.'

'Why do you say that?' She felt strangely indignant on Erika's behalf.

'All the boys know it.' He laughed defensively.

'Well I'm not like that!' said Magda defiantly. 'If you really liked me, you'd appreciate that and respect me.'

'I do like you.' He sounded childlike, suddenly – anxious to please. 'And I respect you. I… love you, Magda.'

It was such a surprising thing for him to say. She had always thought him incapable of any kind of emotion.

'And you?' he asked, nervously, just like any lover.

'We've known each for other a long time,' she said, sensing a subtle shift in their struggle. It was he who was anxious now; she who had the power. She paused… 'Of course I'm fond of you.'

'Really?' He sounded hopeful, pathetically so.

'I'd better go,' she said, seizing the moment. 'But I'll see you next week.'

She reached up and kissed him fleetingly on the cheek, then disappeared round the side of the building where her bike was parked. As she pedalled furiously away, she turned around. He was standing in the middle of road, watching her.

The following morning she left early for Munich. The sky was heavy with snow, and dark grey clouds hung threateningly over the city. Magda's hands were cold as she grabbed the metal handle bars and cycled towards Marienplatz. As she entered the ancient square she was shocked to see slogans painted on the old town hall: '*Hitler: Mass Murderer*' and '*Freedom*'. She remembered Max and the others discussing the possibility of leaving messages on landmark buildings at their last meeting. The group had argued about it – better to stick with the leaflets, some had said, than risk everything by painting signs on buildings. Clearly Max, or one of the others, had decided to do it anyway.

From Marienplatz, Magda cycled north towards the university, up Theatrestrasse past the Feldherrnhalle, guarded day and night by teams of SS soldiers. Everyone who passed – either cycling or walking – was required to salute the Führer. Usually Magda avoided this humiliation by doing a little dogleg and diverting down a tiny side-street just before the memorial, but this morning she was anxious to get to the university as fast as possible. As she cycled past the guards, she noticed the words '*Down With Hitler*' smeared in black paint down the side of the building. A group of women in headscarves and long skirts – Russian slaves, judging by their clothes – were already busy trying to scrub it clean with buckets of water, but they were making little headway. Magda, watched by the soldiers, raised her hand gingerly in salute.

She was breathless by the time she arrived at the end of Saskia's road. The worst of the wreckage from the October bombings had now been cleared away, leaving sizeable gaps where the apartment buildings had once stood. But there was still debris on the road, forcing her to climb off her bike and wheel it through the bricks and shattered masonry. At Saskia's house she rang the bell, but there was no reply. She pushed the door of the big apartment building and found that it was on the latch. Leaning her bicycle against the hall wall, she lurked near the concierge's ever-open door. The woman was stirring something on the stove and did not immediately notice Magda. When she turned round, she looked startled.

'What do you want?' she said, angrily. 'Standing there, spying on me.'

'I'm not spying, really. I'm sorry. I was looking for Saskia. I rang her bell but there's no reply.'

'Haven't you heard?'

'Heard what?'

'They've been arrested… her and that good-for-nothing.' She gestured with her thumb, pointing upstairs.

'Max, you mean?'

'Yes… that man she lived with in sin. They should be ashamed – both of them. They got what they deserved.'

'Where are they?'

'I don't know, do I? They were taken away. It's a disgrace. Gestapo all over the house… and the rent not paid.'

Magda backed away tearfully, bumping her bike down the steps. She stood in the street wondering what to do and where to go. Logic told her to go straight home, but she was frightened for her friends. She leapt onto her bike and headed for their basement meeting-place. She approached it cautiously, and stood on the opposite side of the road checking for any signs of the Gestapo. Confident it was safe, she crossed the street, her heart thumping, and peered through the grubby windows. It was dark and empty – the chairs were standing on the tables and the lights behind the bar were switched off. She noticed a little handwritten sign on the door: *Closed until further notice.* She climbed back onto her bike, and cycled towards the university, praying she would find someone – anyone – that she knew, but the area near the fountain, where Saskia and her friends often met, was deserted. She waited for a while, but eventually, as snow began to fall, wheeled her bike miserably back on to the road, and cycled back to the station, where she caught the first train to Augsburg.

She arrived at the farm just after lunchtime. Snow was falling thickly as she wheeled her bicycle up the lane towards the house. The herd were in their winter quarters and she could hear them in the barn, lowing gently. The familiar sounds of the farm calmed her a little, and she felt relieved to be safely back home.

As the farmhouse came into view she saw an unfamiliar black car parked outside, with a swastika flag on its wing. She thought about getting on her bike there and then and cycling away. But she couldn't leave her parents to deal with the situation. She leaned her bike against the farmhouse, and stood outside listening. She could hear raised voices coming from inside. Her heart racing, she opened the door.

Two Gestapo officers – their dark uniforms in stark contrast to the cosy red and white gingham of the kitchen – were sitting opposite her parents. Otto was leaning against the kitchen range, as if casually warming his back.

'Magda!' Käthe leapt to her feet, but one of the officers – a tall thin man with black hair slicked back on his scalp, got up and pushed her back down on her chair.

Magda took in the scene, her heart thumping in her chest.

'Hello,' she said, trying to sound innocent. 'What's going on?'

Her father took advantage of the fact that the officers and Otto were all now looking at her, leaving him temporarily out of their eyeline. He looked pointedly at Magda, and drew an imaginary knife across his neck. '*Whatever you've been up to,*' he was trying to say, '*be careful.*'

'You are Magda Maier?' The tall officer was studying her.

'I am,' she replied, confidently.

'We have reports that you have been consorting with traitors.'

Käthe gasped and rushed to her daughter's side, knocking her chair over onto the floor.

'No!' she said, grasping Magda to her. 'She's just a child, barely sixteen. Don't be ridiculous.'

'If she has done nothing wrong, she need have nothing to worry about,' the second officer said, calmly. He was older than the first, with a plump, ruddy face. He looked like a shop-keeper, Magda thought, or a country doctor. But his voice was cold.

'Sit down,' he said to Käthe, who obeyed meekly.

'Why are *you* here?' Magda asked Otto.

'He has spoken up for you,' the plump-faced officer said. 'He seems to believe that the reports we've had are mistaken.'

Magda smiled at Otto. But the thought that he might be seeking to protect her, concerned her. He would expect some kind of recompense, of that she was sure. Her mouth was dry and she was desperate for something to drink.

'So what do you have to say?' the first officer demanded.

'I don't know what you're talking about,' she said, wandering slowly to the sink. She turned on the tap, which rattled and wheezed, and bent down, cupping the water in her hand before drinking half a mouthful and wiping her mouth.

Keep calm, she said to herself, feeling her heart slowing.

'You have been meeting with known traitors in Munich. Do you deny it?'

Her mind was whirring. 'I have visited Munich occasionally, yes,' she said, glancing over at Otto. 'I want to go to university there after the war.'

The tall officer smirked. 'To university?' he said, witheringly. 'And who do you meet there?'

'No one really. Well… other students sometimes. But they are all older than me, so we're not friends really, but they give me advice and we talk about the courses they are studying.' She shrugged, as if to say, *so what?*

'Do you discuss politics?'

'Politics? Sometimes.' *Be careful,* she said to herself. *Tread very carefully…*

'And what exactly do you discuss?'

'What it will be like after the war. We're all young – we want it to be over – to have some fun.'

'Sit down, please.' The plump-faced officer stood up now. He pulled out a kitchen chair for Magda.

She sat down, trying to breathe. The officer let his hand drag across her back as he settled her in her chair. Her parents, facing her, were white-faced, their mouths set in thin lines of anxiety. Otto regarded her with a look of relaxed detachment.

'You are a member of the League of German Girls?' the plump-faced officer asked at last. Magda nodded.

'We are told that you are rather rebellious.' He consulted a note-book. 'At least, that's what your team leader Fräulein Muller says.'

Magda tried to look relaxed, and forced her mouth into a smile. 'I'm…. I'm a bit of free spirit, I suppose. The Fräulein doesn't like that. My cakes aren't very good.'

'Do you support the National Socialist cause?' the tall officer asked.

'Of course!' she said with as much enthusiasm as she could muster.

He looked over at Otto, who nodded discreetly.

'It's not true about her cakes,' Käthe said, enthusiastically. 'She's being modest… she always takes a cake or biscuits to meetings and village celebrations. She's such a good girl. *Kirche, Küche, Kinder*… that's her. She only went to Munich for the first time with her troop. They went to a rally. She'd never been before. She's a country girl at heart.'

The plump-faced officer regarded Käthe with disdain and sat down at the table.

'We have reports,' he said, turning back to Magda, 'that you have befriended someone called Saskia Schafer. Is that correct?'

There was clearly no point in denying it, Magda realised. 'Saskia… I've met her, yes. I didn't know that was her surname. I've only met her once or twice. She is studying philosophy, and I am interested in that subject. We just met one afternoon at the university, by the fountain there. It's very beautiful – do you know it?'

'There is a café,' the officer continued, checking his notebook, 'the Café Leopold in Giselastrasse. Do you know it?'

Think… think… 'No,' she said, firmly.

'Are you sure?' The officer with the plump face regarded her cooly. His eyes, she realised, were almost black. Her heart was beating loudly, so loudly she imagined they could all hear it. Had she said the wrong thing? She was banking on the fact that she had only been to the café twice, and hopefully no one in the group would reveal it.

'Yes I'm sure. I've never heard of it.'

'You stayed with Saskia one night,' the taller officer said, glancing down at his own notes. 'We have a report from the concierge of her building. She keeps good records, that old woman.'

'Yes. That's right. The enemy bombed the city one evening. I was intending to come home that night – do you remember, Mutti?' Her mother nodded, supportively.

'I'd never stayed away before, but the bombers came, and we had to go down to the cellar. It was awful. The buildings all around us were hit; there were people killed – little children looking for their mothers in the street.' She looked around the group, her face a picture of anxiety and sadness, hoping desperately to garner sympathy.

'Oh my poor *Liebling*,' Käthe said, as if on cue.

'Do you know what Saskia is really doing in Munich?' the tall officer asked.

'I don't understand… she's a student.'

'Her family are well known for their anti-Nazi views. Did you know that?'

'No!' said Magda, with conviction.

'Did you know that Saskia Schafer is involved with an organisation called the White Rose?'

Magda's mouth felt dry again. 'No… No I didn't. I've never heard of it… what is the White Rose?' Her mind was racing… did she still have copies of the leaflets in her room? Maybe a few, although she remembered posting some when she was last in Munich. Her hands felt sweaty and she involuntarily rubbed them against her skirt.

'They are seeking to overthrow the government,' the tall officer went on. 'They are a revolutionary group.'

She feigned shock. 'No! I cannot believe it. Not Saskia, surely. I don't know her very well, but she seemed so nice and sweet.' She glanced at her mother, whose eyes were filled with tears.

'You expect me to believe,' said the plump-faced officer, standing up and pacing the kitchen, 'that you met this girl and her revolutionary friends and they never discussed their political views at all?'

'Yes… I mean no… they never discussed their views with me, no. They thought I was a baby, really. They used to laugh at me.'

The officer came to a halt opposite Magda. He stared at her, his mouth twitching slightly, his black eyes, unblinking, boring into her soul. He turned and motioned to his colleague, who stood up, adjusted his jacket and put on his gloves.

'Well… we will leave now,' plump-face said. 'But we will be watching you, Miss Maier. Otto here has told us that you are an enthusiastic member of the League of German Girls. He has spoken up for you. Do not give us cause to come back here. This is a very serious matter, do you understand? Treason is punishable by death.'

'Yes… yes of course.'

'And stay away from Munich.'

When the officers and Otto had gone Magda sat at the kitchen table, shaking. Her mother made a cup of hot chocolate and put it in front of her.

'You must tell us, Magda, what you have done and who you know. We will understand,' Käthe said. 'But you must tell us everything.'

'I can't,' Magda said. 'I don't know that much really, anyway. And what I do know, I want to keep from you. Better that you know nothing…'

'Promise me that you'll keep away from them,' her mother implored her.

'Yes,' Magda said, knowing it was a lie.

The following Saturday, she rose early before her parents were awake and cycled once again to Augsburg where she took the train to Munich. It had snowed in the city overnight and the white walls of the university building merged into the hard-packed snow on the ground below. Even the fountain had frozen into a bulbous icy blue sculpture. She waited all morning, stamping her feet to keep warm, blowing into her hands. She was just wondering if she should give up and go home, when a girl named Monika, who had only attended the meetings occasionally, pushed her bike over the snow.

'Monika!' called Magda.

The girl wheeled around, her face stricken with terror.

'It's all right,' said Magda. 'It's only me – Magda.'

'You shouldn't be here,' said Monika. 'It's not safe. Haven't you heard what happened? We're all being watched.'

Magda felt a momentary sense of panic. 'I'm sorry. I see now that it was stupid of me to come, but I had to know what's happened to Saskia and the others.'

Monika, her eyes glistening with tears, looked around to check if anyone was watching them, and reassured they were alone, led Magda down a narrow alley next to the university building.

'They were executed. Didn't you know? Saskia, Max, Willie… all of the leaders. Tried and executed by guillotine the same day. No chance of appeal.'

Magda began to sob. 'No… no I can't believe it.'

'The authorities said they were trouble-makers who had defied "the spirit of the German people". Everyone involved has been rounded up. I don't know why I've not been arrested yet, myself. I'm terrified in case someone talks and my name comes out. I'm going to leave Munich… I'm going back home to Hamburg. I'd rather risk the bombs in the North, than the Gestapo here.'

'I'm sure nobody would give you away,' said Magda. 'They are all so brave and loyal…'

'Maybe,' said Monika, fighting back tears. 'But who knows what you'd do or say under torture. I don't want to die, Magda. I know Max said we had to be prepared for anything, but now… now it's come, I can't face it. I'm not as brave as they were.' She wept, falling into Magda's arms.

'Look,' Monika said eventually, wiping her eyes. 'I'm leaving today; you should too. Don't come back here, Magda. Get away from here… back to the countryside while you still can.'

She kissed Magda fleetingly on the cheek before pushing her bike out of the alley. Magda followed a few moments behind.

The hard-packed snow made wheeling her bike difficult, but she persevered, dragging it tearfully across the white lawns and out onto the road. She thought of her friends, Saskia and Max, and how beautiful they had been; how brave to the very end. As she cycled fast down Ludwigstrasse, tears pouring down her face, she found herself once again next to the Feldherrnhalle. The remnants of the slogan remained. The poor Russian slaves had been unable to wash it away. *Down With Hitler,* it said. 'Down with Hitler' Magda muttered under her breath, as she cycled towards the station. 'Down with bloody Hitler.'

Chapter Eighteen

Gosforth
July 1943

The sun was just coming up, casting long crisp shadows over the neat gardens of Gosforth, as Imogen walked back home after her night shift. The sky was a cloudless blue and the intensity of the dawn chorus almost came as a shock, after a night on duty in the plot room with its hushed tones and orchestrated order and politeness. As her fellow Wrens and officers calmly moved shipping around the map, out in the North Sea sailors and merchant seamen battled the elements, risking their lives against German U-boats and sniping aircraft.

Imogen had managed to complete her first year at university, but at the age of nineteen it became compulsory to join one of the forces. She had done her initial six weeks' Wren training and was now working as a plotter at Askham House – a mere fifteen minutes' walk from her home. Working eight-hour shifts, the plotters received signals through their headphones giving them the location of every merchant and naval ship in the North Sea. They transferred that information onto a huge horizontal grid map called a Cassini grid, using numbered cubes to mark the position of each ship or submarine. It was interesting work – not as fulfilling as architecture of course – but Imogen was happy to 'do her bit' and grateful that she had, at least, been appointed to a section where she felt she had a chance to use her talents.

Joy had also decided to join the Wrens and on the day of their preliminary interviews, they sat nervously together in the waiting room. Joy, who had been working for the Leader of Newcastle City Council as a secretary, was regaling Imogen and the other candidates with the story of how she broke the news that she was leaving.

'He was absolutely livid,' she told Imogen. 'Went quite purple in the face. "It's a reserved occupation",' he blustered. "You can't leave me…"'

'"Well sir", I said. "It's not that I want to leave, but I do think it's awfully important that we all do our bit, don't you?" He shut up after that.'

'Well I'm so glad you're here,' said Imogen. 'It would all have been rather intimidating without you.'

'You're going to miss university though, aren't you?'

'Dreadfully,' said Imogen. 'I'd just begun to feel I was getting somewhere. But, well – like you – I must do something for the war.'

'Have you heard from Freddie since that day – when he popped into the studio?' asked Joy.

'No,' said Imogen quietly. 'He made it quite clear when we last met that he wouldn't be in touch. So joining up is part of a new start. The chance to have new experiences. And… well, if we're meant to be together, maybe we will – when it's all over.'

'Well I can't wait,' said Joy, cheerfully. 'All the nice girls like a sailor!' She laughed gaily.

'Joy, really, it's not about men!' said Imogen, glancing nervously around at the other candidates in the waiting room.

'I don't see why not, Ginny. We're bound to meet some gorgeous officers and be swept off our feet. Think of that.'

'Oh Joy, you really are ridiculous. We'll have our jobs to do. We'll probably never even meet an officer.'

'Well it's all right for you, Ginny. You've always had your fair share of gorgeous men, but I've not had your luck. And I'm rather keen to meet a lovely man in uniform.'

*

As Imogen sat opposite the interviewing officer, she fiddled nervously with the cuff of her sleeve.

'Languages?' the officer asked.

'I beg your pardon?' said Imogen.

'Languages – do you speak any?'

'Yes, sorry… French and German – just higher certificate, but I'm not bad.'

'Shorthand and typing?'

'Yes, a little,' Imogen said, somewhat reluctantly, 'but I've never used it.'

'But you've done a course?'

'Yes. My mother insisted I did one when I left school, before I started university. But I'm not very good.'

The senior Wren smiled a little, and Imogen inwardly cursed her mother, hoping desperately that she would not be sent to the typing pool.

'And what are you studying at university?'

'Architecture.'

The Wren looked up at Imogen, briefly, before returning to her notes.

'Right, that's all. Wait outside for your medical – and send the next person in please?'

Accepted for training, Imogen was delighted to discover she had been assigned to the plotting room.

'I'm so relieved,' she told Joy. 'You know how I hate typing. I'd have loathed that. It was plotting or signals for me, and I'm quite happy with plotting.'

'Well I'm very pleased too,' said Joy. 'I'm a jolly good typist and fully intend to become the best "writer" they've ever had.'

*

Imogen, back from her night shift, let herself into the hall, and went through to the kitchen where Edith was already up, riddling the stove.

'Morning Miss… you just back?'

'Yes, Edith. You're up early.' She sank down onto a kitchen chair and removed her shoes. 'Thank goodness, another shift over and done with. I'm on evenings tonight. So I'll be leaving again around four.'

'You poor thing,' said Edith. 'You must be exhausted. Why don't you go upstairs and get into bed, and I'll bring you some cocoa.'

'Oh Edith – you are an angel,' said Imogen.

She left her shoes in the hall, hanging her coat over the bottom of the banisters, and walked upstairs in her stockinged feet. She removed her uniform, laid it on a chair, and climbed into bed. Either Edith or her mother had left a stone hot water bottle in the bed for her, and although the heat had begun to dissipate, her bed was nevertheless warm and cosy. She was vaguely aware of someone putting a cup down on her bedside table, as she drifted off to sleep.

Standing in the hall later that afternoon, Imogen called out to her mother. 'I'm off now Ma… back just after midnight. Tell Daddy not to put the chain on, won't you?'

'All right, Ginny. Oh… and darling,' her mother called out from the drawing room, 'don't forget we've got a few people for supper tomorrow – you are off duty aren't you?'

'I'm not sure. I think I'm on days tomorrow so I should be free in the evening.'

'I do hope so,' said her mother, 'I think Freddie is coming.'

Imogen was grateful it was a busy evening in the plotting room. Convoys of ships were being moved up through the North Sea towards Rothsay and Scapa Flow and she hardly had time to have a cup of tea, let alone think about Freddie. The thought of him treating her with polite disdain in front of her parents was unbearable.

The following evening, she arrived back from work just after eight o'clock to find the guests had already arrived. With no time to change, and feeling sick with nerves, she checked her reflection in the mirror above the hall table, fished her hairbrush out of her gas mask case, brushed her hair and came into the drawing room with as much aplomb as possible.

Marjorie McMasters and her husband Jock were there, but there was no sign of Freddie – or Philip, or Jonno for that matter. Secretly, Imogen was relieved.

'Good evening all,' she said.

'Good evening Imogen,' said Marjorie. 'You do look smart in your uniform.'

'Oh,' said Imogen, 'thank you. It could be a lot worse, but it's a bit scratchy. I read somewhere that Diana Churchill's uniform was specially made for her out of doeskin, lucky thing. Still, I can't complain. Mummy had mine altered at her dressmakers, so it does at least fit properly.'

'Dubonnet, darling?' asked Joe, standing beside the drinks tray.

'Yes Daddy, thanks. How are the boys?' Imogen asked Marjorie.

'Oh all alive, thank goodness,' said Moira. Jock raised his eyes heavenward.

'Well that's a blessing,' said Rose. 'It must be such a worry. I'm so lucky that Imogen is still here with us.'

'Although how long that will last, I don't know,' said Imogen, provocatively.

'Why?' asked Rose. 'Are they moving you?'

'Nothing's been said,' said Imogen. 'But people do talk about being posted around the country. Anyway, don't worry – looks like I'll be plotting shipping in the North Sea for the foreseeable!'

'I gather you saw Freddie,' said Marjorie, pointedly.

Imogen blushed. 'Oh yes – when he was home for a few days before his posting.'

'Yes, he mentioned you'd met. He said you were doing very well – he thought your design was splendid.'

'Did he?' said Imogen, smiling. 'That was sweet of him. We didn't see each other for long. And he couldn't tell me much about his posting, but it all sounded jolly exciting.'

'It's all a bit hush-hush,' said Marjorie. 'But I know he…' she paused, choosing her words carefully. 'He made of point of saying that if I saw you, to tell you how lovely it had been to see you – and that he was sorry. I'm not sure what for…' She stared pointedly, at Imogen, willing her to explain.

Imogen swallowed hard. She could feel tears hovering. Rose sat, her drink held aloft, waiting expectantly.

'It was nothing, really,' said Imogen. 'Just that he had to rush off, that's all,' she looked around the room. 'I'll just go and check on Edith, shall I?'

Later that night, when they'd gone, as she lay in bed, the hot water bottle warming her icy feet, she thought about Freddie and what he had been trying to say. He'd told her that she must forget him. Was he now trying to tell her that he hadn't really meant it? It was unfair of him, she thought, to be so confusing. She had tried so hard to do as he'd asked. She hadn't forgotten him, exactly, but she was able to spend whole days without thinking about him, and the longer it went on, the more determined she was to try even harder. She rolled over and made a silent resolution… to expunge him, completely, and live for the day. Because, as Freddie had said, who knew what the future might bring? No one knew what to expect the following week, or the following day, for that matter. Life itself was uncertain and all anyone could do was get on with it.

Chapter Nineteen

Färsehof Farm
July 1943

Magda's grief at the loss of her friends did not diminish with time. Instead, as spring turned to summer, and the sun ripened the wheat and barley growing in the fields, her sense of injustice at what had happened to them – at the terrible loss of their lives – became almost unbearable.

Alone in her room, she took out Karl's letter. Written all those years before, explaining the evils of National Socialism and where that could lead, it now seemed so prescient. The thought that the White Rose Movement had been so swiftly snuffed out, that her friends' lives had been so harshly exterminated, dominated her every waking moment. She felt guilt, of course, at having survived. But the fact she had denied knowing them to the Gestapo – like Judas denying Christ – seemed the worst sin of all. She wavered back and forth, caught between guilt and relief. What would have been the point of admitting everything – just to be executed like the others? Better, surely, to remain alive and do her best to support the Movement and – with luck – live to see the overthrow of the National Socialist government.

Her parents, of course, knew nothing of this. On the surface, she appeared to immerse herself in village life. She rose early and helped her father with the milking; she cycled to school and worked hard at her lessons. She was determined to do well in her Abitur – the qualifying test for university admission. In the

evenings she helped her mother in the kitchen. She was relieved
when school broke up for the summer, and she could plunge herself
into farm work. It was harvest time and the day began at dawn
and finished when the sun fell behind the horizon. She helped
scythe the wheat, rolling the crop into stooks, before bringing it
into the barn to thresh. Dutifully, she milked the cows and tidied
the barns, clearing space for the winter feed. The work was hard,
but somehow liberating. When she was physically exhausted she
could almost forget about politics, her friends and even the war.
It all seemed a long way away. The only involvement she had with
other young people was at the weekly Hitler Youth meetings –
something she could not avoid.

After her interrogation by the Gestapo, Otto had made it quite
clear that he expected something in return for his loyalty.

'You are very fortunate,' he had said that day to Magda, after
the officers had left.

'I don't know what you mean?'

'I hope you weren't lying to them.'

'No,' she had said, firmly. 'But thank you… for speaking up
for me. I'm grateful, obviously.'

'I hope you are,' he had said, walking towards the door. 'Maybe
we can go to the next meeting together.'

'Yes,' she said, feebly. 'Yes of course.'

Now, he was always waiting for her when she arrived and
frequently wanted to walk her home. Sometimes she would allow
it, and endure his kisses and fumbling with her shirt buttons at
the farm gate.

'I have to go,' she would say, unwrapping herself from his
arms, 'I've got to be up at dawn… I must go in now. I must help
my father.'

She knew he was frustrated by her reluctance, but it was hard
for him to argue with her, when she was so obviously doing her
duty by her family. But as she said goodbye, she was aware of the

longing in his eyes, and it frightened her. How long she could keep him at bay she didn't know.

She came downstairs one evening wearing a pale blue dress and the brooch Otto had given her all those months before.

'You look very pretty,' said Käthe who was gutting fish at the table. 'Where are you going?'

'A dance in the village with Otto.'

'With Otto… but I thought you didn't like him?'

'I don't. But I need to keep him… on my side.'

'What does he know about you, Magda? Ever since those officers came here… you've behaved strangely. What did you really get up to in Munich?'

'Nothing Mutti. I just met some people. They were… different.'

'What do you mean – different?'

'They didn't… agree with everything.'

'You mean they were revolutionaries.' Her mother put down her knife, and wiped her hands on her apron. 'Did you know they had these dangerous views? I can't believe you met with these people and knew what they were doing! Are you mad?'

'Karl is working against the government,' Magda said, defiantly.

'Yes, and risking his life in the process, I imagine. You don't have to copy him, you know.'

'I couldn't if I wanted to, could I? He's in England, whereas I'm stuck here.'

Her mother looked hurt. 'Is that what you think? That you are stuck here with us? Well, I think you are lucky. Lucky that you escaped from that group just in time. And I'm sorry if you're bored here with your father and me. We are just trying to keep you safe.'

Magda ran over to her mother and hugged her. 'Mutti… I'm so sorry. I didn't mean to be unkind. Of course I'm happy to be with you and Papa – lucky to live on the farm. I just feel guilty about my friends, about Karl, about everything.'

She squeezed her mother tightly.

'Ouch,' said her mother, pulling away. 'Something stuck in my chest.'

'Oh, it's this brooch. Otto gave it to me – he insisted I wear it tonight.'

Her mother frowned slightly.

'What is it?' Magda said, 'What's the matter, Mutti?'

'Oh… nothing. It must be a coincidence.' Her mother returned to the kitchen table and picked up the fish, peeling away its backbone.

'What coincidence?'

'That brooch – it looks familiar, that's all.'

'Does it?"

'Yes…but it can't be the same. The one I remember had some matching earrings.'

'I have the earrings but I don't wear them; they pinch.'

The blood drained from her mother's face.

'Mutti – where have you seen the brooch before? You have to tell me.'

Her mother bit her lip. 'Dr Kalman's wife, Ester.'

Magda sat down suddenly at the table, touching the brooch.

'Dr Kalman had the brooch and the earrings made for Ester as an anniversary present – to go with her eyes. A jeweller in Augsburg made them for him, that's why I know… they're the only ones. Why wouldn't she have taken them with her when they left?' She looked down at Magda.

'Oh my God,' said Magda, pulling at the brooch, ripping her dress as she tore it off. 'How could he?' she said, putting it on the table, as if it were a poisonous insect. 'He must have stolen it from them before they left the village.'

'Yes. Oh but Magda don't say anything to him about it. He already has his suspicions about you and you mustn't make him angry.'

'He disgusts me,' Magda said, leaping to her feet. 'He's not a brave soldier. He's a cheap thief, and I hate him!'

She ran upstairs, slamming her bedroom door behind her.

A little later, as she lay on her bed, she heard the clipping sound of Otto's boots as he marched across the yard. She heard his loud voice down in the farmhouse kitchen; his noisy guffawing, as he made some sort of joke to her mother. She heard her mother laughing nervously, before she called upstairs to Magda.

'Otto's here.'

Magda remained, face down, on the bed. She called downstairs, her voice muffled by the quilt.

'I'm sorry. I don't feel well.'

She heard Otto's heavy tread on the stairs; he pushed open her door.

'Magda, what do you mean… you're not well?'

'I feel sick,' she said, turning her red, tear-stained face to look at him. 'I'm sorry. But I can't come.'

'It's my last night.'

She looked at him, confused. 'What do you mean?'

'Haven't you heard? Our brigade – we've been called up. We leave tomorrow…'

He held his hand out to her, opening the fingers, revealing the brooch nestling on his palm. 'You forgot this… put it on.'

'It was pulling my dress,' she said, 'I had it on earlier, but I took it off again.'

'Wear it,' he said firmly. 'Get ready, I'll wait downstairs.'

*

Her fingers shaking, she pinned the brooch to her lapel. In her mind's eye she saw Frau Kalman, her beautiful eyes – the eyes Lotte had inherited – filled with terror as she stood holding her son on the concourse outside Munich station. What had Otto said about them that day? *They were nothing… just scum.* If it was true that he was leaving tomorrow, she must just get through this evening. Just one more evening, she thought, and with luck, she might never have to see him again.

Part Three

Victors and Vanquished

1944 – 1945

Four years ago our nation and empire stood alone against an overwhelming enemy, with our backs to the wall…. Now once more a supreme test has to be faced. This time the challenge is not to fight to survive but to fight to win the final victory for the good cause…
King George VI, radio address, 6th June 1944

Chapter Twenty

Snow fell silently, carpeting the roads, pavement and gardens in deep drifts. The normally busy streets of Belsize Park were silent, as people trudged down the roads heading into town. Imogen climbed out of bed, recoiling as her naked feet touched the lino. Regretting that she had not brought a small rug from home to put on the floor, she pulled on her woollen dressing gown and slippers, grabbed her towel and wash bag, and ran down the freezing hall to the communal bathroom. Finding it locked, she leant against the wall, jiggling, her legs crossed. Inside the bathroom, she could hear Joy gargling.

'Oh do hurry up Joy, for goodness sake,' said Imogen. 'I'm desperate out here…'

She heard the sound of the lock being slid back and the door opened. Steam billowed out into the hall.

'I've just had a bath,' said Joy, wrapped in a small towel. 'But the water's still lovely and hot. Jump in. I'll just finish my teeth and then leave you to it.'

Back in their icy room, they dressed as quickly as possible, in their uniform of black stockings, dark blue skirt with its kick pleats, white shirt, tie and jacket.

'God it's cold,' muttered Imogen, sitting at the cluttered dressing table she shared with Joy. Bowls of face powder, lipsticks, hairbrushes and rollers competed for space. 'The snow's coming thick and fast now,' she said, peering out of the bay window as she powdered her face. 'Do let's ask that woman if we can have a little fire in here. We've got a perfectly good grate… and I'm not sure I can take another night like that.'

'She'll never let us have one,' said Joy, peering into the dressing table mirror over Imogen's shoulder as she combed her hair. 'You know what she's like. "Fires may be lit only in common parts,"' she said, imitating the landlady's sing-song voice.

'Oh well, we're just time for breakfast, and at least the dining room will be warm, thank goodness,' said Imogen.

The two girls had lived in their chilly boarding house in Belsize Park for one week and were still getting used to both the house and its rules, and the geography of the capital city. Situated in the north of London, Belsize Park had at one time been a comfortable middle-class suburb. Since before the war many of the large Victorian houses had been divided into flats, or were now taking in 'paying guests'. Their boarding house fell into this category and was filled with a motley collection of refugees and military personnel. Not exactly a home from home, but there was a sort of communal spirit.

'Morning girls,' said Nigel, a naval attaché who had moved in the previous week. 'Sleep well?'

'Not likely – our room is like ice,' said Imogen, smearing her miniscule portion of butter onto a piece of clammy white bread.

'You can always bunk up with me if you're cold,' Nigel said, smirking.

'Nice try, you letch,' said Joy, pouring tea. 'Eat up Ginny, or we'll be late.'

As the girls ran upstairs to collect their hats and gas masks, their landlady – Mrs Palmer – called after them.

'I hope you won't be late again tonight. It's most inconvenient having to let people in after I've already gone to bed. I like the door to be bolted by ten.'

'We'll try,' Imogen called out. 'But it all depends on our work…
I'm sorry.'

She heard Mrs Palmer muttering 'bloody war,' to herself.

Mrs Palmer was a sour-faced woman in her late fifties, who
employed two young girls to clean the 'common parts' – as she called
the hall and landings – and serve in the dining room. She appeared
permanently disgruntled, as if the war and all its consequences had
been sent specifically to irritate her.

On their first evening, as Imogen and Joy sat, anxiously, in the
unfamiliar dining room, waiting for their minimal supper to be
served, she announced that if there was any more bombing, she
would close up and leave. 'It's really a disgrace,' she said, as she
slammed two bowls of thin tomato soup in front of her new lodgers.
'How we're supposed to carry on I have no idea.'

Imogen and Joy had giggled as she left the high-ceilinged dining
room. 'Blimey,' said Joy, 'she's a bundle of laughs…'

They had been transferred a week earlier from their postings
in Gosforth to the headquarters of a new department, based in St
James's, London.

They received their transfer papers on the same day and rushed
to find one another.

'Ginny,' said Joy. 'I'm moving to London.'

'Me too,' said Imogen. 'Where are you going?'

'Norfolk House.'

'So am I!' said Imogen. 'How extraordinary! What's it about,
do you think?'

'They're putting a team together for a new op… something a
bit secret, that's all my supervisor said. They're taking girls from the
RAF, the ATS and the Wrens – writers, plotters, radio operators,
the whole lot.'

'Why us?' asked Imogen.

'Don't know – but it's exciting isn't it?'

'Yes… very,' said Imogen.

'You said you wanted a new start,' said Joy, 'looks like someone was listening.'

After their initial excitement, their farewell at Newcastle station with their families had been emotional. Standing on the platform, Imogen's father Joe hugged her so tightly she felt she could hardly breathe.

'I've bought you both lunch in the first class dining carriage,' he said, kissing the top of her head. 'Your table's booked for one o'clock, so don't be late… and enjoy it. It might be the last good meal you get for a while.' His voice was strong and compelling, but Imogen felt his tears as he kissed her goodbye.

The lump in Imogen's throat made speaking virtually impossible. 'Thank you, Daddy,' was all she could say.

Her mother, who was always calm in a crisis, hugged her daughter, saying simply, 'I'll be with you in spirit always, darling. Be brave, be strong, and don't be too naughty! Remember – I'm very proud of you.'

Fighting back her own tears, Imogen kissed her mother's soft cheek. 'Oh Mummy, I feel just as scared as when I was sent away to the Lakes. I'll miss you so much.'

'And I'll miss you too,' Rose said. 'But just remember what fun you had in the Lakes. It made you so… self-reliant. And you've been selected for this post because you're good at what you do. *You* should be very proud of yourself. Now off you go, and don't forget to write!'

Hanging out of the carriage window, Imogen watched as her tall, angular father took the arm of her tiny, straight-backed mother and together they walked towards the barrier. Imogen's heart was filled with tenderness. Her parents, who had always been such stalwart supports, always there in a crisis, suddenly seemed so alone and vulnerable. Swallowing back tears, she wondered fleetingly if that might be the last time she ever saw them. But as the train finally pulled away from the station and they crossed the bridge over the Tyne, she pushed all negative thoughts to the back of her mind and settled into her seat.

'It's just like evacuation day, isn't it?' said Joy, excitedly. 'Except without the labels round our necks!'

When they arrived at the shabby Victorian house in Belsize Park later that evening, they were relieved to discover they would be sharing a room. But as they looked around at the tired lino, the cold, empty grate and the thin bedding, their initial excitement turned to anxiety.

'Oh Joy,' said Imogen, dropping her case on the floor. 'It's a bit grim… we'll be all right, won't we?'

'Of course we will, darling,' said Joy cheerfully. 'Never mind the décor… we're going to have a fine old time.'

In contrast to their shabby lodgings, their offices were in an elegant Georgian townhouse in St James's. Unusually, they discovered that men and women from all three services – Army, Navy and RAF – would be working together. After a cursory inspection of the layout of the building, they were asked to sign the Official Secrets Act, which unnerved them both.

'Everything done or said in this building is top secret,' said the Chief Petty Officer when they arrived. 'Is that clear? Your work here will be of vital national importance.'

Both girls nodded, nervously, and signed the paperwork.

'You will see the word "BIGOT" stamped on all documents,' continued the officer. 'You will come to understand the significance of that in due time. Now, if you go up the first floor you'll get your assignments.'

Joy was sent, predictably, to the writing room, where women worked long hours typing up notes from the various senior personnel in the building. All top quality secretaries in their own right, their work was vital to the project. Imogen, who had worked as a plotter up in Newcastle, was shown into the private office of one of the senior naval staff, Admiral Spalding.

'Come in Wren Mitchell,' he said, standing politely as she entered. A tall man with fair hair and kind pale-blue eyes, he indicated a chair opposite his desk. She sat down, nervously.

'You've travelled down from Newcastle, I gather?'

'Yes sir – yesterday.'

'Digs OK?'

'Yes… perfectly, sir.'

'And you've been working as a plotter up there?'

'Yes…'

'Quite of lot of traffic up there, I'd imagine. North Sea's a busy place.'

'Yes sir… but it's been interesting. I enjoyed it very much. I was lucky, because my parents live in Gosforth, so I was able to live at home.'

'And you're training to be an architect?'

'Yes. I completed my first year at the School of Architecture in Newcastle – Kings College – it's part of Durham University. But then it was time to join up, so I joined the Wrens in June, did my training and became a plotter.'

'And why did you choose the navy?'

'Oh, you know. Quite a nice uniform…' She smiled, and then blushed at having made such a trivial remark. 'But seriously sir, I like plotting – it suits my brain.'

'You speak languages too, I gather?'

'Oh, yes. Just higher certificate – French and German… but I have quite a good command of both.'

'So, quite a talented young lady.' He smiled.

'Oh, I wouldn't say that,' she said, blushing.

'Do you type, by any chance? Take shorthand?'

'I do, sir, yes. My mother insisted I did a short course when I left school, before I started university. I really didn't want to do it… and I can't pretend my speeds are exactly brilliant.'

'Well, I'm sure we'll manage.'

Imogen looked surprised.

'Shall we make a start?' the Admiral asked.

'On what, sir?'

'Dictation. There's a pad just there on my desk. Your plotting will come in handy down the line, don't worry about that, but for now, I need someone to work just for me… Someone I can rely on. I have a feeling you might be just the ticket. But it'll be hard work. And all very hush-hush. You're not to speak of anything that you see or do in this building, and particularly in this room. Do you understand?'

Imogen nodded.

'And you've signed the relevant forms, I presume?'

'The Official Secrets Act? Yes, sir. We did it first thing this morning.'

'We?'

'Myself, and my best friend, Joy. It was rather a miracle really. She's a really good typist – top notch. Perhaps you ought to have her instead of me?'

He smiled. 'Go on…'

'Well, she worked for the council in Newcastle after we left school, then she joined the Wrens when I did. We've known each other since we were eleven. We were evacuated to the Lakes together. So when we heard we'd been transferred to London it was rather a miracle.'

The Admiral smiled.

'Good, I like to think of my staff having friends. Nice to know we get it right sometimes. Now… that memo?'

*

Much to her relief, Imogen discovered that her work involved a lot more than shorthand and typing. She took minutes of meetings and occasionally translated documents for her boss. She also liaised with other departments, often in person. Those journeys around the capital meant she gradually became familiar with London's geography. But the bombing in London was something she could never completely get used to. There had been air attacks in Newcastle of course, but nothing had prepared her for the weekly devastation that London endured at the beginning of 1944. She and Joy learnt never to leave the house without their gas mask boxes, where they kept a toothbrush and spare underwear, in case they had to stay overnight at work. A basement room had been arranged with narrow bunk beds where they would join other staff, sleeping fitfully in cramped conditions. Imogen kept a spare nightdress and a clean shirt in her office drawer and became used to washing in a basin in the ladies' lavatories early in the morning before a full day's work. In many ways it reminded her of sleeping in the dormitory at school.

The staff at Norfolk House somehow continued with their work through repeated bombing raids. One day at the end of January sirens sounded and they hurried down to the shelters in the basement of the building. When they emerged a few hours later, they were told the Houses of Parliament and New Scotland Yard had both taken a direct hit.

A few days later, Imogen had only just returned from delivering some important papers to the war office, when the sirens sounded once again, accompanied by the incessant firing of anti-aircraft guns. Later, emerging from the shelter, she discovered the area had been subjected to a phosphorous incendiary attack, causing damage even to 'The Fortress' – the war office's reinforced concrete extension. The following day, as Imogen emerged from the tube station on her way to work, another bomb fell on Whitehall, a second in Horse Guards Parade and one even in St James's Park itself. When she finally arrived at the office, she discovered her building had been miraculously spared, but rumour had it that the windows of No. 10 Downing Street had been shattered.

That evening, over dinner at their digs, Imogen and Joy discussed her 'near miss'.

'I spent half the afternoon in the shelter at the War Office yesterday,' Imogen told Joy. 'I had to take some papers over for General Eisenhower. Top Secret… for his eyes only. It seems the Americans are gearing up for something big.'

'How exciting,' said Joy.

The landlady's daughter, a frail skinny girl named Phyllis, clattered into the dining room and put down two unappetising bowls of oxtail soup in front of Imogen and Joy. They waited for her to leave before continuing.

'I suppose we shouldn't really be talking about this, should we?' whispered Joy.

'No… you're probably right,' said Imogen, looking around at the other diners. 'But as long as we're careful, it should be all right. At least we've finally found out what BIGOT means: British Invasion of German Occupied Territory.'

Joy nodded and slurped her soup.

'The frustrating thing is,' said Imogen, 'I don't really have any more of the details.'

'I'd have thought,' said Joy, 'with old man Spalding being virtually in charge, you'd know everything?'

'Well my problem is that I have all the pieces of the jigsaw laid out in front of me, but no idea how they fit together.'

'From what I can see in the typing pool,' said Joy, 'there's a lot of chat about troop movements. Portsmouth's been mentioned.' The landlady's daughter returned and removed their used plates. Ginny and Joy glanced meaningfully at one another.

'We'd better keep quiet,' whispered Imogen, when Phyllis had gone. 'We don't want to be strung up for revealing state secrets.'

*

Back in their room, they lay on their beds, on either side of the bay window.

'I'll tell you what,' said Joy. 'Why don't we go out? I'm not sure I can face another evening staring at the ceiling.'

'What, now?' asked Imogen. 'Why not read your book? It's freezing outside.'

'I've finished my book,' said Joy. 'Besides, it's freezing inside too, and at least a pub will be warm.'

'Well that's true,' said Imogen, swinging her legs off the bed.

'And… I've yet to meet my dream man.' said Joy. 'Most of the officers at work are old enough to be my father. And who knows, the dreamboat might be lurking in some pub somewhere. So come on Ginny – let's go to that big pub up on Hampstead Heath – The Spaniard's Inn. Someone told me it's the oldest pub in London and it always looks rather beautiful from the outside.'

'But it's miles away,' protested Imogen. 'Can't we just go to that one on the corner?'

'Oh no,' said Joy. 'Nigel the letch is bound to be in there.'

'Maybe he's your dreamboat,' said Imogen, smiling.

'Don't you dare!' said Joy. 'He's positively rancid. Have you seen his hands? So small and clammy.' She shuddered. 'No… I've decided. We're going to the Spaniard's.'

As Imogen and Joy pushed open the Inn's door, they had to fight their way through the tightly packed crowd in order to reach the bar.

'Two gins, please,' Joy called out over the heads of other drinkers. The barman busied himself with another customer. 'Excuse me…' she shouted indignantly.

'Joy… keep your voice down,' said Imogen.

'Why should I? He's ignoring me.' Then, ducking under a man's arm, she forced her way to the front and shouted loudly at the barman. 'Excuse me… I want a drink.'

'May I help you?' asked a tall dark-haired man standing next to her; he had a strong foreign accent.

'Oh, that's awfully kind,' said Joy, then shouting towards the barman's back, added: 'We just can't get his attention.'

'Two drinks for the ladies,' said the young man.

'All right Fritz – I'm coming,' said the barman.

Joy and Imogen looked at one another, silently mouthing 'Fritz'.

'Fritz?' said Joy, as the man handed them their drinks.

'Not my real name,' said the man, smiling. 'It's his little joke.'

'But you're not English, are you?' said Joy, sipping her gin and tonic.

'No, I'm not.'

'So are you going to tell us where you *do* come from?'

Imogen kicked Joy in the shin.

'What?' said Joy. 'There's nothing wrong with asking, is there?' she said to the young man.

'Nothing at all,' he said. 'Come and join my friends.'

He led them over to a group of men sitting in a corner. They all stood politely as the women approached, and bowed slightly.

'Good evening,' one said.

'Good evening,' Imogen replied.

'Please,' said the young man, 'sit with us.'

Joy and Imogen sat and looked around at the group.

'Well…' said Joy, 'this is rather jolly – where are you all from?'

They glanced at one another before the dark-haired young man spoke again.

'We are all from Germany… but before you have us arrested, we are on your side.' He smiled.

'Gosh,' said Joy. 'I had no idea.'

'Oh Joy,' said Imogen, 'it's like the POWs in the Lakes. Sergio – do you remember? He was an Italian POW,' she explained to the men, 'He worked at our school as a gardener.'

'And on a local farm,' Joy butted in. 'He rescued Ginny here – carried her down a mountain when she broke her ankle – it was awfully romantic.'

Imogen blushed, 'I twisted my ankle and it wasn't a mountain, just a steep hill.' The men laughed.

'So what's your name?' Joy said to the young dark-haired man.

'Karl. And this is Wilhelm, and Dieter, Werner and Ernst.'

The men nodded, politely.

'Well it's jolly nice to meet you. I'm Joy and this is my friend Imogen.'

'So what are you all doing here, in Hampstead?' asked Imogen.

'We moved here well before the war,' Karl explained. 'Two of us are students, Dieter and Werner both got out in thirty-six – they're Jewish, you see.'

'And you all met up in London?' asked Joy.

'Yes. We are émigrés, you know – we cling to each other.'

'And were you interned?' asked Imogen.

'Wilhelm and I were at first, yes. But over time, when they saw we were not a threat, we were released.'

'Well, good for you,' said Imogen. 'Joy and I only moved down to London a few weeks ago. We're from Newcastle originally.'

'You're in the Wrens?' Karl said, noting their uniform.

'We are,' she said. 'But we really can't say any more than that.'

The émigrés drank vodka and told stories of their early lives. They had all left so much behind – jobs, families and loved ones.

'Don't you worry about what's happening to everyone back home?' Imogen asked Karl.

'Of course, all the time. I worry about my parents and my little sister, Magda. She was just a child when I left. She'll be eighteen now. But they live in the countryside and I hope they won't get into any trouble. The cities are taking the worst of it… the bombing and so on.'

'It's so awful,' said Imogen. 'They bomb us, we bomb them. It seems that it's always the innocent who suffer.'

'Oh come on,' said Joy, raising her glass. 'That's enough depressing talk. Here's to all of us – and to the end of the war.'

'To the end of the war!' they chorused.

Chapter Twenty-One

The farmhouse kitchen table was covered with rounds of cheese, sides of ham and loaves of bread intended for the market in Augsburg. As Magda and her mother wrapped the produce, her father stacked it all away carefully in large baskets. Pulling on his winter coat he picked up a fully laden basket and went outside to pack up the cart. The yard was icy and Helga, the mare, slithered slightly on the cobbles.

'I don't know why you have to go all the way to the Augsburg market,' Käthe said, as Pieter came back inside for another load. 'We know the cities are targets for bombs and I worry about you. Why not just sell to the village?'

'Because we won't make any money selling to the village,' Pieter said pragmatically. 'Now stop worrying and pass me that cheese.'

When the cart was loaded up, Magda, wearing her mother's fur coat and hat, her hands already freezing in her woollen mittens, covered the produce with a canvas sheet and then climbed up next to her father.

'Goodbye Mutti,' she shouted to her mother. 'See you later.'

As Helga trotted happily along the road, Magda looked up at the leaden sky. 'It looks like snow,' she said, pulling her muffler up around her mouth. Her breath felt warm and comforting.

'It's almost too cold to snow,' her father replied. 'I worry the market will be empty.'

As they trotted into the ancient market square just before half past seven, he was reassured to see fellow stall holders were already setting up. They parked the cart near their chosen pitch, and tethered Helga to a nearby lamp-post with a nose bag attached to her bridle. The market area was icy and slippery and they struggled to unload the cart, but finally, just after eight o'clock, they were ready.

Magda had left school the previous year. Still determined to go to university, she had been forced to defer her place as she was required to do some kind of war work first. She was offered a job in the factory crèche in Augsburg, but Pieter persuaded the authorities that his daughter's labour would be more valuable running the family farm, as he had lost all his young casual male workers. Magda was in no doubt how lucky she had been to be able to remain at home and work with her parents.

Business in the market that morning was slow. Women wrapped up in wool coats and shawls shuffled past Pieter's stall examining the cheese and bread on offer, but not buying.

'They won't find better cheese anywhere else,' Pieter said irritably, as yet another potential customer walked away empty-handed. 'Hopefully when the workers from the Messerschmitt factory clock off for lunch, business will pick up.'

'I'm sure it will, Papa,' said Magda, who was busy trying to cajole an elderly woman into buying something.

'It's delicious,' she urged her.

'I don't know,' said the woman, reluctantly.

'Try a little piece,' said Magda. She was cutting a sliver from the cheese, when an air raid siren went off.

'We must find a shelter,' Pieter shouted to his daughter.

'I don't know where to go,' Magda replied, panicking.

The shoppers at the market scattered, running in all directions.

'Come over here,' Pieter called to Magda, 'let's lie under the cart.'

'What about Helga?' said Magda, holding onto the mare's bridle. 'Won't she be frightened?' The mare, tethered to the lamp-post, began to shake her head, whinnying pitifully, as the sound of enemy aircraft approached.

'She'll be all right,' Pieter said. 'Get under the cart, quickly. The planes must be heading for the factory.' He wrapped his arms around his daughter. 'Let's hope they hit that and not us.'

As the planes arrived, sweeping over the city like a vast flock of angry birds, they let loose their load, the bombs crashing to the earth, causing the ground to shake so violently that loaves of bread and rounds of cheese fell off the table onto the snowy cobbles. Magda covered her ears with her gloved hands, trying to drown out the terrifying sound of pounding and explosions. German anti-aircraft guns filled the air with their hacking replies. Masonry fell, crashing into the square. They heard glass shattering, the desperate screaming of people as they were hit. Finally, the planes flew away to the south, leaving in their wake an almost eerie silence, interrupted only by the moaning and wailing of injured people. Magda and Pieter crept out from their hiding place. They were met with a scene of devastation – entire buildings had collapsed across the market square leaving yawning gaps; broken glass was strewn everywhere, mixed with shattered masonry and timber; and all around were the pink and red body parts of human beings, their blood spilling scarlet onto the icy white pavements.

'My God!' Magda said. 'Look at it. There are so many injured.'

Her father began to pile cheeses onto the cart.

'Help me load up… quickly,' Pieter said, harnessing the horse.

'Shouldn't we stay and help?' asked Magda, staring around at the people moaning in the street. A woman came running into the square screaming, her face smeared with blood, her hands held out in front of her. Magda ran towards her and realised that she had lost her eyes. She put her arms around the woman and guided her to the Town Hall steps.

'Sit down, and wait here,' she said to the woman, as she looked around for someone to help.

'Magda,' her father called out, walking towards her, 'we must go… the planes might come back. We're safer in the country. Come quickly.'

'But we can't leave her,' said Magda, gesturing to the woman.

'She's one of hundreds, probably,' said Pieter softly. 'I'm sorry, but we can't help them all.'

He dragged Magda away and lifted her, protesting, onto the cart as snow began to fall, covering the jagged edges of the bombed buildings with a thick white blanket. Climbing up onto his seat, he cracked his whip and the mare, Helga, trotted obediently up the street, past the damaged buildings and the people calling out for help. One or two young men tried to stop the cart – to commandeer it, presumably for the wounded. But Pieter raised his whip, and spurred the horse on. Once they were out of the town centre, he slowed to a trot. Magda looked back. The horizon was dominated by fires, leaping from damaged buildings like a wall of flame.

'The fires are terrible,' she said. 'Why don't they put them out?'

'Why do you think?' said Pieter. 'It's too cold. I suspect the fire hydrants have frozen solid.' As they passed near the factories to the south of the city they could see that they too had been badly hit.

Back at the farm, they unloaded the cart, and put the mare in her barn with some fresh hay and water.

'Good girl,' said Magda, removing her bridle and throwing a thick winter blanket over the mare.

'Didn't I tell you!' said Käthe, as they came into the kitchen. 'No more trips to Augsburg – promise me.'

Later that night, as the family prepared for bed, they heard the unmistakeable rumble of planes flying overhead.

'Papa,' said Magda, running to her parents' room, 'they're coming back.'

'I knew it,' said Pieter. 'They're going to take out that factory; make sure it never gets back to life.'

Bombs began to fall – some close to the farm. Magda, terrified, jumped into her parents' bed.

'We should go to the cellar, Pieter,' said Käthe, 'we can't stay here.' Together the family pulled on coats, and went down with a couple of candles to the cellar where they huddled in the cold for the rest of the night, listening as wave upon wave of Allied planes flew overhead towards Augsburg.

The following morning, just after dawn, Pieter and Magda went out onto the farm to inspect the damage. The ground was covered with snow glinting in the morning sunshine, the sky a brilliant blue. They trudged across the yard and checked on the herd in the barn. The cows lay in companionable groups on the thick winter straw. One or two struggled to their feet when Magda and her father arrived.

'They're all right,' said Magda. 'I can't see any damage.' They left the barn, and walked further down the track, inspecting the fields on either side until they arrived at the boundary of their farm.

'Let's go on a bit further,' said Pieter. 'I'm sure I heard some kind of explosion nearby.'

On the other side of the road, in a little patch of woodland near to where Magda and Karl had so often set up their camp, lay the tangled wreckage of a plane – like a terrible scar on the pure white landscape. The nose of the plane had sheered right off as it crashed through the forest, tearing off the wings and the tailplane which lay twenty yards away.

'Don't go near it,' said Pieter, holding onto Magda's arm. 'It might explode…'

'I don't think so,' said Magda, calmly. 'It would have gone up by now. Besides, it's covered with snow.'

'It's a British plane,' said Pieter. 'We should tell the authorities.'

'No… not yet,' said Magda. 'There might still be someone alive.'

She yanked her arm free and crept towards the main body of plane. A young man had been thrown free. He lay face down, his blond hair matted with snow. She touched his icy neck feeling for a pulse, but it was obvious he was dead.

'Magda… come back. It's pointless,' said Pieter, but Magda persisted. The door of the body of the plane had been thrown open and she reached up and peered inside.

'Oh no,' she said, recoiling. 'There are four or five of them in there. All dead by the looks of it. They obviously didn't have a chance to jump. I wonder why.'

'Come away, please,' said Pieter, as snow began to fall again.

'They're just boys, Papa – not much older than me. How awful that they should die like this.'

'They were intent on killing our people – maybe they deserved it.'

'No Papa,' said Magda, 'you can't think that way. All death is terrible, and there is something so sad about these boys, lying here, hundreds of miles away from their families… dying alone.'

'Well there's nothing we can do about it. Come on – we must get back. The authorities will deal with this.'

As he pulled her away, she held up her hand.

'What was that noise?'

'Nothing,' said Pieter, 'come on.'

'No… I heard something – a sort of moaning sound… over there.'

She walked towards the nose of the plane. Still inside the crumpled cockpit was a young man, his arm and leg clearly broken, his face covered with blood.

She touched him and he moaned again.

'Papa,' she called out, 'one of them is alive. We must get him out.'

'Magda, don't be ridiculous,' her father said, coming to join her. He looked at the boy and shook his head. 'He'll be taken prisoner soon enough.'

'Please Papa, help me. It might be hours till anyone comes. He'll be dead by then in this weather.'

Pieter, torn between his desire to save his own skin and his daughter's pleading, reluctantly went back to the farm and returned with the horse and cart. Between them, father and daughter dragged the young man, groaning, onto the cart.

'I'll stay in the back with him,' said Magda, covering the young man with an old piece of canvas.

As they were just turning onto the track that led to their farm, another horse and cart came towards them on the main road. It was Erika's father – Gerhardt.

'Someone said a British plane had come down over there,' he called out to Pieter.

'Yes,' said Pieter. 'I just passed it.'

Magda, her heart beating loudly, checked the young pilot was hidden from view.

'Is it on my land?' Gerhardt asked.

'No I don't think so. It landed in that bit of woodland between our two farms,' said Pieter.

Gerhardt shrugged. 'Got what they deserved,' he said, trotting off.

Käthe ran out of the farmhouse as soon as the horse and cart drew up in the yard.

'Where have you been? I woke up and you'd both gone. I panicked.'

'We found a British plane,' Pieter said, jumping down and holding the mare's bridle. 'Magda has brought an airman back here.'

'What? Are you mad?' said Käthe furiously. 'Magda – take him back… take him back now. We can't have him here.'

'No,' said Magda, firmly. 'It might have been Karl. You'd want someone to help him, wouldn't you, Mutti?'

'But Magda – the authorities are already upset with you.'

'Don't be ridiculous,' said Magda. 'That was a long time ago. Help me Mutti… We'll get him into Karl's room.'

'No!' said her mother. 'Not there.'

'Mutti, what's the point of keeping it like a shrine? Help me take the boy in – please.' She looked desperately between her two parents.

'You can put him in the barn,' Käthe said. 'Then at least if someone finds him we can swear we knew nothing about it.'

'No Mutti – it's too cold. He'll die out there. Besides, do you really think people would believe we knew nothing about it? Everyone knows we're in and out of our barns every day. He'll be safer inside where we can keep an eye on him, trust me.'

The boy drifted in and out of consciousness as they hauled him upstairs. From time to time, he called out.

'It's all right,' Magda said calmly, as she settled him on Karl's bed. 'We'll look after you.'

He was slender and tall, his feet almost falling off the end of the bed. He wore a sheepskin flying jacket and boots, and his flying helmet had slipped off, revealing bright red hair and a gentle face. As he opened his amber-coloured eyes he saw the family standing staring at him and recoiled, terrified.

'It's all right – we won't hurt you,' Magda said in English, sitting on the bed next to him. 'I have a brother about your age. He's in England. This is his room.'

The young man appeared to relax a little. 'Thirsty,' he muttered.

'Mutti, get him some water.'

Once Magda had fed a few sips of water to the young man, she checked him for injuries. 'I think he's broken his arm, and his leg,' she said to her mother. 'What can we use to mend the bones?'

'A splint, you mean?' asked Käthe. 'God knows, I don't. This is madness – trust me. We will all live to regret this day. We'll all be shot.'

Pieter went downstairs and returned with two straight lengths of firewood.

'Go and find a piece of cloth we can tear up into strips,' he instructed Käthe. 'Can you feel the break with your fingers?' he asked Magda.

The young man whimpered as Magda gently helped him out of his flying jacket. His arm hung limply at his side as she carefully removed his shirt and ran her cool fingers along his arm. 'Yes… it's here. On his forearm.'

'That's lucky,' said Pieter. 'It should heal faster. A break near the shoulder would be difficult. We'll tie a piece of wood along the forearm with fabric strips. But first, we'll need to make sure it's straight. We have to pull it into position.'

'How do you know all this?' asked Käthe, coming back into the room with a handful of cloth.

'I saw it done in the first war. One of us must stand behind him, holding his shoulders. I'll do that. Käthe – go back downstairs and get some schnapps.'

'You want a drink now?' she asked.

'Not for me, you stupid woman – for him!'

She returned a few moments later with a bottle of schnapps and small glass.

'Pour some into his mouth. Magda, you must pull his hand away from his forearm, like this…' he demonstrated on his own hand, 'until you feel the bones slot back into position. Otherwise it will heal all wrong.'

He sat behind the man, and braced himself against the wall.

'I'm going to pull your hand,' Magda said to the airman, 'I'll try not to hurt you.'

He grimaced. 'Just do it…'

She pulled his hand and manipulated the bones of the forearm, until she felt them slot into position. The man cried out in pain, his face contorting.

'I'm so sorry,' said Magda.

'Tie on the splint now,' her father instructed. She lay the piece of wood along the man's forearm and her mother tied the cloth strips around it.

'Now… more schnapps. Then we do his leg,' said Pieter. Together they removed the airman's trousers and once again, Magda ran her fingers along his shin, until she found the break. Once more they manipulated the limb and fixed the splint in position.

The young airman lay back on the pillow exhausted, and attempted a smile.

'Thank you,' he said, weakly.

'We'd better clean him up,' Käthe said. 'I'll go and get some water.'

'What's your name?' the young man asked Magda in English, as she wiped his face and hands clean.

'Magda,' she replied, putting the bowl back on the floor and covering him with the quilt. 'What's yours?'

'Michael,' he replied.

'Well Michael – I'll bring you some food now, then you must sleep.'

Downstairs in the kitchen, Käthe rounded on her daughter.

'You will get us all killed. Do you understand what you have done?'

'What else could we do?'

'Leave him there. He'd be a prisoner. He'd get medical attention, it would be fine.'

'Do you really believe that? I don't. If the Hitler Youth had found him, they would have shot him for target practice.'

'Magda… don't be ridiculous,' said Käthe.

'You don't understand, Mutti. You don't know what they're like. I cannot stand by and watch someone being murdered, like an animal. He's a human being, Mutti – like us.'

*

Käthe finally relented, but she spent a sleepless night worrying that his presence in the house would put them all in danger. Over breakfast the following morning, she suggested, once again, that he should be put out into the barn.

'I beg you not to do that, Mutti,' Magda pleaded. 'It's a crazy idea – he's far more likely to be found out there.'

'Well,' said Käthe reluctantly, 'if he stays, then we must have some rules.'

Magda nodded.

'He must never come downstairs at all,' Mutti insisted, clearing their plates away. 'We can't run the risk of someone turning up and finding him here.'

'It will be all right,' Pieter said phlegmatically, 'as long as he stays upstairs.'

'And he never must be left alone in the house,' Käthe added, putting an apple cake on the table.

'Why?' asked Magda.

'Think about it… if someone comes to see us when we are all out in the fields – a friend, or the post boy – they might go upstairs, looking for us and they'd find him.'

'All right,' said Magda. 'One of us stays here at all times.'

'And I'm not cooking for him, either,' Käthe said gruffly.

'I'll do it,' said Magda eagerly.

'You!' said Käthe. 'You can't even boil an egg!'

'I'll learn,' said Magda. 'You'll see!'

Later that morning, when her parents were out on the farm, Magda slipped silently into Karl's room and stood gazing at the tall red-haired young man lying peacefully in her brother's bed. She had hoped he would be awake so she could give him a piece of apple cake and find out a little more about him. But he was fast asleep, his eyelashes fluttering wildly, his good hand protectively holding his broken arm. He would be their secret, she decided – their act of kindness in this terrible war. She would protect him and bring him back to health. It was what Karl would have wanted, she felt sure. She left the cake on the floor by the bed and slipped out of the room, shutting the door quietly behind her.

Chapter Twenty-Two

St James's, London
March 1944

At 7 p.m. Imogen tidied her desk and put the cover on her type-writer. She knocked on the Admiral's door and peered around it.

'Just off now, sir… if that's all right?'

'Of course. I had no idea it was so late. Off you go. See you tomorrow.'

Coming downstairs into the main hall, she noticed a tall young man waiting at the reception desk. He was wearing an American army uniform.

'Ah Miss Mitchell,' the desk clerk said, 'this gentleman is here to see Admiral Spalding. I wonder if you'd be so kind as to show him up. Lieutenant Andersen has an appointment – it's in the book.'

'Of course,' Imogen said, wondering why the Admiral had not alerted her to this meeting.

She led the man up the stairs and along the corridor to the Admiral's office.

'I'm sorry if I interrupted your evening,' he said, gently. 'You were obviously on your way out.' He gestured towards her coat and hat.

'That's quite all right. I've got nothing planned – except a long hot bath,' she laughed. 'The Admiral's office is just this way.'

While the two men had their meeting, Imogen got on with some office work. About nine o'clock, with her stomach rumbling and her mind wandering to the bath she hoped to have, the door to her boss's office opened. Lieutenant Anderson emerged, closing the door quietly behind him.

'Good, you're still here,' he said, cheerfully. 'I was hoping you would be.'

'I thought I ought to stay,' said Imogen. 'He sometimes likes to dictate notes after a meeting.'

'He's a lucky man. I wondered – if you don't mind me asking – if you'd already had dinner? If not, would you like to join me? I could eat a horse…'

She blushed, flattered to be asked out. 'Not sure I can rustle up a horse,' she quipped, 'although having said that, judging by the meat we usually get, it probably *is* horse.' She laughed. 'I'd be delighted to join you. Thank you. Not much waiting for me at my digs – I've missed supper now. Just give me a minute to make sure he doesn't want anything else tonight. I'll see you downstairs, shall I?'

Outside in the street, the weather was unseasonably warm.

'I'm staying at a little hotel just round the corner,' he said, 'we can get supper there.'

As they entered Brown's Hotel in Albemarle Street he was greeted by the receptionist.

'Good evening Lieutenant. How are you this evening?'

'I'm well thank you. We're just going to the dining room – I hope it's still open.'

The wood-panelled dining room of the hotel was arranged with small tables covered with white cloths. It was discreet and elegant, and Imogen instantly regretted not having put on her lipstick before leaving the office. Since starting work in St James's she rarely had the chance to eat out. A Lyons Corner House with Joy was usually about as glamorous as it got.

Settled at the table, Imogen inspected the menu. It seemed impossibly luxurious to someone who had only eaten rationed food for the previous four years.

'Gosh,' she said, 'what a choice! Potted shrimps… I can't remember when I last had those!'

'Well, have them now,' he said. 'Have whatever you want – it's the least I can do. It's all good – simple, but excellent quality.'

The Lieutenant poured Imogen a glass of red wine.

'How lovely,' she said, taking a sip. It was soft and warming. 'I'm rather ashamed to say I've hardly ever drunk wine – my father's more of a whisky man.'

'Well I hope it's good,' said the Lieutenant. 'It's a good vintage.'

'Thank you… it's delicious. Now, I can't keep calling you "Lieutenant". What's your name?'

'Benjamin. But people usually call me Ben.'

'And I'm Imogen – or Ginny to those who know me.'

He raised his glass to her. 'Great to meet you, Ginny. I'd have been eating all alone, yet again, if it wasn't for you.'

'So you live here? How lovely. Is that normal for American officers?'

He smiled, and sipped his wine.

'Sorry,' she said, blushing, 'I didn't mean to pry. I know one's not supposed to ask questions these days. Pretty much everything that happens at our office is top secret too.'

'Yes. I'm afraid that applies to me too. All I can say is that I'm with the American army and I've been sent over here to do a piece of work for the Allies. That's about it.'

'Right,' she said, nervously. 'It makes conversation a little difficult, doesn't it? What did you do before… before the war?'

'I was at college in Washington, and then grad school – Yale – where I read law. My folks come from Virginia. My father is a diplomat. As a kid we travelled quite widely – all over Europe in fact.'

'That must have been wonderful,' said Ginny, tucking into her potted shrimps.

'Sure,' he continued. 'We lived in Paris, Geneva, Rome, of course… and further afield. We had a spell in the Middle East.

But when I was older, I was sent back to school in the US so I only went to these places in the holidays. When I left Yale I was trying to decide what I should do, when the war came along.' He refilled their glasses. 'What about you?'

'Oh well, not quite so exciting I'm afraid. I was brought up in the North East of England – a place called Newcastle. My father and mother are Scottish; she was a teacher before she married, he's an engineer, so we've travelled a bit too – but not to quite such exotic locations. Carlisle for a bit, and the Dartford Tunnel I seem to remember, when I was very little.' She laughed nervously. 'Then we moved back to Newcastle, and when the war started I was still at school, so I was evacuated to the Lake District.'

'What was that like?'

'Quite good fun, really. It's a beautiful place... have you been?' He shook his head.

'It was a bit lonely at times,' she went on. 'I'm an only child and very close to my parents. But well, you know, you get on with it, don't you? When I left school, I went to university.'

He raised his eyebrows. 'Really?'

'Don't look so surprised,' Imogen said, bristling slightly.

'No, forgive me. I didn't mean anything by it. What did you study?'

'Architecture. I'm going to be an architect. But with the war and all that, I had to join up when I was nineteen, so I joined the Wrens. I was a plotter... am a plotter, really. But I got transferred to Admiral Spalding's staff just after Christmas. To this day, I'm really not quite sure why... why he chose me, I mean. He says I'll go back to plotting eventually. I do hope so, as I'm a terrible typist.'

'He speaks very highly of you,' said Ben. 'Perhaps he doesn't mind so much about the typing.' He smiled.

'Well I don't know about that. All I do know is that I type memos and letters, and make calls to government departments, and really haven't the faintest idea what's going on, which is probably just as well as it's all top secret.'

When they had finished their dinner, Ginny leant back in her chair.

'My goodness, I've not had blowout like that for years! My mother's a wonderful cook, and she and our maid at home – Edith – they do make delicious meals. But shrimp and beef and… what was that pudding?'

'Îsles flottantes,' he said.

'Oh! French for floating islands – how clever. I've never heard of it, but it was… stupendous. However did they get hold of so many eggs?'

'I guess they have connections,' he said, smiling. 'Would you like coffee?'

'Do they have coffee here too?'

'Sure. It's not the best; it's not American, but it's bearable.'

'I'd love some – although I can't be too late. My landlady is awfully strict. She has been known to bolt the door. Then I have to throw stones at my friend's window.'

'Where do you live?'

'Belsize Park. Sort of north-east of here.'

'Let's have coffee in the lounge, shall we, and then we can see about getting you home.'

As they walked together along Piccadilly towards Green Park tube station, a girl stepped suddenly out of a doorway. Her painted face was momentarily lit up by torch light.

'Want a good time, Mister?' she said to Ben. He put his arm protectively around Imogen's shoulder.

'No… no thank you,' he said.

'What did she mean?' asked Imogen, innocently, as they walked briskly away.

'Oh… you know.'

'No… I don't know.'

'Ginny, she's a "lady of the night".'

'Oh!' said Imogen, blushing, grateful for the blackout.

At the entrance to the tube station she put out her hand.

'Well, thank you so much for supper – I did so enjoy it.'

'You don't get rid of me that easily,' he said. 'I'll see you home.'

'Oh you mustn't to do that – it's miles out of your way.'

'No, really, I insist. I kept you out this late; it's the least I can do.'

The tube was surprisingly busy and they were forced to stand, pressed against one another. The train screeched noisily as it lurched violently around a corner, and Imogen lost her footing. Ben, holding onto the overhead strap, put his free arm around her to keep her steady.

'Thank you,' she said, blushing.

'That's OK,' he said softly.

She should have felt uncomfortable, standing in the arms of this stranger, but he made her feel safe.

As the train rumbled east towards Trafalgar Square, they found a seat at last. Suddenly, as they approached the station, there was the distant rumble of a falling bomb somewhere nearby.

'Oh no!' said Imogen. 'Not another one.

'Do we get out?' asked Ben.

'I'm not sure. I've never actually been on a train during an air raid.'

As the doors opened, there was the sound of an explosion directly overhead and all the passengers poured out of the train, and threw themselves down onto the platform. Benjamin wrapped his greatcoat protectively over Imogen, and they lay together in the dark, listening to the muffled sound of bombs exploding above, and of their hearts beating in time below.

When the raid appeared to be over, people stumbled to their feet.

'Maybe we ought to stay down here,' said Imogen anxiously, looking around her.

'No,' said Benjamin, standing and offering her his hand. 'Let's get up there and see what's going on.'

Emerging from the tube station, they stumbled into Trafalgar Square. There was a gaping hole on the south side of the square where a bomb had fallen. Nelson's Column was miraculously unscathed, but a bus nearby lay on its side and Imogen could see bodies lying on the pavement as if thrown out of the bus by a giant hand. Wardens were setting up a cordon around the area.

'We should help,' said Imogen.

'No,' said Ben. They could hear ambulances clanging towards them. 'They've got it covered… we should get you home.'

The bus service had finished for the night, and they were forced to walk, lit only by the moon, up Regent Street and past the BBC in Portland Place. And as they walked, they talked… about their early lives, their hopes and dreams, their past loves. It was as if their shared experience had forged a bond between them.

'So,' he said, as they walked towards the park, 'have you ever been in love?'

'Maybe…' she said. 'Yes… I think so.'

'Who was he?'

'An old friend. I've known him all my life. I thought the feeling was mutual, but now I'm not so sure. What about you?

'I was engaged once. My parents introduced us. She was rich… I'll say that for her. But money's not everything and when I joined up, she broke it off.'

'Were you very upset?' Imogen asked, thinking fleetingly of Dougie.

'Not really… it made me see that she wasn't the right person. She can't have loved me very much, can she?'

'No, I suppose not.'

'So let's get back to your man.'

'He's not my man. I thought we had something between us, but when he joined the RAF and went away, he told me to forget him.'

'Why?'

'He said he might get killed, and he didn't want me to be hurt.'

'He sounds like a good guy – unselfish…'

'Yes,' said Imogen. 'I suppose he is. But it's very hard, you know? I suppose I wanted him to declare himself to me before he went away; to tell me he loved me. But instead, he told me to get on with my life and forget all about him.'

She wiped a tear from her eye with the edge of her sleeve.

'I'm sorry,' Ben said gently, offering her his handkerchief. 'This war has made a lot of people do and say things they didn't know they were capable of.'

'That sounds heartfelt,' she said, wiping her eyes. 'Have you done things you didn't know you were capable of?'

'Maybe. My life has certainly gone in a direction I wouldn't have expected when I was law student back in Yale. The thing about war is that it makes you look at life differently, don't you think? It changes your priorities.'

They walked on in silence for a little while, as Imogen brooded about Freddie's last words to her. She felt embarrassed, and angry with herself, that so many months later, he still had the power to make her cry.

'I'll wash this, shall I?' she said, holding out Ben's handkerchief.

'All right, thank you. At least it means you'll have to see me again – if only to give it back to me.'

She laughed. It felt nice to be wanted.

Skirting the edge of London zoo, they heard a curious low grumbling sound.

'What on earth is that?' Imogen asked.

'A camel, I think,' said Ben. 'I remember the sound from my time in the Middle East, as a kid.'

'How extraordinary,' said Imogen. 'I had no idea we had camels here, in the middle of London. And during a war too.'

'Have you been to the zoo?' Ben asked.

'No, never.'

'Maybe I'll take you.' He took her hand as they crossed the road. It felt natural and comforting, she thought, and left it there. As they walked on across Primrose Hill, he put his arm around her and she relaxed into his body.

'I live just up there,' she said, when they got to the end of her road. 'That large house with the covered porch.'

He stopped and turned her towards him.

'I've had a wonderful evening,' he said.

'So have I,' she replied.

He leant down and tentatively kissed her on the cheek.

'I'd like to see you again,' he said.

'Of course,' she said, brightly. 'I've got your handkerchief, remember.'

'That's right. Well I'm very short of handkerchiefs so it better be soon.'

'All right – I'll wash it tonight.'

She gazed up at him, and he leaned down and kissed her lips – tenderly, softly at first.

'I hope that was all right,' he asked.

'Absolutely,' she said, reaching up and wrapping her hands around his neck, pulling him towards her. He kissed her again – a long lingering kiss – and Imogen felt herself melting into his body, inhaling the scent of his skin.

'I don't want to let you go,' he whispered into her hair.

'Neither do I,' she said, 'but I really ought to go in.'

'Can I see you tomorrow?' he asked.

'I'll be at St James's all day.'

'Maybe we can have supper again; would you like that?'

'I would, thank you.'

He wrapped his greatcoat around her, an act of such tenderness that it brought tears to her eyes, and they kissed.

'I really must go in now,' she said, dreamily.

'I know. Just not quite yet…' He kissed her again, and then again.

Reluctantly unwrapping herself from his arms, she ran up the stairs to the front door and turned around. The collar of his greatcoat was up around his ears. He looked dark and somehow mysterious, she thought.

'Goodnight,' she called out.

'I'll be seeing you,' he said, striding away down the street. As he turned the corner of the road he looked back and waved.

Chapter Twenty-Three

Färsehof Farm
March 1944

A few days after Michael had been brought to the house, Käthe and Magda were preparing lunch in the kitchen, when there was a knock on the door. Opening it, she found two soldiers standing in the yard.

'We're looking for a missing British airman,' the first soldier said. 'Have you seen anyone nearby… perhaps hiding in the barns?'

'No,' said Käthe, nervously. 'Why would we?'

'The plane down the road. It's a British Lancaster bomber. There are six dead but there's one crew member missing. '

'How do you know?' asked Magda, peering over her mother's shoulder.

'Because there should be seven bodies and there are only six.'

'Perhaps one of them jumped out,' Magda suggested.

'No, there are still seven parachutes in the plane. Someone got away.'

Magda shrugged her shoulders and retreated back inside, praying that Michael, who was still asleep in the room above, wouldn't wake up and make a noise.

'Well, keep a look out,' said the second soldier.

'We will,' Käthe said, brightly.

Käthe and Magda watched anxiously through the kitchen window, as the soldiers wandered into the dairy.

'You see, Mutti,' whispered Magda, 'the barns are the first place they look – he's safer in the house.' Her mother glared at her.

'We would all be safer if he was not here at all,' muttered Käthe.

The soldiers continued to search the outbuildings – checking the machinery barn and inspecting the yard, before finally walking back down the track towards the main road.

When they were sure the soldiers had gone, Käthe rounded angrily on her daughter.

'What if they had insisted on searching the house?'

'Well they didn't,' said Magda defensively. But she knew her mother was right to be worried. If they decided to come back and search inside, they would be bound to find him.

When she took Michael his lunch, she found him struggling to swing his legs out of bed.

'What are you doing?' she asked.

'I heard,' he said. 'They're looking for me. I have to go.'

'No!' said Magda. 'You can't go yet.' Sat down on the edge of his bed. 'Your leg is too weak – you couldn't walk ten metres.'

'But it's not safe for you. It's not fair.'

'Don't worry about us,' she said handing him a plate of bread and cheese. 'I know,' she said, suddenly leaping to her feet. 'We'll take you upstairs to the attic. There's a hatch in the eaves that leads to a smaller secret attic. My brother and I used to hide up there all the time. If you drag a piece of furniture, or an old box in front of the hatch, you'd never know it was there. It's a bit cold, but at least you'll be safe. Could you climb a ladder do you think, if we helped you?'

'I think so... just about – yes.'

When her father came in from the fields, he agreed to help move Michael upstairs. Pieter climbed into the attic and, holding onto Michael's stronger arm, hauled him up, while Magda pushed and guided from below.

Once he was installed, Magda arranged the bed for him in the tiny space, and blacked out the window in the main attic that overlooked the yard.

'Otherwise someone might see a light from up here,' she explained. 'At least now you can have a candle at night.

Over the next few weeks, she spent as much time with Michael as she could. Up in the attic, away from the main house, they felt secluded, as if they were in a world of their own. She found an old rug and laid it on the floor. Amidst the old packing cases she created a little nest for them both. She set a bowl and jug of water next to his bed and brought him all his meals. Climbing up the attic ladder with a basket of food in one hand, she would haul the small chest of drawers away from the hatch and crawl through into the dusty space. While he ate, she would sit on the floor next to his bed and they talked. Her English soon grew more fluent, as he taught her new words and phrases. But gradually she came to realise that if he was ever going to escape successfully through Germany, he would need to learn her language.

One evening she arrived with supper for them both, along with two glasses of beer.

'I thought we could share our meal,' she said, putting the food and beer down on the floor.

'That would be lovely,' he said, hauling himself up in bed. 'I do get a bit lonely up here.' He winked at her and she giggled.

'But,' she said firmly, 'We are going to speak in German.'

'How?' he said, sipping his beer. 'I can't speak a word.'

'How will you escape then?' she asked logically.

'You're right, of course.' he said.

'Let's begin with something simple. I'll teach you how to order a beer and a ham sandwich.'

Later, when the lesson was over, and she was packing their supper things back into the basket, he reached over and held her hand.

'Thank you,' he said.

'That's all right.' She stood up, stooping in the low-ceilinged space. 'We'll do some more tomorrow.'

'Do you have to go now?'

'I ought to,' she said, reluctantly. 'My parents…'

'Yes of course,' he said.

'I suppose I could stay a bit longer.' She put the basket over by the hatch and knelt down on the rug next to the bed.

'That doesn't look very comfortable,' he said. 'Sit next to me.'

'All right.' She sat down on the narrow bed.

'Tell me about your brother,' he said. 'Did he join up when the war began?'

'No, he'd already moved to England. He hated our government and everything they stood for. I agree with him. I joined a revolutionary movement myself – the White Rose in Munich. They were students, and they tried to stand up to Hitler, but they were all executed last year.'

'You are an extraordinary girl,' said Michael. 'Full of surprises. How did you manage to avoid being captured?'

'Luck, I suppose. I was interviewed by the Gestapo. But I told them I didn't know what the White Rose were up to – and they believed me.'

He lay back on his pillow, and gazed up at her. 'You are one of the bravest girls I've ever met. *The* bravest girl, come to that.'

'No I'm not,' she said, blushing. 'I'm just… what is it that you say… "bloody-minded".'

He laughed. 'Yes… you're bloody-minded all right. I've never met anyone so stubborn and wilful.' He suddenly sat up… and kissed her. She had only ever been kissed by Otto – an experience that she had found repulsive. His kiss had been suffocating, but Michael's kiss was soft and gentle. It made her feel as if she was alive. She had wanted to go on kissing him forever; to lie in his arms and feel his smooth body next to hers. Was this what love really felt like, she wondered?

'Magda,' he said, pulling away. 'I'm sorry. I shouldn't have done that. I shouldn't take advantage of you.'

'Take advantage… what do you mean?'

'I shouldn't have kissed you. Apart from the morality of the situation, you're too young.'

'I'm nearly eighteen.'

'But your parents… what would they think?'

'What's it got to do with them?'

'You've all been so kind to me, I shouldn't abuse that kindness.'

'But I liked it,' she said, childishly.

'So did I,' he said, sinking back onto his pillows. 'Now be off with you. Go on – back downstairs.'

Reluctantly, she got off the bed, crawled through the hatch, looked back at him, and blew him a kiss.

'Good night, Magda,' he said firmly.

The following morning she laid his breakfast out on the floor and sitting on the edge of his bed, poured him a cup of coffee from a flask. She had picked some early spring primroses and put them in a little jam jar next to his bed.

'They're pretty, spring must be coming,' he said, hauling himself up on the pillows.

'It's already April,' she said, laughing. 'You've been with us for four weeks now and the landscape is changing every day. That's what you notice when you live on a farm. It's such a beautiful day outside, and you haven't seen the sun for so long – I thought I'd bring some to you.' She smiled shyly.

'Tell me what you're going to do today,' he said, sipping his coffee.

'Well,' she said, 'I've already done the morning milking and when I leave here, my father and I will be sowing new crops, now the weather is warming up.'

'I wish I could help you,' he said. 'I feel so useless lying here, while you're all working. And I'd love to learn to milk cows.' He laughed. 'I was brought up in the country – not on a farm, but I love the rural life.'

'It's harder than it looks,' she said. 'In the middle of winter, when your hands are frozen and you're trying to milk the cows and you can't even feel your fingers – then you wish you were anywhere but living on a farm.' She laughed.

He glanced shyly at her, taking in her blonde hair, her slender arms.

'You don't look strong enough for farm work,' he said. 'You're so... delicate.'

'Delicate!' she said, leaping to her feet. 'I'll show you how delicate I am. Give me your strong arm, not the broken one.'

'What?' he asked. 'What torture do you have in mind now?'

'Arm wrestling... come on. Or are you scared I might beat you?'

'Right,' he said, handing her the cup of coffee, which she put on the floor. She pulled an old wooden crate nearer to the bed, and while Michael sat on one side, she knelt on the other. She nearly managed to bring his arm down, but he pushed back at the last minute and slammed her arm down on the crate. Laughing, they collapsed back on the bed.

'Kiss me again,' she said coyly.

'Magda...' he stroked her cheek. 'Are you sure?'

'Yes – of course I'm sure.'

'Magda,' he whispered into her neck. 'I adore you – you do know that, don't you?'

'And I love you, Michael,' she murmured, overwhelmed with joy. 'I know I've only known you for a few weeks, but I really love you. I want you...'

He kissed her again, lying her down on the narrow bed, stroking her limbs, her face. She felt her body burning up with desire for him.

Afterwards, they lay together for a while, wrapped in each other's arms.

'Magda,' he began.

'Don't say anything.' She lay in the crook of his arm, her head resting on his chest. His skin smelt sweet and she felt safe and warm.

'Magda. Look…'

He shifted his weight onto his strong arm, lifting himself up onto one elbow. He gazed down at her.

'I'm not sure we should have done that. You've been so good to me – you and your family. You saved my life, and I'm so grateful. But I want you to understand something… whatever happens, I do love you.'

'It's all right,' she said. 'I know. And I know, also, that you have to leave one day. I understand.'

'Do you? You're such a wonderful girl. You're so wise and mature. Your brother is doing his duty back in England. And I must do mine. When I'm strong enough to get away, I must try to get back to my unit somehow.'

'What is your plan? Where will you go? You can't walk all the way back, can you?'

'I can walk part of the way – at least into Switzerland. Lake Constance is not that far away, is it?'

She shrugged. 'A few hundred kilometres.'

'Oh I see. Well, I could take a train, or a bus? You've taught me how to buy a ticket.'

'But you have no map.' She was clutching at straws, putting obstacles in his way.

'I do have a map, as it happens.' He reached over and pulled out a silk handkerchief from his flying jacket pocket, printed with a map of Europe.

'See – it's pretty isn't it? And very useful too; and I have a compass. I'm a pilot, Magda – I'll find my way.'

'But you're bound to be picked up, and shot. What would be the point of that?'

'So what do you think I should do?' he asked, stroking her hair. Stay here in the attic with you for the rest of the war? However appealing that is, my darling – and believe me Magda, it's very appealing – I can't do that.'

Knowing Michael would be leaving in weeks, if not days, they were desperate to spend as much time together as they could. As soon as Käthe and Pieter left the house, Magda would rush to the attic, where they would make love – sad, tearful love sometimes, after which Michael would kiss the tears from her cheeks.

'I will come back,' he promised, stroking her cheek and holding her in his arms. 'Once this war is over, I'll be back for you. We'll marry and have children and I'll help you run the farm.'

Then she would lie in the crook of his arm, inhaling his scent and weeping. It felt as if her heart was being ripped out of her body.

One afternoon in May, while her father was out in the fields and her mother had gone to the village, Magda crept into the attic.

'Michael. Why don't you come downstairs? If you're ever going to escape, you should practice your walking.'

'Your mother wouldn't like it.'

'My mother's not here. She's gone to the village and will be gone for a couple of hours at least. It will be fine,' Magda said, 'trust me.'

Michael, wearing an old pair of Karl's trousers and a shirt of her father's, clambered down the attic ladder. His leg was stiff and ached, but it felt good to be able to stand up straight, and walk, or at least hobble, down the stairs into the kitchen. The rooms in the house seemed so bright compared to the dark attic that he had to shield his eyes.

'How does your leg feel?' Magda asked.

'Stiff. It hurts. But after spending so much time in that little attic, where I had to stoop just to stand up, it feels good – thank you.'

He smiled broadly and held out his arms to her.

'Now,' she said, 'you'd better sit down here. We left your boots upstairs, but it doesn't matter – my father has an old pair down here by the door.'

'Are we going outside?' he asked.

'Yes – the sun is shining and it's such a beautiful day.' She retrieved her father's old work boots from beside the front door; Michael sat on a kitchen chair and slipped his feet into them.

'They're a bit big too for you,' said Magda. 'But you should be able to walk well enough.' She draped an old jacket of her father's around the airman's shoulders and guided him out, and round the side of the house, into the vegetable garden.

'Sit down here… on this little seat,' she suggested.

Her father had made the wooden bench some years before. He and Käthe would often sit there together, after they'd finished digging, admiring their handiwork.

Michael closed his eyes, feeling the sun warming his face. Birds sang in the apple trees and bees buzzed gently in the warm air. Chickens clucked contentedly around their feet, pecking worms from the half-filled vegetable beds.

'It reminds me of home,' Michael said, taking her hand, and kissing it.

'You've not told me much about your home.'

'It seems so far away. Sometimes I wonder if it's all a dream.'

'Try to tell me. I'd like to know.'

'Well… we live in quite a large house, on the edge of a little village, near the south coast of England. We can see the sea from the garden. As a boy I used to lie on the lawn and watch the changing colours of the Channel – grey mostly, but in the summer it changed to a beautiful blue that matched the colour of the sky.'

'It sounds lovely,' said Magda.

'We have a vegetable garden too – it's my mother's pride and joy. We have an orchard and chickens that run around. She grows asparagus – it's the talk of the county.'

'We grow asparagus,' Magda said brightly. 'Look… here.' She crossed the garden, and pointed to the stubbly spears of asparagus pushing through the brown earth.

'So you do.' He admired her boyish figure, her long limbs, always a little tanned, even after a long hard winter, her golden hair glinting in the sunshine.

'Come over here,' he said. 'I want to kiss you.'

'No,' she replied playfully. 'Your leg's much better… you come to me.'

He hobbled over to the other side of the garden and they kissed.

'I love you,' she said.

'And I love you, too,' he replied.

She began to cry.

'Magda,' he said gently, 'what's the matter?'

'You know what's the matter. I know you'll be leaving me soon.'

'Not leaving you. It's not you I want to leave. But yes… I can walk, just about. I can't justify staying much longer, can I?'

They stood together in the warm sunshine, their arms wrapped around one another, Magda leaning her head against his chest.

'Let's eat out here,' Magda suggested. 'It's nearly lunchtime. We could have some bread and cheese and a glass of beer. Would you like that?'

'I'd love that. Let me come and help you.'

'No, it's OK. You enjoy the sun. Keep the chickens company. Sit down – I'll bring it to you.'

As she reached the garden gate, Michael called out to her.

'Magda…'

'Yes.'

'I want you to know how grateful I am… for everything you've done for me.'

'I know,' she said. 'I'll see you in a minute.'

She was washing her hands at the sink, a tray laid on the table behind her with bread and cheese and two glasses of beer, when she saw a familiar figure walking into the farmyard. Panicking, she ran across the kitchen intending to lock the door, but he had seen her already through the window.

'Hi Magda!' Otto called out.

Reluctantly, she took a deep breath, and opened the door.

'Otto… What are you doing here?'

'Well… that's a nice welcome for your boyfriend.' He was wearing the dark leather coat of an SS officer. He looked taller somehow, more threatening – filling the doorway, blocking out the light. She stood rooted to the spot, willing him to go away.

'Aren't you going to invite me in?' He asked.

'Oh… yes, of course.'

She stood back as he strode into the kitchen.

'You're having lunch?' he said, noting the tray.

'Oh… no. I was just laying it out for Mutti and Papa.'

'Where are they? I'd like to say hello.'

'They're out,' she said.

'Then why have you laid a tray?'

'For when they get back… it's a surprise.'

His constant questioning had always irritated her. He frowned slightly.

'Well, if they're not here, maybe I could eat it? I'm starving.'

'Yes, of course. Sit down.'

'It's on a tray. Let's go into the garden and eat it there.'

'No!' she said, abruptly. 'Let's eat in here. It looks lovely but it's really quite cold outside.'

'All right,' he said, shrugging. He sat down heavily on a chair and drained one of the glasses of beer. She brought over a fresh bottle and topped it up.

'When did you get back?' she asked, as casually as she could.

'Last night. I'm just home on leave for a few days.'

'That's nice,' she said, feebly. 'Your mother must be pleased.'

'Yes, I suppose so. And what about you? What are you doing?'

'Farm work… I'm helping my father. All the local men have gone off to fight, so he needed me here.'

He began to eat the bread, tearing chunks off with his hands, pushing the cheese into his mouth. She topped up his glass again.

'Beer?' he said. 'What are we celebrating?'

'Nothing. As I said, it was for my parents.'

'But they are not here. Why would you pour beer for people who aren't even here?'

'Why not?' she replied as calmly as she could.

'It will go flat,' he said dismissively, 'you know that, surely. You're not that stupid.'

She laughed nervously. 'Maybe I am…'

'Aren't you eating?' he asked, draining his glass again.

'I'm not that hungry.'

She kept glancing towards the door, praying that Michael would not come looking for her.

'You seem nervous,' Otto said, 'what's the matter?'

'Nothing,' she replied. 'I'm fine.'

She forced herself to eat something, to sip the beer, and smile.

'Have you missed me?'

It was such an absurd question, she thought. How Otto could continue to believe that she liked him seemed incredible.

'Yes, of course,' she lied. 'What's it like – being in the SS?'

'Not so different to the Youth. I've been promoted already.' He banged the insignia on his shoulder. 'Obersturmführer,' he said proudly. 'They've made me an officer.'

'Well done,' she said.

There was a clattering noise outside.

'Who's out there?' asked Otto, leaping to his feet.

'No one,' Magda said, her heart racing. 'It must be a cat, or one of the chickens knocking something over.'

'I'll go and look. I noticed a crashed plane down the road. You can't be too careful.'

He opened the kitchen door and went out into the yard. Magda followed him, intending to distract him, but he ran straight round the side of the farmhouse and into the vegetable garden.

'The noise came from here,' he called to her.

'Well… there's no one here now.' She looked around, wondering where Michael could have gone.

Otto stalked around the garden, peering into every corner.

'Otto, there's no one here,' she insisted desperately. Suddenly, out of the corner of her eye, she spotted Michael dragging his bad leg, hobbling across the farmyard towards the barn. It would be just like Otto to insist on searching the whole farm. Desperate to distract him and give Michael a chance to escape onto the road, she walked over to Otto, and leaned towards him, entwining her fingers around his.

'Come back inside. My parents are out now, but they will be back soon. We have a little time…'

He grinned, revealing his large white teeth, and together they walked slowly across the garden, only stopping for Otto to study a pile of broken flowerpots. 'This must be what I heard,' he said, picking up the terracotta fragments.

'Yes, I told you. It's just the cat, or one of the chickens. Come…' she pulled him towards her.

Inside the kitchen, Otto pressed her against the wall and kissed her violently. Every sinew in her body ached to push him away, to struggle, but she let him kiss her, praying that as he did so, Michael would make his escape, down the track towards the road, over the fields, out of the valley and away. He was wearing her father's clothes and perhaps could pass as a local. But he had no money, no papers. His compass and silk map were still upstairs in the attic. His chances of survival were slim at best. But at least Otto wouldn't get him. Not that day. She could save him from that at least; and as Otto's hands slid beneath her clothes, as he panted at her neck, murmuring her name, as he forced himself inside her, she cried out – not with ecstasy but in pain.

When it was over, she leaned against the wall, shaking.

'I'm leaving tomorrow,' he said, buttoning his trousers. 'Shall I see you again?'

'No,' she said. 'No, I don't think so… I have things to do.'

He shrugged dismissively. She heard the sound of the horse and cart trotting back into the yard. Her racing heart slowed a little as she heard her father's voice chatting amiably to his beloved mare.

'Your father's back… I'd better go.' Otto clicked his heels at her, as if saluting a senior officer. She almost laughed at the absurdity of it. But as she heard him stride away across the yard, she fell onto the floor and wept.

Chapter Twenty-Four

St James's
April 1944

The pace of work at St James's had increased over the previous couple of weeks and Imogen frequently found herself working late into the evening, her back aching from long hours hunched over the typewriter. One evening, as her fingers thundered across the keyboard, she was looking forward to the warm bath she would have back in Belsize Park, when there was a knock at the door. She had been waiting all day for a stack of documents to be sent over from the War Office.

'About time…' she muttered. 'Come in,' she shouted briskly. To her surprise, Benjamin put his head round the door.

'Hello,' she said, 'what on earth are you doing here?'

'Well that's a very nice welcome.'

'I'm sorry,' she said hurriedly. 'It's just I was expecting some paperwork, and not you. How did you get in, anyway?'

'I had a meeting down the hall with one of your team.'

'Oh,' she said. 'You are full of surprises, aren't you?'

He smiled enigmatically. 'Well, if you're too busy to see me…?'

'No… not at all. I suspect the documents I was waiting for aren't going to arrive this evening. I was just trying to get ready for a big meeting we have tomorrow morning.'

'If you're sure? I was hoping we could have supper together. I have to go away tomorrow for a few days.'

'That would be lovely. Just give me five minutes to sort myself out here. I'll meet you downstairs, shall I?'

*

Outside on Piccadilly, the scent of blossom from the trees in the park floated on a warm breeze. Imogen instantly relaxed and took Ben's arm.

'How lovely it is,' she said. 'I've been shut inside all day; I hadn't realised what a beautiful evening it was.'

'A beautiful evening for a beautiful girl,' he said romantically.

'You're very sweet, but rather corny,' she laughed, as they walked past the entrance to Albemarle Street. 'Aren't we going to your hotel for supper?'

'Not this evening,' he replied, teasingly. 'I have a surprise for you.'

The stately lobby of the Grosvenor House Hotel seemed a haven of peace. Arranged around the high-ceilinged space were little groupings of plush furniture where people in evening dress sat drinking cocktails.

'What on earth are we doing here?' asked Imogen.

'This is my surprise…'

She looked at him quizzically.

'They do special dance nights,' he went on, 'dinner and a dance for a good price, trying to encourage business, I guess. I thought you'd enjoy it.'

The floor of the ballroom was filled with couples, some in full evening dress, others in uniform. Imogen looked down at her sensible black shoes and dour Wren's uniform, and felt a childish disappointment that she was not wearing an elegant silk gown.

'It's so glamorous here,' she said, as the waiter guided them to a corner table. 'I just wish I was wearing something a bit more suitable.'

'You look beautiful,' Ben said as they sat down.

'Thank you. But a long silk dress, like the one I have at home, in Newcastle – that's what I should be wearing.'

'I'll tell you what,' he said. 'Next time we go dancing, I'll buy you a beautiful dress, all right?'

When the band struck up 'In the Mood', he stood up, offering Imogen his hand.

'Come on,' he said. 'Shall we?'

As he held her on the dance floor he made her feel like she was the best dancer in the room. When they finally left, and stood outside on Park Lane, he took her in his arms and kissed her.

'I love you Imogen,' he said. She knew he was waiting for her to say the same. She wanted to – desperately. But something held her back. He was handsome, charming, kind, generous. Why couldn't she just say it?

'I love being with you too,' she said, evasively.

Back in Belsize Park she crept in to her room, trying not to wake Joy.

'Did you have fun?' asked Joy, sleepily, from beneath her eiderdown.

'Yes,' said Imogen, taking off her uniform. 'It was great fun – Ben's such a thoughtful man.'

'Do you love him?' asked Joy.

'I suppose I do,' said Imogen.

'You suppose?'

'I must do, mustn't I? He's everything a girl could want. Now go back to sleep.'

But as she brushed her teeth in the bathroom down the hall, as she put on her nightgown and unpinned her hair, she wondered why she couldn't just abandon herself to loving him. He was everything a girl could want… it was true. And yet… something was missing.

Imogen didn't see Ben for two weeks. She thought about him from time to time, but was so immersed in her work she didn't really miss him. There was a palpable air of excitement in the offices at St James's; a sense that the end was in sight. Finally, in the last week of May, Imogen was summoned to the large meeting room on the first floor overlooking St James's Square. She and one other note-taker were the only junior staff in the room. Around the long mahogany table sat the most senior military men in the country, the Chief of Staff, the Allied Naval Commander, the First Sea Lord and the Air Chief Marshall. Most excitingly of all, at least as far as Imogen was concerned, was the presence of the Supreme Allied Commander himself, General Dwight D. Eisenhower.

The meeting had been arranged to agree on the final details for the cross-Channel invasion of northern France by the Allies. Codenamed 'Operation Overlord', everything was being planned down to the minutest detail. Crucial to its success was an intricate understanding of Germany's coastal defences along the French coast. Thousands of high-resolution photographs from reconnaissance aircraft of what was known as 'Hitler's West Wall' had been sent back to Whitehall. They revealed a steel barrier made of scaffolding erected one hundred and fifty yards out to sea. Behind this sat a double wire fence and a zig-zag of concrete anti-tank barriers with protruding steel prongs. Behind that, on the beach itself, stood a three-foot-high barbed wire fence and three anti-tank defences: a ditch, a concrete anti-tank wall, and an array of concrete blocks. On the dunes overlooking the beaches were fortified gun emplacements and the beaches had been sown with mines.

In England, teams of American and British engineers had duplicated these defences, in order to find a way to defeat them. The first heavy equipment that would come ashore in Normandy would be the bulldozers.

'Well, I think that concludes everything,' General Eisenhower said to the meeting. 'I'd like to thank you all for your outstanding work so far. I believe we have every chance of succeeding. Our double agents are working tirelessly to persuade the Germans that our real assault will be made on the Pas de Calais. As far as I can see we are poised to take the Germans by surprise when we land in Normandy. My only worry is your unpredictable British weather. Pray for sunshine, gentlemen. God bless you all…'

The offices at St James's were to be closed within hours – or at least, left with just a skeleton staff. As Imogen hurried back to her office to type up her notes, she took one last look at the map room. This small office was covered from floor to ceiling with postcards, Michelin guides and maps of the French coast. In addition to the professional reconnaissance photographs, an appeal had been made asking members of the public to send in any information they had about the Normandy coast that might help with planning the invasion. Imogen had helped to arrange the display, and had enjoyed studying the postcards and photographs. Having never gone abroad herself, she was fascinated by the pictures of seaside villages along the French coast with romantic sounding names – Le Havre, Cherbourg and St Malo. Taken before the war, they showed holidaymakers enjoying fine weather. There was one particular postcard that she loved – of the harbour town of Le Havre – nestling around the edge of a beach. Adapted, she thought, from an original black and white photograph taken in Edwardian times, it had since been colourised and the sea was a vivid shade of turquoise. On the yellow ochre sandy beach were children in smock dresses playing with their mothers, men dressed in navy blazers and white boaters, ladies in bathing dresses tentatively dipping their toes into the water. Imogen often fantasised about what it would be like to dip her own toes into that water – so different from the chilly, grey North Sea she had known as a child. The display was soon to be taken down. It seemed such a waste, Imogen thought, so she slipped the postcard, slightly guiltily, into her pocket and closed the door.

Arriving back at her office she found the Chief Petty Officer waiting for her.

'As soon as you've typed up your notes and distributed them, you need to pack up the office. Get everything into boxes – files, maps – everything. You'll find boxes down in the basement. It's all coming with us, and we're leaving first thing tomorrow.'

'Tomorrow, ma'am?' Imogen asked.

'Yes, tomorrow… well don't just stand there. Get organised. And you'll need to clear out of your digs tonight as well.'

'Yes ma'am,' said Imogen, suddenly panicking at the prospect of how much she had to do.

'Present yourself here tomorrow morning… at 0700 hours.'

'Yes ma'am,' Imogen said. 'But where are we going – if I might ask?'

'Portsmouth – where else, you silly girl?'

Imogen spent the rest of the day parcelling up all the files and documents she and the Admiral had gathered over the previous few months. Late in the afternoon, he poked his nose into the office.

'Ah good,' he said, 'I'm glad you're here.'

'Yes, sir. Is there anything I can do for you?'

'No… carry on. I'm just sorry I won't be around to help you. I've got rather a lot of meetings to attend today.'

'Of course sir.'

'And I also wanted to say thank you, for all you've done.'

'It was my pleasure, sir,' said Imogen, glowing with pride. 'A real pleasure.'

'Good, well carry on – and I'll see you down in Portsmouth.'

That evening, back in Belsize Park she found a letter waiting for her from her mother. She had a pang of guilt that she hadn't written home for several weeks. As she ran upstairs to her room, she ripped it open, skimming it for news. Her father was well, but troubled, as usual, by his indigestion. There had been some bombing down by the docks. Her eyes flicked to the final paragraph.

Marjorie told me yesterday that Freddie is doing well, but she's very worried about him. He's flying operations over Germany. Something quite secret I gather. The planes are called 'Flying Fortresses'. They sound rather romantic don't they? I was surprised there was no message for you, but I suspect he has a lot on his mind.

I hope work is going well – do take care of yourself darling, and please write soon?

Much love,

Ma

Imogen leant against the door of her room, musing on this latest piece of information. Freddie hadn't even asked after her. It seemed he had finally forgotten all about her. Well, she thought, slipping the letter into her gas mask box, that was fine, she had a boyfriend now – a charming American who adored her, who couldn't do enough for her. And sometimes in life you just had to accept that what you had once hoped for, was not to be. What did her mother always say? When one door closes, another door opens. Perhaps Ben was that door.

She found Joy surrounded by a sea of clutter.

'I don't know where to start,' said Joy. 'I can't believe we've acquired so much stuff.'

'I know,' said Imogen. 'We just have to be organised. I'll clear the dressing table and you start folding all the clothes. We'll get it done.'

'I don't know why it all has to be done in such a rush. Another day wouldn't hurt, surely?' said Joy. 'Although I'll be glad to get out of this place. It's just rather bad timing – I had a date tonight.'

'Who with?' asked Imogen, as she put her toiletries into a washbag.

'Werner.'

'Werner?' said Imogen. 'That German man we met in the pub? I thought it was Karl you had your sights set on.'

'I did, originally,' said Joy. 'But Karl's so serious – charming and clever, certainly, but with very little sense of humour. But there's something about Werner. He's very funny, and quite brilliant. I think he'll make a marvellous husband.'

'But Joy – have you actually been out with him?'

'Yes. Several times.'

'You've kept that quiet,' said Imogen.

'You're not the only one with a boyfriend, you know. Besides, you've been rather preoccupied lately.'

'Oh Joy,' said Imogen, sitting down on the bed amongst the muddle of clothes. 'I'm sorry. I have been preoccupied – you're right. But seriously Joy, are you sure about this. Isn't Werner a communist?'

'Yes, sort of. He certainly has very firm views about trade unions for example. But I think he's right. Workers ought to be protected.'

'But marrying him? I mean isn't it all rather sudden?'

'War has a funny effect on people,' said Joy, defensively. 'But I have a good feeling about him. He's the marrying kind.'

'And does he feel the same way?'

'I don't know,' said Joy, grinning. 'I think I ought to ask him, don't you?'

'Well I admire your pluck.'

'And what about you?' asked Joy, folding her nightclothes into her suitcase. 'How's your American?'

'He's well. At least I think so. We've not managed to see each other that much recently. He had to go away for while – he's got something big going on.'

'Well you must try to see him tonight,' protested Joy. 'You don't know when you'll be back in London.'

'You're right,' said Imogen. 'I don't even know if he's back, but I'll give him a call as soon as I've finished packing.'

There was a queue for the public phone in the hall of the lodging house, but Imogen eventually got through to Brown's Hotel.

'Could I speak to Lieutenant Anderson, please?'

There was a pause before his voice came on the line.

'Ginny? How lovely to hear from you. I only just got back today. Is everything all right, darling – where are you?'

'I'm at my lodgings… but I wanted to tell you something; we're shipping out tomorrow.'

'So soon?'

'Yes, it's all been a bit of a rush. We were only told this morning.'

'Where to?' he asked.

'Well I suppose you'll all find out soon enough.' She checked none of the other lodgers were listening. 'Portsmouth,' she whispered.

'Ah,' he said, 'the big push.'

'Exactly. I've just packed up the office and all my things here and we're meeting at seven tomorrow morning. I'm so sorry, Ben. I don't know when we'll be back.'

'Can I see you before you go?'

'I don't have much time.'

'Could you come here? I have a late meeting in my office in Mayfair that I can't get out of, but I could meet you back at the hotel in an hour or so.'

'Or you could come here?'

'It would be better here,' he said gently. 'It's quiet – we could be alone.'

Like many girls of her age and class, Imogen was still a virgin. This was not an especially moral decision, in spite of the fact that her mother had impressed upon her that she should 'save herself' for her future husband. Rather, it was a practical problem – it was the fear of getting pregnant that had always held her back from making any kind of physical commitment to a boyfriend. She felt anxious as she entered the swing doors of Brown's Hotel – fearing the night manager might assume she was a 'lady of the night' by simply asking for Lieutenant Anderson at the reception desk.

'I'll just ring up now, Madam,' the manager said, looking at her askance.

She needn't have worried. Instead of inviting her to his room, Ben met her in the lobby and insisted they went to the bar. She felt so relieved that she wanted to kiss him on the spot.

In spite of the late spring weather, a coal fire had been lit in the bar. They sat on either side, nursing their drinks.

'Are you looking forward to going?' he asked.

'I don't know. I've never been to Portsmouth. Heaven knows what I'll be doing. But I suppose it will be exciting.'

'They haven't told you what your duties will be?'

'No… nothing. I'm utterly in the dark.'

'I'm heading off too.'

'Back to America?'

'No, no… to Europe.'

'To France?' she asked.

'Maybe… all over, really.'

'We might never see each other again,' she said, reaching over and taking his hand. She had a momentary frisson of anxiety at the thought that this relationship could be plucked away from her – just as she had come to terms with it.

'Don't be so dramatic,' he laughed. 'Of course we'll see each other again. I know where you'll be, remember? With General Eisenhower; you shouldn't be hard to find.' He picked up her hand and kissed it.

'You do say the most romantic things,' she said.

'Not to everyone – just to you.'

'Ben,' she began. 'I really do have to go soon. I'm so sorry…'

'I know sweetheart,' he spoke softly, linking her hand with his, their fingers intertwined. 'Before you do, I want to say something.'

'Go on,' she said.

'I've never met anyone like you before. I didn't know girls like you existed.'

'Don't be silly,' she blushed.

'No, I don't think you understand how special you are. You're beautiful – that's clear for anyone to see. But you're also smart, funny, brave… you're everything a man could want.'

Freddie slipped uninvited into her thoughts, but she pushed him away just as Ben reached over and kissed her cheek.

'You must know that the one thing I'm burning to do right now is make love to you, don't you?' he whispered.

She blushed, partly with embarrassment, but she was also aware of another sensation – her body aching with desire for him.

'But we're both going away tomorrow,' he said, leaning back in his chair, 'and I want to do what's right – for both of us. Most importantly, I don't want to break your heart.'

'That seems to be the story of my life,' Imogen said. 'Men leaving me, in order to protect me.'

'I'm not leaving you. You're leaving me!'

She laughed.

'No, what I'm saying is this,' he continued. 'Maybe we should get through the next few months. And when we meet again, hopefully it'll all be over, and then we can be together properly – forever.'

'What are you trying to say, exactly?' she asked.

'Well… I've been thinking about it for a while. You know I told you my dad was in the diplomatic service?'

'Yes, I remember,' said Imogen.

'Well I asked him to send something over to me… in the diplomatic bag.'

'How thrilling.'

'I have it here in my pocket. I'd like to give it to you tonight.'

He slipped his hand into his jacket pocket and brought out a small jewellery box.

'Ginny, darling – if we both make it, I can't think of anyone I'd rather be with for the rest of my life than you.' He opened the box. Nestling against a purple velvet cushion was a diamond ring set with dark blue enamel.

'It was my grandmother's,' he explained. 'It's Napoleonic, I think. Does it fit?'

She looked up at him, bemused.

'You're asking me to marry you?'

'I am… will you?'

'I don't know,' said Imogen, slightly flustered. 'It seems so sudden – I don't really know what to say…'

He slipped the ring onto her finger. 'Say yes, darling.' He adjusted the ring, which was clearly too large for her.

'We can get it made smaller,' he said hurriedly.

'Yes, of course,' she said, staring at the ring. 'Ben, are you sure about this?'

'Never surer of anything in my life.'

'But I'm leaving London in eight hours' time,' she said, checking her watch. 'The tubes will stop soon, and I still have to finish my packing, and get to the office by seven.'

'So go,' he said. 'But first… tell me you'll marry me?'

'Yes,' she said, uncertainly. 'I suppose so… yes, of course. I'd love to marry you.'

'We'll have a wonderful life together – I promise. We can live anywhere you want.'

'Can we?' she said, already standing up, picking up her gas mask. He put his arms around her.

'I wish you didn't have to go.'

'I know. I feel the same. It seems all wrong – to be leaving now.'

He kissed her.

'I suppose… I could come upstairs – if you want?' Her heart was racing, she felt anxious, but brave at the same time.

'Do *you* want to?' he said.

'Very much.'

The next morning when she woke it was still dark. She peered anxiously at her watch on the bedside table. It was ten to five. She sank back onto the pillows and gazed at Ben lying so peacefully, sleeping beside her… studying the way his chest rose and fell with his breath, the way his dark hair fell over his eyes. He lay with his hand thrown out across the bed, looking so relaxed and beautiful. She went into the bathroom, taking her clothes with her. She washed cursorily, swilling her mouth with water and dressed hurriedly in the half-light, worried that she was going to be late. She found a writing pad on the desk and scribbled a note to him.

Sorry I had to leave. Didn't like to wake you. I love you…
Ginny XXX

She stood, briefly, in the doorway and looked back at him, before shutting the door, and walking briskly down the corridor. She was relieved to find the reception desk deserted and pushed out through the revolving doors onto Albemarle Street, shielding her eyes against the sharp early morning light. She ran to the tube station, praying there would be no delays to the trains. The platform was deserted and she was grateful for that; she wanted to be alone with her thoughts. She felt a tinge of guilt about spending the night with Ben. But she pushed it aside. This was wartime, after all, and they were engaged. There was nothing wrong, surely, with showing the man you loved how you felt?

Her train came in and she sat down, choosing a corner seat, hugging herself, blushing slightly at the memory of their lovemaking.

It had been tender and affectionate, but both of them had been tired, and a little nervous. She was embarrassed at her ignorance. He had found it touching – to be the 'first'. He had covered her face in kisses and she had truly felt, in that moment, that he was the most wonderful man in the world. But their happiness at finally being together, was inevitably tinged with sadness. He had gazed into her eyes long after they had finished making love, 'drinking her in', he'd said.

'I'm going to imprint every part of your face and body onto my mind to feed on while we're apart.'

It had been such a romantic thing to say, she had been swept away by the emotion of it all. But now sitting on the tube heading for Belsize Park, she looked down at the ring he had given her, and wondered what she was doing. The ring was beautiful certainly, but they hardly knew one another. He was exciting, glamorous, handsome and fun to be with. But he was also secretive and mysterious. She hardly knew him.

She was jolted out of her thoughts by the guard announcing her station.

'Chalk Farm… Chalk Farm.'

She leapt off the tube and ran back to the house in Belsize Park, arriving breathless at her bedroom door. Joy was sitting at the dressing table, brushing her hair.

'Good morning to you too, stranger,' she said, turning around. 'Imogen Mitchell… You naughty, naughty girl…'

'Oh shut up, Joy. Spare me the lectures, please. Just let me pack…'

Sitting with all the other Wrens in the back of lorry heading for Portsmouth later that morning, Joy whispered to her friend.

'Tell me all about it then. Was it marvellous?'

Imogen showed her the ring.

'My God… engaged! Oh Ginny, how exciting!'

'I know,' whispered Imogen. 'It seems mad, really. I hardly know him.'

'Well, after last night, I imagine you know him pretty well.'
Joy giggled.

'I don't know what came over me.'

'I do,' said Joy. 'He asked you to marry him, he gave you a
gorgeous ring, you might not see him for months, so you did what
any one of us would do.'

'So you're not too shocked.'

'Darling, of course I'm not. But I'm a bit worried – you don't
seem very happy.'

'Oh I am,' said Imogen. 'It's just… it's been a bit quick, you
know? How was your evening, anyway? Is Werner the man for you?'

'Oh yes I'm sure he is. Werner is divine. But he's off to Europe
too, any minute now. Some secret op.'

'And will you see him again?' asked Imogen.

'I fully intend to,' said Joy.

'Well I hope you do,' said Imogen. 'It seems we're all heading
somewhere, and who knows where we'll all end up?'

'I know,' said Joy. 'Isn't it exciting!'

As the naval transport meandered its way up the long drive to
Southwick House, the Wrens peered out of the bus's windows,
craning their necks to get a better view of their final destination.

'Gosh,' said Joy. 'It's pretty glamorous.'

'Isn't it?' said Imogen, admiring the extensive grounds as they
swept up the drive. Well-stocked flower beds edged the well-
trimmed lawns. On the perimeter towering rhododendrons jostled
for space next to a pair of arching copper beeches.

'Goodness,' said Joy, as the bus pulled up in front of the elegant
white Georgian house. 'I think we've rather landed on our feet here.'

Filing out of the bus onto the gravel drive, they were met by
a senior Wren.

'Right… follow me,' she said, leading them away from the elegant house and gardens towards a row of wooden Nissen huts in the grounds. She reeled off the names of the first hut's inhabitants.

'Andrews, Aspel, Carr, Davies, Edwards, Hutchinson, McIntyre, Mitchell, Peabody, Proctor…'

The girls stepped forward as their names were called, Joy and Imogen amongst them.

'Dump your bags,' the officer told them, 'and then meet me in front of the house. You've got ten minutes!'

Imogen and Joy, relieved to be billeted in the same hut, grabbed two bunks next to each other.

'The beds aren't too bad,' said Joy, bouncing on hers.

'And at least it's not too cold,' said Imogen. 'But there is a rather a strong smell of newly sawn wood.'

'Yes,' said Joy, giggling. 'It smells like the inside of my dad's shed.'

'Well, come on,' said Imogen. 'Let's put our things away quickly, and then we'd better get back to the house and find out what we're going to be doing.'

As she put her washbag into the bedside cabinet, she removed her engagement ring and placed it on the shelf.

'What are you doing?' asked Joy.

'It's too big for me,' said Imogen. 'I'm bound to lose it.'

'Well don't leave it there,' whispered Joy, looking around. 'You might not find it's there when you come back.'

'Oh surely no one would…' Imogen said.

'Well you never know,' Joy insisted.

'I'll wear it on a chain round my neck, then,' said Imogen.

'It seems rather a shame,' said Joy. 'No one will know you're engaged.'

'That's true,' said Imogen, realising that was precisely what she wanted.

*

'One or two ground rules,' the officer said when the girls were all gathered together in front of the main house. 'This is a top secret location. You are not to leave the grounds under any circumstances, unless travelling in a naval bus. Is that clear? Anyone found breaking these rules will be up on a charge.'

'Yes ma'am,' they chorused.

'Right – assignments.'

As Joy and Imogen waited for their names to be called, the front door of the grand country house opened and two familiar figures emerged, deep in conversation. They stood chatting together on the large stuccoed front porch – one smoking a cigarette, the other a cigar.

'Look,' whispered Imogen to Joy. 'It's Churchill… and Eisen-hower!'

'I say,' said Joy, 'how thrilling.'

'No talking in the ranks,' said the officer, peering over her clipboard.

'Right – Wren Carr.'

'Yes ma'am,' said Joy.

'You're to report to the main house – the admin block is in there. They'll show you where to go.'

Joy raised her eyebrows at Imogen, gripping her hand, and whispered excitedly. 'See you later. I'm off to chat with Winnie and Dwight!'

'Wren Mitchell.'

'Yes ma'am.'

'You're to report to Fort Southwick immediately. Admiral Spalding wants to see you.' She looked at Imogen over her glasses, as if disapproving of this apparently 'special' treatment.

'Fort Southwick, ma'am?' asked Imogen, a little confused.

'It's about ten minutes' drive away – there'll be a bus along in a minute. Wait here.'

*

The fort stood on a windy hillside overlooking the bay of Portsmouth. As Imogen stepped out of the bus she took in the vast seascape. Seagulls screeched overhead and floated on the thermals towards the grey sea merging on the horizon with the grey-blue sky above. Weak summer sunlight glinted on the water, and laid out beneath them was an array of naval ships all painted in a matching shade of battleship-grey. The fort itself was a red brick construction complete with fortifications and battlements. Built in the early part of the nineteenth century, along with four other forts ranged along the coast, it had been designed to protect the city. Now it had been secretly converted into the operational headquarters for the invasion plan.

A Wren officer came over to meet her.

'Wren Mitchell?'

'Yes ma'am.'

'Welcome to the Citadel. I'll take you to the Admiral now.'

She opened a pair of metal double doors and led the way down a steep spiral staircase.

'It's a long way down,' she said to Imogen, over her shoulder. 'One hundred feet down to be precise. It's all going to feel rather strange at first, but you'll get used to it. And the good news is – it's completely impenetrable. They could drop a bomb on it, and we'd all survive.'

'That's rather comforting,' Imogen said, trotting behind, as the officer led her along a long, gloomy corridor, lit only by infrequent single lightbulbs.

'This is one of the two "freeways",' the officer said, indicating a corridor that disappeared into the distance. 'In total, there are thousands of yards of intersecting corridors, but if you get lost, work your way back to one of the freeways – they lead from the front to the back of the building, so you should be able to navigate your way from there.'

Imogen stared down the freeway as it disappeared into the gloom.

'Over seven hundred people work down here,' the officer continued, as they passed numerous office doors – all firmly closed. 'Everyone's doing something vital and top secret. The idea is that no one knows what anyone else is doing, so no one can give the game away. You won't be allowed to discuss your work, and no one else will discuss theirs with you – that's how we manage to keep a lid on things. So,' she said, stopping outside an innocuous-looking wooden internal door. 'The Admiral's in here…'

The Admiral was sitting behind a small oak desk in a cramped windowless room. Box files that Imogen recognised from their offices in St James's were piled from floor to ceiling. He leapt up, when she came in.

'Ah! Wren Mitchell, do sit down.'

'Thank you, sir.'

'Got here all right, then?'

'Oh yes, sir.'

'Good. Now, I wanted to explain something to you. You've been a great aid to me, but I know you've missed your plotting.'

'Oh no sir, not at all,' Imogen said, embarrassed. 'I've been more than happy to do whatever's needed.'

'Good – because what's needed now is an excellent plotter, but more than that, we need someone with a fine brain, attention to detail, and an ability to work fast under pressure, and keep quiet about it.' He looked across at her and winked. 'Think you can manage?'

'I think so, sir.'

'Good, then let's get over there. The ops room is just next door.'

Imogen's first impression of the underground operations room was that it was dark and stuffy – not unlike the plotting rooms she had worked in before. But whereas the plot room in Newcastle had been filled with other Wrens, all wearing headphones listening for signals on which to base the movement of shipping, here there was an air of studied concentration on the faces of the dozen or so men who sat, or stood around a large central table. A bank of signal operators sat along one edge of the room.

'Gentlemen, can I interrupt for a moment? I'd like to introduce Wren Mitchell. She's been working with me on the plans for the invasion and I have every faith in her.'

The men glanced up momentarily. One or two smiled; most simply nodded before resuming their work.

'They're a good bunch really,' the Admiral whispered, showing Imogen to one corner of the table.

'This is your perch. You'll be working for the Senior Staff Officer – Commander Pierce.'

The Commander looked up at Imogen and smiled. 'Welcome,' he said, politely standing up. 'I hope you have a love of hard work.'

'Oh yes,' said Imogen cheerfully.

'Well, your place is here, behind me,' the Commander said. 'I'll hand you the signals, and then you need to plot everything on a chart. We're quite cramped down here, as you can see. You'll have to share some of the table with the Staff Navigating Officer.'

The SNO, an unsmiling man, peered suspiciously up at Imogen. 'I trust you'll take no more space than is necessary,' he said.

'I'll certainly do my best, sir,' said Imogen.

'Well sit down, Wren Mitchell,' said Commander Pierce. 'We'd better go through what needs doing.'

'Good luck,' said Admiral Spalding, squeezing her shoulder. 'I know you won't let us down.'

Chapter Twenty-Five

Färsehof Farm
May 1944

Magda woke early as the morning sun streamed through her bedroom window. Feeling queasy she lay quietly, clutching her stomach, hoping it would subside. But experience had taught her that she would only feel better if she was actually sick. She staggered out of bed and threw up into the china basin in her room. She rinsed her mouth with fresh water from the jug and lay back down, covering herself with the feather quilt.

It was six weeks since Michael had left. Six weeks since Otto had taken her against her will, in the kitchen. From the beginning she was determined to put what had happened with Otto out of her mind. What he had done was appalling, and yet it felt inevitable – the culmination of something that had been building up since they were young teenagers. She couldn't forgive him for what he'd done; in fact, she despised him for it. And there were times – in the middle of the night, or when she was walking the herd into the barn for milking – when she had flashes of disturbing memories – how he had held her by the wrists, how he had forced his way, painfully, inside her. She did her best to smother these memories, preferring to think about Michael, about the happy times they had had together, and more importantly, whether he had got safely back to England.

*

When Otto had left, on that fateful day, she had had sunk down onto the floor and wept. But minutes later, hearing Helga clip-clopping back into the yard, she had hurriedly dried her eyes, and stood at the kitchen window, watching as Otto stopped to chat with Pieter. The young man made some sort of joke, jerking back his large blond head as he laughed. He shook her father's hand – like any polite young man who had been visiting his girlfriend. Her father, cautious and watchful, nodded politely. Her instinct had been to run into the yard and tell her father what Otto had done – to beg him to avenge her. But more important than punishing Otto, was helping Michael, who was out there somewhere on the farm.

So she wiped her eyes and when she was sure Otto had finally left, ran upstairs and collected a few things for Michael. She went first to Karl's room and took the rucksack he had used for their camping trips and stuffed it with a jumper and some socks from his chest of drawers. Up in the attic she found Michael's compass and his silk scarf map. She collected his flying boots and put them into the bag too. She considered bringing his flying jacket, but it was too recognisable as RAF. Back down in the kitchen she wrapped some bread and cheese in a napkin. Slinging the pack over her shoulder she walked through the yard. Her father didn't notice her; he was preoccupied as always, chatting to Helga, settling her, removing her bridle. Searching for Michael, she went into the dairy, and gently called his name.

'Michael… Michael are you here?'

She heard a shuffling sound from behind a bale of straw and he peered over the top.

'Magda – thank God. Who was that man? He looked like SS. Is everything all right?'

'Yes,' she said bravely. 'Just a man I know. He came to visit me. I'm so sorry.' It was pointless telling Michael what Otto had done. What, after all, could he do about it?

'I saw him coming up the path and I just knew I had to make a run for it.'

'Thank God you did. He heard a noise coming from the garden and went out to investigate. I was so worried. I managed to persuade him to come back inside, and then I saw you from the kitchen window running across the yard. I thought you'd left for good.'

She began to sob and Michael came over and put his arms around her, kissing the top of her head.

'I'd intended to. But I got as far as the lane, and realised I couldn't leave without saying goodbye.'

She smiled up at him. 'Why don't you come back inside? You don't have to leave now.'

'Magda,' he said, 'you know that would be madness. That man might come back. Besides it's time… I have to go. We can't put it off any longer.'

'I know,' she said, gently, handing him the rucksack. 'I've brought you some things.'

'Of course you did – you wonderful girl.'

'Inside is your compass and your map. Also some food and your boots. You won't get far in those,' she indicated her father's old boots – two sizes too large for the young man. 'But I worry someone might recognise your own boots as RAF.'

'Not if I put the trousers outside. At least they fit me. Thank you, Magda.'

He sank down onto the hay and changed his boots.

'I've got some money for you too – it's everything I've got.' She handed him some folded notes. 'It's not much, but it's enough for a train ticket, at least part of the way. But you must be careful; you have no papers. You can't afford to be stopped.'

'I know. Darling Magda… thank you. I will repay you, I promise.'

'Just come back – that's all I want.'

He folded her in his arms, kissing her cheeks, her forehead, her lips.

'Magda!' Her father was outside in the yard, calling her.

'I must go,' she said.

'I should thank him,' Michael said.

'No – don't. He'll understand. You're right about Otto; he might come back any time – it's exactly the kind of thing he does. Then he would find you chatting to my father in the yard. So… just go. I'll explain everything to my parents. Go out of the back of the dairy – cross the field over there, and then over into the woods on the other side of the road. There's a stream at the bottom. Follow it – it takes you past the village and on, westwards.'

'I understand. You'll thank your parents for me?'

'Of course.'

He clung to her, kissing her one more time. 'I love you, Magda.'

'And I love you… now go.'

She watched him through a crack in the barn wall as he hobbled across field, hiding behind the hedge to make sure no one was coming, before crossing the road and running off into the woods.

'Well thank God for that,' Käthe said when she came back from the market and heard Michael had left. 'I thought he'd never go.'

'He was a good boy,' said Pieter.

Magda smiled at her father. 'You liked him?'

'Of course. He seemed straightforward, honest, kind…'

'I just hope he makes it…' Magda said, anxiously staring out of the kitchen window. Her mother glanced at her father.

'Well…' she said to Magda, 'he's not your problem any more. You did what you could – we all did, but it's time to put ourselves first and think of the farm.'

Over the following weeks, Magda threw herself into her work – up at dawn with the herd, and falling into bed again, exhausted, soon after dusk. Her mother noticed how tired she seemed, but it was only when she heard Magda vomiting one morning, that she finally confronted her.

'*Liebling*,' Käthe said over breakfast. 'I heard you being sick again this morning. That's the second time this week.'

'Yes,' said Magda, sipping a cup of black tea. 'I must have eaten something.'

Her mother nodded. 'Maybe…'

When Magda came in after the morning milking, her mother was alone in the kitchen, skinning a rabbit.

'Oh Mutti, could you do that later? It makes me feel so sick.'

'Well, don't watch,' her mother said harshly.

'Mutti!' said Magda. 'Don't be so mean.'

Her mother rounded on her.

'Magda Maier… do you have something to tell me – about you and that airman?'

'No! I don't know what you mean.'

'Do you deny you had feelings for him?'

'No!' Magda's eyes filled with tears. 'I don't deny it. I loved him.'

'Loved him! An enemy airman we took in and gave sanctuary to. And now look at you – a fallen woman, living in my house.'

'What are you talking about?' said Magda impatiently, pulling a chair out from the kitchen table and sitting down.

'Well,' her mother said, wiping her bloodstained hands on a cloth. 'I would have thought it was obvious! Do you deny you are pregnant?'

Magda looked up at her mother in amazement.

'The thought of you and that man…' said Käthe, pacing the room, '… having sex under our roof. He treated you like a cheap tart, and you were only trying to help him. I hate him!' Käthe picked up her meat cleaver and chopped the head off the rabbit with one violent stroke.

Magda trembled while her mother ranted.

'You think I'm pregnant?'

'Yes!' Käthe said, turning round and jabbing the knife in the direction of her daughter. 'Why else are you being sick each morning? Are your breasts tender... did you have your period last month?'

Magda began to cry. She sobbed... her head in her hands. 'Oh no – do you really think so?'

He mother raised her eyes to heaven.

'I can't be... surely not.'

'You silly, silly girl.' Käthe turned her back and began to wash her hands.

'Oh, Mutti I can't be. We were careful.'

Her mother swung round, her face white with fury. 'So you admit it?'

'We love each other, Mutti.'

'Oh do you? He loves so much he leaves you high and dry – pregnant with his child. I don't call that love. I call that desertion.'

Magda sobbed at the kitchen table while her mother jointed the rabbit.

'It might not be his,' Magda said finally.

'What are you saying? How many men have you been with? What kind of whore are you?'

'Mutti, Mutti... please – you don't understand,' Magda said between gasps of crying. 'Something happened, the day Michael left.'

'What?' her mother asked.

'Somebody came here, while you were both out. '

'Who?'

'Otto.'

'Otto?' Her mother put down the knife, and sat down opposite her daughter. 'What happened, Magda? Did Otto find him? Is that why Michael left?'

'No... he didn't find him. But I was with Michael in the garden.'

'You took him outside... after all we agreed?'

'I know, I know. It was stupid, but it was a lovely day and he needed some sunshine – he was so pale. We sat outside in the vegetable garden. I went indoors to get some lunch and Otto arrived out of the blue.'

'Magda! If he'd found him, he would have had us all arrested.'

'I realise that. But Michael must have seen Otto dressed in his SS uniform.'

'The SS!' said Käthe. 'He's in the SS now? Oh my God, Magda.'

'So I kept Otto inside, and Michael got away, thank God. But Otto, you know what he's like, always suspicious, he thought he'd heard something in the garden and insisted on going outside. Michael had escaped to the barn by then, but I had to distract Otto, to stop him from searching everywhere – to give Michael a chance to get away.'

Magda began to pace the room, weeping piteously.

'What are you saying? What are you telling me?' Käthe walked over to her daughter, her arms outstretched. 'Come, *Liebling…* come to me. What is it? What happened?' She pulled her daughter to her and held her head against her breast, stroking her hair. 'Magda, Magda,' she murmured. 'Tell me, *Liebling.*'

'Otto – he made me… he forced himself on me, Mutti.'

Magda spent the rest of the afternoon in her room, sobbing helplessly into her pillow – her heart broken by the loss of Michael and the certain knowledge that her mother was right: she was pregnant and alone. She had destroyed her life – her chances of going to university, of breaking free of the farm. It had all been wiped out by the existence of this child growing inside her.

'*Liebling…*' it was her mother, knocking on the door. 'Can I come in?'

'No!' Magda cried. 'No… leave me alone. I don't deserve your sympathy. I'm a fool – an idiot. What was I thinking?'

'Magda…' her mother said gently, through the door. 'I under-stand – I do. You loved this young man – I see that now. But if it was Otto who did this to you… your father will kill him.'

'No…' Magda cried, rushing to the door and opening it – her hair wild, her face stinging with salty tears. 'Mutti… I beg you. Don't tell Papa – please.'

'Magda,' Käthe said, holding her daughter's hands, 'we can't keep it from him – he will notice soon enough…'

Later that evening, as she lay on her bed listening to her father sweeping the yard, hearing the door to the kitchen slamming shut and the muted voices of her parents deep in conversation, Magda dragged herself from her bed. She felt exhausted, her eyes red and raw from crying. She splashed water on her face, and brushed her hair. She would go downstairs, and explain everything to her father. He loved her, she knew that. He would understand, and she would get through this – somehow.

Coming quietly downstairs she stood listening at the kitchen door.

'I don't know which one I hate more…' Pieter was saying, his voice uncharacteristically harsh and so unlike her own dear, gentle father.

'I know,' her mother said gently. 'But at least she loved Michael – whereas Otto, he's always been a bad lot, an evil boy. She swears she and the English boy were careful. But Otto… he had no thought for her. They say he got Erika pregnant and then deserted her, did you know that?'

'That bastard,' Pieter said. 'I'll kill him. I'll kill him.'

Magda listened as he stamped across the room. She heard the jangle of keys as he unlocked something.

'Pieter…' her mother was saying. 'Please calm yourself – put the gun down. Otto's not even in the village any more. He went back to the front the next day. What are you going to do – travel hundreds of miles to hunt him down?'

Magda pushed open the kitchen door, just as her father sank down onto his chair, the shotgun laid across his lap.

'Little Magda – my little girl,' he sobbed. 'We weren't here… we let her down, Käthe. What shall we do?'

'Mutti… Papa…' she stood in the doorway – a ghostly figure, her blonde hair a halo of gold above her pale face. She knelt down by her father and lifted the gun carefully from his lap, placing it on the floor. 'There's nothing you can do, Papa. If I'm pregnant then I shall have a child. And yes, it's true – I don't know who the father is. If it's the child of one, then I will be happy. If it's the child of the other, I don't know what I will do… but either way, it's not the child's fault, is it?'

'Oh Magda,' her mother began.

'No, Mutti, it's all right. I've had all afternoon to think about it. And I'm not going to feel sorry for myself any more. Terrible things happen in war. People are killed and maimed, whole families are destroyed. Right now, cities are being bombed, thousands and thousands of people are homeless, whole communities have been imprisoned, and worse. But we are safe, at least for now, on the farm. We have food, water, and a roof over our heads. And all that's changed is that I'm expecting a baby, just like millions of other women. We must just go on, and one day – Mutti, Papa – one day this will all make sense, I promise.'

She hugged her father to her, as he sobbed into her shoulder like a child being comforted by his parent.

Chapter Twenty-Six

Fort Southwick, Portsmouth
June 1944

Imogen's initial disappointment that she wasn't working in the main plotting room with other Wrens, was soon replaced by a real enthusiasm for her new job. As the only Wren amongst a group of high-powered naval officers, she felt a little lonely at times. With no other girls to chat to, she was certainly isolated, but at lunchtime she had a chance to meet other Wrens in the cramped underground NAAFI canteen. And the Commander was a hard-working man whom she came to admire and respect. He rarely left his post and was unfailingly polite. She soon got to grips with her role – keeping a chart of the movements of every single vessel that formed the invasion fleet.

One afternoon, she returned from her lunch break to find the Commander waiting patiently at her station. Standing next to him was the Prime Minister, Winston Churchill.

'Ah, Wren Mitchell, I wonder if you could show us your chart, please?'

Her hands trembling, she laid out her chart, revealing a complete breakdown of every ship, landing craft, motor torpedo boat and minesweeping vessel in the invasion fleet. The great man, puffing on his cigar, leant over the table with the Commander and together they studied the chart. Imogen stood anxiously to one side, hardly daring to breathe, terrified the Commander might spot an error. But he smiled up at her and winked.

'Excellent,' he said.

Imogen exhaled audibly. 'Thank you, sir.'

She felt a combination of relief and pride that the Prime Minister had taken the trouble to come down into the bowels of the operations room and examine her work. After a few moments he too looked up at her.

'Very good,' he said. 'My daughter, Diana, she's in the Wrens… very well done.'

Imogen glowed. 'Thank you very much, sir.'

'Well, Prime Minister,' said the Commander, 'if you've seen enough?'

Churchill nodded, exhaled cigar smoke, and left.

That evening, as they lay in bed after lights out, Imogen felt compelled to say something to Joy about Churchill's visit.

'I had a visitor today,' she said coyly.

'Oh yes,' said Joy, who was reading a book by torchlight.

'The Prime Minister came down to see what we were doing.'

'Winnie! Really? He walked past our office earlier, but I didn't actually meet him. You are lucky – what was he like? Did he say anything, or shake your hand?'

'Not really. He said well done, which was nice, studied my work, blew cigar smoke in my face, and left.'

'Well, I think I'd take that as something of a compliment,' said Joy.

As the weeks went on, the strict instructions to stay in the grounds gradually eased. All the staff worked long hours, but on their rare afternoons off they were allowed to visit the pretty red brick village of Southwick for a game of tennis, or a much-needed walk.

Occasionally they travelled further afield to Southsea, catching one of the battered naval buses, nicknamed 'liberty boats'. If the weather was nice, they sunbathed on the beach, and on a rare evening off went to see Joe Loss and his orchestra on the pier. As Imogen listened to the band playing 'In the Mood', she was reminded of the evening she'd spent with Benjamin dancing at the Grosvenor House Hotel. She had a momentary surge of affection for him. Most of the time she was so immersed in her work that she hardly thought of him at all. But somehow, listening to the band, she recalled how he had put his arms around her, how beautiful he had made her feel. She missed him, she realised.

'Are you all right, old thing?' Joy whispered, noticing her friend sniffing slightly, and dabbing at her eyes.

'Yes,' said Imogen. 'I was just thinking about the last time I heard that song. I was at a dance with Benjamin.'

'You must miss Benjamin terribly,' Joy said, as they waited later that evening for their transport.

'I suppose I do,' said Imogen. 'To be honest, most of the time I'm working so hard I hardly have time to think. But this evening, listening to that band, brought it all back. Made him more real, if you know what I mean?'

'I think so,' said Joy uncertainly, as they climbed aboard the bus. 'Do you mean he doesn't feel real most of the time?'

'Yes… It's as if he was someone in a dream. It sounds mad I suppose, but meeting him and getting engaged, it was all such a whirlwind. I sometimes wonder if I made him up.'

'I've not heard from Werner since we left London,' said Joy. 'And I know I didn't make him up. We went out a few times; he was fun and I liked him a lot. But now I wonder if I'll ever see him again. And there was me thinking we might get married one day. I'm such an idiot.'

'Oh Joy,' said Imogen, squeezing her hand. 'Perhaps we just ought to put them both out of our minds. There are more important things to think about, after all.'

'You're right,' said Joy. 'Work has to be uppermost now. And from what I can see – at least from the messages I type – the big push is coming any day now.'

From the beginning of June the weather grew unseasonably grey and overcast. Joy and Imogen regularly woke to the sound of rain hammering against the Nissen hut windows.

'Not again,' said Imogen, as they climbed out of bed. 'I wonder how long this is due to go on?'

'Not only is it a bore,' said Joy, 'but it makes the whole operation a bit of a no-go, doesn't it?' She pulled on her shirt and stared gloomily out at the rain. 'I typed out some missive yesterday,' she whispered. 'They're waiting for another weather report from the Chief Met Officer.'

Down in the operations room Imogen could sense the tension. In the bowels of Fort Southwick they had no way of knowing what the weather was doing hour by hour, but everyone was keenly aware that the invasion's success depended on clear, dry conditions. The Commander was unusually short-tempered with Imogen, and at lunchtime she decided to avoid the underground canteen with its sense of claustrophobia and catch the bus back to the military canteen parked in the grounds of Southwick House. Queuing up for her tea and sandwich, she was relieved the weather had brightened up since that morning and some of the Wrens were playing a cricket match against the officers on the lawns of the house. As she watched the match, and sipped her tea, a large Rolls-Royce Phantom drew up in front of the house. Welcoming the car were Admiral Ramsay and General Montgomery standing on the front steps. Out of the Phantom climbed King George VI. The three men shook hands and disappeared inside the house.

'Looks like something's up,' said a rating standing next to her.

*

The following morning at 0415 hours, the decision was taken. The invasion would take place the next day – 6th June. The excitement on the base was palpable, and after breakfast, the Wrens combed the lawns of Southwick House for four-leaf clovers to give to their commanding officers.

'I've got one!' Joy shouted.

'Are you sure?' said Imogen, disappointed to have been beaten to the task by her friend.

'Yes, come and look.'

Imogen examined the tiny plant lying in Joy's palm. 'You're right! You've found one – a real four-leaf clover. Do you know I've never seen one before? I always thought they must be a myth. Well done, Joy. But do keep looking – I must get one for Commander Pierce.'

Imogen continuing scouring the grounds.

'I've got one!' she called out triumphantly.

'It's quite ridiculous,' she said to Joy as they walked towards the house, 'but the thought of not being able to give a four-leaf clover to Commander Pierce this morning seemed unbearable. As if the success of the landings had anything to do with such a daft superstition!'

'I know,' said Joy. 'But you've got one now. And he'll be pleased – you wait and see.'

In the Operations room, Imogen laid her four-leaf clover on the table in front of the Commander.

'What's this?' he said, looking up at her, rather grumpily.

'A four-leafed clover, sir. We've all collected them – all the Wrens. We wanted to give them to you this morning.'

'Well that's very thoughtful, Wren Mitchell, I must say. I don't like to think we need luck. After all, we have planning on our side. But this morning, I think I'll take all the luck's that's going.'

*

Standing on the roof of Fort Southwick as the vast fleet of ships and minesweepers sailed majestically out of the wide bay, Imogen felt a huge sense of elation and pride. The sea shimmered an opalescent grey-blue in the milky sunlight; overhead thousands of gliders were towed out over the Channel, like a vast flock of birds darkening the sky. Once in France the gliders would disgorge their cargo of paratroopers who would jump behind enemy lines, seize vital positions and, God willing, link up with the Allied forces landing on the beaches. It was a plan of such complexity, such daring and bravery that Imogen, watching with the other Wrens, had tears of pride in her eyes.

Back in the operations room the team worked tirelessly for the next twenty-four hours, as they plotted the progress of the invasion force. When they finally took a break, they all felt deflated and exhausted after the excitement and anxiety of the previous few months as the adrenalin gradually seeped away.

When Imogen finally lay down, fully clothed, on her bed she fell instantly asleep. She was woken by Joy rushing excitedly into the Nissen hut.

'Imogen, Imogen.' Joy threw herself onto her bunk, and shook her friend. 'Wake up! Oh do wake up, Imogen.'

Imogen stirred. 'What is it?' she mumbled.

'They're asking for volunteers to go to France!'

Imogen rolled over and studied her friend, sleepily.

'To France?' she said. 'They want *us* to go to France?'

'Yes!' said Joy. 'They've put a list up on the noticeboard in the entrance hall of the main house. It's filling up already – so do come on! Get up and let's get our names down.'

'Do you really want to go to France?' Imogen asked, dragging herself out of bed and trying to locate her shoes.

'Well I don't want to spend the rest of the war typing boring missives from one commander to the other. So yes, I do want to go, don't you?'

Imogen sat up straight and ran her fingers through her tousled hair. She felt a glimmer of excitement spreading through her body. 'Yes,' she said, 'I suppose I do. You're right – what else would we do?'

As neither girl was yet twenty-one, their parents' permission had to be sought. Imogen wrote an impassioned letter home to her mother.

Dearest Mummy and Daddy,

I do so hope you are both quite well. It seems an age since we last saw one another, and also since I wrote to you both. I'm sorry for such a long silence. It's been rather difficult of late to find the time to write. For the last two months I've been stationed down in Portsmouth – helping with the planning of something very important. I imagine you can guess what it was. I've been dying to tell you, but it's all been rather top secret; we weren't even allowed to tell anyone where we were based. Do you remember when I last wrote I had to give my address as Naval Party 1645, Base Fleet mail office, Reading? Well, my dears, that was a complete fib! I was actually living in a Nissen hut in the grounds of a beautiful house called Southwick on the outskirts of Portsmouth. We worked long hours and I felt, truly, that I was doing something important. I even met Mr Churchill and saw the King once or twice.

Now, before I come on to the purpose of my letter, how is my beloved Honey? Is she still behaving? Not getting too many treats I hope. She does so love your biscuits. And how is Edith? Is she well? And you and Daddy – how is Daddy's indigestion? I do hope you're not being too bothered by the war.

Mummy, I am writing to ask a huge favour. I've been asked if I'd like to go over to France as part of Admiral Ramsay's advance party. We're to help set up communications and so on for the senior staff. They will be writing to ask

*your permission. Please grant it? I beg you. I know you'll be
worried about me, but really – nothing can be as dangerous
as living in London during the bombing. I promise to try to
write again as soon as we get to Northern France.*

*Joy is hoping to come with me. If you speak to Mrs Carr
– do beg her to agree also. I'd so hate to go alone.*

All my love,

Imogen.

PS Have you heard how Freddie's getting on?

As she wrote the postscript, she realised she had still not told her
mother about Ben. Instead she had asked for news about Freddie.
In some way, her parents and Freddie were always linked, whereas
Ben seemed alien to the family. Either way, she thought, fingering
the ring that hung on a chain round her neck, it wouldn't be right
to break the news of her engagement in a letter.

Permission was quickly granted, and once they had been equipped
for their journey – kitted out with bell-bottom trousers, square-
necked tops, jerseys and fawn duffle coats - they were allowed a
short leave before they departed for France.

'What shall we do?' asked Joy as they collected their kit from
Portsmouth docks. 'Go to London? Or back home?'

Imogen felt conflicted. If they went to London there was a
chance she might see Ben. Perhaps if she saw him she could rekindle
what she had felt about him before she had left for Portsmouth. On
the other hand, if they went home, she would see her parents and
maybe she would hear news of Freddie. He might even be there.

'I don't know,' she said. 'I'd love to go home, obviously. But the
thought of going back into the war when one had been at home
with all that love and comfort and nice food – how could we do it?'

'Because it's our duty!' said Joy pragmatically. 'We've been chosen to go to France and we're lucky. Did you see all those others – the ones who didn't get chosen – all crying their eyes out when they realised their names weren't on the list, poor things. Oh Imogen! It will be so exciting. But we ought to go home and see the aged p's first, don't you think?'

'Don't you want to see Werner in London?' Imogen asked.

'I'd love to of course, but I'm not even sure he's there. He was planning a trip abroad when we left. Why don't we stop off in London and stay in a hotel just for one night? If Ben and Werner are around we can meet up, and then we can head off the next day for Newcastle. How does that sound?'

After the relative calm of Southwick House and its neighbouring villages, London seemed frantic and filthy. Imogen and Joy checked into a small hotel in King's Cross. The rooms were dingy and the beds uncomfortable, but it was cheap, and had the advantage of being next to the station and their early morning train to Newcastle. Once they had dumped their luggage, they went down to reception to call their respective boyfriends.

'I'm afraid the Lieutenant checked out several weeks ago,' said the receptionist at Brown's Hotel.

'Did he leave a forwarding address?' Imogen asked. 'I'm his fiancée you see, and I've been away myself.'

'No, I'm sorry.' The girl on the other end sounded sympathetic. 'I do have an office number for him though, if that would help?'

Imogen had never been to Ben's office, although she remembered him mentioning his office was in Mayfair the night he took her to the dance at the Grosvenor House Hotel. But he'd never given her his office phone number and as she dialled the number she realised her fingers were trembling; she was anxious suddenly at the thought of seeing him again.

'Can I speak to Lieutenant Andersen?'

'Who is this?' The man's voice on the other end had an American accent. He sounded guarded and suspicious.

'My name is Imogen. Imogen Mitchell – I'm Benjamin's fiancée.'

'I'm sorry, ma'am,' the man said after a few moments. 'I can't help you.'

'Isn't this where he works? The hotel gave me this number. He left it for emergencies, apparently.'

'I think there's been a mistake.'

'But you're in Mayfair aren't you?' Imogen persisted. 'It's a Mayfair number – I recognise it, and I remember him telling me he worked in Mayfair. This must be the right place. I just want to know how he is, and where he is?'

'I'm really sorry,' the man said. 'You are mistaken.'

The line went dead.

'It's very odd,' Imogen said, when she found Joy in reception. 'The man at the other end denied all knowledge of Ben.'

Joy began to sob.

'Oh Joy!' said Imogen, sitting down and cradling her friend in her arms. 'What on earth's happened?'

'He's married,' said Joy between gasps.

'Who's married?'

'Werner, of course. I just called his number and this woman answered. She said "he's away". She wouldn't tell me where. I said I was his girlfriend. She laughed at me!'

'Oh Joy, I'm so sorry.'

'She said I was an in idiot. What was it? "An idiot to believe him." And not to think I was the first. She was German too.'

'Oh dear,' said Imogen. 'What will you do?'

'Forget him, I suppose.'

In the middle of the night they were woken by the sound of sirens. The hotel guests gathered in reception in their nightclothes and were taken by an anxious hotel manager down to the hotel's wine cellars. When they staggered out an hour or two later, they discovered the raid had been a revenge attack for Operation Overlord. Over two hundred unmanned bombs had been launched from Calais, over seventy of which had made it to London, wreaking horrific damage all over the capital.

The girls dressed and packed hurriedly, grateful to be escaping to the relative safety of the north of England. The train travelled painfully slowly, stopping periodically in sidings deep in the English countryside. But finally, as the sun was setting, they crossed the Tyne and pulled into Newcastle station. Imogen had sent a telegram to her parents telling them to expect her, and they were waiting on the platform with Joy's parents.

'Imogen,' her mother said, holding her tightly. 'I'm so glad to have you back.'

'I'm so glad to be here,' Imogen sobbed into her mother's shoulder. It was as if all the tension and anxiety of the previous few months, and the terror of the previous night's bombing, had simply evaporated as she was held in her mother's delicate arms.

Imogen and Joy had four days in which to relax and enjoy themselves before they had to return to Portsmouth, and Rose was determined to spoil her daughter. She had made a special supper using a large portion of their weekly ration, and the fire had been lit in the drawing room. Imogen had a long hot bath and changed into a simple summer dress. As she lay on the sofa before dinner, the fire crackling in the grate and a large Dubonnet and soda by her side, Honey the dog jumped onto her lap.

'Now, it's completely up to you,' her mother said, 'I've not arranged anything – but we could go out into the country if you like – for a walk along the coast perhaps. Alnwick is lovely at this time of year.'

'It's good just to be home, Mummy,' said Imogen, stroking her dog's ears.

'Or we could see friends?' her mother went on, brightly.

'Rose,' said Joe, 'leave the girl alone. She just needs time to rest and unwind.'

The following morning, as Imogen ate a boiled egg and toast in the morning room, her mother noticed the ring hanging from a chain around her neck.

'That's a pretty thing,' she said.

Imogen blushed, her fingers darting to the ring.

'Oh… this. Yes.'

'Where did you get it?' her mother asked.

'It's rather a long story,' said Imogen.

'Well,' said Rose. 'We have four days.'

When Imogen had finished telling her mother about Ben she was relieved that Rose did not express either surprise or annoyance that she had kept him secret. She simply asked: 'Do you love him?'

Imogen gazed out of the window and onto the garden. Her father's beloved rose beds were in full bloom, the lavender hedging attracting clouds of bees.

'I don't know. I think so. To tell the truth, it was all so quick. He's lovely Mummy – really lovely. Handsome and clever – he read Law at university. His parents are diplomats; they live in Washington.'

'Those are all admirable reasons to like someone,' Rose said. 'But if you marry someone, Imogen, you need to know you will love them forever. You will love them for all their foibles, all their faults, as well as for their gifts and advantages in life.'

Imogen mused on this.

'Yes. You're right of course.'

'It didn't work out with Freddie, then?' her mother asked perceptively.

'I don't know,' Imogen said, standing by the window. 'I really loved him, you know. I was on the verge of telling him so, but when we last met he told me I shouldn't wait for him; that I should get on with my life and be a fine architect. He told me that he might not make it and he didn't want to break my heart.'

She turned and looked at her mother.

'He sounds as if he was being eminently thoughtful and sensible,' her mother said, pouring them both another cup of tea.

'I suppose he was,' said Imogen, sitting back down at the table. 'But at the time I felt so hurt. I thought he didn't care. When Ben came along he seemed so romantic and devoted; he swept me off my feet – literally. He seemed so exciting and mysterious. He *is* mysterious, in fact. I tried to ring his office the other day and they denied all knowledge of him. Don't you think that's odd?'

Her mother sipped her tea.

'I think you have a lot of thinking to do and that now is not the time to be making big decisions.'

'Are you saying I should break it off with Ben?'

'No,' Rose said. 'But don't allow yourself to be rushed into anything either. It seems to me that you have a great deal to find out about this man – and marriage should never be undertaken in a mad panic. If he loves you, he'll understand and respect that.'

'Thank you, Ma. You're right, as always.'

*

One week later Imogen and Joy stood excitedly on deck, the salty wind blowing in their faces, watching as the Normandy coastline came into view.

'Isn't it exciting?' said Joy, taking Imogen's arm. 'France at last – who'd have thought it?'

'I know,' said Imogen gazing at the grey-green water of the harbour. She thought back to the turquoise sea in the postcard of Le Havre she had taken from Norfolk House all those months before. 'It's just not quite the way I had imagined.'

'What do you mean?'

'I suppose I had a vision of an idyllic little holiday village. From here all I can see is bomb damage and the beach littered with broken-down machinery. It all looks so grey and sad.'

After clambering off the boat using rope netting and ladders, the Wrens were driven by transport lorry across country, arriving late in the day in a bomb-damaged town in Normandy. Billeted together in an empty room in an uninhabited house, Imogen and Joy did their best to make it comfortable with their roll-up beds and travel bath. They had been issued with a tiny stove and a few packets of dehydrated food, and in spite of the fact that the room was dirty and uninviting, Imogen had a renewed sense of purpose. The Wrens set up their headquarters at a converted factory, and as they arrived each day, she felt proud to be part of this band of brave young women.

At the end of August the Allies liberated Paris. As soon as word came through, the Wrens were ordered to pack up the base and move to the capital city. Their new headquarters would be a chateau in the suburbs of Paris.

Imogen wrote a brief letter home to her mother.

Dearest Ma,

We leave Normandy today and head for Paris. To be frank, I'll be glad to go. The deprivation in northern France is terrible – ruined towns, food shortages, bombed out houses, and the people look so sad and downtrodden. In Paris we will be living in a chateau! Can you imagine? I can't say much more, but wish you all well.

I love you and miss you and I'll write once we arrive.

All my love,

Imogen.

PS: no personal decisions taken on any front – I thought you'd be glad to hear!

Chapter Twenty-Seven

Färsehof Farm
September 1944

Magda pushed the last of the herd out of the milking parlour and into the yard. The cows ambled clumsily into one another, rubbing their soft noses together. Pieter, standing on the edge of the yard, held open the gate to the field.

'Push them this way!' he shouted.

'All right,' Magda said, slapping the backside of the last loitering cow. 'They're coming.'

The slowly setting sun cast long shadows across the yard and the air felt fresh and soft. As the last cow skittered off, her hooves clattering across the cobbles, Magda felt her child move. It was a soft, gentle motion – not quite a kick, more a sensation – a little fluttering, like a butterfly. She touched her stomach over her apron, anxious to experience the sensation again through her fingers. Her mother, standing at the kitchen door, called out to her.

'Magda… are you all right?'

'Yes Mutti,' said Magda, 'I'm fine, really.'

At nearly five months pregnant, Magda did, indeed, feel well. She was over her morning sickness and had entered the second joyous trimester of pregnancy. Her skin glowed and her hair was lustrous. She was not surprised at how well she felt. As a young woman she took good health for granted. But she was relieved that her attitude to the child she was carrying was also so positive. She had been so determined to live her own life after the war – to go to university, to follow in her brother's footsteps, to live an independent existence – and now those dreams had been shattered. She would be a mother by the New Year, to a child with no father – at least not a father she was likely to see again. If it was Michael, she feared he would already have been captured, and possibly killed. Even if he survived, the chances of him ever returning were diminishingly small. She would be simply a pleasant memory in the young airman's wartime experience that he could look back on with affection, before returning to his former life in the soft English countryside. If the baby was Otto's then she actively prayed that he would never return… that he might die in a blaze of patriotic glory, so she could be left in peace for the rest of her life to bring up her child alone. Curiously, this sad state of affairs did not induce any sense of self-pity or resentment. Rather, as her belly grew, so too did her love for her fatherless child.

Her mother was waiting for her in the kitchen when Magda came in from the milking.

'I should take over some of your work,' Käthe said. 'You shouldn't be doing the milking any more. I worry something might happen. One of the cows might kick you.'

'Oh Mutti,' Magda interrupted, impatiently. 'Don't make such a fuss. I'm fine. I'm far better at milking than I am at cooking, you know that. We'd all be eating terrible food if I was in charge of the kitchen. What is for supper, by the way? And please don't say rabbit… again.'

'We are lucky to have rabbit,' her mother replied sternly. 'So many people are starving. At least here in the countryside, we have food.'

'I know; I know we're lucky. You're right, I'm sorry. I'm just a bit tired. I'm going to lie down for half an hour, if that's all right.'

'Yes of course. I'll call you when your father comes in.'

Lying on her bed, feeling the child squirm inside her, she closed her eyes and fell asleep within minutes. She woke to the sound of something knocking against her bedroom window. Befuddled by sleep she roused herself, reluctantly. The child within was sleeping too and Magda was annoyed that they had both been disturbed.

She knelt on her bed, and peered out. It was almost dark. The sun had long since sunk over the horizon, leaving just a pale apricot haze that merged into the inky darkness. Beneath her window stood a bearded man wearing a shabby overcoat and cap. It was difficult to tell his age, but he looked like one of the vagrants – deserting German soldiers mostly – who appeared from time to time on the farm, looking for food or shelter. She opened the window.

'What do you want? If you want food, my mother will give you something.'

'Food would be wonderful,' the man said, 'if you can spare any… little monkey.'

'Karl!' she screamed. 'Is that you?'

He removed his hat, revealing over-long unkempt hair. But in spite of the dirt and the beard, there was no doubt it was her brother.

'Karl!' she shouted. 'Wait there. I'm coming down.'

She ran downstairs, and into the kitchen.

'Mutti, Mutti… it's Karl! He's outside.'

Her mother dropped the rabbit she was jointing onto the kitchen table.

'Karl… here?'

Together they ran into the yard. Karl held his arms out to his mother who fell into them, sobbing. 'My baby, my baby,' was all Käthe could say.

Magda danced around, desperate to hold him.

'I can't believe it,' she said, 'you're back… you're really back.'

As he hugged his mother, smiling broadly over her head at his sister, they were interrupted by the familiar clip-clop of a horse and cart.

'Quick,' said Magda, 'come inside. It's probably just Papa coming back from the field, but it might be our neighbour, Gerhardt.'

She pushed Karl and her mother through the farmhouse door and slammed it shut, peering through the kitchen window into the yard.

'Go upstairs,' she whispered to her brother.

'But can't I have a hug first?' he asked.

'Later. Go… quickly!'

A few moments later, she heard Pieter's voice talking calmly to his beloved mare as he led her into the barn.

'It's all right,' she called up to her brother. 'It's only Papa; you can come down.'

In the kitchen, she hurled herself at him.

'Oh Karl… Karl. I thought we might never see you again.'

'I know, little monkey,' he said, grazing her hair with his lips. 'You're not so little any more, are you?' he said, as released her. 'And where are your plaits?'

'I chopped them off – I got fed up with you pulling at them,' she laughed, as he ruffled her short hair.

'Magda…' he said, noticing her swollen stomach for the first time.

'Yes!' she said calmly, 'I'm pregnant. And no, it wasn't deliberate, and no – before you ask – I'm not married, either.'

He looked momentarily dismayed, and stroked her cheek tenderly.

'It's all right,' she said. 'I'll tell you about it later, but not now. Sit down here facing the door. I can't wait to see Papa's face.'

Pieter was a man of routine. Each evening, when he returned home, he removed his boots and put them side by side at the door. He took off his long waistcoat and hung it on a peg. That evening was no different, except when he turned around he appeared bemused, as if he had seen a ghost, or a vision.

'Hello Papa,' said Karl quietly. 'I've come back.'

Pieter's face crumpled with emotion as Karl walked over to him. Taller by a head than his father, he held him, stroking his hair as Pieter sobbed into his son's chest.

'It's all right,' Karl soothed him. 'I'm all right. And we're together again – at last.'

The family sat up long into the night. Magda, desperate to avoid spoiling Karl's homecoming, deflected all his attempts to discuss her own situation.

'No,' she insisted, whenever he turned to her. 'I'll tell you later. We'd rather hear about everything you've been doing.'

'It's so hard to sum it all up,' he said, sipping the glass of schnapps his father had poured in celebration of his son's return. 'I left university as you know; I was interned at first – as an enemy alien. But my tutor at Oxford persuaded the authorities to let me work on his own farm. He knew where my real sympathies lay – that I was no threat to them. He even got to me write an academic paper or two while I was there – on economic theory. He was a good man and stood up for me. He had...' he paused, searching for the right words, '... contacts with various organisations. I was put in touch with them and now I'm working with the Americans and the British. I'm part of a group of agents – that's really all I can say. Even that is too much for you to know for your own good.'

'You're going to be working for the Allies against our own government?' Käthe asked, aghast.

'Yes Mutti. They need fluent German speakers, with intimate knowledge of the local area.'

'But it's so dangerous, Karl. You might be captured, or killed.'

'If I was a soldier fighting here I might also be captured, or killed. We are at war, Mutti. Death is everywhere. But I'd rather die for a cause I believe in, than for a government I despise.'

*

Much later, as Karl sat on Magda's bed, she told him about Otto and Michael.

'I loved Michael,' she said. 'He was the sweetest man I'd ever met, apart from you.'

He squeezed her hand.

'Even though I didn't want him to leave, I helped him get well enough to travel. I knew he would have to try to escape back to England one day. He'd always told me he would – it was his duty.'

Karl nodded.

'One day – it was such a beautiful, sunny day – I persuaded him to come outside into the garden; it was the first day he'd ever left the house. I thought we could have lunch outside... and then Otto arrived.'

'I remember Otto,' Karl said, 'a little blond boy – bad-tempered, a bad loser.'

Magda smiled. 'Yes, that sounds like him. He's nearly twenty now, and over six feet tall, but he's still bad-tempered and a bad loser. Ever since you went away he's... pursued me. He seemed to have this crazy idea that I wanted to be his girlfriend. I never encouraged him, I promise. I hated him, to be honest. But in the end, it was only by pretending to like him that I could save Michael's life. Otherwise, he would have found him on the farm. I knew what Otto was like – like a dog with a bone – never giving up, always so suspicious. He and I were in the kitchen and we heard a noise from outside. I knew it was Michael trying to get away. But Otto insisted on going out and looking around – to find out what had caused the noise. I brought him back into the house to distract him. I had to give Michael a chance to get away. That's when it happened.'

'You're saying he raped you?'

She nodded, her eyes filling with tears.

'I don't know what to say,' Karl said softly. 'War is vile, men are vile. War is initiated by men, to satisfy the ambition of men. They don't think about the human beings at the centre of it, of the women and children who suffer. You are as much a victim of war, Magda, as the Jews in the concentration camps.'

'No!' said Magda, firmly. 'I don't believe that. My friend Lotte – she's a real victim. She and her family were driven away from our village, sent to Munich and then taken God knows where. But I'm still alive, Karl. And all right, I'm pregnant and I don't know who the father is. But there's a chance it's Michael's child. And I love Michael. So whilst I wouldn't have chosen to have a child now, I must try to be happy about it, don't you think?'

Karl kissed his sister.

'When did you get to be so wise?' he said, stroking her hair. 'But we should both go to sleep now. We all have work to do tomorrow. I have to set up my radio equipment somewhere. It's not safe down here in the house.'

'You can use the attic,' said Magda enthusiastically. 'We put Michael up there – in our secret attic – do you remember?'

'Yes of course. Can you help me move my things up there?'

'Can't you at least sleep in your own room?'

'No. It's not safe. If anyone turned up I'd be too obvious. Everything needs to be out of sight. People must believe I'm still in England. But I'll sleep in my own bed just for tonight. And I'll explain everything to Papa and Mutti tomorrow. Will they understand, do you think?'

'Mutti will complain. She's afraid of everyone and everything. But Papa will support you. He hates the government as much as we do; he won't let you down.'

'I thought as much. Goodnight then, little monkey.'

'Goodnight big brother. I'm so happy to have you home.'

Chapter Twenty-Eight

Paris
September 1944

As their open-sided transport lorry headed for Paris, the Wrens were greeted by cheerful civilians hailing them as saviours. From time to time road blocks or bomb craters in the road forced the lorry to come to a juddering halt, whereupon they would be surrounded by local people wanting to shake their hands.

When they finally arrived at Chateau La Celle St Cloud – which was to be their home for the foreseeable future – they could hardly believe their luck. Set amongst unkempt classical gardens, the gold-coloured chateau overlooked a lake and reminded Imogen, as they rumbled down the long drive, of a forgotten castle in a fairy tale.

'My goodness,' said Joy, standing up in the transport. 'We seem to have arrived in heaven!'

'Don't get your hopes up, Cinderella,' said Imogen. 'I suspect we won't be in some grand bedroom on the first floor, but will be sleeping in a wooden hut somewhere in the grounds.'

'Thought so,' said Imogen, as the Wrens were shown to a set of wooden huts that were to be their dormitories.

'There's an ablution room at the far end,' the Quarters PO called out. 'I've managed to get hold of an old copper, so as long as there's enough firewood around the place, we should be able to heat up some water and you can all get the occasional bath. It's one of those canvas ones – not the best, but it's better than nothing.'

Imogen raised her eyes heavenward, as she threw her kit bag onto her bunk.

'See?' she said to Joy. 'I told you.'

The Wrens went to work each day in a naval bus. The new head-quarters of the Allied Expeditionary Force was another chateau in a suburb of Paris called St Germain en Laye. Chateau d'Hennement had been used by the Germans as their own headquarters while they were in Paris, and as soon as they moved in, the Wrens took huge pleasure in clearing all the grand rooms of Nazi memorabilia. A pair of naval ratings made a vast bonfire in the grounds, and the girls dragged Nazi, flags and portraits of Hitler out of the building, and threw them onto the fire.

The work was straightforward enough. Imogen worked for Admiral Ramsay himself – leader of the expeditionary force – and her duties were similar to the ones she had performed for Admiral Spalding. She organised his diary and liaised with other departments. In the summer months the chateau was a pleasant enough place in which to work. The grand rooms were draughty but they would play the occasional game of bowls or cricket in the grounds, or take picnics outside and sit in the overgrown gardens. Occasionally they got 'a pass' and were allowed to go into Paris itself. Gaggles of Wrens would wander the streets, marvelling at the clothes and dousing their wrists with exotic perfumes.

On their first outing, Imogen and Joy visited the department store Galeries Lafayette.

'Isn't it heaven?' said Joy. 'Just look at these clothes – so beauti-fully made. I've not seen anything like it since before the war.'

'Yes,' said Imogen, picking up the label on a chic summer suit, 'and look at the prices. I'm afraid our Wren's wages won't nearly cover it.'

On the ground floor they wandered amongst the scarves and gloves.

'These are more in our price range,' said Imogen, trying on a dark red silk scarf and admiring herself in the mirror. The colour brought out her red lips and contrasted well with the navy of her uniform. She handed a dark green scarf to Joy. 'Try this on,' she said, 'it will bring out the hazel in your brown eyes.'

'But green's your colour…' said Joy.

'Normally, yes – but I fancy a change.'

'It does look lovely,' said Joy, fingering the silk scarf. 'But would we be allowed to wear them?'

'I think so,' said Imogen. 'Even the petty officers in France seem to wear a little flash of colour. It's as if the rules don't really apply here.'

'And maybe a pair of matching gloves?' suggested Joy, trying on a pair in the softest leather.

Feeling suitably elegant, the pair crossed the river and wandered the Left Bank.

'Shall we have coffee?' asked Imogen noticing a café called Les Deux Magots. 'This place looks rather inviting.'

Issued with cigarettes as part of their ration, they sat on the pavement, smoking Gauloises and drinking coffee, watching as people wandered by. A girl wearing a belted raincoat and headscarf scurried nervously past. As she bumped into an elderly lady walking her little dog, her scarf slipped, revealing a stubbly shaven head. The elderly woman picked up her dog, and clutching it to her bosom, spat at the girl. Others in the café muttered and shouted abuse.

'Poor girl,' said Imogen. 'Fancy having your head shaved like that. They do it to women who had affairs with Germans under the occupation.'

'I feel sorry for her,' said Joy.

'So do I,' said Imogen. 'Who knows what we'd all do if we were desperate enough?'

*

As autumn turned to winter and the weather grew colder, the Wrens spent their lunch hours gathering firewood to burn in the empty grates of the chateau. Back in the unheated Nissen huts, bathing in the portable baths became less and less attractive.

'Crikey,' said Joy one evening, 'you've got to be pretty desperate to get in the bath. It took ages to fill it up and it's so draughty in there! And not just that – at least four girls came in to use the lavatory while I was sitting in the altogether.'

'Oh Joy,' said Imogen. 'You are funny. Did you leave the water in there? I wouldn't mind getting in now. It's over a week since I had a proper wash.'

Throughout those weeks, Imogen immersed herself in work. She felt completely disconnected from her previous life. It was as if she had been caught in a parallel world where her family and friends, apart from Joy, had ceased to exist. Her days seemed filled with a combination of hard work and survival. But one afternoon, after a meeting with the Admiral about his plans for the following day, a letter arrived for her.

'Letter for you, Wren Mitchell,' the post boy said, putting the lavender envelope on her desk.

She knew at once who it was from, and slipped it into her pocket to read later that evening.

> *My darling Imogen,*
>   *I was so happy to get your letter. I completely understand that it must be difficult to find the time to write – and even harder to get letters sent back to you, particularly now you are in France. I do hope that all is well and that you are taking care of yourself. I really cannot imagine what your*

life must be like living over there. It seems such a long way away from everything we know and love. Are the local people kind? Have you managed to go into Paris yet? I worry that the Germans might fight back… there is talk of it. Do your people have plans to get you out if that should happen? I try not to think about it but pray for you every day. I cannot tell you how precious you are to us.

My darling I thought I would bring you news of our friends and family. Your cousin Ella has become engaged – to a charming naval officer – an artist. How they will afford to live I do not know. They are both so gentle and without any apparent ability to earn a living. Daddy's brother's children in Canada are all fighting – as you know. Young Bob is tragically in a Japanese war camp. We pray for him nightly too.

And I have news of Marjorie's boys. Jonno is in Italy – in Sicily I believe. Philip appears to have survived like the cat with nine lives. He's lost two destroyers but survived both episodes apparently unscathed. And Freddie is working with a new unit – something rather secret, I gather. He's based in East Anglia with 214 squadron. He wrote to Marjorie and asked after you, which I thought was nice of him. Perhaps he is still interested, after all? I told her that you had gone to France, but really could tell her nothing more. Perhaps you might write to him and tell him your news?

With all our love,
Mummy and Daddy

Imogen smiled as she read her mother's letter. In her subtle way she was ensuring that Imogen should not close the door on Freddie. But looking again at the last paragraph, she felt confused. Was Freddie just being polite by asking after her, or was he trying to tell her something – and if so what? She was uncertain whether she should write to him, in part because she was fearful of rejection, afraid that she might have misinterpreted the message. Besides, technically she was already engaged to Ben and should an engaged woman write to another man? But the more she thought about it, the more illogical that seemed. How could writing to an old friend be considered disloyal in any way? Freddie deserved her friendship and loyalty too. So one night, when Joy was asleep, snoring gently, Imogen took out a piece of writing paper and her fountain pen.

> *My dearest Freddie,*
>
> *It's been so long since we saw one another. I received a letter from my mother and she told me that you are part of a new squadron. Do write and tell me what you're doing, if you're able to. I'm in France, near Paris. Can you believe it? I never thought I would get the chance to travel abroad, let alone have such an exciting time. But the war, I'm slightly ashamed to say, has opened so many doors for me. It's as if my life before – my aspiration to go to university, to study, to become an architect – is completely in abeyance. I understand now, what you said to me that night when we last met in the pub in Newcastle. You were right, of course. One cannot be entangled emotionally with others during a war. Normal feelings of love and tenderness, even of deep friendship, are impossible when everyday life is so uncertain. Please take care. I know you are a sensible person and won't take unnecessary risks, but if your flying is as bad as your tennis, I fear for you!*
> *All my love,*
> *Your friend,*
> *Imogen*

She fretted about this last line. Whether it rang the right note. Was it too cheeky to refer to his poor tennis style – or even heartless?

She hoped he would infer what she had intended – a private joke, an affectionate intimacy.

The letter sat on her bedside cabinet in its envelope for several days, as she debated whether or not to send it. It seemed to muddy the waters, to draw her inexorably back into her old life, and that concerned her. She also became illogically superstitious and fretted that by sending him the letter she might cause some terrible accident to befall him. That people would say 'he got a letter from a girl he knew and that very day was shot down'. This thought – that she might disturb the balance of his mind, or upset his concentration – tormented her.

'Aren't you going to send that letter?' Joy asked one day as they were getting dressed.

'Yes, I will. I just don't know if I should?'

'Why on earth not?' asked Joy, sensibly.

'It's hard to explain. I worry that I might upset him, throw him off.'

'Oh don't be ridiculous,' said Joy. 'He'd love to hear from you, you know that.'

The following day was 11th November – Armistice Day. The staff at Chateau d'Hennement were buzzing with the news that Winston Churchill was due to arrive in Paris that day to lay a wreath on the tomb of the unknown soldier.

'We've got a pass,' Joy reminded Imogen. 'What luck! Shall we go and pay our respects?'

'Absolutely,' said Imogen. 'Maybe we could find a little café somewhere and have something to eat afterwards?'

As she put on her coat and non-regulation dark red gloves, she picked up her letter and debated whether to post it. She put it on the bed, as she tied the dark red silk scarf around her neck. Checking her reflection in her small compact mirror, she picked up the letter and slipped it into her coat pocket. In the entrance hall of the chateau, waiting for the transport, she put it into the post box. As it slipped from her fingers, she felt a sense of panic – as if she had done something irrevocable.

'Come on slow-coach,' Joy said, excitedly, tugging at Imogen's sleeve. 'We don't want to miss the prime minister, do we?'

Paris was filled with people desperate to mark this solemn occasion. The girls got caught up in the vast crowds gathering on the Champs-Élysées. Anxious not to get separated, they clung to one another as they were swept along with the throng, finally coming to a halt near the front of the vast column of people stretching back as far as the eye could see.

As Winston Churchill stood solemnly next to General de Gaulle in front of the Arc de Triomphe, Joy tugged at her friend's sleeve.

'Aren't we lucky?' she shouted over the crowd.

'Yes,' said Imogen. 'I think we are… we're part of history. I just wonder if normal life will ever be able to live up to this?'

Chapter Twenty-Nine

Färsehof Farm
December 1944

Karl told his family very little of what he was doing, but it soon became clear that he was part of a wider organisation of German-speaking agents who had been dropped into their home country to work against the authorities. Their orders were to link up with other resistance groups, and send back details of German troop movements and power plants, factories and transport depots – anything that could be targeted by Allied bombing raids.

He had parachuted into Bavaria carrying false papers and a small portable transmitter developed specially for American spies working in Germany. The 'J/E', as it was known, used high radio frequencies which were undetectable by German shortwave radio operators. When he wasn't out in the field, he spent his time sending and receiving signals, or transmitting military intelligence to Allied planes flying over Europe. Up in the attic, he monitored BBC programmes which from time to time contained special coded messages. Operatives were alerted to imminent mission information when they heard the opening bars of Sinding's 'Rustle of Spring'.

Magda was drawn inexorably to the attic each day. Sometimes she would crouch furtively outside the hatch, hoping to overhear some secret message being relayed on the transmitter. She became familiar with the classical music that seemed to provoke her brother into activity. He would turn up the volume a little and start scribbling in his old notebook.

'What's that music?' she asked, clambering into the attic one afternoon, with a cup of coffee for Karl. 'They seem to play it a lot on the radio…'

He held his fingers to his lips as he continued his note-taking. When he'd finished he found her lying down, uninvited, on his bed.

'You ought to leave,' he said irritably. 'I don't want you involved in this.'

'But it's always the same music,' she persisted.

'If you're so clever, I'm sure you can work it out.'

'Is it a signal?'

He smiled enigmatically at her and sipped his coffee.

'A signal to tell you to listen to the radio?'

He shrugged. 'I'm not going to tell you.'

'That's it, isn't it? That's really clever. And the programmes – they are code, yes… giving you information?'

'Get out of the attic now,' he said, in mock indignation.

'I don't want to,' she said petulantly. 'It's boring. Can't I stay here for a while?'

'If you insist,' he said, turning back to his notes. 'But don't interrupt – agreed?'

'Agreed,' she said, lying quietly on the bed.

'Magda!' He threw his pencil down and swung round to face her. 'I know you too well – you'll never give up, will you? All right… you want to talk, then let's talk. the White Rose – I do know a little about them already. What I don't know is how you got involved with them.'

'Well,' said Magda, propping herself up on his bed, 'I'll tell you, shall I? It started one day when I went to Munich with the Hitler Youth. I got separated from the others. No, that's not true. I ran away, actually. I wanted to look at the university – I was hoping to go there after the war. I met a girl there called Saskia. She introduced me to the leader of the White Rose. After that we met several times... I went to some meetings, and distributed leaflets for them in Munich and Augsburg. I liked them. I admired them hugely – but sometime in '43, they were discovered, or betrayed. They'd started to take a few risks. Anyway the authorities caught them and executed them the same day.'

'Thank God they didn't find out about you,' Karl said, sitting down next to her and wrapping her in his arms. 'You took a huge risk, getting involved.'

'The Gestapo came here, looking for me, you know. But Otto defended me. Can you believe that? He was a senior member of the Youth then and they trusted him.'

'They let you go?' Karl said, with surprise.

'Yes, I know, it was a miracle. I convinced them I was innocent...' She smiled.

'You're very brave,' Karl said, kissing the top of her head, 'or very foolish. But either way, I'm not surprised. I knew you would be as keen to fight against the authorities as I am.'

'I miss it, if I'm honest. Mostly I miss them – Saskia and the others. They were my friends and such good people and they gave me hope – you know?'

He nodded.

'I promised myself – the day I found out they'd been killed – that if I survived, I'd do something to help the cause. But truthfully, since then, I've not really done anything.'

'Except help an enemy airman,' her brother said gently. 'You took a huge risk doing that.'

'Yes,' she said wistfully, her hands stroking her swollen belly. 'The point is,' she said, sitting up eagerly, 'I could help you now; I could take messages – spy for you. No one would suspect me. I come and go as I please on my bike.'

'Magda,' he said. 'I appreciate it, I really do. But look at yourself. You're about to give birth. It's just not safe.'

'I think it makes me safer. Who would suspect a pregnant woman?'

The logic of her argument did not escape him. He smiled.

'You always could wrap me round your little finger,' he said. 'I'll think about it… all right? Now get out of the attic.'

The following Saturday, as Magda finished the milking she came into the kitchen to find her brother sitting, unusually, at the kitchen table.

'Hello,' she said. 'Is there any coffee left?'

'Yes.' He tipped the last of the coffee into a cup, and slid it across the table to her. 'Magda…'

'Yes,' she sipped her coffee.

'I've been thinking.'

'Yes.' She sat down opposite him at the table.

'Do you think we could go somewhere together today? You would be good cover for me.'

'Yes,' she said immediately. 'Of course. Where are we going?'

The door to the yard opened, as Käthe came into the kitchen, bringing with her an icy blast of cold air.

'My goodness,' she said, stamping her feet, and rubbing her hands together. 'It's cold out there. Magda, you'd better stay indoors for the rest of the day. Your father and I will do the milking this afternoon.'

'It's all right,' said Magda. 'I'm going out with Karl, anyway.'

Karl threw a warning glance at his sister. It was a look that said, 'don't say anything!'

'What do you mean?' Käthe asked. 'Karl, what are you thinking – getting your pregnant sister involved in your mad schemes?'

'It's not dangerous, Mutti,' said Karl. 'We're just going to Munich. I need to check out a rail depot. We think it's being used for troop movements and I have to send some information back to London.'

'And why does Magda have to go?'

'A man and a pregnant woman – we're less likely to be stopped.'

'So, you are using your sister now?' Käthe asked furiously.

'Mutti!' Magda interjected. 'I offered to go with him. I want to help.'

'Haven't you done enough? You could have got yourself executed last year along with those student friends of yours. Think of your child Magda, even if you won't think of yourself!'

'I am,' said Magda calmly. 'I want my child to be born in a country where she can be free and not live under tyranny.'

She left the kitchen, and returned a few minutes later, wearing her warmest winter coat and fur-lined boots.

'Come on,' she said to Karl. 'Let's go.'

In spite of her apparent bravado, Magda had a growing sense of anxiety as the train pulled into Munich station. A guard had checked their tickets on the train, barely noticing 'the couple' in front of him – a man of indiscernible age, with a shaggy beard, travelling with his pregnant wife.

Karl had whispered when the guard had left the carriage, 'I told you – we're invisible.' But Magda wasn't so confident.

The station itself was filled with soldiers. They had their kit bags with them and were clearly being moved to another location. Most looked tired and bedraggled, Magda thought. As the brother and sister approached the entrance, intending to walk across to the Botanical Gardens, two SS officers stopped them.

'Papers,' one of them said, holding out his hand.

Karl's forged papers represented him as a munitions worker – a reserved occupation which exempted him from military service, and explained his lack of uniform.

'What are you doing here in Munich?'

They had their cover story ready.

'We are visiting a cousin,' Karl said. 'She lives on the other side of the Botanical Gardens. We have not heard from her for some weeks and are worried about her.'

Magda sensed the soldiers' mistrust.

'Oh dear,' she blurted out, suddenly bending forward and clutching at her pregnant belly. 'Oh… I think it's starting!' She sank dramatically to her knees, moaning and wailing.

Karl knelt beside her. 'Quick,' he said, looking up at the soldiers. 'I must get her to the hospital – can you help us?'

'Get her to hospital yourself; we're not bloody ambulance drivers,' the soldier retorted impatiently, handing back their papers. Karl helped Magda to her feet, supporting her as she staggered out of the station, panting and moaning theatrically. When they were well away from the station, Magda grinned broadly at her brother, murmuring. 'I'm useful, aren't I?'

'You are, little monkey. You are very useful indeed. Now come on, let's get to work.'

Back home at the farmhouse that evening, Karl radioed the position of the rail depot. It had been clear from their observations that afternoon that the depot was being used to move large numbers of German troops around the country.

Back downstairs in the kitchen, he and Magda told their parents their story.

'She was wonderful, Mutti,' laughed Karl. 'I believed the baby was coming myself. She should be an actress.'

As she listened, Käthe silently ladled chicken onto their plates. 'You're both fools – taking such risks. I don't want to hear any more about it.'

The following day Karl had a message.

'It worked, little monkey,' he said to Magda, when she brought him his hot chocolate. 'By tonight that depot will be a pile of rubble.'

*

On Christmas Eve Käthe asked her daughter to accompany her to church.

'It's Midnight Mass. Pieter won't come with me – he says he's too tired. And Karl can't come, obviously. But you could come with me. Please Magda?'

'I don't know,' said Magda. 'I hardly ever go to church any more, you know that. Hitler and his henchmen have destroyed my Christian faith, I sometimes think.'

'But Father Krämer is still a good man,' urged Käthe. 'You know he has hung on to his beliefs. He has never given up.'

The pastor belonged to a branch of the Lutheran faith known as the 'Confessing Church'. Believers rejected the idea of worshipping the Führer in deference to their allegiance to scripture and to God. One or two of their leaders had become quite infamous – helping Jews out of Germany, professing their desire to overthrow the regime. But most pastors, including Father Krämer, preferred to remain unobtrusive – offering support where they could, without risking their lives and those of their flock by being too outspoken.

'We should support him,' Käthe persisted. 'Please come with me… and get your unborn baby blessed.'

'Oh all right,' said Magda, reluctantly.

In her room she put on her warm coat and fur boots and as she turned to go, automatically picked her bible off the shelf and slipped it into her coat pocket.

*

The white walls of the church glowed in the flickering candlelight. As Magda and her mother walked along the aisle searching for a vacant pew, it seemed a haven of refuge from a dangerous uncertain world. Walking the length of the aisle to find a seat, Magda overheard snatches of muttered conversations.

'There goes Magda Maier… she's pregnant, you know.'

'Who's the father?'

'No one knows.'

'Some say it's that Hitler Youth boy – Otto Schneider.'

There were two free places in the second row, next to the centre aisle. Magda sat down and looked around her. On the opposite side of the aisle, she was startled to see Otto's mother, Emilia Schneider, who nodded her head politely at Magda, her face stern and unsmiling.

The service began. There were traditional carols, followed by a sermon and communion, after which the pastor began his final reading. 'Matthew chapter one, verses eighteen to twenty-five,' he intoned. Käthe nudged her daughter to follow the text.

'Look at your bible, Magda – get it out,' she whispered. Dutifully, Magda removed the bible from her coat pocket, and found the relevant lines. '*She will bring forth a son, and thou shalt call his name Jesus: for he shall save his people from their sins…*'

She felt her child kicking. It would not be long now, she thought, before she had her own baby. She put her fingers over her belly and felt the baby's little foot, or perhaps a hand, pushing against the skin. There was another kick and a sharp cramping pain, unlike anything she had felt before. She winced and clutched at her stomach, dropping her bible to the floor. It spun away from her, out onto the polished marble aisle, just as the priest finished his reading… '*And he called his name Jesus*'. Magda breathed deeply, recovering from the pain. She looked around for her bible, and saw it lying on the floor next to Frau Schneider, who leant down, picking up the bible by its cover. The book hung for a second in mid-air, and Magda watched in horror as the letter – until then safely secreted in the pocket – slipped out as if in slow motion, floating down onto the grey and white marble floor. In her panic, Magda could only dimly hear the priest recite the Lord's Prayer, echoed by the mumbling congregation, their eyes closed in reverential prayer. She edged along the pew towards the aisle, desperate to retrieve the secret letter, but her mother gripped her arm.

'Magda, what are you doing?' she whispered. 'Stay where you are.'

'No, Mutti.' she whispered back.

'Amen,' intoned the Pastor, concluding the service. Frau Schneider, sitting with Magda's bible on her lap, opened her eyes and spotted the letter lying on the floor by her feet. As she picked it up, it fell open – either by accident or design. She glanced at it briefly, before slipping it back inside the bible and handing it across the aisle to Magda, with a polite nod.

Outside the church, it was snowing. The villagers said their hurried goodbyes, shaking the pastor's hand, wishing one another a happy Christmas, before heading back to their homes. Magda tugged at her mother's arm.

'Mutti, we must go… now.'

Her mother looked irritated. 'In a moment… I just want to chat to a couple of people.'

Otto's mother emerged from the church to see Magda waiting alone outside.

'Good evening Magda,' she said. 'Have you seen Otto at all?'

'Otto? No…' said Magda nervously.

'He got home this morning. He's been given a few days leave – he's been working very hard. He's been promoted again, you know.'

'Has he?' said Magda, trying to sound calm. 'He was very pleased with his last promotion, I remember. He told me all about it when we last saw each other in the spring.'

Otto's mother glanced down, pointedly, at Magda's swelling stomach.

'The baby – when is it due?'

'Soon,' said Magda, blushing. She felt ashamed, anxious, desperate to escape from Emilia's disapproving glance. To her relief, Käthe joined the group.

'Hello Emilia,' said Käthe. 'Happy Christmas to you.'

'And to you Käthe… and all your… growing family,' said Emilia, acidly.

'Mutti,' Magda whispered, tugging at her mother's sleeve. 'We really must go.'

Her mother finally relented, and they set off back to the farm, across the snowy fields. Once they were both safely out of earshot, Magda exploded in anguish.

'Oh Mutti!' she cried. 'Otto's mother saw Karl's letter… the one he sent from England which I hid in my bible. I know she read it, not all of it, but enough to know he's a traitor.'

'But how did she see it?' Käthe asked, looking bewildered.

'It fell out of my bible!' Magda shouted. 'I'd forgotten it was there. How could I be so stupid? I dropped the bible and the letter fell out.'

'Oh my God,' said Käthe, quickening her stride. 'Let's think… let's think. He said he was in England in the letter. But there's nothing to suggest he's here, is there?'

'No. But she's Otto's mother. If she tells him about it – you know how suspicious he is. Oh Mutti, what have I done, keeping the letter? Why didn't we destroy it? Why did I bring the bible with me tonight? Why did you ask me to come to church?'

*

The two women hurried home, opening the front door in a frenzy to find Karl and Pieter, calmly sharing a bottle of schnapps at the kitchen table.

'Karl, Papa,' Magda blurted out, 'something's happened.'

'What is it, little monkey?' said Karl gently. 'Sit down…. Have a drink.'

'Oh Karl,' sobbed Magda. 'I'm so sorry.'

'What?' asked Karl. 'What is it?'

Magda hesitated. Her mother poured them both a glass of schnapps, and drained hers in one draught.

'That letter you sent me at the start of the war… do you remember? Telling us you were staying in England; that you couldn't fight for the Germans.'

'Yes, vaguely,' he replied, 'it was a long time ago.'

'I kept it…' she said.

Karl stiffened, and put his drink down on the table.

'I told you to destroy it.'

'I know. The thing is – I couldn't… Please forgive me.' She began to cry again.

'Darling – little monkey,' he said, kneeling at her feet and cupping her hands. 'Tell me… what's happened?'

'I kept the letter in my bible. It's been there ever since you sent it – years now. I took the bible with me tonight to church – I'd completely forgotten it was there, you see? The baby… it moved, kicking me… and I dropped the bible, and the letter fell out. Otto's mother, Emilia, picked it up. She read some of it… enough, anyway.'

'I must leave – now!' said Karl, suddenly standing up. 'I'm putting you all in danger.'

'But why?' asked Käthe. 'The letter said you were in England. Why would they look for you here?'

'They won't, necessarily. But they will search this house for evidence that you have been involved in my treachery in some way.' He paused, looking around. 'Is there anything else that might incriminate you, Magda? You must think.'

She wiped her eyes and began to pace the kitchen.

'No! I don't think so.'

'That article,' Pieter said, 'which Karl sent to us from the British newspapers – about the Jews being gassed – what happened to that?'

'We burned it,' said Käthe. Pieter looked at her suspiciously. 'Really, we did. I promise, Pieter,' she insisted.

'And what of the White Rose leaflets, Magda?' asked Karl. 'Do you still have any of those?'

'Yes… a few,' she admitted guiltily. 'They're upstairs.'

'Go… bring everything down now and burn them. I will go up and dismantle the attic.'

'But why?' begged Käthe. 'We were going to have a lovely Christmas together.'

'Not this year, Mutti,' said Karl. 'I'll be out of here in half an hour.'

'But where will you go?' asked Magda.

'I'll find somewhere. There's a network in Augsburg. There are people I can go to. Don't worry about me. Just forget everything I've told you. And look after yourselves.'

Chapter Thirty

Paris
Christmas 1944

As Christmas approached, the Wrens at Chateau D'Hennement did their best to create a sense of festive cheer. Joy, along with some of the other writers and telegraph operators, gathered up branches of holly from the grounds. They persuaded one of the servicemen to cut down a fir tree and erect it in the vast entrance hall. They had no decorations or spare candles, but made white stars out of pieces of paper and hung them on the tree.

'Do come and look,' Joy said, coming into Imogen's office.

'I can't,' whispered Imogen, her hand over the telephone mouthpiece. 'I'm waiting to speak to someone in Brussels – the Admiral's off there after Christmas.'

'Well come when you can,' said Joy, 'it looks so lovely.'

'It's really beautiful, darling,' said Imogen, half an hour later. 'Well done, but it's still absolutely freezing in here. Can't we get any more firewood together?'

'I think we've used all the spare firewood up,' said Joy. 'One of the girls is threatening to set fire to the furniture a bit later.'

'Well we could burn that tree,' said Imogen.

'Oh not yet… not till Twelfth Night.'

'Oh Joy,' said Imogen, 'you're such a romantic.'

*

The snow lay in deep drifts. One morning as they drove to work at Chateau d'Hennement, the naval bus skidded on a steep road and nearly ended up in the river. When they finally arrived, having pushed the bus back onto the road, Imogen found a telegram waiting for her on her desk.

*ATTN WREN MITCHELL, FIANCÉ DEMANDS
URGENT MEETING AT EIFFEL TOWER 24 DEC
1600 HOURS BEN*

The telegram, which should have been a delightful surprise, was in reality unnerving. Imogen and Benjamin had not seen each other since before she'd left for Portsmouth. So much had happened in that time, and yet he had written to her as if nothing had changed. Perhaps, for him, nothing had. But for Imogen, the ambivalence she felt about Benjamin grew stronger by the day. Re-reading the telegram she tried to analyse it.

At the start of their relationship he had represented some sort of security, but since her time in Portsmouth and France she had learned to be so self-reliant, she no longer felt she needed to be protected by a man. Ben was charming and handsome, certainly – but was that enough to maintain a relationship? And then there was the crux of the problem: his work – whatever it was – created an impenetrable wall around him that made her wonder if she really knew him at all. He was, in every sense of the word, an enigma. Now, this cheery telegram 'demanding her presence' gave her no happiness; it simply made her feel resentful that he should expect her to drop everything and rush to meet him in Paris.

*

As she waited in the hall for the transport to Paris, Joy ran down the stairs.

'Ginny – you're not leaving without saying goodbye.'

'Oh, I'm sorry. I just don't want to miss the bus.'

'Let me look at you,' said Joy, standing back to admire her friend. 'Trousers – today? To meet your fiancé?'

'Oh, it doesn't matter what I'm wearing,' said Imogen, looking down at her naval bell-bottom trousers and fur boots. 'It's cold. I just don't want to freeze to death.'

'I suppose you're right. And what about your ring? You're not even wearing it.'

'What about it?' asked Imogen irritably.

'Well you ought to have it on, at least!'

Imogen reluctantly took the ring off its chain and slipped it onto her finger. It felt even looser than before.

'I must have lost weight,' she said, taking it off again. 'It'll fall off if I wear it.' She hung it back on the chain around her neck.

'Well, I hope his feelings aren't too hurt,' said Joy.

'Well if they are, he clearly doesn't have enough to think about.'

As Imogen approached the Eiffel Tower she could see the French tricolour flying from the top – returned to its rightful place after the retreat of the occupying German forces. As an aspiring architect, and daughter of an engineer, Imogen was fascinated by the tower. It was said that Hitler had wanted to destroy Paris as the Allies approached – to leave nothing but a pile of rubble. But Dietrich von Choltitz – the German general who surrendered the city to the Free French – had disobeyed those orders. Now as Imogen stood in deep snow in the shadow of the tower, she felt grateful for the General's act of disobedience. Sometimes, she thought, a love of place is greater even than a love of country. Stamping her feet to keep warm and blowing into her frozen hands, she checked her watch; it was already after four o'clock and there was still no sign of Ben. Irritated that he had chosen such a windswept place for their reunion, she saw him walking towards her. He seemed taller than she had remembered. His greatcoat collar was turned up – just as it had been that first night they'd met.

'Imogen – darling,' he said, wrapping her in his arms and kissing her. 'I can't believe it. It's been so long – let me look at you.'

He held her by the shoulders and studied her. She felt foolish, suddenly, and self-conscious.

'Ben,' she began. 'It's lovely to see you, but could we go somewhere warm? I'm absolutely frozen.'

'Of course,' he said, 'I was going to see if we could go up…' He glanced towards the top of the Eiffel Tower.

'What – in this weather?' she asked.

'Well… not if you're cold.'

'Well, it's freezing down here. I imagine it will be arctic up there. There's a bar I know,' she said. 'In the Sixth – Les Deux Magots; do you know it?'

'Yes,' he replied, 'I know it well.'

They walked along the edge of the Seine, the icy wind blasting across the river, creating white horses on the surface of the water. They passed the Quai d'Orsay station, before cutting through to Rue de l'Université and on to Rue Jacob.

'You seem to know your way around,' he said, impressed. 'I was hoping to introduce you to Paris myself.'

'Well, in the end, I discovered it for myself.'

Les Deux Magots was busy. The waiters were, as usual, surly and supercilious, but Ben persuaded them to find him a quiet corner table. Once they were settled he ordered champagne.

'Certainly, Monsieur,' said the waiter, bowing obsequiously.

'What are we celebrating?' Imogen asked.

'Isn't it obvious? Us, my darling.'

After the waiter poured the champagne, he arranged the bottle in an ice bucket, wrapping a white napkin around its neck like a mother tucking up her child in bed.

'Voilà Monsieur,' he said to Ben, bowing low once again.

'Bottoms up!" Ben said, raising his glass to Imogen. 'Isn't that what you say in "jolly old England?"'

'No, not really,' She felt irritable. Perhaps it was the cold, or the obsequious waiter, or simply that she felt slightly patronised by Benjamin. He looked a little disconcerted.

'Well… you look wonderful. A bit thinner maybe?' He reached across the table and took her hand in his.

'Yes, well… there's not a huge amount to eat – a chocolate ration, and sometimes the villagers take pity on us and invite us to dinner.'

'Your ring,' he said. 'You're not wearing it.'

'Oh that.' She removed her hand from his grasp, and loosened her silk scarf, fishing out the chain from around her neck. The diamond ring glittered in the lights. 'It's too big for me, and I was scared of losing it.'

He smiled, obviously relieved. 'Well, we must get it altered. Maybe while I'm here in Paris.'

'Maybe,' said Imogen. 'But I'm very busy, you know. The Admiral's travelling right after New Year, and I've got a lot of organising to do.'

'Sure,' said Ben, sensing her reluctance. 'No hurry. I'll be leaving too – on the second or third of January.'

'Oh I see,' she said. 'Not staying long, then?'

'No. I don't think so. I'm just here for the holiday, to see you, obviously, and to have a couple of meetings.'

Amidst the noise and bustle of the café, they sat in awkward silence, as the waiter replenished their glasses.

'Imogen,' Ben began, when the waiter had finally gone. 'Is there something wrong?'

'No, it's fine,' she said, sipping her champagne.

'Ginny – I know you… there is something bothering you. Tell me.'

'I tried to call you… after D-Day,' she began. 'Joy and I had a few days leave before we came to France, and were going home; but we stopped in London for a night. I thought I might be able to see you.'

'That would have been nice,' he said, refilling their glasses.

'I rang the hotel. They told me you'd left, but there was no forwarding address.'

'I told you on our last night that I was leaving. I said I'd find you, don't you remember? And I did, didn't I?" He squeezed her hand again.

'They gave me a phone number for your office.'

'Really.' His normally effortless smile faltered a little.

'I rang it. But the man on the other end denied all knowledge of you.'

'Well it must have been a wrong number,' he said calmly.

'I don't think so. I got the impression he knew you – and it was a Mayfair number, and you did once tell me you worked in Mayfair.'

'So do lots of people, honey. Ginny, stop worrying about it.' He downed his glass of champagne and poured himself another.

'The thing is, Ben… it made me realise something. I don't really know who you are.'

'What do you mean?'

'Who do you work for, exactly?'

'I've already told you – I work for the Allies.'

'Do you?' She pulled her hand free of his. 'I'm beginning to wonder who it is exactly that I'm engaged to. All of us work with some sort of secrecy, but with you it's different. Even your own office denies your existence.'

'Imogen… Ginny… I do exist. I'm here with you now. And I love you – that's all you need to know, isn't it?' He put his glass down and fixed his gaze on her, as if willing her to believe him.

She looked across the table at his blue eyes and his soft mouth. She wanted to believe him. Feeling a momentary longing for him, she blushed at the memory of his hands stroking her body, of his lips on hers, of him inside her.

'I don't know, Ben,' she said, looking away. 'It's all so confusing. We've been living separate lives for so long.'

'I know,' he said. 'It's been hard. But there's no rush. Let's spend the next few days getting to know each other again. And when the war is over it will all make sense. You must just trust me, Imogen. I know it's a lot of ask of you, but please believe me – I love you and that's really all that matters.'

Imogen spent Christmas Day itself with the other Wrens and officers at the chateau. They played hockey in the snow, and afterwards, desperate to keep warm, set fire to a gilded chair in the drawing room fireplace. It was an act of pure vandalism, but as it went up in flames, they all cheered, disgracefully. They drank rum and local wine, and smoked cigarettes; they ate a simple meal and shared their chocolate ration. It was fun and relaxed, and Imogen felt part of an important team, almost as if they were her family. On Boxing Day evening she and Ben had arranged to have dinner at the Brasserie Lipp on Boulevard Saint-Germain. The walls of the restaurant were decorated with colourful ceramic tiles and mirrors, and they ate ham and sauerkraut and drank white wine. After dinner, they stood kissing on the edge of the wide boulevard. Imogen shivered as an icy wind blew around them.

'Come back to my hotel,' Ben murmured into her hair. 'Please.'

'I can't,' she replied, 'I've got to get back tonight. I'm on early duty tomorrow. I'm really sorry.' There was a part of her, she realised, that was relieved she couldn't stay.

'I don't know why I bothered to come to Paris,' he said irritably. 'It's as if you really don't want to see me at all. I'm leaving in a few days.'

'That's not true at all,' she said. 'I'll see you before you go, honestly. What about New Year's Eve? Let's meet then.'

'Why not before?'

'The Admiral's off to Brussels on the 2nd and there's just too much to do…'

'Fine,' he said coldly, 'if that's the way it has to be.'

'Oh Ben,' she said impatiently. 'Don't be so childish. I have responsibilities – I can't just do what I want. I'm in the services, you must understand that.'

'Yes, of course I do.'

'You're lucky,' she went on. 'Your work, whatever it is – this dark secret you're involved with – leaves you a free spirit. But I work for someone, I have a senior officer, lots of senior officers in fact, and I have to get back there now.'

On New Year's Eve, as she prepared to go into Paris Joy lay on her bed watching enviously.

'Where's he taking you tonight?' Joy asked.

'A restaurant called Le Procope, apparently. I've not been before, but he said it was good – "swanky" was the word he used.'

'You are lucky,' said Joy.

'What are you all doing, anyway?' asked Imogen, applying lipstick and tying her silk scarf around her neck. 'I'm sure you'll have lots of fun back here.'

'Oh I think a few games are being planned,' Joy said. 'Then we're going into the village. Some of the locals have invited us for supper – isn't that nice of them?'

'That does sound lovely,' said Imogen. 'I rather wish I was coming with you.'

'Oh don't be daft,' said Joy. 'You're off to meet your handsome fiancé and to eat dinner in a lovely restaurant. You'll have a wonderful time.'

'Maybe,' said Imogen, pulling on her coat.

Le Procope was indeed a swanky restaurant and Imogen slightly regretted not taking more care with her appearance.

'It's the oldest restaurant in Paris, or so I'm told,' said Ben, as he ordered a selection of wines to drink with their meal.

'Well it's certainly very beautiful,' Imogen agreed, admiring the saffron-coloured walls and chandeliers.

'My mother can't wait to meet you,' he said, as the waiter poured white wine into crystal glasses.

'Oh,' said Imogen, uncertainly. 'That's nice.'

'She's suggested we live with them, initially. They have a big house outside Washington. You'll be really comfortable there. They're going to love you.'

'Outside Washington,' said Imogen. 'I thought you mentioned once that we might live in New York.'

'Yes – well maybe one day. But my work will take me away from home a good deal. I'd like to think of you being taken care of by my parents.'

'I don't need taking care of,' said Imogen. 'And why will your work take you away? I thought after the war you were going back to the law?'

'Yes, well… that was the original plan but things have changed. I can't talk about it, and you don't really need to know, but you'll love Washington.'

'What do you mean – I don't need to know?' She felt patronised and irritated.

'I just mean that things are uncertain right now – that's all.'

'The thing is, Ben,' said Imogen, putting down her glass. 'I have plans of my own… I want to be an architect. I need to finish my degree.'

'Really?' he said, beckoning the waiter to order more wine. 'I didn't realise it was so important to you. I suppose you could try to get into a university in Washington.'

'Of course it's important,' she bridled. 'I loved my course in Newcastle. I'm not giving it up.'

'Sure,' he said cheerfully. 'But you might change your mind. We might decide to start a family instead.'

Imogen felt a chill running through her as she sipped her wine and tried to imagine this future existence in a house outside Washington with Benjamin's mysterious parents.

At the end of the meal, two large plates of îsles flottantes were laid with a flourish on the table.

'In celebration of our first dinner together,' Ben said, pouring each of them a glass of syrupy Monbazillac.

'Oh,' said Imogen, 'I remember. How delicious – thank you.' The pudding was too sweet and Imogen, a little drunk, felt slightly nauseous as she spooned it into her mouth.

After dinner they wandered through the quiet streets of Saint Germain, finally ending up at his hotel. Imogen reluctantly allowed herself to be persuaded to go upstairs with him.

'You will use something, won't you?' she said, as she lay woozily on his bed. He had begun to slowly remove her jacket, her tie and shirt.

'Of course I will,' he murmured into her hair.

'I mustn't get pregnant.'

'I know,' he said, lying next to her on the bed and kissing her. She felt his hands slipping beneath her bra, felt his breath hot on her neck. She clutched at his hand, moving it away. 'I mean it, Ben…'

He stopped suddenly, and leant on his elbow. 'All right – but we are engaged… would it be so terrible?'

'Yes,' she said emphatically, struggling to sit up, 'it would. It would be the end of everything.' She began to pull her shirt back on over her shoulders.

'Ginny, what are you doing?'

'I'm sorry. I'm so sorry Ben, but this isn't working.' She swung her legs over the edge of the bed and began to zip up her skirt. 'I did love you once – at least I thought I did. You're handsome, you're clever and extremely charming – why wouldn't I fall in love with you? But the problem is, I keep having to convince myself that you're the right one. And I shouldn't have to do that, should I? Now… being here with you again, I've realised something very important. I don't want to get married. I don't want to live in America with your parents. And I definitely don't want a baby – not yet anyway. I have a job, an important one. I'm here in Paris for a purpose, not to have a love affair.' She stood up and undid the clasp on her necklace, slipping off the ring. She held it for a moment before handing it to him.

'Don't do that,' he begged. 'Please Ginny – I want you to keep it. You'll change your mind. It's this war – when it's over, we'll be fine again. Don't you see?'

Imogen tied her scarf around her neck, pulled on her jacket, and stepped into her boots.

'You're right – it is partly the war. But the real problem was thinking I'd fallen in love with you in the first place. The war made me do that; I was swept away by the romance of it all. You were charming and thoughtful, and the idea that we might never see each other again made me act recklessly. Getting engaged was madness, and I'm really sorry about that.'

As she stood by the door of his tiny scarlet bedroom, she looked back at him lying on the bed, with his dark hair flopping over his blue eyes, his chest smooth and firm.

'My mother said something to me when I last saw her. She told me that when you marry someone you have to love all of them – their faults as well as their gifts. The truth is, I don't even know what your faults and gifts are… you're a complete mystery to me. I understand that whatever you're doing for the war is a secret – and I respect that, I really do. I'm sure your work is vital to national security, but the secrecy that surrounds you means I never really feel I know you. And you don't really know me, either – otherwise you'd never have suggested we should live with your parents, or that

I'd abandon my degree, or be happy to have your baby, instead of doing my duty here in Paris. To you I'm just a romantic ideal – a pretty British girl from a nice enough family who you think will slot into your life; whereas the truth is I'm an independent woman with aspirations and ambitions of my own. And I'm sorry to say I just don't love you enough to give everything up for you. So… goodbye Ben. I'm sure you'll find the right girl. And take care of yourself in your secret world.'

Chapter Thirty-One

Färsehof Farm
Christmas 1944

Magda woke to hear the sound of dogs barking in the yard. She looked out of her window, and in the darkness could make out a group of soldiers accompanied by a pair of aggressive-looking Alsatian dogs. The men were banging on the door of the farmhouse and shouting. She heard her father's voice as he stumbled, sleepily, downstairs.

'I'm coming, I'm coming…'

Magda followed him downstairs.

The soldiers rushed into the house as soon as Pieter opened the door. Ordering him to sit at the kitchen table, they opened cupboards, pulling out china, plates and cups; they emptied drawers – tipping their contents violently onto the floor. Käthe, hearing the commotion, rushed downstairs. She too was pushed down onto a chair in the corner of the room and ordered to keep quiet. The family watched in horror as the soldiers trampled over vases and ornaments, crushing them carelessly beneath their boots. They shook the Christmas tree in the corner of the kitchen until the ornaments lay smashed in a myriad of brightly coloured pieces of glass on the tiled floor.

'Please… just tell us what are you looking for?' Käthe begged. 'If we have it we'll show you.'

The soldiers ignored her, moving their search upstairs, emptying wardrobes, tipping out drawers, flinging beds over on their sides.

Linen, books and clothes lay in untidy piles. Karl's framed diplomas were thrown on the floor, the glass smashed. The soldiers found their way to the attic – already expertly emptied by Karl. They found no trace of his presence – just a couple of boxes containing things that Pieter intended to mend one day, a broken chair, and an upturned crate where Karl's transmitter had once stood.

The family had been instructed to wait in the kitchen while the search was completed.

'Magda Maier – you are under arrest,' the first soldier yelled, coming back into the kitchen.

'No!' cried Käthe, leaping to her feet. 'She is expecting a child. You can't take her. She's done nothing wrong.'

'We have evidence that she has colluded with the enemy. Come with us,' he ordered. Terrified, Magda began to put on her boots with trembling fingers. As one of the soldiers gripped her by the arm, his other hand on the latch of the door, the Alsatians outside struck up their loud barking once again. Magda heard a man's voice shouting, a dog whimpering. The kitchen door flew open, throwing the soldier against the wall and in strode Otto in his SS uniform. The soldiers saluted instantly.

'Heil Hitler,' they said in unison.

'Heil Hitler,' Otto responded brusquely. 'What's going on here?'

'We are taking this woman in for questioning. We have reason to believe she is working with the enemy.'

Magda, wearing only her nightdress, her pregnancy evident to everyone, winced as the soldier once again grabbed her by the arm. Otto gripped the man's wrist and removed his hand firmly.

'Wait outside,' he said to the soldiers.

'But we have orders from—' one of them objected.

'I don't care who your orders are from,' Otto interrupted. 'Get outside now!'

When they had gone, he held out a chair for Magda.

'Sit down – please.'

She sat, her heart racing.

He looked around at the chaos in the kitchen.

'I'm sorry,' he said gently to Käthe. 'They have made a terrible mess.'

She began to cry. 'My Christmas tree! All my decorations…'

'Oh Käthe, for heaven's sake,' said Pieter. 'Sit down, woman.'

'Why did you not tell me?' Otto asked Magda softly.

'About the baby, you mean?'

He nodded. 'My mother told me last night. I didn't know what to say. She asked if it was mine. Is it?'

'Oh Otto, of course,' Magda said. 'Who else's could it be?'

His face softened a little. 'I told her. Magda's my girl. But you should have told me yourself.'

'You were away fighting. I didn't want to bother you.'

'But it's our baby, Magda.'

He knelt then at her feet and took her hand in his. 'Magda, you know I've always loved you – since I was twelve and you were ten. All that time, I've loved you and only you.'

She blushed, in spite of herself, more in disgust than pleasure.

'Marry me – please?' he pleaded. 'Marry me now, today, while I'm home.'

'But the soldiers… they want to question me.'

'Oh that,' he said with irritation, standing up. 'Just some trumped-up charge. I'll get rid of them. It was your brother's letter. My mother told me about it. I said, "If Magda had anything to hide, why would she take it to church? She's not stupid." But my mother reported it anyway. I told her – it's pointless. It's Karl who is the traitor, not Magda. I came down here to make sure nothing would happen to you.'

'But… it's true about my brother – he is fighting against the Germans.'

'I know,' Otto said. 'And your honesty does you credit. But he's your brother, and you love him, so you kept his letter – I understand that. But he will be punished, Magda, make no mistake.'

Käthe began to whimper on the other side of the kitchen. Otto looked at her impatiently, as if she was interrupting his train of thought. She stopped abruptly.

'So,' Otto said, turning back to Magda. 'What do you say? Will you marry me? I spoke to my commanding officer and asked for his permission.'

'You've asked him already… before you asked me?' She couldn't help being argumentative.

He father looked at her and shook his head – as if in shame, for what she was being forced to do. Her mother, in spite of her weeping, forced a smile.

'Of course,' he said. 'It's the rule – permission must be sought.'

Magda bit her lip. 'Yes,' she said, glancing nervously over at her parents. 'I'll marry you.'

Otto pulled Magda onto her feet. 'Oh Magda, that's wonderful. I'll go and tell the pastor now – let's see if he can do it today. I have to go back to the front tomorrow.'

'Today?' Magda asked.

'Well – no time like the present.' Otto grinned.

'And what about them?' Magda asked, nodding towards the yard, where the soldiers were waiting.

'I'll talk to them. I'll explain there's been a mistake. I'm their superior officer and will take responsibility – it will be all right.'

Perhaps because Otto was an SS officer about to go back to war, or perhaps because he was keen to legitimise Magda's baby, the pastor agreed to a hurried wedding at three o'clock that afternoon. Magda wore a pale yellow cotton dress that belonged to her mother, stretched to bursting over her nine-month bump. She carried a simple piece of mistletoe as a bouquet and, as Otto slipped a ring onto her finger, he whispered, 'This is everything I've ever dreamed of.'

Then, as the pastor declared them husband and wife, Otto took her in his arms and kissed her. Together they walked back up the aisle watched only by her parents and Otto's unsmiling mother, Emilia.

The wedding breakfast – such as it was – had been hastily arranged. Käthe had done her best to tidy the house. She had wrung the neck of a chicken and roasted it in the oven. But her Christmas tree had no decorations and there was no wedding cake or champagne, only a glass or two of schnapps to toast the 'happy couple'.

That night, as Magda and Otto lay together for the first time in her narrow bed, he stroked her breasts, his hands wandering up her thighs.

'I want you so much,' he breathed.

'Otto, don't,' she begged him. 'I'm too big… it's uncomfortable… please…' She thought he would take her, anyway… rape her again. But instead he paused and lay looking at her, stroking her blonde hair away from her face.

'All right,' he said. 'I understand. Our baby is a big boy. He will be strong and blond and blue-eyed – like you and me. A perfect Aryan child.' He kissed her chastely on the forehead and they lay together in the moonlight. Finally, in spite of herself, Magda slept and the following morning, she woke to find he was gone, leaving a note on the bedside table.

Good morning my dear wife.
I must leave. I have to report early for duty. Take care of yourself and of our child. All my love, your husband, Otto

Magda's waters broke on New Year's Eve. Three hours of urgent, painful contractions followed, and the baby was born at two minutes after midnight on the 1st January 1945. The moment she saw her daughter, Magda knew the baby was Michael's.

As she lay back exhausted on the pillows, her little child gazed up at her new mother, her dark blue eyes searching Magda's soul.

Oh Magda,' said Käthe, sitting down beside her, exhausted by her duties as midwife. 'She's so beautiful.'

'She is, isn't she?' said Magda.

'Can I hold her?' asked Käthe.

'Yes of course.' Magda held the child out to her mother, who wrapped her in a soft white blanket and gazed at her. 'She's so pretty,' she cooed. 'Look at her hair.'

Suddenly she looked up at Magda, her eyes wide. 'Oh Magda,' Käthe said. 'She has red hair. Do you think she is…?'

Magda nodded.

'Oh no,' said Käthe. 'What will Otto say?'

'I don't know, Mutti,' said Magda. 'And at the moment I'm too tired to care.'

A few days later, as Käthe pottered in the kitchen, there was a loud knocking on the front door. Waiting outside was Emilia, Otto's mother.

'I heard the baby had been born,' she said accusingly. 'I am surprised at you Käthe – not coming to tell me yourself. I had to hear gossip about it in the village.'

'Oh, I'm so sorry,' said Käthe apologetically. 'Please come in out of the cold. We've been so busy, as I'm sure you realise.'

'Can I see the child?' said Emilia, removing her coat and looking around for somewhere to hang it.

'Oh yes, of course,' said Käthe nervously, taking Emilia's coat and hanging it over the back of a kitchen chair. 'But she's sleeping now. Maybe you could come back another day?'

'No,' said Emilia. 'I've just walked all the way from the village in the snow. The least you can do is let me see my own granddaughter.'

Magda, who had been snoozing upstairs, the baby gurgling in the crook of her arm, woke to see Emilia's bright blue eyes inspecting the child.

'Well!' Emilia said sternly. 'Her eyes are blue. But the hair! Where did all that red hair come from?'

'It's funny, isn't it?' said Magda, trying to sit up. 'We were just saying, weren't we Mutti, that Papa had red hair as a child.'

Her mother nodded nervously.

'Hmmm,' said Emilia disapprovingly. 'Well she's very pretty, certainly – although Otto will be disappointed; he had set his heart on a son. What is she to be called?'

Magda, who had not until then actually named her daughter, said, unwaveringly: 'Michaela.'

'Michaela!' Emilia was aghast. 'Is that not a Jewish name? You can't call her that.'

'I like it,' said Magda defensively, looking at her mother for support. 'We like it – don't we, Mutti?'

Her mother smiled weakly. 'Yes. It's unusual, I agree. But it suits her.'

'Well,' said Emilia, 'I hope you've told Otto. You will have to get the child baptised without him, I suppose. Have you heard from him?'

'From Otto? No, not since the day after we were married.'

'If he writes,' said Emilia, already heading for the door. 'I'll tell him about the child – and the name.'

A few weeks later, Magda received a letter from Otto. It was brief and to the point.

Dearest Magda,

   Relieved the child is born and you are well. When I get home we will, I hope, make plans to have another... a boy this time.

   Your loving husband,
   Otto

She was grateful he had made no mention of the name. But his letter disturbed her. The prospect of Otto coming back to her was not something she had ever considered. She had married him simply to avoid a worse fate – namely, arrest and possible execution. The idea that she might actually have to spend the rest of her life tethered to a man she loathed suddenly became tangible... and unbearable.

The person she most longed to spend time with was Michael. But she had no way of knowing if he was even alive... and any attempt to try and find him would only result in further trouble. For now, she resolved to simply get on with her life – caring for Michaela, praying for Michael and Karl's safe return, and hoping with all her heart that she could somehow extricate herself from her disastrous marriage to Otto.

Chapter Thirty-Two

The morning after Imogen broke up with Ben, she woke with a sense of overwhelming relief – as if a huge burden had been lifted from her shoulders.

'But I don't understand,' said Joy over breakfast. 'I thought you loved him?'

'I thought I did too,' Imogen said, 'just not enough. He was handsome and educated and spoilt me with lovely meals. But I didn't really know him. Everything was somehow so… superficial. He asked me to marry him so quickly, and I still don't know why I said yes. I was hurt, I suppose, about Freddie. I thought this charming man would help me to forget about him. But somewhere, deep inside, I knew it wasn't right.'

'But Ben did love you,' said Joy.

'Yes, I think he did, in his own way. But the more we talked, the more I realised he wanted to put me in a box – his little wife safely tucked away at home with his parents. I don't want a life like that. And if he really loved me, he'd have known that. I have ambitions of my own, and they don't include living with someone else's parents and having their babies, while they disappear to do a job that I couldn't even be trusted to know about. I felt belittled. You do understand, don't you?'

'And what about Freddie? Have you heard from him?'

'No,' said Imogen, flatly. 'But that's not the point. Maybe I'll never see Freddie again; but you can't marry someone else as a sort of consolation prize. I just have to believe that I will meet someone who I can love completely and who loves me too – for all my faults and foibles.'

The following day, a bag of post was delivered for the Admiral. It had been held up over the Christmas period. Imogen unpacked it, finding long overdue letters, memos and other missives. But right at the bottom, she spotted a familiar envelope. It was a letter from Freddie. Dated October 1944, it had been originally posted three months earlier, and the envelope was covered with scrawled addresses, indicating it had been forwarded several times. She ripped it open.

5th October 1944
Blickling Hall,
Norfolk

Dearest Ginny,

How lovely to get your letter and how right you are – my tennis is as terrible as ever! You'll be glad to hear, however, that my flying is improving, which is fortunate because otherwise I'd have ended in the drink several times by now. As you can see from my address I'm now based in Norfolk – we're part of a new squadron. I can't tell you much more than that, as I'm sure you realise, but things are going well. Believe it or not I'm now a fully-fledged officer in charge of a magnificent plane called 'The Flying Fortress'. She's a beauty – big and bold and feels like home whenever I get behind the controls.

I'm glad to hear you've landed on your feet in Paris. You lucky thing! I hear it's wonderful and I long to go there myself.

I spend my life flying thousands of feet up in the air over places I yearn to visit. One day maybe you can show it to me?

I'm so relieved you understand what I was trying to say when we last met. It wasn't easy to say. You know, I think, what I feel for you. No one can hold a candle to you and that's the truth. You're a very special girl Ginny and I'm lucky to know you. You must know – from your own work – that there's a feeling in the air that this thing is nearly over. The Germans are losing ground everywhere. One more big push and we'll win. The end's in sight and with luck we'll all be together again soon.

Take care of yourself dearest Ginny, and here's to the end of the war.

All my love,
Freddie

It wasn't a declaration of love, but it was as much as she could hope for in the circumstances. At that moment she knew she had been right to finish with Ben. It was Freddie she still loved, and reading between the lines perhaps he loved her too. She was smiling, and re-reading Freddie's letter with tears in her eyes, when the Admiral arrived.

'Is everything arranged,' he asked, 'for tomorrow?'

'Yes, sir,' she said, slipping the letter into her office drawer. 'Your plane leaves at 0900 hours from the airport down the road. I've arranged a car to collect you at 0830. You should be in Brussels by lunchtime.'

'Good. And everything all right with you?' he asked affectionately.

'Oh yes, sir. Everything's very good indeed, actually.'

'Excellent. And you all had fun last night – New Year's Eve and all that?'

'Yes. The others went into the village. I went to Paris.'

'It lived up to expectations I hope?' he asked with a smile.

'It was decisive, thank you sir.'

'Very good,' he said. 'Well, I'd better get on.'

'I'll put a file of papers together for you, sir – to take with you tomorrow.'

That evening she wrote back to Freddie, explaining that his letter had been delayed. It was a happy letter filled with news of her work and her life in France. She told him how much she enjoyed working for the Admiral.

> *He's one of those men who says a great deal with very few words. I'm sure you know what I mean. He's utterly loyal and kind and courteous to everyone around him.*

Of her life with the other Wrens, she wrote:

> *We live in a hut in the gardens of a chateau. It's freezing and rather grim, but somehow we just get along. We played hockey in the snow over Christmas – can you imagine? It was marvellous. And we have a beautiful ballroom, and put on dances – Scottish reeling is popular! Write soon.*
> *All my love,*
> *Ginny*

The following morning it was snowing hard. As Imogen dressed, putting on her old fawn duffle coat and boots, she picked up her letter to post at the chateau. She thought fondly about Freddie and realised that if she had received his last letter before Christmas, she would probably have ended with Ben straight away. Now, she felt free to return his affection. It was too soon to declare love, but they had a chance to allow their relationship to develop over time, and she had a feeling of optimism as she clambered into the bus heading for work.

The bus took its normal route between Chateau St Cloud and their work headquarters in Saint Germain en Laye. The road was icy, and at one point got stuck at the bottom of a hill. The Wrens had to get out and push.

'We've got to get a move on,' Imogen said to the driver, anxiously checking her watch. 'The Admiral's leaving in half an hour and I've got to give him some papers.'

'I'm doing all I can,' replied the driver irritably. 'Push harder.'

When she finally arrived at the chateau, the Admiral had already left. The file of papers she had collected for him still lay on her desk.

'Damn,' she said under breath.

Imogen was typing up some notes, when a rating rushed into her office.

'Have you heard the news?' he asked breathlessly.

'No,' she said, suddenly anxious. 'What is it?'

'It's the Admiral. His plane crashed as they were taking off – snow, or ice on the propellers, or something.'

'Is he hurt?' asked Imogen, instinctively putting on her coat, preparing to go down to the airfield to help.

'Oh no,' said the rating, 'he's dead I'm afraid… they all are – no survivors.'

Imogen felt numb at the news; the Admiral had been such a kind man. In spite of her grief, she worked tirelessly – helping to arrange his funeral in the cemetery opposite Chateau d'Hennement. All the senior military Personnel were invited, and there was a flurry of excitement when General Eisenhower arrived in his jeep, his outriders wearing their customary white helmets, gauntlets and gaiters.

'Here come the snowdrops,' whispered Joy when they saw his party arrive.

Imogen, in tears, barely noticed her friend. In gently falling snow, the funeral party assembled – the Admiral's family first, then the top brass, and finally the Wrens.

'He was such a good man,' Imogen whispered to Joy, at the graveside, 'I just can't believe he's gone.'

The following day his family were due to spend some time alone at the graveside before flying home to England. Imogen and some of the other Wrens went out to the cemetery to check everything was tidy before the family arrived and found the grave covered in over a foot of snow. As they shook the snow off the wreaths, the air was filled with the scent of fresh greenery and Christmas roses.

Over the following weeks, Imogen and Freddie struck up a correspondence.

In spite of the war, and the constant danger he was in, his letters were filled with positivity. He was busy and loving life.

> *We play squash every day if we can,* he wrote, *especially when waiting for an op to start. It helps to fill the time and use the adrenalin.*

He included a charming drawing of Blickling Hall – a stunning little pencil sketch of the Elizabethan building, which clearly demonstrated his enormous talent. Imogen replied, sending him a drawing of Chateau d'Hennement – a complex Neo-Gothic structure with turrets and crenellations, its arched windows edged in pale coping stones. She was proud of her sketch; it was almost as good as his, and she expected a letter by reply – perhaps with some encouraging comment about her drawing ability. But as the weeks went by, none came.

In early April, she received a letter from her mother.

Gosforth

My darling Imogen,

Not to beat about the bush, I have news of Freddie McMasters. I thought you'd want to know as soon as possible that he's MIA. He was shot down a couple of weeks ago – somewhere near Stuttgart. The RAF have let his parents know, and Marjorie is in terrible distress, as I'm sure you can imagine. There's no way of knowing what happened exactly. His plane did not return to RAF Oulton, so one assumes it was shot down. None of his fellow pilots saw it happening, so information is sketchy. We can only hope and pray that he and his crew got out in time.

Do write to Marjorie. I'm sure she'd appreciate a kind word at this terrible time. And pray for Freddie.

Your loving mother

Imogen burst into tears as she read her mother's letter. She lay on her bed sobbing. Joy, returning from the bathroom, rushed to her side.

'Darling – what on earth's the matter?'

'It's Freddie,' said Imogen. 'He's been shot down over Germany. He's missing.'

'Oh no,' said Joy. 'I'm so sorry. I know how fond you are of him.'

'I'm not just fond of him, Joy, I love him. And I never told him, not really. And now he might be dead and he'll never know what I felt.'

'Oh Ginny,' said Joy, lying next to her friend and wrapping her in her arms. 'You can't be sure of that. And he did know you love him – he's always known. Don't lose faith. Missing is not actually… well, you know.'

Imogen looked up at her friend. 'You think he might be alive?'

'Yes, I do. I don't know him, of course, but from you've told me about him, Freddie McMasters won't go down without a fight.'

Chapter Thirty-Three

Färsehof Farm
March 1945

The RAF bombing raids over Germany were increasing. The main targets were oil refineries, railways and marshalling yards. A bomb dropped on any of these would disrupt troop movements and frustrate the development of armaments and equipment. 100 Group, based in Norfolk, supported these raids with countermeasures: Flying Fortresses, filled with jamming gear and Geman-speaking radio operators, flew high above waves of Lancaster bombers intercepting the Luftwaffe's own intelligence and diverting German pilots away from the real raids. As a result, more of the Allied planes got through to their targets, and the destruction was widespread. Increasingly smaller towns and villages were also targeted – whether to simply destroy the morale of the German people, or because the Allies had information that German troops were suspected of sheltering in village schools and halls.

In those early months of 1945, Magda was often woken in the middle of night by the sound of planes rumbling overhead on their way back from a raid over Augsburg or Munich, flying very low to avoid the night fighters and German flak. She would take the baby into bed with her, to soothe her.

One night she woke with a start, as a bomb exploded nearby. Her father knocked on her door moments later.

'Magda, Magda! Wake up. We should get down to the cellar, now. Quick, *Liebling*.'

The family sheltered for the rest of the night down in the cellar, listening to the roar of planes and the crashing of bombs. When they emerged, shakily, early the next morning, they found one of their barns – where they stored the tractor and other machinery – had taken a direct hit.

'Oh my God,' muttered Pieter as he and Magda inspected the damage, rubble spilling into the yard. 'What are we supposed to do now?'

'Well just be grateful it wasn't the milking parlour. We could have lost the herd,' Magda said pragmatically.

Käthe came running out of the house, weeping. 'Oh no! I can't believe it was so close – it could have been us! Or the house!'

'Well it wasn't,' said Magda, hugging the baby to her chest. 'I'm going back inside to get dressed. Mutti, will you look after Michaela, while I help Papa clear up? And we've still got to do the milking.'

They rescued as much of the equipment as they could and stowed it in the milking parlour. The cows, which had not yet been turned out into the fields for the summer, were milked by hand, as usual. As the herd rested on their bed of straw in the barn, Magda went outside and sat on the stone bench in the yard, her face raised to the sun. Daffodils and snowdrops poked their way through the melting snow at the edges of the fields. In spite of the bombing, she had a sense of optimism.

In the late afternoon, she offered to go into the village to collect some supplies.

'You look after the baby,' she said to her mother, 'I'll do the shopping. I need a walk.'

'Be careful,' Käthe said, as she left.

'Oh Mutti,' said Magda, as she threw her coat on over her old trousers and jumper. 'Stop fussing. The planes have gone now; they won't be back for a while.'

As she crossed the fields and entered the village, evidence of the previous night's bomb attack was everywhere. Parts of the village square had been virtually destroyed, including the haberdasher's shop run by Herr Wolfahrt, which was now reduced to a mangled pile of broken stone, glass, roof tiles and oak beams mixed with rolls of fabric. Magda joined a group of villagers, Otto's mother amongst them, staring in dismay at the bombed-out shop.

'Poor Herr Wolfahrt,' said one old woman, 'he was such a good man.'

'Did they manage to get out in time?' asked Magda.

'No!' said Emilia angrily. 'Poor Herr Wolfhart, his wife and her mother – they've all been killed.'

'Murdered in their beds,' said the first woman.

Emilia nodded vigorously. 'You're right,' she said. 'It's murder.'

'I'm really sorry to hear that,' said Magda. 'He was a good man. Our farm was hit last night too – just one of our barns, thank god.'

'Is the baby all right?' asked Emilia.

'She's fine thank you – we're all fine.'

A small group of bedraggled strangers wandered helplessly into the damaged square.

'Who are these people?' Magda asked Emilia.

'They've come across from the town on the other side of the valley,' Emilia said. 'It was completely destroyed last night – razed to the ground. They have nowhere else to go. Some have relatives here, or friends. We will have to take them in, although how we will cope, I don't know.'

The village grocery just off the main square had survived the bombing with just a broken front window. The owner was sweeping up as Magda arrived.

'I'm not really open yet,' he said irritably. 'What do you want?'

'Just some flour,' said Magda. 'And sugar if you have it.'

'We have no sugar,' said the owner. 'The flour's over there – but don't blame me if there's glass in it.'

Magda paid for the flour and was just about to leave, when a young girl came running into the shop.

'Come, come quickly,' she called out, wildly.

'What is it?' Magda asked.

'Some men – some English airmen; they've captured them. They're threatening to kill them.'

'Who is?' said Magda.

'The village boys – Anton, Hans, Christoph,' said the girl.

'They're in the Hitler Youth, aren't they?' Magda recognised the boys' names from her own time in the organisation. They were younger than herself – no more than sixteen or seventeen. 'Where are they?'

'Near the school.'

The lane outside the school was thronged with people. Magda fought her way through the crowd and was alarmed to see five British airmen standing in their stockinged feet in the centre of a ring of Hitler Youth boys. Without their boots, the airmen seemed particularly vulnerable. The boys, egged on by the crowd of adults, were punching and kicking the men.

'Kill them, kill them,' the crowd jeered. 'Murderers, murderers.'

Magda looked around frantically for someone to take control. The mayor stood impassively in his doorway, observing the scene.

'Herr Weber,' Magda pleaded. 'You must stop this. It's not right. These men are prisoners of war; they aren't allowed to be treated like this.'

'What can I do?' he shrugged helplessly. 'A group of us arrested them last night when they landed. I had them all locked up in the cellar of the school. I was keeping them for the Gestapo to deal with later. But someone must have let them out.

The sun was just setting over the horizon, and one or two of the crowd lit torches, their flames licking into the darkness.

'They've brought them here to kill them,' Magda insisted. 'Surely you can see that. You must stop this.'

'How can I?' Herr Weber said. His thinning grey hair was plastered over his skull, his pale grey eyes red-rimmed and bloodshot and his breath smelt strongly of schnapps. He was utterly powerless, Magda realised, and would do nothing to help.

On the other side of the lane, next to the mayor's house, was an old barn that was used sometimes for village dances. Magda glanced inside and saw in the torchlight – to her horror – five ropes hanging from the rafters with nooses at one end.

She shouted above the noise of the mob. 'Stop… stop this. We mustn't do this. Please.'

One or two spat at her, their faces contorted with anger and hatred.

'They deserve it. They're murderers – all of them.'

The airmen looked around frantically for an escape route. Two of them suddenly bent double, and charged head first into the crowd. They broke through, and ran up the narrow lane towards the square. Taken by surprise, the crowd splintered, some racing after the two men. The remaining three airmen took advantage of the confusion, and ran in the opposite direction towards the church. The rest of the crowd surged after them and within minutes Magda heard the sound of gunfire. Her heart pounding, she raced to the churchyard, but the mob had already dispersed, evaporating into the night. She found one airman slumped in the entrance of the church itself, as if he had sought sanctuary in the holy place. He had been shot in the head and his fair hair was matted with blood. She gently rolled him over, and wept as she touched his pale unlined face. He was no more than nineteen or twenty, she thought.

Regretfully she left him and went in search of the others. She found a second airman draped over the cemetery wall, as if he had been shot in the back attempting to jump over it. She felt for a pulse in his neck, but there was nothing. The man's eyes were wide open. She closed them, stroking his head as she did so. The third man had died on top of a grave, shot three times – once in the head, twice in the torso. The churchyard was eerily silent, except for the awful screeching of the crows that lived high up in the black alder trees.

Magda stumbled back down the lane towards the village school. The mob had dispersed, and the mayor's house was firmly closed up for the night. Even the torches in the barn had been extinguished, leaving just the five nooses swinging from an overhead beam. Relieved they had not yet been used, Magda hoped the two remaining airmen might have survived. They had run off in the direction of the square. Might she find them huddled in a quiet corner somewhere? She set off, peering down the tiny lanes on either side of the road. Within minutes she spotted the body of a man wearing RAF uniform. He had been beaten so viciously around the head that he was unrecognisable. She sank to her knees, feeling in vain for a pulse. 'I'm so sorry... I'm sorry,' she wept.

It seemed so terrible to leave his body lying there in darkness, but without help, she could do nothing else? As she walked briskly through the now-deserted village there was no sign of the fifth man. She prayed that somehow he had escaped – to the woods, perhaps, that surrounded the village.

She could hear the baby crying as she walked up the track to the farm.

'Magda, where on earth have you been?' Käthe shouted, jiggling Michaela frantically in her arms. 'I've been so worried – and the baby is starving.'

She handed the baby to Magda, who sat down at the kitchen table, unbuttoning her blouse. As the baby pawed frantically at her breast, gulping and gasping, the milk flowing out of her tiny mouth, Magda burst into tears.

'*Liebling,* what is the matter?' Käthe asked, kneeling beside her. 'Tell me.'

'Oh Mutti. Something terrible has happened in the village.'

'What? Is it the bombing?'

'Partly – yes. The village was hit and poor Mr Wolfahrt and his wife and her mother are dead.'

'Oh no,' said Käthe. 'He was such a nice man.'

'I know,' said Magda, 'And I'm sorry. But more terrible even than that… there were some British airmen – they've been murdered.'

'What do you mean?'

'Their plane was shot down nearby, and they were taken captive. The mayor had them locked up in the cellar of the school – he was waiting for the Gestapo to come and take them away. But a group of Hitler Youth boys broke into the cellar and were threatening to lynch them – they had the nooses all ready in the village barn. Three of the Englishmen broke free and ran towards the churchyard, but they were shot. Another ran towards the village, but they chased him and beat him to death.' Magda sobbed as her baby suckled.

'You saw this? Why didn't you come home straight away?' Käthe demanded.

'I wanted to help them.'

'It's always the same with you. Putting yourself in danger for others. What have they done for you, these men?'

'They risk their lives for us,' she said, drying her eyes with her sleeve. 'Now they've lost their lives, in the worst way possible.'

'Well… I have some sympathy with the villagers,' said Käthe. 'They come over here, bombing our towns – even our own barn. It's terrible. Nice people like Mr Wolfahrt get killed. Why shouldn't these Englishmen suffer too?'

'Don't you realise,' Magda said calmly, 'we are bombing their towns and villagers too? The British suffer as well, you know. Don't you ever listen to Papa's radio?'

'It could all be propaganda,' said Käthe.

'Oh Mutti – don't be so blind! Remember what Karl told us – about how he was treated in England, looked after on a farm, given work to do.'

'Well he was on their side,' Käthe protested.

'They didn't know that at first,' said Magda. 'Besides, it can never be right to take the law into your own hands – lynching people. Do you think the British would do that? I don't think so. It's completely immoral.'

She swapped the baby over to her other breast. The child settled happily – pawing and sucking.

'I don't think we have any right to preach about morality, Mutti.' Magda continued. 'It is we who have murdered thousands of innocent people; we who have been complicit and allowed terrible sins to be done in our name. Do you have no shame – for our country and what we have done? If not, then I'm ashamed of you.'

Magda stood up, the baby still suckling, and went upstairs, slamming her bedroom door.

Chapter Thirty-Four

Magda woke with the early morning sun streaming onto her face. She checked the baby was sleeping in her cot, then pulled on her trousers and a jumper and, grabbing her apron from behind the farmhouse door, went outside into the yard.

The weather over the previous few days had been warm and dry, and she and Pieter had just turned the herd out into the fields. As she walked down the track to collect the cows, she picked a few primroses growing in the hedgerows and stuck them in her apron pocket. Since the murder of the four British airmen, she had been haunted by memories of their eyes staring into space, of their contorted features and bleeding bodies. Now as she listened to the birds singing, and felt the sun warming her back, it seemed incredible to imagine such horror taking place just a mile or so away. It could have been Michael left for dead in the churchyard.

Back in the milking parlour, the cows lined up patiently, gazing at her with their orb-like dark eyes, eyelashes fluttering coquettishly. Settling herself on her stool to milk the first cow, she thought she heard a curious rustling sound. She peered around the barn but could see nothing unusual. Perhaps it was a crow, she thought, flapping around in the rafters. As she squeezed the cow's udders, feeling them full and soft beneath her fingers, milk squirting into the pail, she thought she saw a sudden movement – a flash of something in the dark corner of the barn behind a pile of hay.

Calmly and quietly, she moved her stool and her bucket along the line of cows, chatting to them as she did so.

'There. That's better isn't it?' she said, whilst keeping one eye on the dark corner.

As she moved her stool and bucket one further time, she saw it again – a flash of dark grey.

'Come out,' she said. 'I won't hurt you, but you must show yourself.'

A young man in RAF uniform emerged from the pile of hay. He smiled nervously.

'*Guten tag, Fräulein… ich bin ein Englischer flieger…*'

'It's all right,' Magda said, 'I speak English. You're in the RAF.'

'Yes.'

'Don't worry. I won't hurt you.'

The young man looked at her with surprise, and sat back down heavily on the pile of hay, clearly exhausted.

'Let me finish the milking,' she said, 'and then I'll take you inside and give you something to eat.'

With the herd back in the field, she led the young man towards the house.

'Come in,' she said, opening the door and kicking off her boots. Her mother was standing at the range, the baby lying wriggling in a cot next to her, her tiny arms and legs raised towards the light. Pieter was eating his breakfast at the table. He stood up, aggressively, as soon as he saw the young man.

'It's all right, Papa,' said Magda, 'he's a British airman. I found him in the barn. He needs something to eat.'

The young man looked around at the cosy kitchen and the baby in the basket. It seemed so utterly domestic and normal.

'Thank you,' he said, his voice filled with relief. 'I'm so grateful.'

He sank down on a kitchen chair and Magda put a plate of bread and butter in front of him. She watched him eat, while she sipped her coffee.

'You were very hungry,' she said, when he had finished. 'More?'
He nodded.

'Mutti – give him more.'

'No,' said the young man. 'No, I shouldn't.'

'It's all right. We have enough.' She pushed the bread towards him and he ate.

'What's your name?' she asked pouring him a cup of coffee.

'Freddie McMasters. Yours?'

'I'm Magda – Magda Maier. You look exhausted,' she said.

'Yes. I am rather.' He ate his food and looked around nervously at the family, smiling occasionally.

Magda sat down opposite him and poured them both another cup of coffee.

'It's all right. We won't hurt you. We're…' she looked back at her parents, '… we're sympathetic. Please… tell us your story – we want to help.'

He began nervously, 'Well… if you're sure?'

She nodded.

'I've been marching for a couple of weeks – me and thousand or so British airmen, soldiers… I reckon we've walked about two hundred kilometres. I was shot down over Stuttgart a few of weeks ago. I got everyone out of the plane and jumped myself. The plane blew up seconds later – I only just made it. I landed in a tree; my parachute got stuck.' He smiled, laughing slightly at the memory. 'It was the most ridiculous thing. I didn't know what to do. It had been snowing heavily, so I reasoned if I just released the chute, I'd probably be OK. So that's what I did – landed in several feet of snow.'

'You were lucky,' Magda said.

'I suppose we were. About half of my crew were rounded up by soldiers. I'm not sure what happened to the others. I hope they got away all right. We were put in prison originally. It was quite rough, but eventually we were taken to a POW camp in Ludwigsburg.'

'That's a long way from here,' said Magda. 'How did you end up in our barn?'

'Ah... well the Allies have taken all the territory west of the Rhine, so the Germans decided to move us south east – hence the long march – and we ended up near here. A few of us, including my crew, got a bit fed up and did a bunk, but we got separated somehow a day or two ago. I expect I'll find them all somewhere around the place.'

'You make it sound very easy,' Magda said. 'You could just leave like that? Weren't you being guarded?'

'Oh yes, well the guards are not very bright. I'm sorry,' he said suddenly, looking around anxiously at Magda's family, 'I don't mean to be rude.'

Käthe was busying herself at the sink, but Pieter had sat down in the large armchair near the range and was listening intently to the young man.

'It's all right,' Magda said. 'No one will take offence. My mother and father – they only speak a little English anyway. And – you should know my brother is fighting for the Allies, and I was part of the German resistance – so we're not big fans of German soldiers, either.'

'My goodness,' said Freddie. 'I had no idea there was a German resistance movement. Your brother – is he in England?'

'He was, but he's been back in Germany for a few months now. He works for American intelligence, sending information back about troop movements and so on. He lived with us for a while, but he had to leave us at Christmas and go on the run. I wish he was here with us now. He would be able to help you.'

'I expect he's got better things to do,' said Freddie. 'I'll be OK. I just need to rest up for a few hours, get my strength back, you know? The Allies are very close now. It won't be long until the whole show's over.'

*

Magda persuaded her parents to let him stay the night and she made up the bunk bed in the attic where Karl and Michael had both slept. Freddie collapsed on the bed fully clothed, and slept for over twenty-four hours. When he woke, it was late morning. Peering out of the tiny attic window he watched Magda chatting to her baby in the yard below. Downstairs, Käthe was in the kitchen.

'Good morning,' he said politely.

'Hmmm,' she said, gesturing to him to sit down. She put a plate of eggs on the table, and he fell on them, even wiping the plate with the piece of bread she had provided.

'*Vielen dank*,' he said, 'Thank you so much.'

She smiled faintly and nodded.

Outside in the yard he found Magda sitting on a log, nursing her child.

'Come,' she said, 'sit next to me.'

'Thank you. Your mother just gave me some eggs for breakfast. They were the most delicious thing I've ever eaten. I'm so grateful.'

'It's our pleasure.'

'It's a lovely place,' he said, looking around. 'You're farmers?'

'Yes… we have a dairy herd, and grow some cereals. Chickens and vegetables too, but mainly for own use. Tell me a little about yourself.'

'There's not much to tell, really. I'm an officer with the RAF.'

'No, I mean when you're not fighting a war – tell me about that.'

Freddie blushed slightly. 'We're trained to say nothing but our name, rank and serial number.'

'I know that,' she said. 'But I'm not the enemy, I'm a friend.'

He smiled and watched her feeding her baby. 'I'm training to be an architect, or at least I was before I joined up.'

'Are you married? Do you have children?'

'No!' he said. 'I'd like to get married though, one day.'

'You don't have a girlfriend?'

'Not really,' he said. 'I do love a girl – except she doesn't know it yet. We've known each other all our lives. What about you?'

'I'm nearly nineteen years old. I would like to go to university one day too. And my daughter is the child of a British airman, just like you. '

'An Englishman?' he said, startled.

'Yes.'

'He didn't…' He blushed uncertain how to say what he was thinking. 'It wasn't – something he shouldn't have done?'

'No! Not at all. He didn't take me against my will – if that's what you're asking.'

Freddie blushed.

'He crashed his plane on our farm last year,' she explained, 'and I brought him home. He had a broken leg and arm, you see, and needed somewhere to get better. His name was Michael – Michael Stewart, and we fell in love.'

'I see.'

'He left me with this little person.' She gazed lovingly at her daughter and tickled Michaela's tummy.

'She's gorgeous,' said Freddie, putting his finger into Michaela's tiny hand. The baby gripped it tightly. 'Michael Stewart,' he said, thoughtfully. 'I'm trying to work out if I know him. I don't think I do, I'm afraid. What was he flying?'

'A Lancaster bomber – that's what my father said. There were several people in his crew. They were all dead, unfortunately. Only he survived.'

'That's awful,' said Freddie. 'What happened to him – if you don't mind me asking?'

'He stayed with us for a few weeks while his leg healed. But I knew he was desperate to get back to England. He was getting stronger each day, although he still had bad limp, and then one afternoon we were outside in the garden, and a German officer

– someone I knew from childhood – came to the house. Michael had to escape in a hurry. I have no idea if he got home safely. I pray he did.'

'I'm so sorry,' Freddie said.

'So, tell me…' she jiggled the baby on her lap. 'What's happening out there? You said when you arrived you thought the war was nearly over. How do you know? We see so little here on the farm. All I know is that our village was badly bombed the other day and…' She trailed off, wondering if she should tell him about the murdered airmen. But her courage failed her – she felt so ashamed of the villagers.

'Well the Americans are pushing in. I can't see the Germans holding out much longer. The roads are filled with lines of people; the Germans are pushing prisoners farther east, but it's madness. There's nowhere to go. The guards have lost all control. They were as hungry as we were. We had no food on the march, just what we could all scrounge. We've eaten some terrible stuff. One night we were put in a barn. The guards of course had to stay outside to make sure we didn't escape.' Freddie began to smile at the memory. 'During the night we had the most spectacular thunderstorm. And there we were snug inside and there they were outside in the pouring rain.' He laughed. 'We ate raw turnips that night – not something I'd recommend. I had the most terrible gut ache – I thought I was going to die.'

'Well you can stay here as long as you like,' said Magda. 'If things are as bad as you say, there's no point in leaving, not yet anyway. Get your strength back. My father has a radio, we could listen to the BBC and find out what's happening.'

'That's kind of you, but I really ought to go and look for my friends. And whilst I don't have a plane any more, I am still in the forces. I need to fight.'

'I understand – but give yourself twenty-four hours at least. OK?'

Reluctantly, Freddie agreed, but the following day over breakfast, he told them he would be leaving.

'You've been very kind, but I must go and see if I can find my crew. Then I intend to go into the village and see if I can take it for the Allies.'

'What?' asked Magda, aghast. 'I don't think you should go to the village.'

'I'll speak to the mayor,' Freddie continued, 'persuade him to fly the white flag. It's the only sensible thing to do.'

Käthe looked anxiously at Magda.

'I really don't think that's a good idea,' Magda said.

'Why not?' Freddie glanced between Magda and her mother. 'Is there something wrong? Something you haven't told me?'

Magda bit her lip.

'Tell him,' said Käthe.

'A couple of weeks ago,' Magda began. 'Before you came, some other British airmen were murdered in the village. I hope they weren't friends of yours.'

Freddie blanched visibly.

'Tell me what happened,' he said calmly.

He sat with his head in his hands as Magda recounted the horror of that night.

'Two of them escaped, at least I thought they had at first. Then I found one of them down an alley – he'd been beaten to death. But one is still missing. When I first saw you in the barn, I thought you might be him. If he's still alive, God knows what state he'll be in.'

'I must look for this man. He must be around somewhere. Have you heard that he's been caught?'

'No. I've heard nothing. But to be honest, I've not been back to the village since that night. I did my best to protect them but I failed. Now I'm a little scared. The villagers are angry about all the bombing and destruction round here. If you go there, I worry they might kill you too.'

'That's just a risk I'll have to take,' said Freddie. 'I'm very grateful to you, but I can't stay here any longer, dodging my responsibilities. Apart from anything else, I'm putting you all in danger. I ought to go and see if I can find this missing chap, as well as my own crew.'

'But you don't know where to look,' protested Magda. 'Let me come with you.'

'Magda,' Käthe said. 'No.'

'Your mother's right,' said Freddie. 'I'm really grateful, but you can't come with me. You're a civilian and you have a baby.'

'Oh, the baby will be all right with my mother,' said Magda, defiantly. 'And I'm practically a soldier myself. I was in the resistance, remember.'

She could tell he was wavering.

'Besides,' she went on, 'I know all the places where they might hide. There are lots of woods round here. If your crew, or the missing airman, have any sense they'll be there.'

Half an hour later, dressed in his full uniform, his hair combed, his face washed, Freddie came down into the kitchen, followed by Magda wearing her old trousers and hiking boots.

'You look very smart,' Magda said.

'Well – I'm on duty,' said Freddie.

'I'm coming with you,' she said.

'Are you sure?'

'Of course.'

'All right then. And thank you.' He turned to Käthe and shook her hand. She smiled faintly. 'Thank you so much,' he said. '*Vielen Dank*. You've been so kind. I won't forget it.'

Magda translated for her mother.

'And I'll send Magda back before nightfall,' Freddie went on. 'If she can just show me a few places where they might be hiding, I promise I won't let anything happen to her.'

Pieter came into the kitchen carrying his shotgun.

'Here,' he said to Freddie. 'Take this.'

'No – I couldn't take that,' said Freddie. 'It's yours.'

'I'll take it,' said Magda, opening the gun expertly and peering down its sights.

'There are spare bullets in this box,' Pieter said to her. 'Put them in your pocket.'

'Come on,' Magda said to Freddie. 'Mutti, look after the baby. Give her some milk if she's starving. I'm sure she'll take a bottle if she's hungry enough.'

'Take this with you,' said Käthe, handing Magda a small package, wrapped in a cloth.

'What is it?' asked Magda.

'Food!' said Käthe. 'For the airmen.'

'Thank you, Mutti.' Magda kissed her mother and stuffed the package into her jacket pocket.

'We'll check the woodland opposite the farm, first,' said Magda, leading Freddie down the farm track. 'I had a camp there when I was a child. It's hidden from the road and no one goes there.'

As they approached the road, a German tank rumbled past, heading for the village. Magda waved cheerfully at the tank driver, while Freddie ducked down behind the low stone wall. Magda crossed the road, and when she was sure the tank had gone, gave him the all-clear. Together they slithered down the muddy bank towards Magda's old camp.

'There's a river running at the bottom,' she told Freddie. 'That's what makes it a good place to hide – there's water, fresh fish, some protection from the weather. It's where I'd go if I had to disappear.'

At the bottom of the hill, in the clearing where she had made camp so often, there was evidence of a recent fire.

'Look,' she said, 'someone has been here. It could just be a vagrant. Spread out – let's see what we can find.' About ten minutes later, Freddie called out. 'Over here. I think I've found him.'

A young man in RAF uniform, his feet bare and bloodied, was huddled beneath the roots of a vast oak tree. He looked frightened and exhausted.

'It's all right,' said Freddie softly. 'I'm here now. I've just escaped from a camp nearby. What's your name?'

'Tom,' the airman said, recoiling as Magda walked towards him, the gun over her arm.

'All right Tom. Now, don't worry about this girl – she's on our side. Look here… we've got some food.'

Magda handed Tom the food parcel. He opened it nervously, then ate ravenously. He looked at both of them from time to time, with terror in his eyes.

'We should take him back to my house,' said Magda.

'I'm worried about your family,' said Freddie. 'There are Germans crawling about everywhere. What if someone came and searched your place and found him? You'd be in terrible trouble.'

'We've managed before,' said Magda. 'And as you say, the Allies are close now. Come, we're wasting time. Let's get him back to the barn. He can't go on much further, anyway – not without boots.'

Back at the farmhouse, Magda came running into the kitchen. 'Mutti, Mutti… We need more food. We found the man who escaped from the mob the other night. It's a miracle he's alive.'

'Oh God,' said Käthe, 'where is he?'

'In the barn – we'll keep him in there for now,' Magda said, as she ran upstairs.

'Where are you going?' Käthe called after her. 'The baby needs feeding.'

'All right,' Magda yelled down the stairs. 'I'll come down in a minute.' She returned to the kitchen carrying a pair of Karl's old boots.

'What are you doing with those?' Käthe asked, handing her the baby.

'Well, Karl doesn't need them, and Tom has no shoes. I hope they fit.'

Back in the barn, Magda bathed Tom's feet, and offered him a bowl of warm milk and some bread and cheese. Soon, he lay down on a bed of hay and closed his eyes.

'You try and rest, all right?' Freddie said to Tom. 'Magda and I are leaving now. I've got to look for my own crew. But her parents will look after you, and we'll be back.'

Tom nodded, sleepily.

'I'll take you to the woods on the other side of the village,' said Magda, as they hurried down the farm track together. 'You might find your people there.'

As they crossed the fields heading for the woods, they heard the distant sound of shelling.

'Is that German gunfire?' Magda asked nervously.

'I don't know,' said Freddie. 'Could be the Americans – or both, more likely. Not much we can do about it now.'

They combed the dense woods for more than an hour, but found nothing.

'It'll soon be too dark to find anyone,' Magda said as dusk began to fall. A herd of deer gathered nearby, nervously keeping their distance, nibbling at the low branches of trees.

'I know, and I promised to have you home before dark,' said Freddie.

'Oh don't worry about that. I'm fine. Let's just keep looking.'

*

Nightfall, when it came, was like a dark blanket enveloping the wood. Only the pale light of a narrow new moon, filtering through the trees, made it possible to see where they were going. Magda heard an unfamiliar crackling sound – something heavier than a deer crunching across the forest floor. Turning towards it, she saw the outline of a tall man holding a machine gun.

'Don't shoot,' she said, her fingers fumbling for the shotgun. Freddie swung round.

'Alec!' he said, rushing towards the man. 'Magda – it's all right! This is my navigator, Alec.'

'Freddie, me old mate! Am I glad to see you! We've been hiding out here for days.'

'Are you all here?' asked Freddie.

'Pretty much. Bob, Mike, Bill, Roger – we're all here. Come and join us, we've got a little camp together.'

Freddie went round the group, shaking hands, slapping the men on the back. 'I'm so relieved to see you all. This is Magda, by the way; she found me in her barn. Her brother is fighting for the British.'

The young men gathered around Magda, and shook her hand. 'Good to meet you,' they said.

'We've just left another one of our chaps with her mother,' Freddie continued. 'Another crew were murdered here the other day, but this guy somehow got away. He's in a bit of a state.'

'My God,' said Alex, 'that's terrible.'

'Come back home with me,' Magda said. 'You can all stay in the barn tonight. Have some proper food. Then tomorrow you must do whatever you think is best.'

'We have to take the village,' Freddie said to his crew.

'We've got no guns,' said Alec.

'What's that then?' asked Freddie, pointing at the German Bren gun.

'Oh this. I nicked this, but it's empty. Still, it looks quite threatening, doesn't it?'

'It does Alec, it certainly does. You fooled me, anyway. Come on then. Let's go back and regroup. Then tomorrow – well, tomorrow will take care of itself.'

Chapter Thirty-Five

Färsehof Farm
April 1945

The following morning the seven airmen sat around the kitchen table eating breakfast and planning their approach.

'There was a lynching in the village a couple of weeks ago,' Freddie explained to his friends. 'The locals are angry, so we need to be careful. So far we have one gun with no ammo, but on the plus side, the Allies are just over the hill to the west. If I can reason with the mayor, or whoever's in charge, and make them see that there is no purpose in fighting on – we might stand a chance.'

'I'll come with you,' said Magda, sitting down at the table with her cup of coffee.

The men looked at one another.

'We can't let you do that, Magda,' Freddie said. 'It's not safe. You've been very kind, but your duty surely is here… with the baby?'

'I can help you. I can explain things to them,' she argued. 'Tell them that fighting now is useless.'

Käthe pulled her daughter away from the table.

'You are not to go. The villagers will never forgive you for colluding. They are angry, Magda. They might lynch you too.'

'These men need me, Mutti. Freddie is sure the war is nearly over. The Allies are so close. I won't put myself in any more danger than I need to, I promise.'

Her mother picked the baby up from her cot.

'And Michaela?' she said holding the child out to Magda. The baby wriggled her legs excitedly, and held her arms out to her mother. 'What happens to her if you're killed?'

'That's not going to happen,' said Magda bravely. 'But if it does – she has you and Papa.'

The airmen shuffled out of the kitchen and gathered in the yard. They watched as Magda hugged her mother in the doorway, stroking Michaela's cheek, kissing the top of the baby's head. Then, slinging her shotgun over her arm, she joined the men.

'Are you sure about this?' asked Freddie. 'The last thing we want is to put you in unnecessary danger.'

'You won't. It's fine,' said Magda. 'Let's go.'

Crossing the fields on their way to the village they clung to the boundary hedges to avoid being spotted. Explosions and the sound of shelling ripped through the air from time to time.

'Is that our boys, or the other side?' asked Bob.

'Well we know the Americans are over that hill,' said Freddie. 'But I've spotted SS in the area, so we'd better watch out.'

As they approached the outskirts of the village, it felt strangely deserted. Walking through the bombed-out village square, Magda noticed a few net curtains twitching as the airmen walked past.

'Where is everyone?' asked Roger.

'Hiding inside,' said Magda. 'The mayor's house is down here.'

Tom hung back, anxiously, as the group walked down the lane towards the school – the scene of the lynching. Magda took his arm; he was shaking, she realised. 'It's all right, Tom – we'll look after you.'

As the group of men waited in the lane, Freddie marched up to the mayor's door and banged loudly on it. There was a deafening silence.

'Knock again,' said Magda. 'I know he's in there. He's scared, or drunk.'

After a few minutes a bolt was slid back on the heavy oak door.

'Who is it?' The mayor's voice was tentative, frightened.

'It's the RAF, sir,' said Freddie, politely.

'Open the door, Herr Weber,' said Magda. 'They're not going to hurt you.'

The mayor opened the door. He had a glass of schnapps in his hand and his red face was beaded with sweat.

'I've come to tell you that I'm taking your village for the Allies,' said Freddie. 'If you fly a white flag, I guarantee your safety. This will become a neutral village.'

The mayor frowned, his hands shaking.

'The Allies are just over that hill,' Freddie said gently, pointing towards the west. 'It's all over, sir.'

Herr Weber nodded.

'Do you have a sheet, or something you can use for a white flag?' Freddie asked.

'Wait a moment,' Muller said, leaving his glass on the hall table, and stomping upstairs. A few minutes later a window opened above and he hung a white sheet out and over the windowsill, where it flapped in the breeze.

'Excellent, thank you sir,' Freddie called up to him.

At that moment, a group of German soldiers came round the corner. Seeing the RAF officers, their hands moved swiftly to the pistols in their holsters, but Alec hoisted his empty Bren gun and pointed it at them.

'*Hände hoch*,' he ordered firmly. They dropped their hands to their sides, and Freddie walked calmly towards them.

'Fighting is pointless,' Freddie said, as Magda translated. 'The war is over – you know that. The Americans are just over that hill. You can't win now. The mayor has seen sense and is flying the white flag. Lay down your arms, and I guarantee your safety. I am taking control of this village for the Allies.'

The soldiers, exhausted from years of fighting and lack of food, studied the young man. One by one they lay their guns down on the road, as Bob and Roger leapt forward and picked them up.

As the men checked the guns, a German tank rolled down the narrow street, coming to a halt outside the mayor's office. Once again, Freddie approached the tank commander.

'I'm the senior officer in charge,' he called out. 'My name is Flight Lieutenant McMasters. Please lay down your arms – I've taken this village for the Allies.'

The German tank crew looked at one another. They glanced up at the white flag and at the mayor, who stood in his upstairs window, surveying the scene. He nodded at the tank crew and they threw their handguns out of the gun turret, where they landed on the ground with a clatter; once again, Freddie's men picked them up.

At that moment an American tank rolled down the hill from the church and came to a juddering halt, facing the German tank. Freddie, sensing what might be about to happen, pushed his crew and Magda down into a basement, shouting 'Take cover,' just as the American tank opened fire. From their place of safety, the sound of the ensuing explosion overhead was deafening.

'Is everyone all right?' Freddie asked as he stood up, brushing off the brick dust and metal fragments from his uniform. He leapt out of the basement and ran across to the German tank. The tank commander lay prostrate over the side of his gun turret. Freddie swung round and strode angrily towards the Americans. The tank hatch opened and the commander emerged, his pistol at the ready.

'What the hell are you doing?' Freddie asked furiously. 'I'm an officer with the British Royal Air Force and have already captured this town and accepted its surrender. Can't you see?' he said, pointing at the flag of surrender hanging from the window on the

mayor's house. 'What's that?' Freddie asked, 'the bloody washing?'
The American smiled, and shrugged.

'It's a bloody flag! That's what it is,' Freddie continued. 'They
had abandoned their arms. What the blazes have you done?'

The American soldier stared, uncomprehendingly, at Freddie,
who called up to the mayor, hiding in his upstairs bedroom.

'Herr Weber, sir.' The mayor peered over the windowsill of the
upstairs window, the white sheet flapping in the wind, his eyes
filled with terror.

'I'm so sorry,' Freddie told him. 'That should not have happened.
We will bury them – all of them – and give them a full military
funeral, you have my word.' Turning to Magda, he asked. 'Can
you do one more thing for me?'

'Of course!' she replied.

'Go upstairs, and ask the mayor for another sheet and perhaps
an old broom handle or something… I need to make a flag for us
to take to the Allies over that hill. Can you do that for me?'

She returned a few minutes later, with a second sheet tied to
the handle of a broom.

'Marvellous,' said Freddie. 'Now, Magda… you really should
go home. Our duty is to remain here – I'm sure you understand
that. We're a small unit, but we have some weapons. And shortly,
we'll get the Allies' agreement that no further harm should come
to the village.'

'If you're sure?'

'I am.' He took her hands in his. 'Magda, I'm so grateful to
you. If I don't get a chance to see you again, I promise to try and
find Michael. I'll tell him what you and your family did for us.
And how beautiful his daughter is.'

Magda had tears in her eyes. 'I won't forget you, Freddie. You
are an honourable man – an inspiration.'

Freddie shook her hand and kissed her lightly on the cheek.

She shook the hands of the other airmen, who thanked her, and as she began to walk slowly up past the school towards the square, she heard Freddie organising three of his men.

'Take this flag – go through the square and across the fields to find the Allies. Follow the noise. Take one of the German soldiers with you. Tell them I sent you. Tell them that this is a neutral village. I want safe passage for all the villagers; no more destruction. Good luck.'

'Aye aye, Skip,' Bill said cheerfully.

Bill, Roger, Tom and one of the German soldiers walked hurriedly, passing Magda, up towards the square, carrying the flag between them. A German jeep careered round the corner from the square and stopped in front of them, barring their way. Magda watched, horrified, as out of the jeep stepped Otto, wearing his long elegant leather coat, the SS skull and crossbones emblazoned on his hat.

She had hoped she would never have to see him again. She had hoped he would die, somewhere, in a blaze of glory. For him to turn up now seemed the ultimate irony – just as the war was finally ending, he would be back in her life. She hung back, hiding in a doorway, hoping he wouldn't notice her. He seemed agitated, shouting at the German soldier. She couldn't make out what they were saying, but she saw the fury in Otto's face. At one point he touched his gun in its holster, but stopped when Bill pointed the machine gun at his head. Clearly furious, Otto climbed back into the jeep and drove at high speed down the lane, screeching to a halt outside the mayor's office. Presuming he was going to speak to the mayor, Magda remained hidden in the doorway, waiting for him to go inside – after which she would make her escape. She heard the jeep door slam shut, and was about to emerge from her hiding place, when she heard the sound of his heavy footsteps walking briskly towards her. She tried to open the door she'd been sheltering against, rattling the handle, but it was locked. There was nowhere to go. Suddenly, he was standing in front of her, red-faced.

'Magda!' he shouted, his hand fidgeting with his gun holster. 'I've been looking for you. I went to your house. I saw the child. Tell me… is she mine?'

Her mouth felt so dry, she couldn't speak.

'My mother wrote to me,' he went on – his face was so close to hers, she could feel his spit. 'She told me – she believes the child is not mine. Is she right? Tell me!'

'Yes, she's right,' Magda said, weakly. A vision of her beloved child floated into her mind.

'It's not just your brother who is a traitor,' Otto said, unbuttoning the gun holster. 'It's you. I've loved you all my life and you reward me like this. You disgust me.' He removed the gun.

'No… No Otto,' she implored him. 'I beg you… don't do that.'

There was a crackling sound in the air, and Otto crumpled at her feet, his big blond head crashing to the ground, blood seeping out over the pavement, spilling over her boots. Tom ran down the hill towards her, a pistol in his right hand.

'Are you all right?' he asked gently. 'I…. had to do something.'

'Is he dead?' she asked Tom. She was pressed against the door, trying to remove her foot trapped beneath Otto's body.

Tom leant down and felt for a pulse in Otto's neck.

'Yes… he's dead.'

Freddie ran over to join them.

'Tom, what on earth are you doing? We're trying to stop the killing.'

'He was going to shoot Magda,' said Tom. 'I'm sorry, Freddie.'

'He's right,' said Magda, stumbling out onto the lane, and away from Otto's body. 'This man was my husband – he had just discovered he was not Michaela's father. He was going to kill me. Thank you Tom, you saved my life.'

*

A few days later, true to his word, Freddie and his men stood respectfully in the village churchyard, the coffins of the German tank crew and the four British airmen lined up in front of them.

'These men,' Freddie began, 'gave their lives for a cause they believed in. They were young men with their whole future ahead of them. They had that snatched away because of the insanity of war. Pray for them and for the people they have left behind. And pray too that this insanity is never repeated.'

Part Four

Homecoming

After the war

Armed or unarmed, men and women, you have fought, striven and endured to your utmost. No one knows that better than I do; as your King I thank with a full heart those who bore arms so valiantly on land and sea, or in the air; and all civilians who, shouldering their many burdens, have carried them unflinchingly without complaint.

King George VI speaking to the nation on 8th May 1945

Chapter Thirty-Six

Imogen pushed through the swing doors of the drawing studio on the first day of term. After several years away, it felt familiar and yet unfamiliar – the pegs hanging by the door, the rows of drawing boards and high stools, the way cool grey light streamed through the double-height windows.

A cheer went up as she entered, and the men in the room stood up and applauded. Imogen blushed, smiled and bowed slightly, uncertain what had prompted such an outburst. Giles came bounding over to her.

'Darling girl,' he said, taking her coat from her and hanging it on one of the pegs. 'I knew you wouldn't let me down – you've just won me a bet! Welcome back.'

He took her arm and squired her across the drawing studio to her old place in the corner. Marion was already there, cigarette between her teeth. She grinned up at Imogen.

'What on earth's he talking about?' said Imogen, sitting down and removing the cover on her drawing board. 'And how lovely to see you,' she added. 'Forgive me – I was so embarrassed by that reception, I quite forgot my manners.'

'No apology necessary, darling. They thought you'd never come back – that you'd be married, by now, to some naval officer and pushing out babies. Giles and I disagreed with them – we've made a few bob, thanks to you. How are you?'

'Relieved to be back,' said Imogen. 'Although there have been times in the last few years when I wasn't quite so sure I'd ever make it.'

'That sounds intriguing,' said Marion 'You'll have to tell me everything over lunch.'

'That would be lovely,' said Imogen, as she gazed around the studio. 'It feels so normal, doesn't it? As if we'd never been away. Rather peaceful, after all we've been through.'

'What? Even with Giles around?'

'Yes… even with Giles.' Imogen lowered her voice. 'I was actually rather pleased to see him. I know we always take the mickey out of him, but I'm really awfully fond of him, and I'm so glad he made it through the war. He was in the Paras wasn't he?'

'Indeed,' said Marion. 'I think he's got a few tales to tell.'

'And what about you, Marion? Did you join the Land Army in the end?'

Marion nodded.

'And how was it?'

'Jolly hard work. I now know more about the workings of a tractor than any woman ever should.'

Imogen laughed.

'I came looking for you one day, actually.' Marion went on. 'Your parents said you were abroad.'

'Yes. Well, it's a long story,' said Imogen, pinning a fresh piece of drawing paper onto her board.

Gradually, as the day wore on, she and the other students got back into the rhythm of university life. But here and there around the studio were empty drawing boards that belonged to young men who hadn't returned to finish their degrees. Young men who had lost their lives fighting Mussolini's men in the mountains in Italy, or who'd died in a prison of war camp in Japan; young men who'd been slaughtered on the beaches, or on the battlefields. Men who had perished twenty thousand feet in the air in the cockpit of a Spitfire, or been shot down and had lain in the mud and the dirt, unburied, unblessed. Young men who had died in the middle of the Atlantic, or the North Sea; who had drowned in engine rooms, or burned to death waiting hopefully to be rescued in oily seas. Their drawing boards remained covered, their pegs by the door unused.

At the end of the day the students left the studio and went down to the pub at the end of the road. Sitting in a snug corner with Marion and Giles, and nursing a gin and tonic, Imogen saw Freddie. He rushed in, wearing corduroy trousers and an open-necked shirt. He was looking wildly around him, as various young men called his name.

'Freddie, over here, I've got you a pint.'

'Freddie, come and join us.'

He held up his hand. 'In a moment,' he called out. 'I'm meeting someone…' When he saw her he smiled – such a wide, broad smile. She stood up suddenly, knocking the table.

'Hey,' said Giles, leaping to his feet and wiping spilled beer off his trousers. 'Careful, darling.'

'Sorry Giles, so sorry,' she said as she ran towards Freddie.

Marion nudged Giles. 'Well, that's another bet you've just lost, I'm afraid. That girl is definitely taken.'

Freddie held out his arms to her as she ran to him. In the middle of the pub, amongst the old lags who shrugged their shoulders, and the young students looking on enviously, he kissed her.

'I thought you weren't coming,' she said eventually. 'I've been waiting all day. I thought something must have happened.'

'I'm sorry, I'm so sorry. It took an age to get my discharge papers. I've been champing at the bit, flying pointless exercises for months, ferrying various big wigs around. Then when I finally got out, the trains were delayed and – oh, anyway, I'm here now. Let me look at you.'

He held her by the shoulders and took in her dark hair, her shining green eyes.

'You look wonderful,' he said.

The boys in the pub began to laugh and then to clap, cheer and stamp their feet. Freddie blushed. One or two of them came over to him and slapped him on the back. 'Welcome back, old mate.'

'We heard you got a DFC. Well done.'

One of them handed him a pint. He took a large swig and taking Imogen's arm, they joined the group. They laughed and chatted and shared stories. They shared their sadness too at those who were missing.

At the end of the evening, Freddie took her hand. 'I've got my car round the corner. Shall we go home?'

'I'd love that,' she said. Standing outside the pub, Freddie put his arms around her. 'Do you remember the last time we stood here in this doorway?' she asked.

'I do. I've thought about it so often. I was such an idiot. To think I nearly lost you.'

'No,' she said. 'You were right. I was too young to understand, then. My head was full of romance. I thought falling in love was simple. But you were just being unselfish, and noble and grown up – because that's the sort of man you are. And it took me a while to understand that.'

'Well, we're together again now,' he said, kissing her hand. 'And I promise, I'm never going to let you go again.'

Chapter Thirty-Seven

Michaela ran into the yard, chased by her mother.

'Come back,' Magda shouted. 'It's time for lunch.'

Michaela giggled, and ran towards the bombed-out barn.

'No, Michaela,' Magda called after her. 'Not in there, you're not allowed.'

Eighteen months after the bombing, the old barn had still not been rebuilt. Pieter had slowly begun to clear away the damaged timbers and had made tidy piles of reusable roof tiles, but the area was still littered with small piles of rubble and broken pieces of machinery. Now Michaela could walk, Magda was concerned she could easily injure herself on a piece of sharp metal, or bit of rough stone.

She scooped Michaela up and brought her back inside, and squeezed her, wriggling, into the wooden high chair her grandfather had made for her.

'Papa,' Magda said, bringing a pot of soup over from the range and putting it on the table. 'We really must clear up the old barn. It's dangerous out there – especially for Michaela.'

'In time, in time,' Pieter said, spooning soup into his bowl from the pot on the table. 'It all takes money,' he said.

'I know,' she said, sitting down opposite him. 'That's why I went into Augsburg yesterday.'

Pieter cut a piece of bread from the loaf. 'Augsburg?'

'Yes. I had a meeting at the bank,' she continued.

Pieter looked up, sharply. 'The bank? Why did you go to the bank?'

'They might lend us some money to build a new barn. They're trying to encourage agriculture and we need a new dairy, Papa, if we're ever going to expand the herd.'

'I don't want to borrow money and we don't need a bigger herd, or a bigger dairy. Our own dairy works fine. We can rebuild the other barn, eventually. Just be patient,' said Pieter. 'We have enough milk for ourselves, and for your mother to make cheese.'

Magda looked over at her mother, standing at the sink. Käthe shrugged her shoulders.

'But Papa,' Magda persisted, 'the country needs milk. If we had a bigger herd and a more efficient dairy, we would have a good surplus and could sell our milk and make more money.'

He slurped his soup.

'Think about it,' Magda said. 'Please.'

After lunch, she took Michaela upstairs and lay her, resisting, in her little bed. She read her a story and slowly the child's eyes fluttered until they closed and she slept. Magda sat down at her desk in the window and picked up her pen and a piece of writing paper.

Liebling,

Our little one is very determined. Mutti says she is like me in her personality and that may be true, but she looks so like you. I see more of you in her each day. The way she smiles whenever I speak to her – even if I'm telling her off! The way she sleeps, with one arm thrown across the bed…

She lay her pen down on the table.

She wanted to speak to Michael so desperately – to tell him about Michaela, and ask his advice about the farm. She'd written to him regularly since the war ended but had never heard back. As she had neither a work nor a home address for him, she had addressed her letters simply to Flight Lieutenant Michael Stewart, RAF, England. Sometimes she worried that the letters were simply not being delivered. Or that he had received them, but had decided to forget her. In her darker moments she worried that he had never made it back home, but instead had been shot or incarcerated somewhere in Germany. As she lay in bed at night listening to Michaela breathe, she wanted so desperately to hold Michael, and for him to take their child in his arms, that she thought she would die of pain. But in the morning, as she put on her boots and went out into the fields to collect the herd, she was once again filled with optimism – that he had survived, that he had got to Switzerland, had been flown home and had spent the rest of the war convalescing in the south of England, dreaming of the girl he loved. He would come back to her one day – of that she was sure.

She looked down at her half-finished letter. It was already after two o'clock and she ought really to be working outside while the light was good. She could finish the letter that evening and post it in the morning.

She checked Michaela was asleep and went downstairs to the kitchen. Her father had nodded off in his chair next to the range. Käthe put her finger to her lips.

'I'm going outside, Mutti,' Magda whispered, as she put on her boots and jacket. The oak beams and timbers from the old barn were too heavy for her to move alone. She would need to get help, she realised, and for that they needed money. But she could make a start on the pile of rubble – sorting out the usable stones and bricks from the damaged ones. As she cleared a small area, she swept the yard clean. She was just leaning her broom against the wall of the house, when she noticed a man wearing an overcoat and trilby hat walking up the farm track. She did not recognise him, but wondered, briefly, whether it might be Karl in some sort of disguise? It would be just like him to turn up unannounced. But as the man drew closer, he removed his hat, revealing dark red hair.

'Michael?' she called out, uncertainly.

'Hello,' the man replied, in English.

Could he have changed so much?

She walked towards him, her heart racing, wiping her hands on her overalls. But as she drew closer, she realised with a sinking feeling that it wasn't Michael. The young man held his hand out to her.

'You must be Magda.'

'Yes. How did you know?'

'I'm so glad I found you. They gave me directions in the village, but they weren't very clear.'

'Have you come far?'

'All the way from England.'

She looked at him, bewildered.

'I should introduce myself. My name is David Stewart. I'm Michael's brother.'

She saw the likeness then – the same dark red hair, the pale skin – and she knew in that instant that all hope was gone.

'You'd better come inside,' she said, fighting back the tears.

Over the rest of the afternoon and long into the evening David told her Michael's story.

'He made it back to England,' David said. 'He managed to cross the border into Switzerland. God knows how. He was so resourceful. He told us he wouldn't have made it without you… the money you gave him, the clothes, the German phrases you taught him. From Switzerland he was flown to England. I was still at school then, but I was allowed home for a few days to see him. It was wonderful to have him back; my mother was so happy, and as far as she was concerned he had been raised from the dead – like Lazarus, you know?'

Magda nodded. Käthe and Pieter sat quietly, listening politely, following the conversation as well as they could.

'He recuperated for a few weeks and then re-joined his squadron. He was determined to go back, even though his leg was pretty badly mangled. And then a couple of months before the end of the war he was on a raid over Hamburg… and was shot down. He was killed pretty instantly, we were told.'

'I can't believe it,' Magda finally said. 'That he got home safely, but then still died.' She began to weep silently.

'He told us what you'd done for him,' David said, looking at Magda's parents. 'You were all so kind. He always said that after the war, he'd go back and find you. I promise that was his intention.'

'I wrote to him,' Magda began, 'after the war. I couldn't risk it before, in case the letters were intercepted. Now I wish I had. He died not knowing how much I cared, or even about Michaela.'

'Your letters were finally passed to my mother. It took a while, I'm afraid, for them to find us – we only received them a few weeks ago.'

Magda nodded.

'I can't pretend it wasn't a shock,' he went on. 'To find he had a child. My mother was very upset – very cross with him in fact, that he had left you in the lurch, so to speak.'

'No,' Magda said. 'No, you mustn't think that. He didn't know about the baby. And we loved each other very much. We always talked about him coming back after the war. That's why I went on writing. I suppose I hoped…'

'When my mother read the letters,' David continued, 'she insisted I came here to find you, and tell you, personally, what had happened to Michael. She would like to help – with the child. Anything you need… anything at all. She'd like to meet her too one day – if that might be possible.'

Upstairs, Michaela woke and began to cry. Käthe left the room, returning a few minutes later with the sleepy child in her arms.

David gasped slightly when he saw her.

'Oh! She's so like him.'

'I know,' said Magda, holding out her arms for her daughter. 'I chose the right name, don't you think – Michaela?'

She sat Michaela on her lap, facing David.

'This is your uncle, Michaela,' Magda said gently. Michaela looked up at her mother, her eyes wide. 'This is your daddy's brother…'

Michaela grinned and held out her chubby arms to David, who picked her up, fighting back the tears. She snuggled into his neck, and he breathed in her scent.

'She's beautiful,' he said.

'We think so,' said Magda.

'We'd love to be part of her life,' he said. 'If you'll let us?'

'Of course,' said Magda. 'You are already part of her life.'

Chapter Thirty-Eight

London
May 1951

Imogen was waiting for Freddie at the foot of the dark oak staircase of The Royal Academy. They had arranged to visit the summer exhibition and afterwards they planned to have tea at Fortnum & Mason followed, perhaps, by a drink and supper.

'Let's see how we feel,' Freddie had said the previous evening. 'If the job interview goes well, I might feel like celebrating.' They had married a few months earlier, and moved down to London. Living in a boarding house on the edge of Hampstead, they were both looking for jobs.

Wearing a dark emerald-coloured coat and matching hat, Imogen waited anxiously for her new husband to arrive. She had been thinking about him all day, worrying about his interview. If he could just get a job, they stood a chance of finally getting a place of their own. As she flicked nervously through a catalogue of the exhibition, she noticed a dark-haired man watching her from the other side of the grand entrance hall. She looked away, but when she turned back he was still there, studying her. It was rather disconcerting, and yet he somehow seemed familiar.

'It's Imogen, isn't it? he said, walking towards her. He had faint accent – German, she thought.

'Yes. That's right. I think I know you – I just can't remember why.'

'My name is Karl. I met you a few years ago with my friends in Hampstead. In The Spaniard's pub.'

'Oh yes. I do remember you now. Of course… Karl. My friend Joy – she rather liked you.'

'Oh,' he blushed. 'I thought it was Werner she liked.'

'Yes, you're right! She did hold a bit of a candle for him, until she found out about his wife.'

'Ah yes. Werner and his girlfriends. He was always rather, how should I say, liberated.'

'Well, that's one way of putting it,' laughed Imogen. 'Where is he now?'

'Berlin I think,' Karl said. 'And how is Joy?'

'Oh she's very well. Living in Northumberland and married to a doctor. She's already got two children.'

'I'm glad – she was a nice girl.'

'And what about you?' asked Imogen.

'I'm very well. I'm still at university, in Oxford.'

'I remember – you were doing a Masters or something.'

'Yes. I finished that a while ago. But I continue with my research.'

'You never went back to Germany?'

'Oh yes, occasionally. I visit my parents and my sister Magda, and her daughter.'

'That's nice,' said Imogen. 'So you have a niece?'

'Yes – Michaela.'

'Well,' said Imogen, uncertain what else she could say, 'it was lovely to see you again.'

'Yes – and send my love to Joy, won't you?' He laughed again and Imogen smiled.

'Yes, of course. Goodbye.'

He wandered over to look at a display of catalogues near the door and Imogen was left feeling embarrassed and slightly irritated that Freddie was so late. It was awkward standing so close to Karl, but not actually speaking to him.

Suddenly, Freddie arrived in a rush, his raincoat flapping wildly, filled with apologies.

'Darling, I'm so sorry. But I have great news!'

'What?' she said, gripping his hands.

'I got the job. It's a small practice up near Marylebone. I start in a week.'

She kissed him. 'I'm so proud of you.'

'Now we just need to get you a job and everything will be perfect.'

She smiled.

'Shall we get the tickets?' he said. 'It's a wonderful show, I hear.'

He guided her to the ticket desk, and then took her arm as they went up the grand staircase towards the exhibition. Standing at the top of the stairs, waiting for their tickets to be checked, Imogen turned and noticed Karl was still watching her.

'Just a moment,' she said to Freddie. She ran down the stairs, opening her handbag as she went, and retrieved a small notebook and pencil.

'I was just thinking,' she said to Karl, 'do let me have your number. It would be nice to keep in touch.'

'Yes, of course.' He took the pencil and wrote his number in her book.

'Karl Maier,' she said out loud. 'Such a lovely name. And what is your sister called?'

'Magda.'

'Thank you. Are you going to the show?'

'Yes. But I'm meeting someone first,' he said. 'We're going together.'

'Oh well,' said Imogen, 'we might see you in there. Goodbye again.'

'Who was that you dashed off to see in such a tearing hurry?' asked Freddie, as they wandered around the exhibition.

'A man I met during the war. A German, as it happens. He was at Oxford, and fought on our side. He was always rather mysterious, you know, about what he did. Now I think about it, he was probably involved in some sort of espionage.'

'How exciting,' said Freddie, gazing at a modernist portrait.

'He's called Karl Maier,' said Imogen, following her husband's gaze.

'That name is strangely familiar,' Freddie said. 'I knew somebody called Maier during the war. A girl – you remember I told you about her? This extraordinary girl I met, when I was on the run. Magda. Yes, that's right; Magda Maier.'

'It's the same person,' said Imogen excitedly. 'He just told me he had a sister called Magda.'

'Where is this man, Karl?' asked Freddie. 'Can you see him anywhere?' He looked around the crowded exhibition room.

'No,' said Imogen. 'He said he was coming to the show with a friend. But I can't see them anywhere.'

'Could we go and find him?' asked Freddie.

'But we haven't seen the show yet,' protested Imogen.

'We can come back and see the rest in a minute,' said Freddie, tugging at her sleeve. 'Please darling. If it is Magda's brother, I'd love to hear how she is.'

'I've got his phone number,' said Imogen, chasing after Freddie as he ran down the staircase towards the crowded entrance hall.

'Can you see him anywhere?' said Freddie, frantically looking around.

'No,' said Imogen. 'He seems to have gone. How odd.'

'Damn,' said Freddie. 'I'd have loved to have spoken to him. To find out about Magda, and see if she ever got in touch with Michael.'

Out of the corner of her eye she saw him. He was walking across the courtyard outside the Academy, his hand outstretched to Karl. He was wearing a dark coat with its collar turned up, and a trilby hat, which gave him an air of mystery.

Karl said something to him, and Ben turned around and glanced towards the Royal Academy. He looked straight at her; there was a flicker of recognition, a glimmer of a smile, and then he put his arm around Karl's shoulder, guiding him away from the building and out beneath the arch and onto Piccadilly.

Over tea at Fortnum's, Freddie mentioned Karl again. 'I'd like to telephone that man, Karl. I'd love to know how Magda is. She was such a lovely girl. Very brave but a bit wild.'

Imogen smiled, and nibbled a scone. She was thinking about Benjamin. Of the way he had looked at her. Of the way he had enveloped Karl, as if he was precious to him – almost like family.

'Magda told me a bit about what her brother was doing,' Freddie said. 'Karl was a spy working for the Americans – did you know that?'

'I think I knew some of it,' said Imogen. 'I knew he was doing something secret. I didn't understand that the Americans were running it though, but it doesn't surprise me.'

'Karl was dropped into Germany to send information back to London. He had a handler,' Freddie went on, 'an American guy based here, apparently. She never told me his name. From what I can gather he was part of the American secret service – it was called the OSS back in the war, but it's the CIA now.'

'I think his name was Benjamin,' said Imogen.

Freddie looked up, quizzically.

'I knew him, briefly,' she went on. 'I never really understood what he was doing in London. But I think I'm beginning to understand now.'

'How extraordinary,' said Freddie. 'That you knew him, I mean.'

'We went out for a while, actually.'

'Really?' Freddie sat back in his chair and studied his wife. 'I'm shocked,' he said, with mock-indignation. 'We've been together for over five years and this is the first I've heard of it! I thought you loved me and only me.'

'I did. I do.' She reached across the table and held his hand. 'I've loved you since the day I met you.'

'So much that you went out with someone else – and a spy to boot?'

'Well I didn't know he was a spy – at least not then. Besides, you told me to forget you. I thought you didn't care.'

'How could you think that?' He picked up her hand and kissed it.

'You stood in that doorway in Newcastle in the rain and told me to "get on with my life". To forget you. So I did.'

He smiled. 'I had no idea you were so literal. So what happened between you and… Benjamin?'

'Not much, really.' She blushed slightly.

'You're blushing! Imogen McMasters, is there something you haven't told me?'

'No. Not really. We went out for a bit and then I gave him up, when we were in Paris.'

'In Paris!' Freddie said. 'I didn't know you were with anyone in Paris. You wrote to me from there and never mentioned him.'

'He turned up out of the blue and took me out to dinner two or three times. He wanted to marry me. Even gave me a ring. Actually, it was some family heirloom or other.' She fiddled with her own engagement ring – a single diamond on a gold band. 'He'd planned the whole thing. At first he told me he was a lawyer and we would live in New York. I quite liked the sound of that, if I'm honest. But by the time we met again in Paris, he seemed to have changed. He was rather cagey about what he was going to be doing after the war, and suggested we lived with his parents in Washington. It sounded so awful and I realised I didn't know very much about him. I wasn't really sure that I loved him at all. So I broke it off.'

'Well, thank God you did!' said Freddie, laughing.

'The next day, I got a letter from you – the first one in years. It seemed prophetic. You sounded so… hopeful about us meeting again, and I realised that all was not lost.'

'I could see the end was in sight by then, I suppose. I realised how much I loved you and I was scared suddenly that I might lose you. And it turns out I nearly did.'

'And all that time,' Imogen said, squeezing his hand, 'I thought you weren't really interested. Then I nearly lost you, when you crashed your plane.'

'I didn't crash – I was shot down. There's a difference.' He smiled.

'You know what I mean.'

'I just hope it was worth the wait – for me I mean. I'm sorry I was such a fool.'

He leant across the table and kissed her.

'Of course it was worth the wait.'

Chapter Thirty-Nine

Magda's village
December 1951

Michaela darted between her mother and grandmother, hiding in shop doors, giggling as she picked up handfuls of snow, throwing it at passers-by.

'Michaela,' Magda called after her, 'behave yourself – come back here.'

Michaela, her red hair peeking out from beneath her little rabbit fur hat, ran happily to her mother, who took her firmly by the hand. Stopping in front of the haberdasher's shop in the square, Magda admired the window, filled with bales of red and green fabric – cotton and velvet – and trimmings decorated with snowflakes and stars. In the foreground was a life-size model of Father Christmas on a sleigh pulled by straw reindeer.

Michaela, enraptured by the scene, tugged at her mother's hand. 'I want to see.'

'All right,' said Magda, 'we'll go inside and buy some fabric and make you a new Christmas dress. Would you like that?'

'Yes, yes,' Michaela jumped up and down.

As Magda rifled through the fabrics, the owner – newly arrived from Augsburg – dug out a dark green velvet.

'This would suit her very well,' she suggested to Magda.

'Fine, thank you. We'll take it. And I'll need some buttons, please – those little pearl ones, and some matching thread.'

As the fabric was wrapped in brown paper, Magda glanced out of the window. A woman wearing a shabby overcoat, her hair greying slightly, walked unsteadily into the square carrying an old-fashioned brown suitcase.

'Who is that?' Magda asked her mother, pointing to the woman.

'I don't know,' said Käthe, glancing up, irritably. Michaela was running around the shop, picking up lengths of fabric. Käthe marched over to her and grabbed her arm. 'Michaela,' she said, pulling her back to stand next to Magda, 'stop running around and stand quietly next to your mother.'

'She looks familiar,' said Magda.

'Oh, I don't know – probably someone's relative coming to stay for the Christmas holiday. Come on Magda, we must go.'

'That will be two marks,' said the haberdasher, handing her the parcel.

'Mutti,' Magda began as they stood outside the shop. 'There's something I'd like to show you.'

'We really ought to get home,' said Käthe. 'Michaela is tired – that's why she's behaving so badly.'

'In a moment. Please. There's a shop on the other side of the square,' she said, leading them across the road. 'It's empty and up for rent. I'd like you to see it.'

'A shop?' Käthe said, with surprise. 'We've got a farm to run, Magda. Why do we need a shop?'

'I've had an idea for some time… just something I'd like to do. Please, just come with me.'

The shop was one of the few buildings that had been left unscathed by the bombing. Half-timbered and painted dark pink, it had a steep roof typical of the local architecture, and an oak front door with two large windows on either side.

'Well it's very pretty,' said Käthe. 'But what are you going to sell here – bread and cheese?'

'No,' said Magda. 'Christmas.'

'What on earth do you mean?'

'I'm going to have a Christmas shop – somewhere that always sells lovely things for Christmas.'

'But it's only Christmas in December. What do you sell the rest of the year?'

'I know it sounds mad, but I think people will like it. After all those years when Christmas was,' she paused, searching for the right word, 'spoiled. Taken away from us by the Nazis. It will be a joyous place. Somewhere to bring happiness to people.'

'Magda,' said Käthe, 'it's madness. Your father will never agree to it. I'm sorry, but we can't afford to take a risk like that. We're just getting the farm back on a firm financial footing.'

'I know,' said Magda firmly. 'Thanks largely to me having the courage to borrow from the bank. I have plans for the farm too, but I'm sure this Christmas shop will be a huge success, you'll see.'

As they left the square it began to snow. Walking down a little side street on the edge of the village, Magda once again saw the woman carrying the suitcase. She looked cold and very alone, Magda thought, standing in front of the old Kalman house. She was staring up at the building, her hand poised on the doorbell, as if unsure whether or not she should ring it.

'Wait a minute,' Magda said to Käthe, 'I'm sure I know her.'

She ran ahead of her mother, and tapped the woman gently on the arm.

'Excuse me.'

The woman looked up at her with dull blue eyes.

'It is you, isn't it? Lotte?'

The woman frowned and stared at Magda.

'Magda?'

'Yes! It's me – Magda.' She threw her arms around Lotte, startled by how thin and frail she felt beneath her coat.

'I can't believe it,' said Magda, standing back to look at her. 'I can't believe you're back, that you're alive. Oh Lotte, where are you staying?'

'I don't know.' Lotte looked up at the house. 'I thought maybe I could move in here, but it seems someone is already living here.'

'Yes,' said Magda, noting the curtains in the windows, the white Christmas roses planted in the window boxes. 'I'm afraid a family moved in some years ago.'

'It was stupid to come back,' said Lotte angrily, her fists clenched. 'I should have realised they would take everything that belonged to us. Now… I have nothing left.'

'Oh Lotte. You must come home with me, with us – mustn't she, Mutti?'

Käthe nodded.

'Our home will be your home now.'

Later that night, after a meal with the family, Magda took Lotte up to the attic where she had made up a bed for her.

'I'm sorry it's not more comfortable,' she said, looking around at the empty space. 'We don't have a spare room. Michaela is in Karl's old room, but I could move in with her.'

'No, it's all right,' said Lotte, sitting down tentatively on the bed. 'This is fine – really.'

'Well, we can make it cosy over time, you'll see.' Magda nervously arranged a little jam jar filled with early snowdrops. 'Look I found these outside… I thought they'd look pretty.'

'Thank you,' said Lotte, quietly. 'It's better than anywhere else I've slept for a long time.' She looked around the attic, touching the little brightly coloured rag rug Magda had put by the bed.

'I can't begin to imagine what you've been through,' Magda said, pulling over a crate and sitting down on it.

'I don't find it easy to talk about it,' said Lotte.

'If you'd rather I left you…?'

'No,' said Lotte. 'Stay… please.'

'Where did they take you – that day I saw you all in Munich?'

'Dachau.'

'Dachau?' said Magda, 'But that's just a few kilometres from Munich. You mean you were so close to us all this time?' She leant over and gripped Lotte's hand. 'Oh Lotte, I'm sorry we couldn't do anything to stop it.'

Lotte smiled up at her. 'It wasn't your fault.'

'Where are your parents, and little Ezra?'

'All gone,' said Lotte. 'My mother was not well from the beginning. She was taken away from us within the first month. We never saw her again. I suppose she was taken somewhere and gassed. My father was put to work in the infirmary; he did his best to care for the prisoners, but there was a typhoid epidemic in '44, and he got ill and died.'

'And Ezra?'

'He worked loading wagons with crushed rock; it was brutal and many of the workers collapsed. Somehow he survived it.'

'And you?' Magda could hardly bear to hear the answer.

'I worked on a herb farm.' She smiled faintly at Magda. 'It sounds nice, doesn't it? But it wasn't. When they decided people were too weak to work there any more, they'd march them to the lake and make them stand in the water for days, until they collapsed. Thousands of people died that way.'

'Oh Lotte…' Magda began to cry.

'Then in the last few months of the war, they moved us. We had to march all the way to Eurasburg, then on to Tegernsee. But we were already so exhausted many people couldn't cope. They shot anyone who was weak, or couldn't go on. Ezra was so brave and kind. He did his best to help people, carrying one woman on his back for miles. One day, a guard pushed them both over onto the ground, and stood over them shouting "Get up… get up." They lay there for a moment, both too tired to move. He shot them both. I thought, that day, I would die myself. I wanted to die. To live without Ezra seemed impossible. But somehow I survived. Then the Americans came. They found a pile of bodies – Ezra and others. They made the guards lie amongst them. They asked us to spit on them. The men did, some of the women too. But I couldn't do it. I didn't want any more of it. No more hate.'

They sat together in the silence of the attic for some time, as the snow fell softly outside, Michaela's laughter floating up from the kitchen.

'You'll stay with us now,' Magda said, finally. 'You're part of our family now.'

'Thank you,' said Lotte quietly. 'I thought I might go to the house and find something to remind me of my parents – a photograph, or clothes, or an ornament. But I suppose the people living there have taken it all, or thrown it away.'

'No… wait a moment,' said Magda, leaping up. 'You do have something.'

She ran downstairs to her bedroom and returned with a small dark red leather box.

'This is yours,' she said, handing it Lotte. 'It was your mother's, I think. Don't ask me how I got it, but I've been keeping it for you.'

Lotte opened the box. Nestling on the dark blue velvet was the silver and aquamarine brooch and earrings her father had given her mother. She looked up at Magda, bewildered.

'How did you get these?'

'Do you remember Otto?'

Lotte appeared to be searching her memory. 'Yes – a nasty boy – blond.'

'That's him. When they drove you out of the village, he took this from your parents' house. He gave it to me, but I knew it belonged to your mother. I never wore it, I promise. I just kept it, in case…' Magda wept, kneeling in front of her friend, '… in case you came back. I'm so sorry. I'm so, so sorry.'

Lotte stroked her hair, her eyes filled with tears. 'Thank you,' she said, fingering the brooch. 'I remember my mother wearing it. She looked so beautiful. Thank you. This means more than I can say.'

Chapter Forty

Imogen stood patiently waiting for her luggage.

'I've got your case, Mum,' her daughter Jennifer said. 'I'll just grab mine, and then we can go.

Installed in their hire car, Jennifer started up the engine. 'Right… we're off. I'll have to get the sat nav working and see if we can find this place.'

An hour and a half later, they drove up the tarmacked drive of the farm. Immaculately trimmed fields lay on either side, filled with a large herd of chestnut and white cows.

The yellow ochre farmhouse had a high-pitched red-tiled roof. The windows were white, framed by dark green shutters. The dark green front door opened and a tall woman with red gold hair streaked with silver, came out onto the drive. She beckoned them to a parking space near a large barn.

Jennifer climbed out of the rental car and held out her hand.

'Hello. I'm Jennifer – Imogen's daughter.'

'And I'm Michaela – Magda's daughter. Welcome. Please, come inside.'

'It's so good of you to put us up,' said Imogen, handing their coats to Michaela.

'My mother wouldn't think of you staying anywhere else. She is very keen to meet you both.'

*

Jennifer and Imogen were shown through to the modern kitchen. An elegant white-haired lady sat very erect in a chair by the fireplace. Lightly tanned, she was dressed in grey trousers and a white silk shirt. She wore pearls around her neck and pinned to her shirt lapel was an aquamarine brooch that brought out the colour of her startling blue eyes.

She began to push herself up from her chair.

'Oh please don't get up,' said Jennifer, rushing forward to help her.

'It's all right,' said Magda. She walked a little unsteadily over to Imogen, and grasped her hand.

'I am so happy to meet you, Imogen – at last.'

The initial greetings over, Michaela showed Imogen and Jennifer to their rooms.

'Come back down when you're ready,' said Michaela. 'You may like to change after your journey. We'll be in the drawing room at the back of the house.'

Imogen put on a dark green dress and stood back to admire herself in the mirror in her room. Her daughter knocked on the door.

'Are you ready, Mum?'

'Yes, come in.'

'You look lovely,' Jennifer said.

'Thank you. I always feel at my best, wearing green,' Imogen said as they went downstairs. Coming into the drawing room, they found Magda and Michaela sitting on either side of the large wood-burning stove. Michaela leapt up as the pair came in.

'Oh good – you're here. Would you like a glass of champagne? Dieter – would you?'

A tall grey-haired man, who introduced himself as Michaela's husband, handed round a tray of champagne.

'This part of the house is an extension,' Michaela explained to Imogen. 'The original farmhouse, when your husband visited us, was very small. In those days it was just a kitchen downstairs, and two small bedrooms upstairs. Your husband, I think, spent a night in the attic. But my mother extended the house some years ago, so now we have this lovely room, and a dining room and a study. It's very comfortable.'

'It's a beautiful house,' agreed Imogen.

Over drinks and dinner, Imogen and Magda spoke of their memories of the war, and of the extraordinary connections between the two families.

'I remember your brother Karl very well,' said Imogen. 'I met him again, you know, after the war. I was with Freddie – we'd only been married a few months and we bumped into Karl at the Royal Academy in London. He was meeting someone – a man I knew, actually. In fact, I had been engaged to him, briefly.'

Jennifer looked shocked. 'You were engaged to someone before Daddy?' she said.

'Yes,' said Imogen calmly.

'Why have you never told me before?'

'I don't know,' said Imogen. 'Because I was very happily married to your father, I suppose. There seemed no point in mentioning it.'

'Mother,' said Jennifer, 'you are impossible. You must tell us all about him.'

'He was American,' said Imogen.

'American. How did you meet? What did he do, this man?'

'Oh we met at the office in London… when I was a Wren. He told me he was in the American army, but it turned out to be a bit more complicated than that.'

'What do you mean?' asked Jennifer.

'I'm not sure I should say, really. He worked with Karl, you see, and I don't know if I'm at liberty to reveal anything about either of them.'

Magda smiled. 'I think – after all this time – it's safe to tell a little of their secrets.'

'Mother?' Jennifer sat on the edge of her seat.

'Well, as far as I know, at least from what Freddie told me – Karl, Magda's brother, was a secret agent for the Allies. That's right, isn't it?'

Magda nodded. 'He was a member of OSS,' she said. 'After the war it became the CIA.'

'And the man I was engaged to was his… what is that word?'

'Handler?' Magda suggested.

'Yes, that's right. His handler.'

Jennifer sat back on the sofa. 'You are full of surprises, Mother.'

'So many people were involved in secret work during the war,' Imogen said. 'I myself signed the Official Secrets Act. I worked on Operation Overlord, but we weren't allowed to talk about it. We knew how to keep a secret in those days, didn't we?' Imogen looked across at Magda, who smiled and nodded.

'We certainly did,' Magda said.

'We took it all very seriously,' said Imogen. 'I never really discussed what I did in the war. Your father knew some of it, of course.'

'You can talk about it now though, surely?' said Jennifer. 'The war's been over for seventy-five years. There is a statute of limitations on these things, you know?'

'Yes, you're right,' said Imogen. 'But I don't suppose anyone would be interested, really. Most of us just got on with our lives after the war. We were so grateful that it was over. Daddy and I were happy just to be alive and to be together.'

Magda nodded. 'I understand that,' she said.

'Freddie and I worked together as architects,' Imogen explained. 'We had our own practice eventually. We had Jennifer, and our grandchildren, and life was busy – even after we retired. Then two years ago, Freddie died, and I've struggled since, if I'm honest.'

Jennifer reached over and took her mother's hand.

'It wasn't until I got your letter, Magda, that I gave any thought to those days. I found a little notebook buried in an old chest, along with my husband's log books and diaries. The day I met Karl at the Academy in London, I had written down his telephone number and next to it I'd written your name – that's how I realised who you were, when you wrote to me. I remembered what Freddie had said about you – how brave you were, how 'extraordinary'. That was the word he used.'

Magda laughed.

'My mother is indeed extraordinary,' said Michaela, proudly. 'She's one of the most remarkable women I've ever met. She's built up two businesses and brought me up by herself. She is the ultimate "self-made woman".'

'Two businesses,' said Jennifer. 'Not just this farm then?'

Magda looked down at her manicured hands and smiled quietly.

'Tell them, Mutti.'

'I had wanted to go to university after the war,' Magda began, 'but I had a child to care for.' She looked across at her daughter and smiled. 'So I stayed on the farm. They encouraged agriculture in Germany after the war, so we were able to expand, although my father was always against it. He grumbled constantly. But I was ambitious. I felt I had to prove myself – a single woman, with a child.'

'My mother is being uncharacteristically modest,' Michaela said. 'She was a little revolutionary in her youth, but grew up to be a stately capitalist lady.'

Magda shot her daughter a dark look.

'As well as building up the farm into a huge business, she started a Christmas shop back in the fifties,' Michaela explained. 'She has shops all over the world now – she's quite a celebrity.'

'How amazing,' said Jennifer. 'But why Christmas?'

'During the war,' said Magda, 'the Nazis took Christmas away from us. They forbade any mention of Christ or Father Christmas. Do you know we weren't even allowed to put stars on our Christmas trees?'

'Why?' asked Imogen.

'The star was the symbol of the communists, or of the Jewish people – both of which were unacceptable. We had to hang little swastikas on our trees.'

'I had no idea,' said Jennifer.

'So after the war, I decided I wanted to put that all behind us. People really love Christmas and they love my shops. When I stand behind the till – which I still do sometimes, I see the joy on people's faces. The joy, and the wonder and the delight. We must never forget the past and all the terrible things that took place, but we can look forward to a better future. That's partly what this ceremony is about tomorrow. It's something I feel I need to do, before I die.'

Michaela reached across and touched her mother's hand. 'Mutti…'

'It's all right,' Magda said. 'We're all going to die, *Liebling*. And before I die, I have to make something right. A terrible thing happened in our village and it's time to make amends before it's too late, and put it behind us. '

'What are the plans for tomorrow?' asked Jennifer.

'There will be a ceremony to commemorate the airmen who were killed in the village. I've invited everyone who is connected to them – their widows and families and the one airman who miraculously survived – Tom. He is coming too, although he is in a wheelchair now. They are all staying in the hotel in the village. There will be a service of remembrance in the church and I have commissioned a plaque with the names of the murdered men, which will be placed overlooking the churchyard where they died. I want them to be remembered, permanently, and honoured.'

'I understand,' said Imogen, 'what Freddie meant about you. He always said you were remarkable, and now I can see why.

The following day, after the service, Magda accompanied Tom, being wheeled by his grandson, into the churchyard where the plaque would be revealed. Daffodils and primroses poked their way cheerfully through the soil.

'Tom,' Magda said, as Imogen joined them. 'I want you to meet Freddie's wife, Imogen.'

'Ah, I remember dear old Freddie so well. He and Magda saved my life, you know.'

'And then you saved my life,' said Magda, bending down and kissing him on the cheek.

She stood up in front of the group, her hand on the small curtain concealing the brass plaque.

'I don't need to say to you good people – British and German – how important this day is to us all… a day of reconciliation. Our two peoples were at war for six years – a war started by the evil rulers of my country. So many terrible things happened here before and during the war. Millions of people suffered and we must never forget their sacrifice. Communities were torn apart, people taken away from everything they loved and cherished, to be punished, tortured and murdered. Even our own village was not immune from terrible acts of vengeance. Four young British airmen were murdered in this village – one near the school and three others here in this churchyard. It was a shameful and cowardly act of violence and one of which I, and the people of this village, are rightly ashamed. For many years I have wondered how to make recompense for this wickedness. You can never make up for a lost life. But I hope that this plaque, which tells the terrible story of these four fine young men, will serve as a warning to others. That life is precious, war is pointless and friendship and loyalty are everything.'

A Letter from Debbie

Thank you for choosing to read *The Secret Letter*. I hope you enjoyed it, and if you'd like to keep up to date with all my latest releases, just sign up at the following link. Your email address will never be shared and you can unsubscribe at any time.

www.bookouture.com/debbie-rix

Like my other novels, this story is historical fiction based on fact. But it is more closely linked to true events than my previous novels, as it's based on some of the real wartime experiences of my parents; my father was an RAF pilot shot down over Germany, and my mother was first an evacuee and then a Wren. I used their letters, diaries and my father's RAF log books to develop the story, and to flesh out the characters of Imogen and Freddie. I wanted more than anything else to explore the humanity that exists in wartime – the acts of selflessness and nobility, as well as the love and loss that affected ordinary people during the Second World War. I knew a certain amount of the bravery of British and Allied troops and citizens from my mother and father, but as I began to research I also discovered acts of great courage performed by those who chose to rebel against the Nazi regime. At the heart of that story is Magda – my German heroine.

If you did love *The Secret Letter* I would be very grateful if you could write a review. Firstly, because I'd love to hear what you think, but also because it could be useful for people who are new to my books.

I'm always delighted to hear from my readers; you can get in touch via my Facebook page, through Twitter, Goodreads or my website.

Thanks,
Debbie Rix

 @debbierix

DebbieRixAuthor

 www.debbierix.com

Historical Note

As a child of the late 1950s, the Second World War was a part of my DNA. Most of the adults I grew up with had fought in the war in some way or other. My mother had been in the Wrens, my father was a pilot in the RAF. He would regale us with stories of his daring adventures over Sunday lunch. His plane was shot down in the last few months of the war. He and his crew escaped just as the plane exploded above his head. His parachute got caught in a tree and he hung thirty feet above the snow-covered ground, wondering how to get down. He eventually pressed the parachute release button and fell unscathed into five feet of snow.

Eventually captured, he was imprisoned and then route-marched, along with a thousand or so other Allied prisoners eastwards for several hundred kilometres. He had many adventures, and suffered some terrible hardships – dropping to seven stone by the time he returned to England – but through it all retained his sense of humour. His stories of that time were full of the pranks the Allied prisoners played on their German captors and were always told with much laughter.

My father kept a diary while he was in Germany – a tiny leather journal he hid in his boot – and this, along with his flying log books and the notes he made later in life have been invaluable source material for me. What shines through is the dignity and respect with which he treated everyone he encountered while he was on the run in Germany.

I am also indebted to Renata Beck-Egninger, a German woman who wrote a book called *The Plaque*, in which she describes a tragedy that took place in a small German town towards the end of the war involving British airmen. That tragedy, and my father's part in it, is one of the real-life events I wished to explore in this novel.

As well as telling his story, most of this novel is told through the eyes of two young girls – one English, the other German. The English character, Imogen, was inspired by my mother's experience of being evacuated to the Lake District from her school in Newcastle. Over the years she has told me much of her story, but I also have the thirty or so letters she wrote to her mother during the war. These gave me a fascinating insight into the stoicism of young people at that time. As the novel began to take shape, I used several of the letters in the manuscript verbatim, only deleting the odd sentence about small irrelevances. What amused me was the juxtaposition of political comment about the war, intermingled with demands for money for food or new shoes!

The other central character in the novel is a young German girl, Magda. Her character was inspired by the real life heroines of the White Rose movement, a group of young Munich University students who attempted to fight back against the cruelty and evil of Hitler's National Socialists.

As these two girls grow up – going from school children at the start of the war, to young women by the end – I have tried to reveal the wider conflicts and complexities of the war and all its horror, through the intimate lives of two families on opposite sides, who both try to retain a sense of morality. As the daughter of two people who went through the war and came out of it relatively unscathed, what I have learned is that my parents' generation had an incredible ability to retain a sense of morality and humanity in the midst of appalling brutality. I hope I have honoured that in this story.

*

I am indebted to those who have taken the trouble to write of their own experiences of life during the war. These are some of the books and articles I have consulted:

- *I Only Joined for the Hat: Redoutable Wrens at War – Their Trials, Tribulations and Triumphs* by Christian Lamb; Pub: Bene Factum Publishing
- *At the Heart of the White Rose – letters and diaries of Hans and Sophie Scholl* edited by Inge Jens; Pub: Plough Publishing House
- *Sophie Scholl and the White Rose* by Annette Dumback & Jud Newborn; Pub: Oneworld
- *The Second World War* by Anthony Beevor; Pub: W & N

Articles:
- 'Nazifying Christmas – Political culture & Popular celebration in the Third Reich' by Joe Perry
- 'Christmas in Germany – a cultural history' by Joe Perry
- 'Strange Bedfellows – an article on the OSS and the London "Free Germans"' by Jonathan S Gould
- The recollections of various wrens who worked on Operation Overlord and were sent to France

I am grateful too for the fascinating insights I received during my various research trips to:
- Fort Southwick near Portsmouth – the underground tunnels which were the headquarters of Operation Overlord in 1944
- The White Rose Museum, Munich
- Munich Documentation Centre, which tells the comprehensive history of the National Socialist Party
- Käthe Wohlfahrt's Christmas shop in Rothenburg ob der Tauber

Acknowledgements

I'd like to say a huge thank you to team Bookouture, especially to my editor, Natasha Harding, for her unwavering support and enthusiasm for this project. I feel blessed to have such an empathetic editor. Thanks too for the support of my fellow writers in the Bookouture Author's Lounge.

I'm extremely grateful to the wonderful media team at Bookouture – Kim Nash and Noelle Holten – who work tirelessly to promote our work.

I'd also like to thank my family. My husband and children are a huge support to me as I research and then lock myself away in my 'shed' to write for months on end. My children have been more than usually interested in this story, as it involves their grandparents, and last summer we travelled around Bavaria following in the footsteps of my father's 'long march' through Germany. As we enjoyed the charming villages and towns of that area, it was hard to imagine the devastation he would have seen in 1945. Finally, thanks to my parents – the inspiration for Freddie and Imogen. My darling Dad died many years ago, but I've long wanted to recount some of his remarkable wartime experiences, and this book has provided me with that opportunity. And lastly, my thanks to my wonderful mother who is now ninety-five and, sadly, quite frail. Her letters to her own mother, her recollections and delightful drawings from her time in the Lake District were the starting point for this novel, and her indomitable spirit shines through the pages in the character of Imogen.